Love Me More:
An Addict's Diary

Love Me More:
An Addict's Diary

Danusha V. Goska

To order additional copies of this book, contact:
Xlibris Corporation
1-888-795-4274
www.Xlibris.com
Orders@Xlibris.com
17742

Readers Comment

With stunning prose and raw power, Danusha Goska has written a chronicle of addiction and a saga of the cultural and social dislocation of immigrants of every kind. Anyone who hopes to understand the human condition should read *Love Me More*. While the clarity of Goska's writing makes it an easy read, the subject itself is difficult. Those who stick with it will be richly rewarded.

Love Me More is a testament to the power of language as slayer and as healer. The Diary itself is a main character.

Love Me More demands that readers push the universal struggle for acceptance to the limit, and perhaps beyond.

> Don Freidkin, filmmaker, *Los MacArturos: Hispanic MacArthur 'Genius' Grant Winners*. San Antonio, Texas

Danusha Goska is one of the finest writers this country has produced in a decade. But this is not what will make people read her. Nor is her intellectual brilliance the thing. It is the coolness of her eye and the warmth of her heart that will connect with her readership. Her absolute honesty. These qualities are so needed, so precious and, in full combination, so sadly absent from the new book tables that they alone will generate controversy and public interest. Her complete lack of cynicism, so striking in such an urbane talent, will cause The Buzz to sound.

I couldn't put *Love Me More* down, as they say. I felt elation as I read its wonderful last lines. The first and last lines of this work are great and great counterparts to one another, a true beginning and a truer end. The end lines utter something universally understood, and are the reader's reward for every painful thing that has come before. The opening lines are truth for the narrator, mysterious to the reader, the motor of the book. Question/Reply: symmetry.

I felt sick reading some of the abuse material. It's blisteringly real. I had a nightmare. This book freaked me out. I had plenty of 'How the hell does she know that?!' moments when I forgot that the book was Mira's story, not mine. That's what I want when I read: total immersion, complete identification.

> Amanda Moody, actress, playwright, *Serial Murderess*. Oakland and Los Angeles, California

Ms. Goska's combination of honesty, keen observation, and kick-ass literary skill make her writing about men and about teaching ring like the keenest, clearest, most purely stuck bell. The way she manages to depict conflict without setting up good guys and bad guys gives these scenes an honesty and resonance that I rarely experience in reading. Depictions of abuse are clear enough to be very effective and disturbing, but are not wrung for every tear.

Mira, *Love Me More*'s protagonist, inspires great love and great irritation. She is unflinchingly honest, insightful, and driven forward by an oft-thwarted passion for life. Her own struggles are paralleled by her experiences teaching international, marginalized, 'special' college students. In the classroom we see her battle for their truths as vigorously as she searches for her own. There's a great deal of material balanced here and the flow from thread to thread is handled beautifully. Pacing was exceptionally good.

Peter Greene, author, *Venango Tales*. Franklin, Pennsylvania

Love Me More is a journey I will never forget, a literary journey somewhat reminiscent of Joyce's *Ulysses*. More than that, it is a clarion cry to anyone in similar circumstances that they are not alone, and they don't have to stay beaten down. Mira's fight towards acceptance and personal happiness is one that everyone can share, and is proof of the endurance of the human mind and heart. *Love Me More* is witty, and forgiving. It is beautifully written, and a joy to read. It's a book of comfort, a harbour for people who have difficult lives. It's a chronicle of a tunnel-trek. It is uplifting. It's a self-help manual that lets people know that it's how you deal with life that measures the quality of it. I look forward to the next book Ms. Goska writes, and the next, and the next. I would like to quote my favorite parts, but it would take pages. I feel I've actually inhabited its scenes and walked its streets myself. Characters are complex and three-dimensional; it's as if I myself know them.

Rowena Lundquist, freelance writer. Surrey, British Columbia, Canada

Love Me More's voice is one that we don't usually hear, a voice that addresses important, but often overlooked, issues: child abuse, class, ethnicity, religion, gender, and size. But this isn't a polemic about the sad state of society. It's the story of an individual struggling to make sense out of her life. *Love Me More* worked for me on lots of different levels. I would recommend this book to anyone wanting to find out what life is really like for that person you pass on the street everyday without noticing.

> Jeanette DeMain, union organizer. Nashville, Tennessee

Love Me More's prose, by turns hilarious and poignant, is always taut and astonishing. Given her subject matter, it is no small thing that Goska's attention to literary craft is so meticulous.

> Simon Stern, editor, *Oxford World's Classics Tom Jones*. Seattle, Washington

There are things that are difficult to talk about and words that are hard to say. Ms. Goska manages both with an honesty, a clarity, and a grace that you will find in few contemporary writers.

> John Guzlowski, poet, *Language of Mules*. Charleston, Illinois

Danusha Goska has an incredible gift: the ability to see beyond the mere word, expression, or act, and through her writing create a work of pure beauty.

> Stuart Vail, Editor/Publisher of *TheScreamOnline, The Online Journal for Art, Photography, and Literature*. Los Angeles, California

for

Kayla McKean

1992-1998

Acknowledgements

First, I thank those whom I will forget to thank; I thank those who, for whatever good, bad, or ridiculous reason I won't be thanking here individually and by name, but who know that they have my gratitude; and, finally, I thank a blessed group: the anonymous. A woman poet who, out of left field, sent me a check for $125, because she was doing well and once, when she was not, someone had sent her a check for $125. The computer programmer who sent me a keeper of an email, "You the best you the best you the best." The woman from Appalachia who sent me a winter coat. The daughter-in-law of an Iowa corn and soybean farmer who wrote to insist, "Keep writing." Thank you.

Thank you, Reference Staff at Indiana University Main Library. You know who Billie Holiday is, and so much more. And you shared it all with me.

Stuart Balcomb, inspiration gave you a priceless work of cover art; you shared it. I thank you.

Peter Greene, Jeanette DeMain, Rowena Lundquist, because I admire you as writers, you are all the more important as readers.

Roman Solecki, it is not just because you survived, and battled, the Soviets and the Nazis, but also because you have provided many with a role model of grace and commitment, that I thank you. Poles like you have let the world know that surrender is never the only choice.

It was an honor to have the author of *Serial Murderess,* Amanda Moody, offer her incomparable intellect, passion, talent and outrage to the service of this work.

Don Freidkin, you deserve a special reward. Alas, all I can offer you is one large Tony's pizza, *with* anchovies.

DEAR DIARY, SOMETHING terrible has happened to me. And the thing is, I don't know what it is.

I've been at the same agency in Manhattan for almost a year now and I haven't taken any of my sick days. I was late once, when a snowstorm knocked out the buses. I immediately got a substitute for the thirty minutes they had to wait for me. I even pull on a pair of pantyhose, once in a while, for special occasions.

My students hoard time at the end of the semester. They carefully clock my rhythms and the scheduling of final exams, evaluations and parties. Like bandits they ambush from the doors of halls I walk to pick up my final paycheck. It's always so weighty, so first-time, so please-assure-me-that-this-was-not-a-risk-wrongly-taken. "You changed my life," they say. "There has never been anyone like you." "Because of you, of that thing you said in class, I know that I will today or someday . . . "

I study their faces as if they were mirrors. The pleasure students get from me is evident. Why don't I feel warmth reflect back? I mime the requisite facial glow, mouth the appropriate kind and guiding words; I sound clear as a bell and am as empty.

Konrad's been sulking after we make love. He seems to want to ask me something. It's lucky I picked an immigrant. He lacks the vocabulary to formulate his question. I silently demand of his back, "Why can't you? Ask me *my* question. The one I need to be asked. I'll go in search of the answer and piece together what's wrong with my life." Occasionally Jim blocks my exit from the supply closet. I listen to Jim complain about his dates. I listen to Konrad whine about his wife. That's enough.

I don't really know when I decided to stop breathing. I turn on the faucet to wet my sponge while wiping up Mel's toast crumbs. It takes a good long while for the water in these old pipes to get hot. This matters. This matters a lot. It's important enough that I put my life on hold while waiting for hot water. Then suddenly I realize I'm not breathing. Or while standing in line to be allowed in to a movie. Or while waiting for Jim to get it over with in the supply closet. I hold my breath. Then I realize what's happening and I try to force myself to breathe and discover that at some point in the past year, or two, breathing became exertion. My chest and lungs and diaphragm, chock-a-block with clanking angles, resist.

I wake in a group and ask myself, "Did I ever want these? How did they come into my life, other than by the same physics that scurry seaweed and Styrofoam around on shore? Do I really care about these people enough to discover her birthday, or his favorite toy? If I left right now, would I need to get in touch with any of them ever again? Am I casting my memories to strangers?"

But this is something I'm supposed to be enjoying. It's certainly something I worked hard enough for: to pass the afternoon at a café with colleagues, to be clean and accepted and indistinguishable. I wear the uniform stitched after study. I speak the Standard English I taught myself with a tape recorder. I do not neglect keeping score. I tally every flat "A," every glottal stop in words like "bottle" and "mountain." No one is winning. I mentally attend my own slide show. I slouch in the back and shoot spitballs at the lecturer. I can't get out of bed in the morning and I've got a solution for Israel. I want to grab my interlocutors and shout, "Give me some solemnity, here! We're at a funeral."

I turn off the TV in late November. I can't abide the Thanksgiving-Christmas-Hanukah-Kwanzaa-New Year joy advertised as all-inclusive. Such ostentatious festal diversity is blind to its own bleak uniformity and exclusion. Pilgrims, Blacks, Jews, Christians, Pagans, but all families. Everyone is reuniting and my single greatest triumph is cutting loose. I never know till the day before what I'll be doing on any big holiday. I live for the day after, when social isolates who require open libraries and supermarkets and regularly scheduled public transport can function smoothly again. We don't get our holiday till the families of every team finally wrap it up for another year.

I rent rooms in houses with people who interview perfectly nice, but who are affected by me the way werewolves are by full moons. Why am I not surprised to discover that Chris is an alcoholic who feels unloved by Mel? How is it that we all gripped our scripts and began to act them out with fury and verisimilitude, defending the little postage-stamp territories we've claimed, before we even knew each other's middle names, hobbies or favorite colors? We invest hours everyday playing tricks on each other, failing each other, trying to save each other. Trying to resurrect the living dead. Trying but not too hard; if we succeeded, our own reason for getting out of bed in the morning would disintegrate.

When I wake up I ask myself, "Can I do justice to this day or should I wait, suspended, for another morning?"

I've always felt like there was something I was supposed to do, that I just kept putting off. I thought in getting away from home that I'd be getting closer to it, but that's not been the case. Some days or years go by that I just have no sense of it at all.

Why does it hurt to put on a shirt, to brush my teeth?

When I was a kid, I didn't need toys; I made dangerous assignations with forsythia bushes, mud castles; I staged essential cuff link dialogues. Even now I can feel that tension and gratification, waiting on the edge of my seat like a first-nighter, "What line will next fall in this cufflink saga?" What were they saying? I wish I could remember what those cufflinks were saying.

What scares me most right now is that this year I crossed off the last thing on the list. The list of life goals I wrote up after They killed Kai. I wanted to see the Taj Mahal, bird-watch and be bitten by scary ants in a tropical rain forest, have an affair with a man from every continent. There was lots more. I've done it all. I thought I'd feel better after.

The scariest thing right now, so scary I don't even want to write it, is that I can't, no matter how hard I try, complete the sentence, "I want . . ." except with the word "food."

So it's food, then. Food is the problem. Or the unseemly pleasure I get from food. And so, I have recruited this diary. I've read all the books. I know how long it takes. If I diet for six months, I will be thin. And then

I'll be okay. To make it easier on myself, I'll write about it in this brand new diary. I'll start tomorrow.

D EAR DIARY, WRITE about food. Where to start?
You're a teacher. Assign yourself an exercise.

Okay. Complete this sentence: "Food is . . . "

Food is joy. Food is memory. Food is home. Its opposite, food's absence, is terror, humiliation. The lack of food is dark. It's alone. It's cold.

Cold. It is really cold today.

Cold chilled our backs in winter through second-hand coats whose useless stuffing clotted near the hems. Cold grated gloveless hands right down to the red. Hunger was no easier in summer. We ran around on empty bellies till we passed out and were carried into shade by older brothers or just the nearest big kid. We revived to jump up and run around on empty bellies some more. School wasn't more advanced; phys ed consisted of a nun with a whistle; the lunch program, shoplifting. But there was no getting around cold. Aunt Bora apologized, "Yes, you can have poppy seed cake but no walnut," late frost had snapped the sap in the trees we sat under, and, as I could confirm by examining the branches, there just weren't any walnuts to be had.

We weren't supposed to be afraid. We were living in the richest country in the world. America fed us, all right; surplus labeled "peanut butter," "powdered eggs," "white rice," and "margarine." Without even such unambitious labels you would've had no idea what to call each plain brown box's contents. The dry stuff tasted like insecticide smells. The greasy stuff coated the tongue vile long after each desperate swallow. The main ingredient of the peanut butter was grease – lard? Vaseline? crankcase lubricant? – that, as Mommy used to joke, had been "waved over" some peanuts. Death by starvation paled to insignificance in the face of aesthetic assault that insulting. I was fainting from stubborn hunger; Kai determined by pulling down my eyelids that I had no blood left. He knelt and tried to tempt into me surplus white rice sauced with surplus margarine. "There's a fire inside of you," he promised, earnestly. "And if you don't eat this, it will go out."

I was thrilled. I was discovering that the hardest males, when scared, can seduce as lusciously as the softest females. But this was one of those rare incidents when Kai was wrong. That fire inside of me would never go out. That fire inside of me was outrage at America for deciding that the poor are so undiscriminating that we will eat things that a well-fed person would not.

But then maybe Daddy would win on the horses. Want was exorcised with the brightness and fullness, extravagance and warmth of a feast. Blood-flecked paprikash spilled from overfilled bowls; the walls were spattered with hot pink borscht stirred too greedily. Oven-fresh rye never survived long enough to cool. The loaf was cracked, sliced thick, slathered with butter that saturated sponge, or pooled in golden pockets of caraway-flecked, hot, sour rye. Pork skins rendered to crackling in cast iron for hours, reducing the air in the kitchen to a mellow, murmured invite to fry up some potatoes and onions and forget. Through the right connections, we knew secret torten allowed only to Viennese masters, and not just; we churned out the mousses of France, Scottish shortbread, hot spiced meats. Food was where I was rooted and the destinations to which I'd someday fly.

Mommy doubled and tripled recipes. There isn't a cookbook in the house without "1 1/2" crossed out and "3" penciled in the margin. Make that "3 heaping." No sin is more despicable than cooking for one. Any limiting of hours I'd fret nursing a yeast dough, money I'd lavish on ingredients, distance I'd travel to buy them, or, God help me, helpings I'd offer a guest, was damned as collaboration with Them. But then the phone would ring. Loan sharks. The good times were over.

Hunger is the essence of poverty, the proof of need. When I escape hunger by feeding, I escape poverty as nametag. I can be a good little workaholic, dedicated to my job, need to be reminded to take sick days. Balance on high heels. Pull on pantyhose. Invest earnings. Stifle my laugh. Lower my temperature. Answer the phone, "It is I." Every time I am hungry I return to poverty as identity. I become who I was when I stood in line for surplus food, America's culinary punishment, its slap in the face of the poor, for committing the faux pas, the bad career choice, of hunger. Every time I am hungry, They win, I lose.

And so, I am a fat woman. Passing time, turning a calendar from one month to the next, has only ever brought me a sense of failure and shame, because I am a fat woman, and I have not yet used that demarcated unit of time as a larva metamorphosing into an acceptable life form. I avoid old friends from Lenappi, people like Arnulfo Baca, and the members of my own family, for years. I'm sure they don't want to see me because I am still a fat woman. Aunt Olga – as I got older, she stopped saying so in so many words, but I'm sure the last time I saw her she showed some deep disappointment in my being a fat woman. I made a silent vow not to see her again until I was thin. But then she died . . .

I scrub Mommy's back. Mommy is insisting that she is a fat woman, has always been, and is therefore ugly. To illustrate, she will tell a story about school, and being called "a big cow." My hands, hungry for contact with her, linger over her body's contours beneath the sponge as we bathe together. Mommy is big boned and a lifetime of doing other women's hard labor has made her hard-muscled, but I do not find fat.
"I didn't do it," she protests. "I didn't ring the nun's little bell –"

God, I hear it now. Her Slovak. She would bite her tongue off at the root before she would speak Slovak, her language, *her* language, to me, the American. But – "little bell." That's Slovak. "*Zvon*" means bell; with the diminutive "*chek*," it becomes "*zvonchek*," "little bell." I learned that from a grammar book. Slavic languages, it instructed, can turn a word, any word, into a more beloved, littler version of itself. You learn that, and you conclude that Slavs see the world through magical lenses and tender senses that render visible the love in every object. Thus the name "Kaiyetan" becomes "Kaitek," "dear little Kaiyetan," and then "Kaitoosh," a son's name as an audible pillow of affection. For America, of course, my big brother is just plain "Kai."

Based on this grammatical knowledge, and its model, you wait, with faith. Someday, you will hear it. You will no longer be "Miroswava," four formidable syllables, or "Mee," the family nickname, or "Mira," the American. You will be "Mirka," "little Miroswava;" you will be "Mirechka," "dear, little." Your lovable inner essence will be seen and called out, by its proper, secret name.

"I didn't ring the nun's little bell. I was scared shitless! I had just

gotten here. I had no idea what was going on in this country! And so, on the first day of school, all the kids ganged up on me, and accused me. The nun kept me after, and hit me, because I didn't answer. But I didn't speak a single word of English! I had no idea what she wanted! When I got home, Mama hit me, too. At first, nobody liked me. They always thought I was responsible. Cause, ya know, I had just come from working in the fields. I was big –"

"And foreign," I add, trickling suds down her back.

She does not hear, not even in memory. *"Eventually, cause I loved school so much, all the teachers liked me. But there was never any money. The coal mines were all spent, and Apa had black lung anyway. And his legs were always sore, from lying in those wet coal shafts. Ask your father. As soon as he got off that boat from Poland, that's where he went. Straight down that hole. And then, it was the Depression. Even Americans couldn't find work. Mama had to send me to New York to cook and clean for a rich Jewish family. 'Who's gonna feed the big cow?' She asked. I was the cow. That was the end of school for me."*

And, in a way, though she's still alive, that was the end of her life story.

I've seen her old passport photo. Mommy wasn't ugly; she wasn't particularly fat. She was big. And beautiful. I've never seen an American with that kind of face: pinpoint pupils encompassed by splinters of glacier ice, opalescent skin with the weird back-lit glimmer of Tatra glass paintings. Before exile to the American mines she'd been raised on goat's milk and raw air; her face was so unfenced it's scary.

Mommy is right about one thing that will never change but grow more and more true each day that I live. *"That's why you're fat. You look just like me."* But I do not possess her strength.

A memory:

I am four years old, sucking on a bottle. Aunt Olga is criticizing Mommy for allowing me a bottle so late, much later than Evie or Kai.

"There's so little I can give her. Let her at least have that."

I am different. I am needy and only food can meet my need.

The world informed me, every day, what was wrong with me: I was a fat girl. I accepted this truth, but I still fought back.

Uncle Buddy picks me up. "Boy, pretty hefty, aren't ya?"
"Yer not so skinny yourself!" I punch his beer belly.

They still tell that story. She's scrappy. A survivor. Don't need to worry about her. We trained her that way; we toughened her up.

Mommy knows I am always hungry. One day she buys chicken. She calls me into the kitchen. "This is chicken, Mee. You remember what chicken is? We had it at my sister Olga's house and you said you liked it. Said, 'Mommy, fix this for me!' This is for you, Mee, cause I know you like chicken." Evie and Kai watch. Mommy tosses the package into the garbage. I run out of the room, screaming. Everyone is laughing.
"You'll have to be stronger than that to survive in this world," Mommy yells after me.
"She's too sensitive," Evie chimes in.

I was too sensitive.

A family reunion. Aunt Eva is slender and works in a Manhattan skyscraper. She has never married. She drinks cocktails. She is a world away from Mommy. Of course. They were born in different countries. Eva is American. I have never heard Aunt Eva complain about not having money. Like the magi, she arrives with gifts: things you can buy in the city, rare things too good for us. Today, it is "chocolate."
My cousins are skinny and their hair shines; their clothes match. Their parents were born in America, and grew up eating food paid for with wages Mommy earned cooking, cleaning and raising children for a rich family. My cousins take a piece of chocolate, or they don't, and go out and play volleyball with a net and a ball they have brought. Lenappi neighbors gather to watch; they have never seen such a thing. I've been fainting too much in sun, lately; Kai is getting cranky about carrying me around. Inside, I sit next to the chocolate box. I've never seen such a thing; so neat, so pretty. I open it up, knowing that I am entering a world of

privilege and coordinated colors. The lining is quilted paper. I finger it. I put a piece of what's inside on my tongue. This is not surplus food. I rocket. I don't especially like this, but I am in thrall. Wanting to repeat the intensity, I do more, and more. The box almost empty, I stop, feeling like a scientist. That was nice.

Aunt Eva enters the room. With the instinct of a Grand Inquisitor (she toys with the idea of becoming a nun), she beelines for the box. She opens it.

"How many did your cousins have?"

"One each, I guess."

"How many did you have?"

"The rest that are gone," I report, not feeling bad, because I don't yet understand. Aunt Eva persists in staring until I do; I obediently shrink. Suddenly I know how Jane McNally felt when she was caught touching herself in kindergarten. I have discovered a taboo by breaking it. And it was finally something that felt good. And I can't have it or do it, like I can't have or do so many things. My body obediently flames up like fall leaves. I know the exquisite heat of frustration and shame.

Aunt Eva shakes her head. "You have a problem. You'd better watch it." She wrests the box away from me, as if I might do it some harm. Indeed I might.

Now I know I am not just the daughter of the man everyone "allows for," the daughter of the alien mother, the cousin who must be re-clothed when she arrives on visits. I am not just the one who plays poorly with others, who gets her cousins laughing or crying too loud or too hard. I am the one with a problem.

Yeah, but . . . Evie ate chocolate. She never got fat. I wish I could put my finger on whatever was wrong with *me.*

Like Aunt Eva, Evie is tall and slim. She gets straight A's. Other girls snap like nature-show hyenas just to sit next to her. She has hiked from our house to New York State via a secret trail in the woods, hills so high I could never make it; maybe there isn't anything she couldn't do. When she spends time with me, I want to hoard every second in my fist.

We are up late playing crazy eights. She has so much energy . . . !

God, I haven't thought of that in years! Evie was always so full of pep. How could two sisters be more different? At first, after I left that house, every time I got a full night's sleep, I felt grateful, and bereft, that I was not in a room where Evie's insomnia kept me groggy throughout the day.

It is impossibly, exotically late – an old black and white Fred and Ginger hour, maybe even midnight.

"I'm hungry," she decrees. She is skinny. She can afford hunger whenever she wants it. I sigh.

"Let's go get some ice cream from the fridge." Ooo, I love it. She calls the icebox, "Fridge"! She probably picked that up from her city friends, Protestant friends. But this is naughty, this is bad. She is rolling out of bed. I am her conscience, her fear.

"Mommy'll kill us!"

She smirks. "Don't get your shorts in a twist over that old bitch." I don't get it, but looking at Evie, her easy swinging legs, how her tan body flatters the baby doll pajamas Mommy bought her for Christmas, I do.

She glides into the kitchen. I scurry after on fat, bare feet, almost tripping over the hem of Mommy's old slip, my nightgown. She takes the box with a proprietary air. She grabs two spoons. She returns to the bedroom.

"But, plates!"

She ignores me.

I find her back in bed, spooning chocolate ice cream straight from the carton into her mouth. She tosses a spoon onto my side of the bed. I've never eaten ice cream from the carton. I've never eaten chocolate ice cream.

"C'mon, poophead."

I hesitate.

"C'mon. C'mon." Mouth full, she thrusts the carton to me. I do it. I'll never taste anything sweeter.

Okay. This stuff seems good; it'll probably prove useful. But they're just memories. I have no way of knowing how they've been altered by time. I need some actual documentation of that era. Let me dig out my old diaries and copy pertinent passages in here.

September 8 *Grandpa died. Evie and me turned the house upside down* *trying to find something right for me to wear to the funeral. Finally we settled on a brown polyester jumper. Aunt Wanda left it from last time she was here. I don't have a nice enough blouse so I had to wear it with no blouse. Also it was a little big for me because it had plumpers, and I don't have those yet. It looked pretty funny but it was the best we could do. It was either that or my school uniform.*

Mommy came up to me as soon as I walked in the door. I haven't seen her all this time cause she's been down there while grandpa was sick. First thing, she grabbed my arm. "Now don't you see how disgusting you are? I don't want my family to see you. Cover yourself. You are so fat." Then I had to go into the coffin room and say good-bye to grandpa with all the cousins, who are skinny and okay, seeing me. Wish I had a blouse to wear with this thing; my arm is all blue now.

October 20 *Evie said if it wasn't for me our family would be normal.*

December 4. *Mommy said if I lose weight, she'll give me one hundred dollars.*

February 2 *Evie says I could be as pretty as her if I lost weight.*

February 4 *Evie bought all kinds of baking stuff and got me to bake cookies with her.*

March 3 *Mommy told me about coffee and cigarettes. "That's the only way I managed to do it. I had to do it while I was carrying you. I got too fat – you were a fat one even from the inside! But I did it; got looking decent enough to go to Olga's wedding, and six months pregnant with you. Just survive on black coffee and cigarettes."*

I have been on a fast for ten days. I can't take the coffee or the cigarettes, so I'm just not eating. It was pretty easy at first. Now I'm going crazy. Mommy has just been shopping. She brought home every food I've ever asked her for, and heard her say, "What do you think, I'm made out of money?" Chocolate-covered nuts. Halvah. Butter and brown sugar. Potato chips. Pizza. She watches as I unpack the groceries.

"You did the best you could," Mommy announces. "Now you deserve to reward yourself."

I don't say anything.

"Stubborn, eh? You always have to make everything so hard."

I am really good; for another day I don't eat anything at all.

Lights that aren't there flash in front of my eyes. Everything's a fuzzy haze, except for the craving for salt, which is pretty sharp. I go to the local market and, not trying to hide, tear open a bag of potato chips and eat them. I leave the empty bag on the shelf. I go home. Mommy's in the kitchen making chocolate-covered pecans. I retreat.

She comes into my room with some almonds. "I don't know what to do with them. Marzipan would be nice."

I spend the night vomiting in the bathroom.

"See? See what you did to yourself? Why do you even try? Maybe it's just time to be satisfied with yourself as you are. You're fat, just like me. Not like your sister. She has what I would call – an American shape. There's nothing you can do about it."

She's really sweet to me. She lets me sleep on the floor in her room. The world is whirling around and whistling. I taste the salt, feel the push and pull of ocean in my mouth and muscles, as if I'd spent the whole day down the shore. Mommy feels like a steady wall I can nail myself to tonight.

I'm so bad, so weak and bad. I went off my diet.

You know, I just know, if Mel read this, she'd say, "Why didn't you get angry? You should have asserted yourself." Mel's so smart that she's clueless. Anger was not an option.

I am four years old, or six, or ten. My mouth turns down. A spark flares in my eyes. It feels good. For an eyeblink, I feel whole. She senses.

"Are you constipated?"

Defiance melts to fear.

"No."

"Yes you are. I can tell by your face. You must be constipated."

"No –"

"Don't you contradict me."

It's too late. Muscles even my big, strong brother Kai knows enough to fear grab me, throw me down, face down, on the bed, tear off my pants, expose my heinie. Branching all throughout the body, sinking into the spirit: being physically overwhelmed by someone stronger, forced to do something disgusting. I am not strong enough. Anger fooled me. She can do this to me. She is better than I am just like God is better than us cause he is stronger than we are and can do anything to us. I swallow that worthless thing, myself. I submit. This tingles: my naked flesh, exposed. I know nakedness is sin. I know anyone passing could see my nakedness through the window. She shoves her thing into me. I know this is very wrong. My skin is not like good people's skin. My skin is a laughable barrier; it is a traitor. Hot water –

"Does it hurt?"

"Mmmm."

"Then it's hot enough."

– flushes through me as if I was a toilet, burns through my entire body. This is an emergency. If something isn't done, I'll cook, I'll burst –

"Does it hurt?"

"Yes. Let me go."

"No. Wait."

I hear the precise ruffle of match strike; the cigarette smoke cracks open my skull; my brain throbs. The smoke nauseates me. A delicate confetti of cool ash sprinkles over the mounds of my upraised ass. Ass. Only nice girls have heinies.

I must like this cause I bring it on myself. If I hadn't been so silly as to show my own bad feelings, Mommy wouldn't have had to do this to me. And it shows she cares. It's the only thing she does when she spends so much time with me, pays so much attention to me, touches me.

"Let me go now, please."

"No. Wait. It has to hurt."

"It hurts."

"Not enough. It has to hurt worse than it does now."

I remember spending whole nights in the bathroom, while the rest of the family slept, trying to fit spasms of breath in between rips of pain. Between spasms, I'd read. *Jane Eyre, Gone with the Wind;* I read all of

Voltaire's *Candide* during one of these shifts. In fourth grade I had to leave class periodically so I could bleed into the toilet. At eighteen I was home-nursing colitis with Kaopectate.

Aunt Olga's house. Puberty has just struck. I hear Aunt Olga and Uncle Buddy talking in the kitchen.

"Well, her baby fat is gone. She's a stunner."

"Yeah, slimmed out nicely. And what a face! She'll be a real heartbreaker!"

Something in my chest writhes like a carton full of night crawlers. No matter how I wriggle, I can't squish this down. They go into the den to watch TV. I sneak into the kitchen and find a coffeecake. I hate coffeecake. I shove it into my mouth, whole, not breaking it down into pieces.

Aunt Olga and Uncle Buddy's nice talk is just like Daddy's mean talk lately. Ever since I got plumpers he's been coming into my room when no one's around and saying mean things. I don't understand all the words, but I do. Anyone who wants to punch me can, and does. Anyone who wants to shove things into me can, and does. Men will grab me, hurt me, shove things into me. Those men who somehow see how alone I am – who drive back and forth, back and forth slowly as I walk to school – those nasty, potato-faced businessmen. "I travel a lot. Sometimes it's nice to give a ride to a young lady like you." I'll never get what I've been craving and planning my whole life – to be left alone. Either I'm a fat girl and ugly, as always, and boys get scared off, or I have this new, slimmed-out body and what-a-face! God! I can't even think about it. Even the church says we can't do anything to stop getting pregnant. That's why Mommy had me – cause she was Catholic and not allowed birth control. She says so.

I eat the rest of the afternoon. Secretively. Aunt Olga and Uncle Buddy never know.

I just lit a candle. I'm sitting on the bed now, wrapped in my granny square afghan.

I wasn't expecting to talk about that stuff. I never do. Anyway, I'm sorry. Right; I'm apologizing to a diary. But I want you on my side, Diary.

We've got a long haul ahead of us, here. Six months without peanut M&Ms.

Hmm: "I want you on my side, Diary." I used the vocative there. I created – or acknowledged? – a being outside of myself, by addressing that being. I named the being, or acknowledged the being's name, by placing a capital 'D' on 'Diary.' I can't use a pronoun; I don't know if 'him,' 'her,' or 'it' works. I so wish we had a gender-neutral third person singular in English. Diary, you are not an 'it,' but, like God, your command of reality transcends a tight orbit around a schlong. Nor are you diluted as human women too often are by custom and self-sabotage. Thus, neither "he" nor "she" honors you, or God.

But there you are, something palpable, outside of me, to be won over, or at least to be told, and, truth to tell, I do want you on my side. I've cut to the chase, in this: "We've got a long haul ahead of us." By using the pronoun "we" I tried to form an alliance by assuming it into existence. I'm talking as if you're with me already. Of course you're not; forgive my presumption. But I do want the victory of winning you over. That's one reason I so rarely tell those stories. I know everyone would side with Mommy. She, so much more beautiful than I. More compelling. More convincing. And no one ever wants to side with the victim. Because "perpetrator" is just a synonym for "winner," and "victim" a synonym for "loser." Where will you stand, Diary, if I tell more such stories – I'm not saying I will. I don't want to put you off. But if I did, where would you stand?

D EAR DIARY, VERY hungry all day. I'm eating three square meals; just making sure not to go over a thousand calories, or snack between. Even so, I'm starving. I was afraid to do anything. Couldn't visit friends; they'd offer me something to eat and I'd frenzy, shove food into my face maniacally; they'd think I was an animal. Couldn't go to a movie; they might eat on screen. Anyway, I'm so hungry I wouldn't be able to decipher the plot. Couldn't read a story. It might mention food.

What do people do all day if they're not doing food?

D EAR DIARY, DISHES much easier to wash. I've cut all grease from cooking. It's better for the environment – no need for harsh detergents. Wonder when I take my daily walks, "If I chew on this sassafras twig, will I be breaking abstinence?" Haven't figured that one out yet. Haven't chewed any sassafras twigs, either.

DEAR DIARY, SUDDENLY I realize that I am going to get old and die. As an active addict I didn't realize that. Performing my changeless food rituals over and over I lived outside of time. Waiting and waiting for someday, the day when I could finally let myself out, when I was finally ready, I've been assuming that someday has been waiting for me.

DEAR DIARY, *"What a cute little doll sat next to me in mass today," Mommy reports to the family. I turn to take the water off the stove, and smile. She has found a way to compliment me within the iron rule that nobody or nothing could change. I pour tea for her and Evie. "She said her prayers so nicely and looked so pretty. She sat just like a little lady. And what fat sausage curls! Shiny blonde hair all done up in a blue ribbon. I'd love to have a daughter like that."*

I don't understand. Mommy never talks about me this way. I don't understand. Why must the iron rule erase me? Is it a matter of having blonde hair? That hardly seems fair. I didn't ask to be born with this stupid brown hair. Was it the sausage curls? The blue ribbon? But then why doesn't Mommy just put a blue ribbon in my hair? I didn't ask to be born with this ugly brown hair! And I sat nicely and prayed like a lady! I have been trying so hard! I want to go back to church and find that girl and mug her; there is no other way. She has already mugged me.

As it happens, I did not return to church to settle the score with that little girl. But I did find her. She's everywhere. I find her in fashion magazines, surrounded by boys at parties. She's married to Konrad. During my teen years she was the star of a television series all women had to like, "The Mary Tyler Moore Show." I recognize her because she is everything I am not, and everything I am she is not. I can't be her. I'm not yet ready.

My cheeks are brushed with ribbons of hanging crepe. Father Malachy is retiring. St. Francis' basement has been transformed. It's as if I've never been here! The music, the long tables covered with purple paper, my shiny dress, and, finally, I have something to stuff in the plumpers.

This is my debutante ball. As soon as Mommy said she was too sick to come and gave me her ticket, as soon as I got here and stood among suited men with freshly shaven cheeks, and women allowing those men to pull their chairs out, I knew. Tonight I would release the refined princess I have been cultivating while watching old movies on TV. My witty repartee will dazzle. My body ripples like a butterfly highway as my performance thrills even me. But the lady with the beehive hairdo is staring, not nice, not happy. "Dear," she whispers, leaning in so that only I can hear. "Actually, you're supposed to eat with a knife and fork." I'd been eating with my hands.

I had to learn so many things. How to use a knife and fork. A hairbrush. Soap and water. Toilet paper. Sanitary pads. Penises. Standard English. And the rules so often conflict. Mel gasped one day when she came into the bathroom to get something out of the medicine chest while I was brushing my teeth. The innocent look I gave her enraged her only more.

"That's *my* toothbrush!" she screamed.

"Ir ir?" I asked, through toothpaste suds.

"Yes, it is," she insisted, displaying her multilingual acumen.

"O," I said.

"Stop it!" she finally exploded. She was actually stamping her feet. It's always been curious to me – how something about me seems to drag out the ugly, desperate and the crude in even the most rarified of ethnically correct suburban aristocracy. Finally getting at least part of her message, I did just that, and spat.

"That's my toothbrush, Mira."

"Yes," I said, after rinsing my mouth.

"You had it in your mouth!"

"Um . . . I was brushing my teeth."

Diary, I'll spare you the rest of our equally repetitive and obvious conversation. What it boiled down to was that I am not to use my housemates' toothbrushes, and in fact, at least they claim so, they never use mine. In spite of the fact that, as I pointed out to Mel, "We all use the same forks. We put those in our mouths."

Mel was astounded when I first moved in with her. "You mean, you're telling me, you don't know how to use a washing machine?" They let me pay rent in cash every month, and wrote out a receipt. At that point I think they just stopped asking. I am too afraid to go into a bank and open a checking account. I just don't know what is involved. I'm too old to be that uninformed.

To help myself master this vast body of material, I review what I've learned so far by critiquing others. For example, as I walk down the street, I judge the thighs of each passerby. If they are smaller than mine, that person is doing it right. "Ah, look at him. Naturally thin thighs. People like him better and always will. Love will come easier. Look at that couple. Would he still love her if she didn't have such thin thighs? They can eat whatever they want whenever they want it. They don't obsess. They have thin thighs." If the passerby's thighs have a larger circumference than mine do, then I can breathe easily, until the next person passes.

Such concentration sometimes drives other matters to the periphery of my consciousness. For example, last night, in the bathtub, I noticed by the smell that the blisters in my feet have become infected. My shoes reached such a state of disrepair that my feet were going straight through to the pavement.

DEAR DIARY, I didn't expect this diet to be so – what? This: today I felt as if I were in a small boat at night on an unfathomed body of water. As if I had no oar; as if I had no sail. As if I were being pushed off from shore by hooded strangers. I couldn't oppose this by imagining myself six months from now thin, happy, playing softball in a park. I've never played softball in a park. I just kept picturing myself alone, forlorn, beside a cold and empty oven, keeping a white-knuckle, grim-lipped hold.

I had just gotten home from work. I was perched on the kitchen table. Pulling out a chair and targeting myself into it was more than I could handle. I was panting into my clenched fist, obsessing: "There must be so much data I'll be needing that I just haven't mastered yet.

What must I study, stuff that people like Mel know; what must I be able to do, that people like her can do, that I don't, that I can't, before I can do it right, before I'm ready? I've been trying so hard for so long, and I still haven't gotten it. Keep focused, Mira. Don't lose the trail. Just lose this weight, and the rest will fall into place. But since that's the answer, being thin, how do I live with this woman who's still fat?"

I heard a key turn in the lock; I heard the door opening, the call of bonding, roisterous males. Damn! Chris is never home this early! I thought I'd have a good twenty minutes to boil the panic down to its more socially acceptable residue of sleep or TV hypnosis. No such luck. Here was Chris, buddies in tow. Owen, who I've seen a lot of, lately; Borders in the mall has his "erudite, yet accessible" bestseller near the door. As usual Owen was dressed worse than Kai when he was going to work in the plant – what kind of academic presentation requires the professor to wear steel-toed boots, anyway? And is it erudition, accessibility, ignorant bliss or ostentation to go days without shaving or committing to a beard? I can't help but think that if Mel found *Owen* using her toothbrush, it wouldn't be a mistake, it would be the cutting edge of a trend. Tailing behind was mascot Dick, the sleepy-eyed bear with the air of sad resignation so thorough one can be sure that Dick never invested in anything before his principled surrender.

"Hiya, Mira, keeping your flowers watered?" Chris asked me, loudly. He always greets me that way when he is in a good mood. I think he means it to convey the intimacy of an in-joke; the only thing is, I have no idea what it refers to. Perhaps it was a line he shared with the last housemate to play the role of Mira.

"Yeah, Chris, hi, how are ya, how are ya, guys, gimme that, I'll get the mugs." I took the six pack from Chris' straightening fingers and fetched the frosted mugs I keep in the freezer. And then it happened. It wasn't what I expected at all.

The different thing happened. The thing I'd been waiting for all day. The thing that was different from being a fat woman, and would only happen to me if I were getting being skinny right, or abstinent from my drug of choice right, or Mary Tyler Moore right, or whatever it is I'm trying to be now. The thing that I could never have predicted this morning cause I've never before walked past the chocolate shop on my way home from work and *not* gotten a quarter pound of pecan turtles to make up for the little cavities in the day, the anticipated hollow silence of bed and night.

The different thing is this: I saw myself. I saw my eyes glued to the floor. I heard my voice as that nasal whimper that Kai used to try to mock out of me. I slammed the mugs on the counter and stared at Chris, Owen and Dick as if I were some voodoo priestess willing them into zombiedom. And I shouted, "Hello, Owen. Hello, Dick. It Is Good To See You."

And they didn't look at me at all. And I got it – whatever changes take place with this diet are gonna be like an episode of "The Twilight Zone." I alone will experience them. The rest of the world will just go on.

The usual word salad was flying from Chris' lips; his tongue was quicker than a mail order Ginzu knife advertised on a late-night commercial, slicing and dicing through more surfaces, putting to flight even fewer vital juices. I watched his hands to time a break to put the mugs down. Pouring too quick and waiting too long meant loss of head, and, whereas Dick was indifferent to head, Owen voiced appreciation of it. I always manage to twist my wrist at the last moment so as to cause some dribbling of foam and Owen's appreciative "ah." Chris paused; I delivered; Owen alone said "Thanks."

"Join us in a beer, why don't you, Mira?" Owen, ever the gentleman planter, invited.

"Um. I don't drink, actually," I said for the millionth time.

"Of course. But sit with us. You always have so much to offer."

I couldn't resist rising warmth at Owen's flattery, although his words were a bit frayed from overuse. I'd sat in on a couple of his lectures and *everyone* has "always has so much to offer" to Owen. I just smiled at his invitation to sit. As Owen could no doubt see, we've got only three kitchen chairs. Chris broke the fourth one night. I assumed my usual billet as sentry at the pantry door, gazing at the back of Chris' sunburned neck.

I've never seen any of my housemates' photo albums; I construct imaginary albums from their bodies, stories, moods, from the half of their phone calls home that I hear as I do dishes. I try to tell their fortunes in reverse.

Chris has tight straw curls behind his bald spot; he gathers the longest bits off his nape into a ponytail. It doesn't look good; ornamentation is not its reason for being. In Chris' slim hips supporting a sprouting pot belly, dusty trophies, and his measured, rueful appreciation of his academic career, I read a boy who was once a state, but not national, athletic star. His finest trophy, the lithe Melville Smith, namesake of America's Greatest Novelist, her willingness to do as he wants, to live off his salary alone, "as the people do," and his pony tail, record that this former golden boy was once as pretty as he was loved. He keeps his few remaining hairs in a talisman on his neck just as he keeps the famous professor's handwritten response to his dissertation framed on his bedroom wall. The response is yellowing and the hairs are frighteningly close to being countable and the dissertation was never bettered and never did lead to that book.

He has told me about the book: *The History of the World.* "No, no," he explained. "There *aren't* any books out there that do this. You see, Mira, this would be a social history. History of the common man, not the kings and the crooks. The common man. Give me a break, you think it's going to be easy to get a publisher for this? They don't want this information out there." So far, the book has not materialized, and has not brought with it the money or the prestige, the fame or the plum academic appointment. But Chris has folk like me to feel superior to, and so he rents me a room in his house.

And then the next new thing happened.

"Chris."

He kept talking.

"Chris –" louder. Sounding like a woman trying to imitate a man.

He kept talking.

"Chris, I believe Mira would like to contribute." Owen smiled at me with the vivid warmth of a cult leader. I was able to resist the flattery this time. Being indulged by Owen just doesn't count – he does it in such a way that it makes him bigger, and you feeling needier than you ever thought yourself to be. I made a sour face, out of reflex. But he did get Chris to shut up for me.

"Chris, um, could, um, could you – I have this question. And since you guys are here, um, maybe you could answer it? I love listening to you guys talk. You talk about things that are really important and that nobody talks about. I mean, work conditions. Class relations. Sexism. Nobody talks about that stuff and it's so important. So I really want to follow you, you know? And be part of – whatever it is, exactly, the work, that you guys are doing. Because what's more important? But – I mean – you use all these words – I mean, I can follow you only so far. Then you get to something like 'postmodernism' or 'praxis' and wham the gate slams in my face. I've asked you a couple times what they mean and you never tell me. And they're not in the dictionary. I've looked."

I wanted Chris to answer. He may be my housemate who never puts the toilet seat down and purposely stomps up the wooden stairs late nights when he knows I have an early Saturday class the next day, but he is so damn verbally elegant. I wanted it from *him*.

So of course Owen jumped in and said a bunch of stuff; Lord knows what. He used the word "irony" a lot. That's another word I think I know what it means but when they use it I get all turned around. To me maybe a joke is ironic. To them even a sandwich can be "ironic." How ironic it is, Owen said, that today, in 1990, postmodern theory is the Ivory Tower's effort to "voice the cry of the oppressed, voice the yearnings of the common man" but actually, because it's so "dense in academic jargon," it shuts "us" out. So, geez, I guess Owen thinks he and I are the common man. I'll be sure to look for him next time I'm taking the bus home from teaching night and weekend classes to immigrants. I couldn't really focus on what Owen was saying cause Chris's annoyed shoulders were shouting at me; I was scared.

When Owen finished I said, "Chris, please don't be mad."

"Why should I be mad, Mira?" he said, without turning around. "Why should I be mad? Because you have this calculated plan to make me look like a didactic hypocrite in front of my comrades?"

Dick sighed deeply. This was all part of the messiness renounced by the wise.

"Oh, grow up." I'm still trying to figure out who said that. All right. I said that. But I'm still trying to figure out who said that.

Dick got up to go. Owen said, "Now let's just . . . "

Chris whirled around. "What?"

"I didn't mean to say that," I began. "There's something going on in my life right now –"

"There is *always* something going on in your life, Mira! You have more going on in your life than Princess fucking Di! 'Please don't stomp on the stairs, Chris, I have an early class.' Who do you think you are, the princess and the pea? Do you think you're the only one in this house who works? I'm so sick of your working class pretensions. Maybe if you treated your housemates with a little affection and respect –" and he always seems so wounded when he says that that it amazes me that he's such an atheist. I mean, he could be a stigmatic, an icon of the bleeding heart of Jesus.

I shocked myself by not apologizing. "Respect? Chris, you grew up with maids, so I can't blame you for this –" I flung out my arm and pumped it angrily at the toaster.

"All right, now what? A didactic parable about the brave little immigrants toasting bread around open fires?"

"Owen, I want you to look at this." Suddenly I realized I could strategically exploit Owen's inability to be more loyal to any person than to his own need to feel morally superior. "Crumbs, Owen. Crumbs. Every morning, he and Mel leave crumbs beside the toaster. And that wouldn't be such a bad thing –" I was halfway out the kitchen door. "But for these –" I lifted up a couch cushion, re-entered. "Owen, do you know what these are? They're not poppy seeds, Owen. They're mouse turds. I have never lived in a house with mice – goodbye, Dick! See you again soon! – not till I moved in here. My mother, she may be . . . difficult, but I tell you, she's so clean, you could perform a Caesarian on her bathroom floor. You people aren't like that –"

"Only a Polak would want to perform a Caesarian on a bathroom floor!" declared Chris. "And don't start. You know I only talk like that to tease you."

"Yeah, very funny. When will you get it that talk like that hurts people? You would never talk about African Americans that way!"

"They're not Polaks!" he shouted. "Everything hurts you! Owen, I'm going to walk up the stairs. You tell me if a normal, rational person like yourself couldn't sleep through it. If someone wouldn't have to be neurotic to be disturbed by it."

I turned to Owen. "I have to clean up after them cause they have never cleaned anything in their lives. And he's always raving about the revolution." Chris returned from his stair demonstration. "You know you walk way louder than that when I'm in bed. Now why can't you walk that softly when you know I'm trying to sleep? How can you bring more justice into the world when you treat your housemates like shit? Give me a break. You won't even share the definition of 'postmodernism.' You know what, Dr. Chris Thaeler? One day I'm gonna find the dictionary that has that word in it and I'm gonna be one up on you. Meantime, clean up your own fucking crumbs tomorrow morning. The maid just quit."

Owen's cheeks revealed the outlines of a quickening summary statement, so I beat a hasty retreat.

Is that getting it right? Or is that just haywire? I was jerking around like a dead insect, but I sure wasn't Mary Tyler Moore. And the thing is, I still feel afraid. Chris and Owen went out to a bar, I'm in the house alone, and I still can't get a breath in or out. It's ten thirty. Where am I going? Where is the boat now?

Miles, what would you say that would make it all all right?

It was ten years ago. I was barely 21. We had been Peace Corps trainees for only a month when you, our teacher, sent us out on our own. "Go to such and such a village. I won't tell you where it is or how long it takes to get there. Live there, teach there, for two weeks. Then come back." Because I was the most scared, and in the worst shape, you sent me to the highest, most remote site. I hated you.

"You can do it," you said. "Locals do it every day."

"But—"

"Just, go," you said.

I hated you some more. I hated you some more at least partly because it thrilled me to see how sad you looked when I did that to you. That angelic ache visible on your face was the only strong emotion I was allowed to draw from you. I think you knew this. I think that's at least partly why you made your pain so visible.

With a pack on my back for the first time in my life, I set out in Nepal, a kingdom without roads, to a place I'd never been. Every rice paddy measured eternity. Every hill punctured clouds. When dusk fell, I could hear the hungry jackals padding behind, salivating.

I hated and I resisted. I had to journey without any notion of the contours of the way until my foot fell. I had no clock to adequately gauge this new form of time: how fast my legs could carry me over a given stretch of earth. I had no idea of how I could or should trust the locals until well after any encounter, and I had tested their assessments against the trail I had just covered. I knew how to say "My name is;" "One, two three four," "Monday, Tuesday, Wednesday," not much more. I had no context for the few words I could make out:

"How far is it?"

"Far. Very far."

"How high is it?"

"High."

"But how high?"

"High."

"And steep?"

"Steep."

"How long will it take?"

"Me? Before rice. You? Maybe after."

"How much after?"

"You will be very hungry."

I wanted some feel of this stage so I could script in advance an honorable surrender that matched my own myths about myself. I needed a history and culture of others' performances at this same task so that I could feel prouder than some whom I found it safe to show contempt for, and more humble than others whom I'd chosen to worship. I wanted archival footage of this trek's version of the Academy Awards so I could rehearse my acceptance speech if I actually did make it. I wanted to prepare in advance the closest thing I had to confidence: "Ha. So what worse have you got?"

You gave me none of those things, Miles. Instead, I had to do what you told me to do. I couldn't talk about going, plan going, worry about going. I had to go. In spite of hating you, I did.

Thank you again, Miles. Good night.

DEAR DIARY, MEL and Chris were sitting in the parlor watching a video. Mel said to Chris:

"This film is drek. The plot is absurd. The acting is terrible. It's not even bad funny."

God, I envied her.

DEAR DIARY, EVEN the exercise part isn't working right. I assume the proper posture: shoulders back, arms open, head high. And I think, "Throat, breasts, belly exposed: an easier target. Any moment uniformed fascists will storm the house and drag me off." I was climbing stairs. Immediately, and as usual, quick images of atrocity, tortured prisoners, echoes of victims around the globe ooze across my mind. These overblown catalysts of terror deform so quick I don't engage or defuse them. And it's not just because they're impermanent and irrational. Unlike memories of Miles, they're not something I want to delay, save and savor. I want these phantoms gone. But ignoring them has never gotten rid of them.

Maybe if I pause and arrest one, I can defuse it. Why? I ask, why this constant association of physical exertion with a desperation to make it be over, why this paralysis that extorts my body's escape to the burrow of numb passivity?

My answer forms quickly and stays articulate: hard beings of impossible size, bulk and persistence are on me. They blot out the other reality in which doing this to a child is unthinkable. Relentless, windmill arms strike over and over. I screw up, like those giant screws that propel ships. I screw up every bit of strength, moral, physical, personal, and spit it out at them. I punch; I kick; I bounce up no matter how many times they knock me back down. They laugh. "See? I told you she never quits." I am amusing.

Just writing this is exhausting me. No wonder I've been AWOL from my body for so long. It's booby-trapped.

I just made a sign and hung it on my wall. "DARE MOVE."

DEAR DIARY, IT'S midnight. A sewing machine is going through my shoulders. When I woke up this morning my jaw hurt from grinding my teeth in my sleep. I tried to talk at dinner; something sharp in my throat twisted my muscles like spaghetti around a fork. My eyelids swelled with tears that would not fall. I lost all joints. I was a solid mass. I moved slowly, stiffly, up here, to my room. Chris was staring, some new expression on his face. The voice keeps saying, "I can make all this go away with a few bites of cookie."

DEAR DIARY, I was in the supply closet at work. My back to the door, I was reaching up on my tippy-toes to get down some index cards for my new phonics project. Some of our students are actually illiterate. How the agency dare take tuition money from these people . . . Anyway, I'm gonna try to teach this one Jamaican nurse's aid to read. I was feeling – okay. I realize I was feeling okay because all of a sudden I wasn't feeling okay. All of a sudden I sensed Jim in there with me. I could feel the hoarding, the forced shortage, of oxygen, of space, of dignity. I grew very angry. I turned around.

Jim's face, usually so full-to-bursting with self-congratulation, withered; he turned aside as neatly as the Moses-parted Red Sea. I walked out, pink erasers, staples, index cards, in hand.

Old Dolores looked up from her coffee. She shoved the floppy Dunkin Donuts box my way. Her eyes pleaded, "Eat it, Mira. Don't die on this hill. We don't want to lose you over Jim's supply closet shenanigans." And suddenly I realized, everybody saw. Everybody knew. Everybody has been seeing all along, and knowing, probably more articulately than I. Everybody had taken stands, and had an investment, had expectations that I'd just keep putting up. Keeping Jim satisfied enough to keep him off of everybody else's back. I felt sick. The kind of sick that makes you pull off the road.

I shoved the Dunkin Donuts box back at Old Dolores. "No thanks, dear," I said, smiling with my mouth only.

I came home and felt great. I didn't want to eat at all. I sat here in my chair, rereading *Jane Eyre*, a pastel winter sunlight flooding the kitchen, resting on the fuzzy tips of the pussy willows I'd put on the sill. Every now and then, I'd close the book and smile. Boy, I was angry back there, wasn't I!

How many people do I want to kill? I'd kill Mel. I'm so sick of those breadcrumbs. Since I haven't been sponging them up every a.m., they've been accumulating, a miniature Sahara on the countertop. I look at it and think of the maids, the houses on Cape Cod; I think that I'm going to go through the day obsessing on Mel's bread crumbs, gritting my teeth, and Mel will never pause to ponder them at all, and I want to kill her. How? A well-aimed meteor. And, in the solemn obituary: "Daughter of prominent family; promising young scholar with body like young deer; hair like harvest wheat; survived by a family of very hungry mice." I want them also to record: "A Paterson storefront gypsy reported that an angel had come to her and whispered 'bread crumbs and a rich girl's chronic, unselfconscious sloppiness' played a role in the death.'"

I wonder if Mel knows that I want her dead? I doubt it. If she did, she wouldn't pour her heart out to me. I wouldn't know about the job offer she's gotten from the West Coast; I wouldn't know that she's factoring Chris' sorry penis size into her decision on whether to accept. I have to admit I was somehow sad to learn that Chris isn't opulently hung.

DEAR DIARY, ME? Remain abstinent from my drug of choice for more than a week? Refuse Jim? Fantasize murder? I feel hyperaware of myself, as if I'm in the company of someone I greatly respected and didn't want to offend, someone whose affection and admiration I want to earn, someone around whom I can't fully exhale. This can't work for long. I want to feel like I'm living my life, not renting it out to that cocky Brazilian bombshell, Sonia Braga.

Tonight, and for how long? Every time I checked the flame under the pot, I could hear Mommy and Evie murmur, "Is it thick yet, Mee?" Every time I stir I sense their eyes on me as I strain every muscle in my arm to propel a wooden spoon through cream puff pastry. The elastic grows more and more stubborn with each slick neat round of egg yolk dropped in by Evie or Mommy. Mommy scrutinizes for any flaw in my technique; if any are found she'll yank the spoon out of my hand, splintering me, "Let me do that." Evie watches to spell me when I can't turn that spoon any more in the rubberizing dough: "Are your arms sore yet? I'll take a turn." The very first words ever written in Polish, they say, were, "*Day at ya pobrusa, a ty pocivay,*" "Give me, and I will grind; you take a rest."

We never went for a walk together. I can count on one hand the number of times we went to a movie together. And Mommy rarely talked to me. I don't feel rooted comfort while walking, talking, with a woman. Those were all new to me and had to be learned. With Mommy I cooked. Every meal I produce is the result of communal effort. I feel Mommy and Evie every time I enter my kitchen. I ponder their reflections, smirk at their jokes, worry over their gripes, make sure, by retelling, that I still remember their stories. These ghostly conversations weigh like dreamtime, tribal rite.

Today was very cold and everything looked so conservative-wool-overcoat, so leafless-tree, I had to force myself to take my walk. I was so touched by what I met that when it was time to go I had to pull myself back in. I encountered nothing you could photograph for a travel brochure. It was just the public park on a cold weekday afternoon. The sun's light was diffuse and merely dutiful. Tufts of bending yellow grasses broke the surface of crusty snow and arched down, casting blue shadows. The rose-red of snowballing and snow-forting brushed the porcelain skin of squealing little kids and parents, too, young, but trying to act like parents. There were Christmas sleds and puppies. Even though I'm not a kid, even though I didn't have one to enjoy this with, I didn't want to go back inside. I climbed the hill and watched the sunset. Pink stretched itself across baby blue sky until it tore and faded. A black lab barked, I have to believe, at the sweet, soft beauty.

No, it was nothing special. But it penetrated me, or maybe absorbed me? It shattered me, or connected me, into memory after memory of my own winters and Christmases, pups and snow forts. It did something to me that no travel brochure vista – London, Paris, Rome – has been able to do. Paris was two-dimensional; I only ever saw its façade. I didn't know what hallway led down that front door. I didn't remember one special hot chocolate in that corner café. I only knew as much of the song as I was hearing, and that was a meaningless fragment. Play a fragment of Jersey winter to me, and I hum the rest, all day, by myself, as it emanates, effortlessly, out of my memory, like the aroma of dried mushrooms slowly filling a room.

Food, as bad as it was when it was bad, still charms. It's familiar. I know it. Abstinence is still the very foreign country.

DEAR DIARY, CLACKETY clackety clack! Do you hear that? To repeat: "The quick brown fox jumped over the lazy dog." That is the sound of your words, Diary, your letters, echoing off the bare walls of a brand new place. I'm writing today's entry hunched over my typewriter on a bare wood floor; the sound waves of your voice are not muted by furniture or curtains. Your key taps echo metallically. I'll clarify: we are in a new apartment.

Owen and Dick were over. Chris was spewing the usual about the conservatism of blue collar workers. I felt so bottled up; he's not blue collar! Never has been! Struggled to speak. Spoke.

Chris announced, "No. You're wrong. You just don't understand." He launched into a little lecture to "explain" to me. I crumpled. My mind was a radar screen displaying every movement of Chris' lips, hands, posture, attitude. When he leaned back, I leaned forward. He monologued for a long time; I didn't change position, not even after my foot went to sleep and I needed to go to the bathroom. Though I disagreed with everything he was saying, I kept offering the petty applause of eye contact and repeated "Uh huh"s.

Suddenly, the strangest thing happened. Sonia Braga walked – no, sambaed – into my body! She gave new orders but they were hard to follow. I gripped my jaw with the force of an industrial vise to keep my head from nodding. I compressed my lips as I worked to erase the Chris radar screen and turn some attention to myself. I discovered that my foot was falling asleep. I unfolded my leg and smacked it back to life. Chris actually stopped talking when I did that.

"You're wrong, Chris," I said.

Owen and Dick began to stare at us as if we were the entertainment. Mel wore a sad and defeated and yet somehow triumphant smile. Chris barked: "You've been weird lately. Everybody in this house thinks so. What's going on up in your room? What are you writing all the time? Just what the hell are you writing about?"

I struggled for the words that would justify everything I've been doing. I struggled for the arguments that would make him see, make him approve, make him like me and allow me to live for another day. Yet, suddenly, Sonia Braga said, "Chris, I never throw my pearls before men who are hung like chipmunks."

Mel spit out her beer. That wasn't necessary; Chris is too arrogant to make the connection. But, anyway, it's his house, you know? And I was renting month to month. So, now, I'm here.

"Here" is a renovated silk mill in Paterson, New Jersey. I'm close enough to hear the Great Falls, the second highest falls east of the Mississippi. The apartment is two stories. Well, it's one story and a loft. I'll sleep up there. I'm using the future tense; I haven't slept up there yet. The windows are eight feet high. They look out on an old brownfield grown over with skeletal, winter-killed sumac. Right below my window runs a little stream – maybe that's what I'm hearing? Not really the falls? – It's foul with junk, but supportive of fish. Yes, I did check, first thing. Didn't see any great birds yet, but I'm keeping my binos on the sill. Wow! There goes a raccoon.

What with first month's rent, last month's, and security, I had to empty out my bank account to get here. Plus, I'll need to buy everything. But it's mine. It's mine. This is the first time I've lived alone. Think I'll go relax in a shower.

Omigod! There's no shower curtain! No rings to hang one on! I hate myself. I hate myself. I'm such a bitch lately, criticizing everyone; Mommy may have been a difficult personality, but we always had shower curtain rings! And I haven't provided myself with them!

Wait a second. Wait a second. I'm not that bad. Maybe I can take a bath . . . if there's a plug.

There is a plug. *My* plug!

DEAR DIARY, "I live in Paterson." Never, ever, did I dream that I'd say those words. When I finally quit food, my drug of choice, I'd no longer be earthbound. I'd travel from Manhattan skyscraper offices to skyscraper parties without ever touching ground. Everything would be black velvet and sparkling silver. That is the elemental scheme of those skyscrapers when you're dreaming from New Jersey; silver lights sparkle in soft black night. But now I have moved from sharing a house with people manifestly better than I in the kind of suburbs Mommy used to clean in, to Paterson. Anyone in New Jersey will tell you that that isn't just a step down, it's a white person's suicide. I grew up ten miles from Paterson but was taught to avoid it as Sodom. Even geography facilitated this shunning by tucking the city in. Paterson is in a valley; the Passaic River almost encircles it; Garret Mountain rises several hundred feet at its southwest end.

When Chris was driving me down here with all my stuff, he got lost for a bit and said, "There's no one to ask."

Of course, people thronged the streets. Blacks. Arabs. Hispanics.

Pale, embittered, sardonic looking – Aha! So there *are* Slavic immigrants in Paterson! I didn't correct what I assumed was Chris' bigotry. I wanted to hear what he had to say.

He went on. "It's a sin what they did to this city," he vowed. "A sin."

"A sin," I echoed, as if I knew what he was talking about. Sometimes asking direct questions gets you nowhere. Sometimes simply agreeing, pretending that you are a member of the club, gets Them talking more, and you get more information. My gamble paid off; he went on. Maybe I'll try this tactic the next time he uses the word "postmodernism."

"You know, in the eighties, Joe used to do organizing in the south Bronx," he said. "Joe wouldn't set foot in Paterson. He says it's worse than the Bronx was. Nowhere near as safe; nowhere near as much hope. Now that's pretty sad. When you're worse off than the worst parts of the Bronx."

"Yeah," I agreed, emphatically, becoming even more curious as to what Chris was referring to.

"And it's especially bad when you think of the history of this place. This whole city should be a museum, a fucking national monument. 1794. America's first factory strike. Right here. Right here in Paterson. Every school kid should know that date. I bet they don't even teach the kids right here on the spot about it.

"And the kids should know. Kids made history in this city. July 3, 1835. Children working the silk mills went on strike for the eleven-hour day, six-day week. And what organized labor did here in the thirties – and what the bastard owners did back – do they want the people to know what this city has to teach? Huh. Look out the window. Look at your answer. They killed this city. Killed it."

I obediently peered out the window. An obscenely beautiful Spanish girl was – well, she was walking, but she was making moves I'd never seen before, moves I'm sure no one in Jersey outside of Paterson would even try. Her dress was a vivid red; the ruffled neck and cuffs and hem were pure Flamenco. Like a hummingbird, she was lighting on the kind of tiny shops I thought malls had killed. An Indian, or maybe Pakistani, stacked shoes in front of a sign advertising "Friendlee Servis!" In a shop for notions, "*Se Habla Español*," the requisite urban Buddha, chomping a cold cigar, manned a hole-in-the-wall newsstand: "Milt's Sundries." A dark, very handsome swain, without any visible self consciousness, supported a suit, a fedora and a pencil-thin mustache. Down to his immaculate pocket handkerchief, he was as swank as if stepping out of a Zoot suit riot. Chris was right; Paterson was dead. But it was evidently enjoying one hell of an afterlife.

D EAR DIARY, I love to walk around downtown Paterson at dawn. It's like Pompeii or Fatehpur Sikri or Anasazi – one of those eerie intact cities caught, like a fly in amber, by disaster. Paterson's unattractiveness to urban renewers is recorded in its architecture. Reform never razed whole blocks. The steel-framed, glass-skinned structure hasn't been invented yet. My footsteps echo against stone, brick, domes, and fossil-fresh billboards advertising nickel burlesque shows. I was admiring the exterior of the former silk mill I now live in. Eight foot tall windows run two feet apart in rows of brick. Each window is set in its own solid slab base; above each arches a two-brick thick capital. Between every two windows a five-pointed, steel star marks the final point of interior support beams. No Greek temple ever created a more elegant façade with fewer lines and curves. What was it, then? Fire? Flood? Invaders? Who was the crook who did her in, and what was his *modus operandi* in assassinating Paterson?

During one of my all-day walks I entered a coffee shop to use their ladies' room. A weathered man at the counter drank soda water. I had to stop and ask. "Soda water? In a coffee shop?" I had found the right guy. He was an old-timer, an old Irishman named Manning. He had bum kidneys, he told me, from decades of working the dye vats. "Yeah," I said. "But nobody does that in Paterson anymore. 'Paterson's primary industries are now crack and welfare,'" I said, fishing for information while trying to sound informed. I was just repeating something a black man at a bus stop had told me earlier when I had wondered aloud to him how anyone in a city with no visible working industry managed to live day to day. Mr. Manning nodded. "Cheap offshore labor," he said. "That," said somebody else, "and all the whites escaping after the blacks came up from the south." The men started talking about Paterson's glory days as "Silk City," about Old City Hall. And so, after a while I went on my way, to make a beeline for Old City Hall.

I found it. I looked up past the winos, the crack dealers, and the stray waste. I held my nose and crossed my eyes. They were right. Old City Hall was as pretty as an architectural extra from Lerner and Loewe's frothy French musical comedy, *Gigi*. It's a mint-condition replica of city hall in Lyon, France. Like Paterson, I've learned, Lyon's silk industry had a long pedigree and a prestigious founder. Alexander Hamilton founded Paterson; he wanted to make power out of the seventy-foot falls. Lyon had been granted its silk monopoly by King Charles VII in 1450. Lyon, like Paterson, harnessed its waters, there of the Rhône, to stir industry. Standing downtown and looking up, I reentered a time when Paterson was run by precious esthetes conscious and careful enough of such cultural sisterhood to commemorate it in Beaux Arts stone.

DEAR DIARY, I walked to the mall, in Wayne, to do some shower curtain shopping. It's about three miles as the crow flies. I didn't ask instructions or use a map; I wanted to get the feel of the route. I figured, I'm in a valley; if I'm walking uphill, I'm going the right way.

Walking past the Salvation Army I was startled by the metallic sheen bouncing off a mallard's head. Focusing on him, I caught, beside him, a camouflaged female. The couple bobbed in the nameless tributary of the Passaic that flows in front of the store, giving it the look of a post-Apocalypse Venice. The mallards took in stride, or in stroke, the varied garbage with which they shared the water. Styrofoam, shirts, car parts, books, springs, spray cans. I worried for the mallards. The black men living under the bridge didn't surprise or concern me in the same way.

I came across The Cedars of Lebanon Deli and decided to visit and buy the most foreign thing. I asked for lots of tastes and settled on the baba ghanoush, a vaguely bluish gel. Maybe I just imagined it to be bluish; I'm always looking for blue food.

Behind a boy, a figure entered in full black veil. She absorbed all light and suggested the contours of a woman's body only fleetingly, when she moved. Somehow I want everything to be more dramatic when I am among Arabs. "Cedars" was just a deli yet I demanded much more than grocery shopping, making change, the satisfaction of something so common as hunger. I wondered; did the Arabs want more when I walked in? Did they want me to be a fallen Western hussy? I don't know, but I imagined everything florid:

"The clerk eyes me with the unforgiving glare of an action news hijacker while asking my bare naked face, 'Anything else, madam?' Behind us, entire families, shopping together, bubble and hiss, cajole and whisper. Arabic: uninhibited glottal lolls; letters consisting of an artful gargling of spit, arguments and allusions to rich poetry go on in this grocery could make English come off as the provincial argot of a band of hunter gatherers, I'm sure. Families part to let me to the counter. For them shopping is the day's entertainment. They'll be here the morning, pinching products in places it never occurs to me to pinch, thus gaining the kind of esoteric knowledge archaeologists can from one whiff of a thirty-five-thousand-year-old camp fire. They tease sweetly out of the hijacker with a reference to his sainted mother a little bit more on the pound than I could ever dream as I watch his hairy knuckles pile up my precise half pound of baba ghanoush, no more. 'Anything else, madam?' Anything? Else! Heavens to Betsy, yes, A thousand and one nights! The Crusades! Hostages! Pistachio groves! The promise and temptation in one taste of that baba ghanoush – smoke, sour, slime, irresistible. Jihad! Scimitars slashing heaven above the head! Damask, Arabesque, harems, slim, naked boys wearing mud-green, diamond-patterned pythons. His eyes searching mine for my next order. 'Will the infidel request what she thinks is a snack but what is really something holy, and that only believers may touch?' His eyes are black, liquid, impenetrable as the Arabian Sea after the fisherfolk have returned with the day's slick finned harvest. 'What are you doing tonight, honey,' just doesn't make it. 'No, thank you.' With heavy regret, eyes cast down in interpersonal purdah, I see the black-haired knuckles neatly seal my dish of baba ghanoush with a white cardboard disk, which will no doubt one day float down the once trout-rich, Indian-run Passaic River . . . "

See what I mean?

Like a bull's eye Paterson's blacks inhabit the center of chromatic unacceptability, Downtown Paterson, the nadir of the valley. Arabs surround them and shade into old Italians, tan from gardening and hauling wares. Sidewalk graffito proclaims, "*Forza Napoli!*" These Italian men, men alone, patronize boxlike cafes offering grimy black and white tiled floors, stale air, wire stools, and "Members Only" status protected with hand-lettered window signs. Here the men argue and sip coffee in front of plates holding two pignoli cookies. How do they keep females so thoroughly out of this world? Off of the sidewalks, out of the cafés, with no nearby public culture that serves women or girls? I don't care how many dirty looks they give me. I'm going to keep strolling down there till I figure that out.

I walked uphill. The welcome sign at the border between Paterson and middle class Wayne was an indictment: "ENTERING WAYNE. KEEP IT CLEAN." On the other side I crayoned, "ENTERING PATERSON. DRESS MORE INTRIGUINGLY." My route proceeded past younger Italians with no tans, but office jobs, private homes and lawns. The spaces between where each can live fanned out. Sounds were further apart and subtler. I walked uphill; everything got bigger; what would have been a storefront on the Italian street was here a picture window; what would have been a playing field in the black neighborhood was somebody's front lawn.

In my new apartment others hear my sigh; last night some guy was beating his woman and, gathered on the street, neighbors provided running commentary. Entering Wayne there was suddenly no sound; there were no children, no proud moms, no hyper-hetero hunks, no fevered soccer fan's sidewalk graffito. I'd entered a better place, but one people aren't allowed to live in. A bomb had gone off. The world had ended. I decided to buy a shower curtain in Paterson, after all, and headed back down.

There's a pass in the ridge right before Hamburg Turnpike dips into Paterson. I stopped there while walking back from shopping. I stood in Brother Bruno's Pizzeria parking lot and watched a waxing moon gain in brilliance as the sky went black. I wanted so badly to point my finger and say to another, "See?"

I walked on towards Paterson through rank grass and over broken glass on the shoulder. A beat-up Chevy heaved into my space. Something more animal pelt than paint sheathed this jalopy, something biological; it was blotched with great liver moles of primer and rust. I composed a spew to greet the male who would jump out and offer me a ride, a party, or whatever he had been able to extrude from his pathetic imagination.

But a woman opened the door. Under Farrah Fawcett hair, behind thick glasses, blinked the smallest and most clouded eyes I've ever tried to see. She was dwarfish, in tight jeans.

"Don't you know it's dangerous to walk where there's no shoulder?"

"Yes, I know that," I said, measuring whether to deploy my "teacher-meeting-a-psycho-on-the-highway" authority or my "I'm-just-a-good-ol'gal-like-you" factory twang.

"Are you a foreigner?" she asked.

"Kind of," I said.

"Get in. I'll take you."

I didn't want to get into that car. Just taking a seat in it would probably soil my pants with dirty car stain. But I didn't want to walk another mile, either.

"My name's Martha Streichert. Just coming from Welfare. Those dickheads don't want to give me my check. You wouldn't believe how these people jerk me around."

"No, I guess I wouldn't."

"So, where you headed? Paterson? I'll take you."

"No! You were going the other way!"

"Don't be ridiculous. It's only my children. They can wait. You can't walk all the way to Paterson."

"I might take the bus," I lied.

"Yeah, I know all about those buses. They're always late, the drivers are living out antisocial aggression, and the passengers sit close and have bad breath. Besides, get a clue, you're white – ostensibly. Get in," she cocked her head toward the car. I followed.

Bending low to avoid the shedding roof, I saw three little faces in the backseat. They looked like a didactic woodcut excoriating the evils of capitalism. They were blue-white as the sheen off a TV screen, and puffy. I wanted to greet them politely; I thought, maybe, that hooking them up to some life support equipment might be a necessary first step.

I leaned over to the woman with the big, blonde hair and whispered, "Are they okay?"

She ignored me, peeled into traffic, fingered the "Asshole!" stupid enough to horn loudly. "You're from Lenappi." she pronounced.

"How did you know?" I asked, surprised and really not sure who to be now.

"Yeah. Now I've placed you. I've seen you around. No one from Lenappi is really white. That's why I said, 'ostensibly.' Hope I didn't offend."

"No one from Lenappi uses the word 'ostensibly,'" I said, testing her identity.

"Your mother would; she's really bright," the woman said. "And she is who she is, so she could carry it off."

"You know my mother?"

"Everybody knows your mother. She's a real hero in that town. And I think my husband knew your brother Kai. Vaguely. They served time together. He was a good guy. Your brother, I mean. I'm really sorry."

"Mm," I said.

"I didn't know him. He was older than I. And way out of my league, I tell you. But he was such a nice guy, everybody was friends with Kai."

I nodded.

"Swell, I've already blown it, haven't I?"

"Red light!" I cried.

"Roger." A pained screech of what used to be brakes. I turned to the kids in the backseat to make sure they weren't flying forward. They hadn't budged. Curare? Electronic restraint anklets?

"Look," she said, turning to me. "I'm charm-impaired. Don't think it's just because I'm from Lenappi; its more than that. It's genetic. A birth defect. That's how it is. Charm deprivation. I'm never gonna change."

"Okay," I said.

The light changed. She jackrabbited forward.

"You know, I've been watching you. I've been waiting to see when you'd do it. You know, what we all did. Get pregnant by the wrong guy, like I did. Not once but three times. Before I finally got the balls to kick him out. Sell out. That's what I am. I treat my life as if it were Kleenex. When you left to go live in some other country, it blew me away. I thought, all right, what's this?"

When she dropped me off, she gave me her number, and made me repeat it to her three times. She asked if I were in the book. "Not yet," I said, "but you can get the number through information. Ask for a new listing."

She said, "Okay," drove a few feet, then braked, jackrabbited back. "Maybe you better give me your number anyway," she called out the window.

I did.

D EAR DIARY, WHEN I woke up this morning, I sent my hands on an expedition under my bed sheets. I plunged splayed fingers into the thick of pubic hair. I rode the heel of my hand up the firm mound of belly, allowed thumb to plumb navel, counted bony ladder ribs climbing to breasts. Cupped breasts, tested nipples, experienced flushing firmness; slid hands down ancient mountain profile from ribs, down waist, up to hip, down thigh. I was exploring, hoping, that by some miracle the fat had disappeared in the night. I used to pray for this as a child. Maybe I'm normal. Maybe today is the day that my life really starts. But the courier's dispatch defied my hope. I was still a fat woman.

Mel and I are different species. We carry different passports. I've watched men converse with both of us at once. They have a completely different personality they use with each of us, in turn, and switch from one personality to the other in the time it takes them to turn their faces from her to me. I get the scary mask, the demon mask. I get hate. Mel gets solicitousness and warmth I never see, unless there's a mirror behind her head.

What men get from looking at Mel, I want to give to Konrad. I hope he and I are still together when I'm finally thin. But I won't be able to give it to him tomorrow. I won't be thin by then. He's coming, and I get to play his disappointment, once again.

Miles, would it have mattered if I had been thin with you, for you? No. No. You weren't that kind of a man. I'm sorry I asked. It was wrong of me.

D EAR DIARY, I don't know why we play it this way. I had mailed the key to his clinic, not to his home, though she knows all about me. I reclined on the couch early and began to drift into sleep and I knew that when I next opened my eyes they would see beauty crossing my floor in the darkness, a swan sifting out of night.

He waited to come until very late, until I had almost fallen asleep, in my white nightgown with the white satin embroidery, waiting beside the window, in the light from the full moon. We are always together for the full moon. She has him every sun.

He was as pale as snow, as cool and as silent. He glided toward me. I was almost asleep. Maybe he is a swan.

Other people look like marionettes next to Konrad. He moves as if propelled on jets of evenly calibrated air, though he is massive; Chris calls him "Mr. Mount Rushmore." And he is somehow always in profile; he has a profile like the prow of a ship. He sat down on the edge of my couch. I thought what I always think. "You are so much better than I."

"Miroswava, as always, you have grown bored with anticipation of me, and have fallen asleep." His voice is so deep, when he spoke, I felt the couch vibrate. Maybe. Anyway, I want to remember it that way.

I opened my eyes fully and looked up at him. He gasped and pulled back. And then I realized; I was looking at him the same way I had looked at Jim. I tried to stop it. "No," I told myself, "this is not Jim, this is Konrad, whom you love. This is not Jim, invading the supply closet; this is Konrad, whom you have invited, prepared for, bathed for, fasted for."

"Mira," he stated. He stated just that: Mira. He was suddenly unsure and he wanted to know what was different.

We haven't seen each other in a month. Much was different. I was in a brand new apartment, in a new city, a dangerous city white people aren't to move to. He could ask about that. He could say, "Mira, I see you are in a new apartment, in a dangerous city. Did something terrible happen that you have sunk to this level? Shall I buy you mace?"

But he never asks; not any more. He had at first, when we first met. Now our relationship was my assignment. I maintained the weather station with its careful record of average and extreme temperatures, barometric pressure, wind speed. It was my job to interpret his one word probe, "Mira," and comfort, protect, inform, anchor, any anxiety, curiosity, need for power, he had expressed.

I reached up and put my hands behind my head, and just lay there, gazing at him in the moonlight.

A smile darted around his severe mouth, like a fish in a sun-dappled stream. I saw it; it was gone. I know that smile. He's such a small-town boy, Konrad; when I first met him, to impress me, he said things like, "I was a member of the best reggae band in Bialystok." He understood my fits of giggles at such comments, but never my love. He concluded everything was that kind of a joke, and he never again wants to be the butt, or to be the last to get it.

So now he thinks I'm playing. He thinks this is a new game. He grabbed the edge of my blanket and ripped it off of me, stood up, stood back, and stared. As he walked away, I noted the click of his heels on my blond pine floor. I thought about what kind of carpeting I might want to get. My thighs were getting cold. I reached for the blanket.

"No," he said, sternly. I always wondered – did his ability to sound frighteningly stern come from being born over there? From serving his mandatory tour in the Warsaw-Pact military? What did they experience, what strength-making initiation, that I would never know – he, my parents? He walked back to the bed, took the hem of my nightgown in his fingers, and began to push it up. I lifted my hips. He nudged my thighs apart and pressed his mouth against my fur-ringed lips.

I put my hands against his hair and pushed hard, trying to lift his head up. "Konrad."

His cheek was taut and cool against the plump warm cushion of my inner thigh. "I don't have much time this time," he said.

"Then let's talk," I said.

Keeping his back to me, he stood up and walked over to my one chair. He sat down. "If I wanted talking, I could have stayed at this tedious party in Park Slope."

I brought my legs together. Suddenly, he *was* Jim. Maybe this was the last chance. I had to take it.

"Let us talk, then, Miroswava," he said. And I could see; this was still a game he was trying to master. He'd talk, and earn his blowjob and his adoration that way, rather than with the worn mystery of his late night appearance and petty sadism.

"What shall I talk about? Well, I have a dentist's appointment tomorrow. You would not believe what communist dentists do to one's teeth. Even if you do pay the bribes. I'm hoping it won't have to be root canal. But that's what I fear. Just like a kid, eh?" He smiled at me coyly. "I know I should have the answer to my own fears of the dentist. I mean, everyone comes to me with their fears. You wouldn't believe the clients I had today! Sometimes I wish that psychologists could be assigned a confessor. Why can't that be you, my little Mirka? After all, we break the other rules together, let's break that one, too, eh?"

"I know that my body is not beautiful," I blurted out. Konrad dropped his head and looked at the floor. I fumbled on. "Your appearance mesmerizes me. You're tall and thin and young and clean; naked you look like Michelangelo's David. Your hair is the color of steel –"

"No one has hair the color of steel," he said, looking up, wearing an indulgent smile.

"Konrad does," I whispered. "Konrad," I said, suddenly loud, like that time I tried to greet Owen and Dick. "I guess you enjoy watching me, too, you've watched me for hours, you've drawn my portrait. You touch me, you grab my bottom and hold, hold, my breasts, even my upper arms, holding them, squeezing them, as if to test them, or remember them, until the next time we are alone together."

He was looking thoughtful. Trying to scope out the rules.

"But, I wonder – I hate – There's a difference between my looking at you and you looking at me. Anyone can see that you are beautiful."

He laughed out loud. "I don't think so."

"You don't have to think. You were born this way."

"I was born a skinny boy in a Third World nation. What is your point, Mira?"

"Please hear me out."

He nodded solemnly.

"I like looking at you because I love you," and when I said that, I realized it was no longer true. But I lacked the courage to go back and insert the past tense. "What I'm trying to ask, is, when you look at me, do you feel like you're slumming? That's what everybody would say. When we touch, I score. When we touch, you're being magnanimous."

He was quiet for a long time. I just kept breathing. My neighbor's music soaked through the walls. I didn't like it; it was mournful; but indulgently so. No catharsis; just wallow. Konrad adopted a reverent look and swayed in time.

"Your neighbor has good taste. This is one of her better albums. Essential, really."

"No," I corrected him, "my neighbor's a guy."

Konrad looked confused for a moment. Then he smiled, slightly triumphant. "Billy Holiday. One of *her* better albums."

"Oh, is that the name of the lady singing? Sounds like kind of a whiner, no?"

"*Wlasnie,*" he breathed out, exasperated. He shook his head. He looked out the window.

I put myself on hold, to wait out my time in Siberia, waiting for the reprieve of renewed warmth, or even eyeshot, to offer me my visa back in. Meanwhile, I conjured the companionship of my own thoughts . . .

. . . the first time I met him, at that party where they burned tiny paper American flags atop the birthday cake, instead of candles. There had been caviar in the buffet, something I'd always wanted to try, but I had no idea what it might look like; I passed it right by and piled up on the Polish ham and mushrooms. Some gorgeous man said to me, "Very good caviar, no?" And I shouldered past him and ran to the buffet table and discovered that it had all been eaten already.

I was finding this new wave of immigrants so strange. I had hoped to meet people like my parents, only younger. Peasants who would talk of a Poland made of earth, woven on linen looms, Polish roads run with gypsy wagons; Polish markets where you bought from Jews. They would talk of this coherently, in English, so I could piece together my past and my identity. My wishes erased what I knew. That Poland had been the victim of a torture-murder. New Poland attended this party: slender young urban men and women in black earnestly debating the poetry of rock lyrics. Cell phone conversations covered who got what Ford Foundation grant. Damn, I thought, these people, even with their accents, are more American than I, they have managed to become American in Poland while my parents in America are still stuck in the Old Country.

Robbed of the excuse of Polish identity I can resort to with Americans, unable to produce the kind of American these Poles craved, I wandered out onto the balcony. Hanging over Manhattan's lights, not in the room, not on the street or land or air, I took off my shoes, and danced. There was no music. I hummed. I was invisible. When I opened my eyes, there was a very tall man, watching me.

He was smoking, and smiling, but his lips were so thin and pale, his chin so taut and severe, I couldn't feel secure in the smile. I wanted to comfort this man. I was wary of this man. I closed my eyes, and the man disappeared. I returned to my music, and my dance.

We discovered, later, that while in my fantasy, he was a sultan bidding for a slave, in his fantasy I was a witch who enslaved men with my puzzling footsteps and hypnotic, jiggling ass.

I did not hesitate. He was Polish, well over six feet tall, obviously brilliant, polite as a priest. My one-liners threw him off balance and making anything that tall teeter – the power was irresistible. That night, I tested how my first name sounded with his last . . .

"Miroswava."

I checked back in to the present. "Yes?" I asked, attentive.

"It always . . . amazes me," he began. "'Amaze'? Is that a strong enough word? Amaze? Astound? What you know always amazes me. What you see. And what you don't know, what you don't see, always amazes me."

"This isn't what I wanted to talk about," I said very fast.

"Of course not. What was it you wanted to talk about?"

"Well, like I said. About – my body. About my body."

He rose from the chair and sat on the edge of the couch. Without meeting my eyes, wearing his professional face, he began lifting my nightgown again. "No," I said, and he said something, in Polish? Or just a mutter? That sounded authoritative, final. My arms rose over my head; he slipped the nightgown off. As his arms rose with my wrists in his hands, his jacket squeaked and crunched. I was completely naked. He had never removed his black leather jacket with the multiple zippers.

He put his hand on my neck. I didn't resist, but I felt also, somehow, defiant. Whatever he's going to do, to say, I'm going to survive it. This one time. And then it never has to happen again. For the last time, I made myself like water.

His hand dropped. I shook. What would it find? My round belly? Creamy, soft, warm, eager to be touched, to be a place of sex, of love. But round. Round. Not flat like the belly of every girl in every fashion magazine, the girl men want, the girl who gets paid a hundred thousand dollars to do nothing but stand in one place and look how she looks. My thighs? My inner thighs, my hands' favorite spot, when I am in bed, alone. Like marble, a microclimate, no matter how hot, always cool. Smooth and responsive but so vast his big, broad hand could get lost between them? Or just all over me, padded, not boney, not at all what is valuable, as he is valuable.

I stretched back and granted permission to his hands. I wanted them to find out for themselves. I shuddered like a prisoner in the dock awaiting the inevitable. His hands dropped to my breasts; they executed a quick fondle. His hands dropped to my pussy. They made some predictable moves. And then his hands grasped my hands and pressed them against his erection. I don't know how else to record this next, except, prosaically: suddenly, I felt very bored.

I got out of bed and put on a light. I can't remember the last time he and I were together in a room with a normal light on. I went into the bathroom and pulled on a T-shirt and jeans. I came back out. Konrad looked, I don't know, less. Thinner. Less handsome. And scared. Really. Little-kid, horror-movie scared. I guess I got it right then that we'd never fuck again. And suddenly, without wanting to, I felt as strong as Jean Arthur as the intrepid girl reporter in *Mr. Smith Goes to Washington*, or, was it *Mr. Deeds Goes to Town*? Shit, it was *both*. Suddenly, without wanting to, I felt strong enough to play the spunky girl in two Frank Capra movies. I began to unpack things from the cardboard boxes and milk crates Chris and I had used to move me over here. Cause, that's what I wanted to do at that moment. That was my agenda. No intro, no careful feelers, any more than Konrad's agenda had had. I followed my agenda. I figured Konrad could entertain himself. For a while, what, ten, fifteen minutes? He sat in silence behind me. I was emptying out the last box of books when he left. When he said the self-conscious Americanism, "See ya," it conveyed as much peevishness as two words can carry.

Well, no. "No." That's what Sonia Braga was saying at that moment, "No." I ran into the hall. "Konrad!" He turned. He looked utterly confused. "Konrad, give me a minute, okay?" He didn't understand. "*Choc na chwile*," I requested, in Polish. "Come back for a minute. Gimme this minute."

Whereas confusion had seemed to compel some minor chary engagement, the understood request apparently drained him of any interest. A bored-looking man in expensive, squeaky leather returned to my fully-lit apartment. "I do not wish to intrude," he said, in that voice he uses with his students, that deep, old world, stiff and accented voice that makes the girls in the short skirts seated in the middle rows sure that they have found the last of the courtly gentlemen; sure that they could crack him.

He stood in the wood-floored entryway. I backed into the tiled kitchenette. We looked at each other. There he was, Mr. Mount Rushmore, everything better than I. And I was flummoxed to confront the sudden, cold, bomb-crater where the shrine of my desire used to rise. Embracing his better-than-me, tall, slender form allured as much as embracing a heron. There had been times when the only quick solution to these passing moments of distaste was our taking off our clothing and rubbing our skins against each other until we could rekindle fire that would consume hesitation. That was the ritual, the sacrificial mass we had developed to honor the irretrievable, innocent magic of our first night.

I had what I had believed that I, a fat woman, could never have. Not just Konrad, but Konrad neither immediately satisfied nor fulsomely adored. No. I had Konrad dismissed, Konrad reeled back, dismissed again, and here. I had it; what would I do with it? Eat it? Fuck it? Taxiderm it and wear it on my neck as a trophy? "I have three things to say to you."

Ah, he was again amused. Talk was a game he could always win. "May I sit?" he asked.

"Please."

"And you?" I was wired, ready to pace, but I knew he couldn't sit if I stood, and I wanted him downed. He took the rumpled couch; I, the chair.

"Tell me why sometimes you come and sometimes you don't come. Tell me why sometimes you say you're gonna come and then don't come. Tell me why you can be so tender, so needy, cling so hard, and then, when I run into you downtown when you are with your friends, you act like you hardly know me. And the thing is, they all know we're fucking. So it's not you're trying to hide that. You flaunt that. You . . . act like you love me. Then, with no warning, you leave. Though we're in the same room. Why."

He put his hands over his face. "If you must know, Miroswava, I fear that I'm using you. When I am cold to you, I do it quite consciously. I do it because it's best for you."

"Okay. No problem there," I confessed, casually. "That's easy for me to buy. So, tell me, why are you warm to me, when you are warm? Why, no matter how long goes between visits, you eventually return? And are like – a boy. As enthusiastic as a boy with a cricket he wants to show a friend, or like a baby, sucking."

"Because –" He cut himself off. I knew I'd never hear the rest of that sentence, hurriedly aborted. I'd have to make do with a more consciously worded answer. "I have always valued you," he pronounced, blasé. "You have many qualities that have been . . . very rare . . . in my life." I narrowed my eyes. I was dying to know what those qualities might be. I was searching for something lost or stolen, that he has some feel for. I wanted to stare into his eyes, to follow his focus, so I can find it myself. "But you judge me too highly," he announced.

"No!" I slammed my fist on the coffee table. "That's not my mistake. You're a star, Konrad. You're a *star*. You don't have to get overnight tenure or live in Manhattan – Don't look so shocked. Yeah, she's told me that's what she wants of you. You told your wife stuff about me, too. We've probably all shared the same germs. I don't judge you too highly. Please believe that. Please.

"But I did fail you, Konrad. I gave you total power. I thought that was love. I resented you when you didn't seem grateful. I'm only coming to realize what a burden it is when you do that to people. I was wrong and I'm sorry."

He looked shocked but confused at what had shocked him. I felt like I was in a Star Trek episode, where someone comes back from the future with information that no one else could know, but which they can't quite deny, either.

"The second thing," I raced on. "Actually, this is maybe still the first thing. Konrad, you keep a velvet rope around yourself. You deny me access sometimes, and even when you let me in, you treat me as someone you let in. That hurts."

His head had been down. When he looked up it was with a whole new face. People wonder how a nice guy like Konrad could be with that wife. He was now wearing her, on his face. I felt the fool. I regretted every self-exposing word I had said. "Miroswava," he hissed. "I am always so – entertained – by you. You are like – and I don't mean this in a negative way – you are like some kind of a fossil. Your heart is so close to the surface. And it appears to matter so much to you. I suppose that is all right for someone who works a part-time job teaching immigrants English and shares a house and has no particular ambitions. But it isn't very adult. We aren't enjoying each other right now, Miroswava. I'm going."

He rose and walked to the door. Well, that's it, I thought. He has nuclear capability, and he's just used it. I spoke quickly, but firmly. "This is the third thing. You're full of shit, Konrad."

He leaned against the refrigerator. Looking slick and bored, he waved his hands. "Oh, yes, yes, I am a bad person." he laughed. He reached into his pocket for a pack of cigarettes. He had a match against the strike strip when our eyes met and he remembered. He sheepishly threw the cigarettes and the matches into the trash.

"Do you understand what that expression means?" I asked. "'Full of shit'? It's an American expression. Maybe you're not familiar with it?" For some reason, I was so proud of myself that I was still seated.

"Yes. I imagine it means that I am a bad person. I'll go," he said.

"No." Why was I still talking? Why was I trying to make him understand? Because I cared, I was finding, I cared. Caring is different than being a supplicant. It's different than giving someone else your power. I revved up to, and slipped comfortably into, teacher gear, which I'd never used with him before, because I didn't want to demean him. "The expression, 'You're full of shit,' means that you are not telling the full truth. You're hiding something from me and from yourself. You're probably doing this because you are afraid. Understand? If you don't understand, I'll explain again." Holy cow! So this was power! I walked into the kitchen, and tugged on his sleeve until he looked at me.

As curtains close over a stage so that players may change costume, his hands closed completely over his face. "Fuck off," he said. I gasped. That was not like him at all.

The casual, almost picnic tone in my voice surprised me. "No, I won't fuck off. If I fuck off, it'll be just like every other time, with you manning the velvet rope, and that's not what I need."

He just stood there, his hands covering his face. There were long moments of silence. Neither one of us moved. I thought to myself, "Well, it is his life, I *should* fuck off" and then, "Oh, too bad." Everything had changed. Suddenly *he* was the invader in *my* psychodrama. And then I heard a strange sound, so unexpected that at first I couldn't identify it.

Even when I saw his face, red and wet, I couldn't believe it. He picked me up and sank down to the kitchen floor. The backs of my wrists brushed against his ivory flesh; he fingered my neck, tucked it into his neck. I trembled. He said nothing. He only cried. I scooted around behind, and wrapped my legs around his waist, and rubbed his back. He laughed through his tears. He turned and embraced me hard, pushing me into the cupboard doors. Suddenly he was someone new again, as needy and physically able to meet that need as any big, strong man. Oh, Good Lord, no, Konrad, please don't turn whatever happened here into some new variation on seduction. I felt his erection pressing into my belly as he kissed my face. I was reminded that I am penetrable. He reached around and undid my bra. And the terrible thing is, it was beginning to make sense that way to me, too. Him, strong. Me, strange. The only possible resolution: fucking. "I don't want to go home tonight," he was growling. "No matter what I do, I cannot please her. There is never enough money. You never talk about money. We connect through the heart, you and I," his teeth clamped onto my left nipple; he began to suck and slurp.

Disengaging gripped flesh winded me, hurt me. I latched my bra. I felt terrified and wild with despair. I didn't have the words to rightly baptize anything that had happened. It would be so easy to write off this night as nothing but embarrassment and futility. But whatever was happening this night between me and Konrad seemed to have some holiness and goodness in it, for me. I wanted to make him see that. I didn't think I could.

When he saw that I was not available, he looked, only, defeated. I was relieved – and I was sad. And I hated myself for my own perversity. I stood up. He did, too. I thrust out my hand, grabbed his, shook it with the vigor of a football coach. I struggled to find words that wouldn't sound triumphal or humiliating. "I would welcome phone calls from you anytime, Konrad, to discuss any topic you feel you need to discuss." And he walked out the door.

Is that it, Miles? Did I do it right? Is that what I was trying to be, when I was trying to be as good as you? Is it being a woman who makes men cry, who rejects getting laid, who's as selfish as all the women I've ever hated? God, it's almost six a.m. I'd better stop now and try to get some sleep.

- Reminder: Go to the Borders store in the mall and find out who Billy Holiday is.

DEAR DIARY, WHY can I feel outrage when I witness some bozo smack his kid in a supermarket, when I see a plant go without water, and yet I starve myself daily? Why is it so hard even to imagine what I might want from a man? So hard to imagine that there is any man alive who could give it? I want a man who will kiss the parts of me that are least like the cover model's. I want a man who will not shrink back as if my body detracts points from his manhood, or is evidence of some secret crime I once committed which he, out of tact, will not address. I like being naked when I'm alone; I want to be naked with the man I make love to, and I want to enjoy it as much. I don't want to have to make love in the dark. I want to be able to turn the lights on my full nakedness and say, "This is my body. I love you. I chose you. You are my first choice. I am ready to use this body for our mutual pleasure. I want you to hungrily, greedily, kiss and fondle every morsel of my body, as I will kiss and fondle all of you. I will caress your features which, if photographed under bright lights and hung in a museum exhibition, would not draw the awed applause of crowds. If you can do the same for me, if you can make sweet, imaginative love to every inch of me, if you can please me as well as food or the breeze on a spring day or hard sweaty work that produces fruit or skinny-dipping in the winter Atlantic or my own self-sufficient fingers, then good, then do it. If not, good-bye."

DEAR DIARY, WHEN you love a man and he loves you and he is with another woman, that other woman is a piece of yourself that you've lost. Do I want to be her? Is my love for, is my fear of, Konrad, a peculiar symptom of my own carnivorous envy?

I'll never forget the first time I saw her, the first time I realized her. I was in downtown Manhattan, sniffing out food. I had bought some *makovy kolach* at Moishe's on Second Avenue. I'd rushed down there after work before they closed for Sabbath; it was a Friday. I began to eat it off the wax paper as soon as I hit the sidewalk.

I looked up; there he was. His appearance arrested me as always. The fabulous man from the party, from the balcony, from the earnest groping explosions ever since. The man I'd been telling all my friends about. There's that hewn-in-rock profile. It's turning. Turning toward a girl. A young and slender girl who was skipping up to him, weaving her arm through his. It's the scars, I think, the three deep scars which he has never explained to me – "It's not a very interesting story" – in his right cheek that make his smile so puzzlingly touching and severe, and his unnatural, uniform, paleness. The turn of his profile toward the girl was an indulgence. He was tall and straight and solemn and not in touch with his own heart. She was young and curvaceous, vivacious and wild. She wanted to do nothing with all of her young sex and energy but pierce this very man, tease a smile out of him, constantly invite him to life. She was wearing a ring. Ah. So he is married. Ah. He is married to her. Aha, I see. Aha.

I was the one thing on the landscape that had somehow escaped the symmetry of nature. I was an insult even to the stars, which nest comfortably in the companionship of constellations. I slunk behind a parked truck with my cake.

Tomek, the artist: "She has the most exquisite eye for color I have ever encountered. When I paint, I hear music. She looks at my paintings and can tell me what music I hear. She is exquisite. Exquisite."

Marek, the writer: "She can get to the gist of one of my stories quicker than anyone. She is gifted with a rare gift, the heart of a child, of an animal, so spontaneous, no one has a heart like that, and only with a heart like that can one fully appreciate what is in one of my stories . . . "

The grad student knew an intellectual; the day laborer told her as strong. And then one night Konrad called me up and told me to return to him the reading glasses he had left at my place; he couldn't do anything without them. It didn't occur to me until later that I should have questioned how he had gotten back to Manhattan without them.

I marched up to the door of his apartment. I'd never been there before. So, I thought, this is Konrad's home. The door was ajar. That was surprising. Who keeps the door of a Manhattan apartment open? I saw him sitting inside, looking strangely sheepish. I said, "Excuse me," to the woman standing in the doorway and I was in the middle of squeezing past her when I suddenly realized what was going on. I turned to the owner of the powerful set of boobs pressing into me. "Hello," I said.

She's short and neckless, with short, dark hair, and lots of makeup. It was uneven; as if, when she wakes up in the morning, she doesn't wash off yesterday's make up before applying more. She was wearing a low-cut burgundy silk blouse and no bra. Though she was cramming her breasts into me, I had to resist the urge to cup them. I cannot believe that anyone, any woman, any celibate monk, any gay man, would not want to do that when as near as weighty, globular, tensile and yet pliant a set of purple-titted beauties as hers. They are so much what the world has panted after for so long. And she gets to wear them twenty-four hours a day. And, no, I didn't see them, but, given her coloring, they'd be purple, or, more precisely, with a ripe eggplant's hue, spread and sheen.

Konrad rose; his shoulders hunched. There was a ridiculous apologetic look on his face. After that, it was hard to get aroused by him for about the next month. "I'm sorry," he said, and I wanted to laugh. I squeezed past her, fished in my backpack, and threw his glasses on the couch.

"Hi, Konrad," I said.

His wife reached out and entwined my fingers in hers. I am always so cautious when I touch people. I am always so aware that most feel my touch as trespass, as affront, perhaps even as obscene supplication. In the tips of her fingers I read that her touch on me was to be felt as a tinsel-wrapped gift I should celebrate, be grateful for, and relax into, but only temporarily. "Come, we must talk, you and I. Husband," she turned to Konrad, "Go away for a while. The 'other woman'" – theatrical – "and I must talk."

After Konrad left I realized that she had an open, half-empty bottle of vodka at the end of her arm. I panicked. I could laugh at and dismiss the wife, but not the alcoholic. I wanted to run. She sensed this before I could express it. She gripped my wrist, flashed me a desperate look, and sank to the floor. I folded up and sat across from her. To the artist, she was an artist, to the student, an intellectual. To me she would play the needy alcoholic, and I would not leave for the next nine hours.

Bits of her story still come back to me, for no reason, because there was no reason in her story. It began with an effort to magnanimously humiliate me: "You were lonely. You thought that he understood you. But I am beautiful, and I can make any man love me. Don't you understand? He is a psychologist. It is his job to talk to lonely people. You are just one of many. Perhaps, for some reason, you're interesting to him now, but when he wearies of that – case study – how can you keep him? He gets hard every time he looks at me. It's always been that way, no?"

"Whatever," I said. "Listen. There's a Night Owl AA meeting near here, at St. Bart's. If you like, you and I can go together . . . "

"Ah, the vodka? It upsets you, no? But your father drank beer, no? Don't look so hurt. Yes, he tells me everything. Drank beer and ate kielbasa and didn't shave and even now the feel of a man's stubble and the smell of beer and sausage makes you – what? Angry? Aroused? Sick? Ashamed? All of the above? I forget.

"Ah, no, no, Mira, your outrage. Thank you for that. I was hoping I would see it. Yes, he has told me all about it. 'She becomes so outraged. She's like an ancient human trapped in a glacier and then released.' Thank you for letting me see it myself. Konrad and I, Miroswava *moja*, with what Konrad and I have seen, have lived through, we can no longer afford the luxury of outrage. Here. Have some. Then you will feel none of those things. Just relaxed, like me."

I rose to go. She grabbed my ankle. "I too have memories that upset me. I am afraid of yellow lights. Yellow lights . . . yellow lights. I have seen my own death. It will take place under yellow light . . . Has he told you? Did you know I was an actress when we met?"

At first, I carefully noted all the details. The "yellow lights, yellow lights." The grandmother, who, she was just sure, was Jewish. "That explains so much . . . " she insisted, chest heaving. The ancestral estate, commandeered by the Communists and turned into an insane asylum, now being contested by her brother, the lawyer, who was married to a lesbian who once had her. She told Konrad about it; he made her arrange it again, so he, hidden, could watch. All stories eventually climaxed with Konrad.

"You see him as so much a man. So big, so strong. I know he is really just a little boy. A little boy, Konrad! You are a little boy!" She cried out the open kitchen window. She pulled her torso back in, waved her arm. "Do you see this place? What a dump, no?"

"No! Anyone in Manhattan is lucky to have an apartment like this . . . "

"Always defending him. Believing in him. Telling him he can do it. That's you. If it weren't for me, we'd be back in Bialystok. You know Bialystok? Of course not. Even if you saw it you wouldn't know it. It would all be picturesque to you. If it weren't for me, we'd be *there*. We'd be in Greenpoint with those cleaning ladies and wetbacks who still line up for bread as if this were Warsaw! I'm the one who made him take that extra job teaching. Not you. You telling him he can do anything he dreams. I'm the one – back in Poland, all his friends had something. Marek was smuggling lipsticks into Russia. Tomek was selling hash. And *him?* Nothing. Nothing. Till he met *me.*"

"I think," I ventured, slowly, "men in love are like a person eating artichokes. They bite and scrape and lip the parts they like. The parts they don't like, the barbs, the choke, the starch, they just toss away, without a second thought. You know Konrad and I are only ever alone together, and only at night. He doesn't show me off to his friends, like he does you. I mean, it's obvious; you're more beautiful, more sophisticated –"

She fingered my hair, "With the right cut –"

"He brings me his dreams in the dark," I asserted. "His dreams of leaving you. Of starting a clinic, of serving the poor . . . and then he tosses away the rest of me, just like he tosses away the rest of you. Women, we're different. We're like a frat pledge closing his eyes and swallowing a goldfish, scales, bones, wriggle, and all. We want the whole man. You and I are not so different, that way."

She was hanging half out the kitchen window. "Yellow lights! Yellow lights!"

Around dawn, she produced her own theory of male love, which, weirdly, like mine had been, was food-based. "Men are like a nose passing a donut shop. A man can't not smell. And you just aren't a donut shop,"

I was with her that far, "my little *Mirechka.*" I gasped and stared daggers at the bitch. Her spell over me was broken. I recognized this not as a fated encounter with one destiny had placed in my path, but as time wasted with the tawdriest kind of gambler. So far her gambles with me had worked; in using the yearned for endearment "Mirechka," she had badly miscalculated. Alerted, I began to realize that she could spew her "fascinating, no?" and "verrrry unconventional" life story forever; that I was not, as she had temporarily convinced me, essential to her continued respiration. I realized that I would never save her, never get her to an AA meeting, nor would I ever burst with my teeth the perfect berry of unearthly love she no doubt hid behind those fierce, half opened eyes and labyrinthine stories. My goal became to convince Konrad of this, also. I rose to go.

As I walked out, a neighbor rang the doorbell to ask her or tell her something about the building's superintendent. He was immediately recruited into the audience on the kitchen floor. I couldn't tell if they had ever met before.

Even if she were sixty and had lost all her beauty she would still be compelling because she's one of those powerful women who has chosen to devote all her power to doing the work of fascinating men. As she talks you can feel her trying to knock you off your center and into her own. If I were the most beautiful woman in the world I could never compel as she; I would feel compromised and unsafe working so hard to charm.

Why did she fear me? As long as I don't know the answer to this, she has something of mine that I want, that I am less without. Why did she fear me, me who refused to be beautiful, who, loving Konrad, demands nothing from him, who renounces hating her, the apparent winner? I offered to leave him several times, to her refusal. "No. He will tire of you soon enough." She wasn't secure enough when she said that. And for some reason, I wanted her to be. I felt more comfortable when I could live in a world in which I knew that her cosmetics and need and tits and carnival, manufactured fascination were stronger than me in my fat and backpack and beat up running shoes. Why?

D EAR DIARY, I don't buy lipstick because it's made from whale products. I don't buy mascara because it's tested by torturing rabbits.

I don't buy new clothes or pantyhose because I think they're silly and trivial in a world where children are starving.

Part of me always wants to lecture women like Konrad's wife. "Honey, while you're spending time trying to find fishnet tights to coordinate with that little cocktail dress, the revolution stalls. You could be licking envelopes or typing tracts or canvassing door to door! Do you want the progressive candidate to lose just so you can look nice? Huh?" And another part of me wants to plead, "Take me on as an apprentice? Just a few shopping trips – if I could only watch you . . . "

That night Konrad's wife tried to shock me. Her performance didn't. The biggest shock I received was when I stepped into their bathroom and saw her well-lit make-up table. It was exotic as an oriental bazaar, with a mess of jewelry pouring out of an open chest and tubes of foundation, jars of perfumes and skin oils, and lots and lots of mascara. Maybe five kinds. I actually took two steps back. It couldn't be that the man I love prefers a woman who doesn't keep a clean house, who tortures rabbits, to *me.*

I have lived, and continue to live, a responsible life of self-denial. Except. All thoughts of declining whales, starving children, atom bombs, evaporate when it comes to food. I won't spend $2.25 on a new pair of stockings for a date; I'd never spend less than twelve dollars a pound for chocolate. I condemn elitism, yet I can't respect anyone who buys family brand ice cream. I belong to the Sierra Club and haven't ever bought a toxic household chemical; I put candy in my mouth that is coated with the same stuff I wouldn't wax my floor with.

Self indulgent. Determined. Crafty. A discriminating member of the cognoscenti. These were words I used to describe the women men preferred to me. I never thought of myself this way.

DEAR DIARY, SO, Diary, how do you like your new home? This big, fat teacher's desk Chris and I just brought you from the Salvation Army. It's the kind with wobbly metal walls that echo like thunder if you kick them accidentally. It's so old that I bet it once served as a shelter in "Duck and Cover" drills. It's as dull and gray as today's sky out my high mill window. A snowstorm conjures. Quilted clouds hover so close one of the sumac staghorns will soon pierce them, loosing fleece. Find that hollow log, or abandoned car, whatever you den in, you fat old urban raccoon! Any minute now!

Not just my mouth or stomach but every part of me is saying, "Give us some sugar and we'll let you off the hook."

While pacing the apartment I paused to glance in the bathroom mirror. I saw sadness caused by a life of addicts and addiction. For that reason I have not given myself the sugar I am craving . . . yet.

D EAR DIARY, WHY do I hate her so violently? The loathing I feel for Konrad's wife is almost stronger, and it is certainly more enjoyable, than any love I ever felt for Konrad. It surprises, and frightens me, that I made this choice. Of the two, I hate the woman.

I'm plunked down on the front stoop. I'm staring long enough to memorize the green hills standing in front of me.

Yes, yes! The hills that brim Lenappi valley. Even nowadays, in my mind's eye, I nestle into their ancient, rolling silhouette, as seen from our stoop, whenever I ponder difficult questions. Why Psalm 121 is *my* psalm.

I'm trying to figure out what is, to me, today's biggest, hardest question. Which do I love? Mommy or Daddy? Other days I ask: "Which do I hate the worst? Mommy or Daddy?" How they treat each other you know it's impossible to love them both. I've gotta make up my mind. Until I do, I won't be ready. I'm straddling the blade of a razor. I gotta decide where to press down, which half of me to cut off.

I sit on the floor, my back against the couch Daddy's lying on. Mommy's words sting. "I don't know why you are so devoted to him! He's a bum and he ruined this whole family!"
Evie takes over. "We once found Daddy lying in a gutter. He couldn't get up. The cops were kicking him in the stomach. Mommy had to pull them off. Are you proud of that?"

"If no one else in the world loves you, I will; if everyone else in the family leaves, I'll stay." My eyes silently promise. But he doesn't look like I want him to. He doesn't look like he won. He looks queasy. His smile says, "Your love isn't enough." I screw my love up. I make it stubborn and strong. I will make it enough.

He would carry me, while the older kids, wearing their fear and resentment in slouched shoulders and glum expressions, walked. He'd sing to me, "Without you, I'd die," while the older kids looked at me and said, "You sucker."

Mommy screamed when I touched her. "Get off my back, Mee! I don't like being handled!" She brought the long-corded phone to wherever I was in the house. "I can't get pregnant again. This last one almost killed me. Please, give me birth control pills – or something." After hanging up she'd turn to me. "See that? You see that? The doctors won't give me the pills, because of all the damage you did to my body." She stopped sleeping with Daddy.

Sometimes he'd sit on the couch after a long day, and pull up his white T-shirt. I've always had long, hard nails. Every detail of those evenings remains something that I cherish: Daddy's black hair, the white cotton of the unadorned T-shirt, the weariness he brought home from working for us, working hard with big steel machines. This stark black and white haloed in the gentle golden light shed by our parlor lamp. The pattern of the scattering moles on his back. How could I feel unconnected? I had the same pattern on my back. That I was asked, me, in a houseful of competent people, me, the one everybody else laughed at. I'd take up my position behind him and feel the pressure on the backs of my nails as, with a dry whine, the long tips scraped across his shoulder blades, down his spine.

Once a week Kai, Evie and I bathed. The runt, I sat in the cold and shallow rear. Through pure male threat, Kai claimed the front, under the faucet, which, if he could, he'd cover with his mouth, swallowing all the hot water, rather than letting me and Evie have any. It was good when it was just me and Daddy in the tub; it was good to sluice hot water from a squeezed washrag down Daddy's back.

Daddy is like me. "Soft," "romantic," "childish," Mommy says. Daddy never talks this way about Mommy. "Your mother is a saint. You've got to appreciate her. You kids don't understand how good your mother is."

Every time I choose the crayons labeled "periwinkle," "thistle," or "carnation pink" to draw a rabbit, Mommy sniffs over my shoulder. Even my friends have to laugh after they ask my favorite color. "Turquoise." "Where'd you get that word?" But it was. It wasn't blue. It was "turquoise." After I saw just the right shade on the "Rocks and Minerals" page in the atlas, I added, "Sleeping Beauty Turquoise, from Santa Fe, New Mexico." Mommy shakes her head. "Just like your father. You both like bright colors. I don't," she proudly announces. I know that my job is to someday grow up to be the kind of person who will prefer dark, one-syllable colors, and that I will not be ready until I do.

Her movies are black and white. I fold clothes. She irons, and roots for John Wayne. He's big, dumb and boring. All these fighting films, Nazi uniforms, sudden gunshots, they're scary. A lid has clamped down over this world. Daddy and I cuddle on the bed and watch screwball comedies. In this world, anything can happen. Paupers marry heirs, because he can dance well, or she is spunky. Daddy predicts the plot of every film after seeing the first five minutes. He's always right. He fought in World War Two. I've never seen him watch films in which people are punched or shot. He's walked out of movies like that after driving Mommy to the theater. He sits and waits in the car, shaking his head, repeating, "Sick. Sick."

Daddy sends away for the literature and then takes us on long trips so we can experience educational things, like Chinatown, underground caves with fluorescent stalactites, the World's Fair. He reads the paper every day. He clips an article, underlines it in red, leaves it on the table, shows it to Mommy. "Will you lay off?" she barks. "Do you think I have time for that bullshit? Somebody has to do the work around here."

When I find a word I don't know, I ask Mommy. "Don't bother me. Can't you see I'm busy?" I ask Daddy. "Gee, I don't know. Can you look it up in the dictionary?" It's a dinosaur. Its cover is red leather; the title is stamped in flaking gold. Its weight presses into my thighs; its covers spill beyond my lap; it squirts dust up my nose. I look up the special word but still can't find it. Daddy says, "Okay, then. I'll give you a ride to the library and you can look it up in the encyclopedia. Then I want you to make out a report for me, so I can learn it, too."

I get into bed with Daddy at night and nestle under his arms. Together we make up fairy stories about wretches, the worse off, the better. Cave dwellers and lepers, in the end, by being true and just and humble, are always redeemed by some kindly and, best, unlikely deus ex machina.

If Deus ex Machina were a horse, Daddy would bet everything we have on it. Mommy brings home paychecks; Daddy gambles. His contributions to the family till come with shock and parties; hers are a boring but reliable dribble. Mommy is a voice, which, if I can wake myself, I get to hear at four in the morning, down in the kitchen, talking or singing to herself, in her own language. That voice is all I will have of her in her day of working two full-time jobs, until Sunday.

My Mommy loves me. She is walking away from me, to go to Sunday mass alone because I wasn't quick enough. I see her dark woolen-coated back up ahead of me on the blue tunnel of snowbound street. I am running over ice on stubby legs. I am out of breath. Everything in the world depends on catching up.

"Mommy!"

I don't have enough air to run like this. I can't catch up. I don't have enough air to make her hear me, to make her see me. She doesn't turn. "Mommy! Mommy!" Her gait is so proud. Even from here, I can see. She is so strong. I hold her face inside of me. It's my support. It's my energy. Nothing in the world could be more different than her proud and steady gait, announcing to everyone on the street just who she is and just what she will and will not take, and my flailing, my running.

"Mommy, Mommy!" Suddenly, I catch up. Kai told me about The Big Bang that gave birth to everything. The center of the universe is the place that's the most solid, with the most heat, power and beauty. I see that now in my mother's face. It's like looking in a mirror that adds what I don't have.

"Okay. You can go to mass with me." I told you she loves me! "Now can you get dressed quicker next time?"

"Yes, Mommy."

So which will I chop off? The choice is made for me. It was so dumb of me to think I even had a choice. I am made into the cause of pain. I am made into the thing that must be chopped off.

I need photocopies of an article for school. I put on my sneakers, count my change, walk out the door. Daddy is suddenly leaning out of it. "Whaddya need?"

I know what is coming. I mumble and try to keep walking. Sudden paralysis. Mommy, cigarette hanging from her mouth, storms out and grabs me. "Stop being such an ungrateful bitch. Your father wants to do something nice for you! For Christ's sake! For once let him!" They only unite like this to knock the earth out from under one of us kids. It is too late.

Daddy takes the article. "Whaddya need? I'll take it to a special place. They'll do the copies up nice."

I plunk down in front of the television set. The day is over for me. An hour later, the inevitable phone call. "I donno. The last time this guy let me do it, but now he says if I do it again, he'll get in trouble. I could ask him, but I might get inta trouble with this guy. Ya want me to ask him? Whaddya think?"

I need those copies tomorrow. I look at the clock. If Daddy drives home immediately, I can still make it to the library. Everything feels slow motion and heavy. I exist in conflicting realities. In one, the clock, my legs, and the library's closing time work efficiently in my favor. In the other, I struggle for the words I can say that will make them not hit me, not hate me. I mumble: "Can you come straight home please?"

The shriek is immediate and as loud as one of the exotics in the birdhouse at the Bronx Zoo. "'Please! Please! Come straight home please!'" I know I don't sound like that, but she is mocking the music in my voice. "She thinks she's Greta Garbo! Who do you think you are to talk to your father like that? 'Come straight home please! Come straight home please!' Who the hell do you think you are?"

Daddy is on the line. "I donno, ya know. I think there's something wrong with my brakes. I was gonna stop and get 'em checked. If you really need it, I could come home now, but I'm afraid with these brakes, ya know? I could get into an accident. Whaddya think? Want me ta come straight home?"

"Could you maybe try again with the man?"

"Awright, if you want me to, but it could be trouble."

Daddy hangs up. I move slowly towards the couch. I continue watching a rerun of McHale's Navy. *The next call comes fifteen minutes later. There is fighting in the background. Hearing Daddy being called a beggar. "He's not gonna let me do it. Whaddya think."*

There is squeezing tension in my body and a burning, maybe of hatred, maybe of humiliation, of knowing, again, that I'm just a pawn. Once again I'll be the stupid kid, who isn't ready, though I wanted so badly to be, because I loved this assignment. I look at the clock. If he left at that moment, if he made all the lights, I could get to the library's ten-cent photocopy machine before it closed. Defying what I know is my fate, I say so.

"I donno. This thing with my brakes, ya know. But if you really want me to do it, I'll do it."

While driving home, Daddy has an accident, and has to spend some time in the hospital.

Mommy stands in the waiting room, telling my aunts and uncles about that little bitch, it's all her fault. "She doesn't appreciate how lucky she's got it. She gets to go to school! She doesn't even show any affection to her father, ever." I feel no affection. I only wonder what's wrong with a girl who can see her father in a hospital bed and only obsess on another F in school. I'm convinced that I cannot feel.

We go for our last drive together as a family. I am the only one who will still sit up front with Daddy, who will still engage him in the current events, philosophical, or religious debates he so adores. After all, it was the movies I watched with him that taught me the workings of plot. It was he who demanded that I never assume I understand any issue before I have debated both sides as if my fate depended on the outcome. It was he who taught me to worship and ritually clip the daily paper. But suddenly I am being screamed at and threatened by a man driving seventy-five miles an hour on a state highway. "You stuck up little bitch know it all! Don't you tell me! Who the hell do you think you are? Just because you got your American school ej jay kay shun. Son of a bitch. Son of a bitch. Why did we even have 'em?" the husband asks his wife.

"Calm down," the wife replies, completely in control. "You know you shouldn't get into these conversations. She always does this to you. What

do you expect? She was the youngest. We loved her so much. Our love was wasted on her."

Daddy didn't just betray me. He betrayed the things we enjoyed together. He betrayed himself, a person I loved. I would never be like him. I would never submit to the hammer. I would never be weak. I would be tough and responsible, independent. I stopped writing. I used, exclusively, the brown, gray, and navy crayons. Every time I went to a movie, read, scribbled a poem on the back of a bus schedule, chose periwinkle, felt some tenderness for the body I was fucking, I knew I was still wrong. I knew I was on the trajectory to eternal hunger and submission to the strong. I sucked in my breath during those movies I allowed myself; protesting, "This isn't life. This isn't my life. This isn't time, yet. I'm not ready. I'll do this today because I need to; I'll be ready, soon, and then my real life will begin."

I ate to kill the fear that time would never come, that I would never be ready. I ate to numb the stress of being who I was not. I ate to numb the grief for my dead self. On the same shopping trip during which I wouldn't buy myself a book of poetry, I would buy a pound of chocolate.

I corner my students who are uncomfortable with themselves because they care, because they cry, or need music, or just need to stare out of the window a lot. "Go with it," I insist. "Trust it. Don't lose it." I never permit myself to hear those words as I speak them. Even so, there is clear indication that my choice did not work out as planned: my doomed push to save Konrad, and my rage at Konrad's wife.

D EAR DIARY, I was trying to read want-ads in the library. The little voice said, calmly and confidently, "Anyone else in this library can have a cookie when he wants it." The battle had begun. I was sure that I would lose. My muscles ached and sagged; I assumed the posture of the defeated. I hunched my shoulders and pressed my lips together like a child who knows that her favorite toy is about to be taken away from her, but who will hold on for one moment more. I felt so ashamed. No one was doing this to me. I was sitting alone in a library, passing as an adult, and, for no apparent cause, I attacked myself, thwarted myself, damned myself.

I began arguing. "Yes, anyone else in this library can have a cookie when he wants it. He can have one cookie. How many people in this library, given the choice, would trade every day for the rest of eternity looking for satisfaction in cookie after cookie?"

The voice didn't have an answer for that, so it evaporated, but my concentration on the want-ads was broken. I began counting the hours until my next meal. Is this what life is going to be from now on? Must something as normal and healthy as hunger pangs be my enemy, or must I be theirs? This struggle again reminded me of how weird, how sick, how different I am. I thought, if I'm this weird, I might as well just go ahead with it. I now obsess on my obsession as much as I formerly obsessed on food. At least with active addiction I know the tiger's steps, and can work around them. I could have promised the voice, "Check out ten want-ads; then you get a cookie." It would have waited. We've worked together for decades; we know these deals are kept. To say to the voice, "No cookies. Your tyranny is over," ignited its wrath and of that I am very afraid.

Merde. I just realized I've given myself away to you, Diary. " . . . trying to read want-ads in the library" indeed.

I wish I could report that I cattle-prodded Jim. Or merely laughed at him. That I whipped off one of those devastating retorts that film heroines have on the tips of their tongues. But I can't. I just saw the assignments for the next semester, and my name was on none of them. I didn't want to talk to Jim, so I went to Old Dolores. I was standing at her desk, waiting for her to get off the phone. She didn't. For a very long, uncomfortable time she didn't. I noticed an empty Dunkin Donuts box on her desk. Jim walked up to me. "Would you like to come into my office?"

"No," I said, suddenly sure that with nothing to lose he'd take one last sloppy lunge. "I'm just here to ask Dolores about the assignments for next semester –"

"Why your name isn't on there. We've just had some fluctuations and we won't be needing your services this next time."

"In the future?" I hated that I asked that. Hated it.

"Probably not then either." The amazing thing is he didn't look personally vengeful; he looked like God banishing Adam and Eve. His outraged, patriarchal glare communicated that my resisting him in the supply closet was a threat to the divinely ordained order. All I could think was, "How I envy that." How I wish I could understand and communicate someone else's causing me pain or even just discomfort as wrong.

DEAR DIARY, I always find it so amusing when people accuse me of being a bookworm. They're more accurate than they know; bookworms are insects that eat books. They are voracious and they are illiterate. I'm dyslexic; most of what I know of books I've pickpocketed by listening to people who can read.

I do read, after my own fashion. Index finger runs under lines, shoving them into place; mouth gutturally sounds out the identity of elusive words. I read a page or so a day, and then, the next day, go back and read that page all over again. Over time, words swim into place. Stories unfold to me as do the hidden texts of a palimpsest – now there's a word I never thought I'd use. In layer after layer of reading and coaxing I understand the story again and again. Maybe in the fourth or fifth reading it comes to me that the word I'd recognized as "banana" was, in fact, "bandana," and my hero's headgear was nowhere near as unconventional as I'd been picturing it.

I think I also used to read books over and over as a child because there weren't enough in the house to satisfy me. This was not boring. Didn't someone once say that you can never step into the same story twice? I'll never forget *Tales of Oki,* a little Scholastic paperback I bought from the book club at St. Francis School. I read a tale or two every night, before going to sleep, for years.

Once upon a time, a poor student rented one slant-ceilinged room above a fine restaurant. Every night for dinner, all he had to eat was plain rice. But as he ate, he would lean out his window, and flavor his meal with the savory perfume wafting up from below. The rich restaurant owner found out, and sued for payment. Wise Oki told the student to run his coins from one hand to the other, the pleasant sound to serve as payment enough for the greedy rich man.

Miles, have I loved anyone since you? Did I love anyone before you? When I had sex with Konrad, did I make it possible by smelling your perfume?

I'd run into the Peace Corps training house and explode. Everything was distorted, like the first European drawings of rhinoceroses. You'd listen. Then you'd repeat my words as if you'd had an invoice of my vision in hand, waiting. You'd just check it all off. And I'd sit there, hearing my heart and my mind in coherent words for the first time.

Miles, it's been ten years. Where are you now?

DEAR DIARY, MOMMY'S birthday. I bus to the mall and enter a card shop, one of the central manufacturing plants for that consensus reality I so insistently envy. I look at all the pretty cards, read the sentimental messages. Are there really people out there who feel these sentiments? Who can rely on them? I'm not one of these people and it is poison to pretend that I ever was. I am some kind of freak orphan with vestigial parents. I am accused again, by my inability to feel any of the sentiments expressed herein. I am as perverse as my parents always said I was. I walk out in a cloud, not sure where I've been or where I'm going.

When I come to, it's days later. What alerts me back to consciousness is the calendar, accusing me again. "You! Time is running out!"

I offered to take Mommy out to dinner. She said okay. I tried to set a day. "Actually, I'm very busy. I'm translating for a batch of Slovak women St. Cyril's brought in to clean houses up in Cupsaw. And I visit the old folks' home every Saturday."

"Please, just . . . name a day."

"Oh, that's all right. I don't need to. You don't have to."

"Call me when you decide." I left her house, knowing I would not get a call. So I called. "Have you decided?"

"If you don't have the time, it's okay."

"Just name a day."

"I'm very busy, Mee. Just forget it."

I called a week later. "Are you free now? Yeah? Then we go today."

I assume that if my new mill apartment ever got broken into the first thing they would go for is my words. I imagine thieves reading this diary. And it's only in writing, in turning Mommy into some code other than life, that I get it that an observer would conclude that I am crazy. In a way, I am. I think of Konrad's wife, of Mel, of Evie. Part of me feels that there are women out there I have to conquer, whose skin I have to peel off and dress in before I am authentically human. Part of me feels that life is something they have and I can only hope to suck off their umbilical cords. But I'll never really be fully human because I'll never be them.

But it's not simply a question of such icky Freudian stuff. If only it were, it would be much easier. Chris said to me once, sounding like he was quoting someone else, "The great tragedy of life is that love does not last." I snorted and felt so much older. "No, my son," I thought. "The great tragedy of life is that it does."

DEAR DIARY, I parked Chris's car in front of the house. It was good of him to let me borrow it. I walked in the always-open back door. I caught sight of Mommy out in the garden, in an open jacket and a loose housedress. She was breaking earth already, and smoking. Her thick dark hair was just brushed back, in no special do. She moved her hand to her hip; the cigarette jut out like an exhaust pipe. She was braced on her wrestler's legs as if awaiting a blow from God, from a tornado, from the inevitable, but never to down her. "This is the last year I'm gonna have a garden," she announced.

"You say that every year," I called out after opening the kitchen window over the sink. She does. I wanted to tell her that I heard her, that I recorded her, as Miles did me.

"Shut that window! You're letting the heat out!"

I shut the window.

Mommy saw that Bob, next door, was outside. She had to bring him some onion sets, to bring him some pickles. To tell him how you can make pickles in your own cellar. To offer him a crock from ours to give it a try. "No. Take it. It's not such a big thing. I'll go get it now. No, wait, I'll get it. After you've had your own homemade, you'll never want store-bought again."

I sat down and grabbed a magazine. She gets them all, and they are always all over the house. God, I miss that. Fresh, glossy prose. How were these ever afforded? I heard the back door slam.

"Damn!" I could hear furious scratching.

"Want some alcohol?"

"I have alcohol!" She screamed. "Benjie, get out of my way, you damn dog." She came into the parlor, thrust out her stout, freckled arm. "This is *not* poison ivy. This is poison oak. It's much worse."

"Mom, we don't have poison oak in New Jersey. I have a book. I can show you —"

"'I have a book! I can show you!'" she mocked, baby talk.

"Want some calamine lotion?"

"I have! There's no use talking to you." She sat down and scratched her reddening arm. Her bra was visible from the armholes of her housedress; this didn't seem like the kind of thing she'd wear to a restaurant for a birthday dinner.

"All right. So, what about what your sister is doing to me?"

"Evie? What's going on?"

"What kind of a daughter would not let her own mother see her own brand new grandbaby?"

Omigod. My Evie, my sister Evie, my leggy fun-loving sister, tanned and smart-mouthed belle of a hundred Jersey shore parties, was a *mother.* Again. I reeled. Inside, thanks to long training . . .

"Everyone shits on my head!" Mommy.

. . . Evie hadn't told me she was pregnant again. When was the last time I'd seen her? When was the last time we talked? But of course Evie's stuck-up behavior would hurt Mommy more than it would hurt me. I'd call Rick, Evie's husband, and in a way he couldn't refuse invite Mommy over there to see her new grandchild. I'd drive Mommy over. I'd sit in the car while she visited.

Mommy didn't show any signs of getting dressed; in fact, she turned on the TV and began watching *The Good, the Bad, and the Ugly.* I decided to give Benjie a bath while working out the execution of my plan.

When I came out of the bathroom, Mommy was on the phone. With me she'd been morose; she was now an animated charmer who couldn't say the wrong thing. I wondered who was on the line, and getting the best of her. A priest? No, even to priests, she's often challengingly crude. An elderly relative? No, she's speaking English.

I knew I'd have to return Chris' car soon. As I had with Konrad the other night, I needed to be assertive with my care. I said to her, "Look. I'll take you over to Evie's house. Let's go."

Rage inflamed her face. I stepped back. My stomach curled against my spine.

"'Who was that?'" she said into the receiver, apparently repeating a question from her interlocutor. "Your sister's here. Here, talk to her."

Suddenly she thrust the phone at me. I heard Evie say, "Don't give the phone to her. I don't want to talk to her. She's such a –" I returned the phone to Mommy just in time for her to catch the tail end of that comment.

"What?" Mommy asked.

I guess Evie repeated her assessment of me. Mommy sighed. She said wearily, wisely, "I know. I know. What we have to put up with for family, right?" And then she went right on merrily charming like some network TV morning host.

While drying Benjie, I eavesdropped on the rest of the conversation. Evie was cajoling Mommy to come visit the new baby, I guessed from Mommy saying over and over, "Oh, no, this is a special time, a time for a husband and wife, for you and Rick. I'd be a burden. We'll give it a couple of days and then your father and I will drive over there."

I stared at the wall.

Mommy gaily hung up the phone, warned, "Don't you let that dog on the furniture!" and went to her bedroom and closed the door. When she emerged she wore a navy blue suit and a white blouse with a built-in scarf at the neck. I took her in in an ill-focused second, and saw that she had lipstick on. "You look nice," I said.

She did. I've never seen a more beautiful woman. "Beautiful" is a euphemism here. Ages before it became popular in rock stars like Madonna, or even proper, Mommy surveyed the world with a hot scowl. Her lipstick was, as ever, bright red. She has always gotten that very right. Thick, dark hair, white, white skin, "fuck you" expression, all take blood red lipstick.

"So, are you here to take me out to dinner or not?" she said abruptly, and she was out the door, her pocketbook swinging, before I could alert myself to realizing that walking out the door was the next thing to do. I pet Benjie, let him kiss me again, and left.

I focused ahead, not looking to my right, where she sat, even when I needed to turn right. She kept her hands on the purse in her lap and on her ever-burning cigarettes. "Where's the ashtray in this car? Oh, never mind." I jerked my leg leftward at one point when I thought I had touched the hem of her dress. To check, I did not lower my face; I looked down, with my eyes only. I breathed out. It was just the hem of my coat, which I had placed between us.

Mommy's curious about the world and anything new; she's never had Indian food. I took her to The Taj, in Montclair. It's quiet, with a careful, effortfully elegant décor. A few Rajasthani miniatures hang on otherwise plain white walls. Here even working class diners can enjoy excellent food they can afford, and a touch of exotica, before getting back, via the turnpike, to their nine-to-fives. I love the place.

The waiter placed us across from each other. Mommy got up and went to the ladies' room. When she came back she sat to my left. I now had an unimpeded view out the window. I looked at the parking lot across the street. I studied customers entering and exiting the supermarket. I wondered if there were a correspondence between the size of the car and the length of time spent in the store. Mommy was across from the restaurant wall. She looked at a Rajasthani miniature. "I wish I could speak their language," she said.

Mommy ordered biryani lamb. I got thali. Mommy talked. "I take the kid as much as I can. You should see her. She is growing up so fast!" It was the kind of thing you say in a long distance phone conversation, in a letter to a boy away at war. Evie and her kid – her kids – live twenty minutes from me by car. "Rick is useless, just useless. But I can see why she married him. He has that plumbing outfit. It's better to bring kids up with shoes than without, as I well know!"

I think it's because I have worked so hard to act like a white suburban lady, at least for short performances. I was dressed like a teacher. I was wearing my black skirt and my white blouse with puffy sleeves and black pumps and pantyhose, the kind of clothes that can only ever feel like a costume to me. So, perhaps, this was why Mommy performed for me as she would before a teacher, a druggist or a nun. She performed the sturdy, noble immigrant who held the teary, undifferentiated children together under one roof through the sheer dint of her Old World determination and Catholic faith. Even her pronouns were wrong. She did not say, "you kids," to me, but "them." Evie was not "your sister" but "my daughter."

"Evie will never have it as hard as I had it. She'll never have to sacrifice for those children as I sacrificed for mine. Evie's kids will never do to her what mine did to me. I support her. I baby-sit every chance I get. And you know what? She had a party last week, wouldn't believe who she had over there, her neighbors, a *doctor*, a *teacher*, who does she think she is? You know. And she didn't invite me. Didn't even tell me about it. Rick told me about it, that loudmouth jerk. That's all right. That's all right. I believe in God. She'll get hers some day. She'll get her comeuppance. I just do what I can. Cause that's how I am. That's how it is in the Old Country. It's not like that here. People walk out on their families here." She almost looked at me. Her look was citing an illustrative example: "the kind who walks out on her family." At least I could serve as show-and-tell item, as well as audience.

"She needs me. That Rick is useless. My daughter, Evie, her water broke in my house. You should have seen it! Who drove her to the hospital? Not Rick. It was Arnulfo Baca from across the street. I went and got him. Rick wouldn't do it. Old Arnulfo Baca, you remember him. He drove about twenty miles an hour! It was so funny. My daughter, Evie, you know, she wanted to kill me!"

"But I won't call her. I won't. You know how it is. You can't do that. People don't do that. You can't say your feelings; you just smile and walk away, and never let them know how they hurt you. If she didn't want me at that party, all right. But then don't expect me to call, right? I'll be over there next weekend for the little one's christening. Are you going to that? Oh, well. Rick won't do anything. I just wonder, who's gonna do all this when I'm dead?"

The lamb goes down between the red lips quick. "Waiter, more water. And how about some ice? This food is so salty. They don't give very big servings here, do they? And this is supposed to be lamb? It's not lamb. It's beef."

"Let's get the waiter," I said. "We'll send it back."

"Don't be ridiculous. Rick is jealous of me. You know? Because she relies on me. She still comes to me. If there is some problem, there she is. On the phone. On the doorstep. A Jeep. Do they need a Jeep? What do you need a Jeep for? Do they live on an unpaved road? No. They live in New Jersey, for Christ's sake. What does he need a Jeep for? No wonder she's worried. How can they save when he's buying like that? I told her, 'Save your money now. You'll be glad later.' Like I did. I saved what I could, with a drunken husband who liked to gamble and kids to take care of, not just my own kids, but my mother's kids, too.

"And now he's redoing the downstairs bathroom? What for do they need a new downstairs bathroom? The old one was good enough. And they could have banked that money, a good six, seven thousand dollars. And he's not even getting the top of the line faucets. He's a plumber. If plumbers can't have the best faucets, then who?"

"You should see that Kimberly. She is so precious. Priceless. That's what she is. She's going to be very smart when she grows up. You should see what she says to me! 'Grandma, I no like soup!' Cause she didn't like the borscht, you know? Well, you can't expect an American kid to like borscht. So, she just didn't eat it. I had to make her a peanut butter and jelly sandwich. Cause that's what they like. You gotta know what these people like. She was folding her arms and stomping her feet like Shirley Temple.

"But Evie's got to get a decent schedule at work. She lets the kid stay up too late, waiting for her to come home. She wanted me over there last night. I said, 'No. Whose fault is it that you have this backbreaker work schedule? Do you want to be a mother or no to these kids?' You know. I never let my work interrupt my kids' sleep. Never. Kids are kids. You got only one chance to do it right.

"And these hours are not hurting just my grandchildren. No. Evie gets it, too. And what I wanna know is, where is Rick? What's his job in all this? I can't always be over there babysitting. I have my own life to lead too, you know. I have the Rosary Society, and counting collections on Monday, and now they've got me translating for Slovak women who come to this country to clean houses and to take care of kids. These women don't speak a word of English, some of them, and they've got them with kids eight hours a day. Imagine that! I'm sorry. This is just too salty. Here. Pack it up and take it with you. God knows what you get to eat in *Paterson*. I'm glad at least you could enjoy your meal."

I thought. Evie could talk to her boss about getting a better work schedule. She's been at that place for ten years; they know her value. They'll give her better hours. Rick may be a jerk but he is a handy man, so he could put acoustic tiling in the girls' bedroom. That way the noise of Evie coming home wouldn't waken them. And, about the invitation, if Evie knew how Mommy felt, maybe she would behave differently. Maybe some intervention could do some good. Mommy is right; she does baby-sit for the kids too much. I could volunteer – if I knew Evie's number. She has an unlisted number and hasn't given it to me yet. I could probably talk to the operator, explain that she is my sister. And I would be asked: "If it is so important that I put your call through, why don't you have your sister's number?" And I decided that, yes, the bigger the car, the more time people spend in the supermarket.

D EAR DIARY, THERE'S something I'm supposed to do that I haven't done yet. I'm not enough, I can't relax, because I haven't yet done this thing. I rush toward it, but it stops me, like a border guard's flashlight. Crashed silence, clotted sound, stalled arrows, rushed paralysis: the rhythm, the percussion, the push, the pull, the in, the out, the ready-set-go of my body's fluids and its airs, of my life goals, of any encounter or even writing in you, Diary.

I make little lists. I cross off each task. This serves no end. I feel as much tension after completion. I can't reward myself, even with satisfaction, even when I've acquitted myself well in a day of breathlessly done chores, or graduating from college *magna cum laude.*

I have wrestled this tension, this need to do even when weary, by exhausting myself with huge amounts of food. I'm not doing that now, and so it won't let go. Tonight I was so jittery; tried to relax, couldn't. Sat down and asked myself why. Held a pen above the page; wrote any words that came into my head. The first: "Not ready."

Feelings of unworth, unreadiness, I've associated with fat. But no. The next: "Salvation."

Have I been waiting to be saved?

"Not to be saved, to save. Mommy. I must save her. I will never have done enough until I save her."

Then I burst into tears.

"How can I save her?"

"By loving her. She needs to be loved. Even if I have to erase myself to love her, I must. Then she can love *me.*"

But Mommy, Daddy, Konrad, they don't want my love. They beckon it forward with waving hands. Then, like a border guard shining his flashlight, they stop it dead. They are loyal to their addictions. "Love me," they say. "When you do, I will reject you." Love threatens addiction. Love exposes the lies that make addiction possible. Love forces the addict to confront: "I am lovable; I am worthy, right now; I have no reason to continue abusing myself. I can take the energy I invest in addiction and invest it in *me*."

Well, good for them. What about me? I'm no longer devoting each day to food, my drug of choice. What do I invest my energy in? What else is there besides tempting those you love, failing those you love, hating yourself and devotion to drug of choice? I have no idea.

I want to be monstrously fat. I want to be twice as fat as I've ever been. I want to lose every contour of my body and become one round ball and roll my days between the oven and the couch. I want to become so fat that no know-it-all busybody will ever suggest to me again, "But you have such a pretty face." or, "But you're so smart . . . " So fat that no matter how dim the lights or lonely the man, no one will ever flirt with me at a party and get me hoping that I can have romance in my life for longer than the length of one afternoon soap opera, minus commercials. I want to live my life in muumuus, capacious as Red Cross refugee tents, without any buttons or zippers or snaps. I want to fling all the belts I own right into the ocean. I want to get so fat that I can at least be something, be something definitively, rather than someone trying pitifully and without success to be something else.

D EAR DIARY, JUST called one of those suicide prevention hotlines. Ten times. Got a busy signal every time. A good thing, cause I have no idea what you're supposed to say to a suicide prevention hotline. Have to study up on this.

Grabbed my Sierra Club magazine and called catalog companies' toll free numbers. Pliant, respectful voices greeted me from Vermont, Wisconsin, Colorado. "How may I help you, ma'am? Why surely. I'd be happy to. You'll be hearing from us in four to six weeks. If there's any trouble, you call right back. Ask for me. I'm Jeff . . . Linda . . . Cathy."

And a Bill, in San Francisco.

"So, what kind of name is Miroswava?"

"It's – Polish? It means, 'the glory of peace,' oddly enough."

"It's really pretty. We're expecting our first-born any minute now, but we have no idea what to name him, her, or it. We're looking for something that isn't just run of the mill, not another Jennifer or Josh."

"You a Polak, Bill?"

"I'm Irish myself."

"Well, how about Colleen? Or Siobahn. I've always loved that name, though it's hard to spell."

"I like Miroswava the best."

"Go for it."

"Say, what kind of weather are you having in Paterson?"

"Drear."

"Yeah, it's been dreary here, too."

"Even over there in California?"

"Even over here in California."

"Let us eat and drink, for tomorrow we may die."

"That's right. Only tomorrow my child may be born."

"Hey, good luck with that. And congratulations."

"Thanks, Miroswava. I'll be getting our appropriate technology catalog to you shortly. Stay well in Paterson."

"You too, Bill. This has been nice. Bye!"

"Bye!"

Damn! I could have touch and bliss with food whenever I wanted it. I can't conjure Them so easily.

DEAR DIARY, I wanted to relax with a bottle of mineral water in front of the TV. "No. You can't do that. There isn't enough mineral water. You'll use it all up. Save it till you really need it. There aren't enough good shows on TV to entertain you. They'll get old and you'll get bored. Then what pleasures will you have?"

A list in mind for a special recipe, I purposely don't buy everything I need. I purposely don't buy everything I need, though I have the money on me. I purposely don't buy everything I need, though I've plenty of time to. "I purposely don't buy everything I need:" this is the first time I'm admitting this to myself. I never questioned it before. "It would be too good if I had it in my house all at once, and I finally prepared this recipe as written."

I put cotton swabs on my shopping list. "No! Did Lewis and Clark have cotton swabs? Did immigrants crossing the ocean make use of cotton swabs? They did without. As can you. Cotton swabs are no necessity. You'll use them all up at once, and then where will you be? You'll want more and more, and then you'll use them up, and then you'll want more and more . . . "

I have something to say. I hold my tongue. I want to smash an empty soda bottle on my table. "Don't do that. It's a temperamental gesture and you forfeit the nickel deposit." I wash three more cups before I turn up the radio, turn three more pages before I turn off the light, test how many times I can count to ten before I go to the bathroom, take up a hobby, tell someone, "You're stepping on my foot."

Last night I'd been working at my desk for hours. Suddenly the alarms went off at Addiction Control Central: "Hunger Pangs," "Taste of Cookies," "Vision of the Last Bakery Visited," and, the pièce de résistance, "Rationalization:" "It wouldn't be so bad if just this once I . . . "

After a good half hour of ricocheting off the walls, I decoded my body as if it were a captured enemy encryption. I grasped each piece of understanding before it faded so that I could sew it to the next one. I had to flash the completed manuscript on a mental screen, and stare at it, open mouthed, struggling to let it sink in: "You've been working all day. You haven't taken a single break. You are so cold you have goose flesh. What's more, you have to pee. Visit a friend. Put on a sweater. Go to the bathroom."

D EAR DIARY, *A decorative scene is painted on an antique dresser. A woman wears a billowing, diaphanous gown that gathers on her upper arms and just under her high bosom. Gold ringlets pile atop her head and spill over cheek, brow, pearl-drop ear. A man of supernaturally long and slender proportions joins her. He is no less pretty and elegant than she. He hands her a long-tailed, emerald bird which balances perfectly on his outstretched hand.*

"Thank you. And your poem. So beautiful."

"Not as beautiful as you, oh daughter of the king."

"You are my sweet man."

"You are my dream."

The bird takes flight. The woman stirs to watch its arch. Her gown catches light. He sighs deeply, then sings. But his song proceeds from my mouth. One day, I am heard.

One day I approach the secret dresser and find Mommy painting it over. She studies my face. I know what she is looking for. I resist producing it. Mining, perhaps, she probes, "You can't get attached to anything in this world. I had to leave my country when I was only a child, and never saw it again. You've got to learn to be strong."

I pity her. "You're such a fool," I think, but do not say. "I don't need you. I don't need anybody or anything."

The sensation: poise on ice, thin, over a still warm pond; flex toes, never relax; arms calculate, like a level, every balance fluctuation. Never allow too many toys, too much attachment to any one thing. Know that they will be on shore when you are speaking in bubbles, negotiating with mud turtles, water snakes, catfish. Learn to take, learn to steal, but never learn to need.

But I did need them. Without their food and shelter I could not survive.

I knew that only the dead have no needs.

I'd been trying to work out some pattern, some logic, so that I would know when it was about to happen, so that I would be able to explain it to others. I am struck by how I can discover nothing different that may have triggered this episode, or been used to justify it. I don't remember the morning of this day; I don't remember its evening. I don't remember what Miss Farrow was teaching in kindergarten. I don't remember if it was winter or spring. But I remember this: coming home from school, walking down the hallway between the kitchen and the bedroom. And, suddenly, she is on me.

"You fat slob! You're not a human being!"

My hands flail out, never strike home. I am as tossed and turned as a handkerchief in a washing machine. Fist strikes spatter over my body. These will soon swell and blossom into blue and purple clouds, streaked with lightening slashes of red veins "I hate you. I hate you! I am going to

kill you!" I tumble to the long thin faux Persian runner that loosely covers
the hall floor. "Go! Get out of my sight, you fat pig!" I am pushed into a
room, a dark room, alone. I hear the door – click – lock shut. I fall to the
floor, grip knees into stomach, lock arms tight round abdomen, try very
hard to press in, to press in, to give substance, connection, ballast. Breathing
fast, hard, shallow, sure struggle is vain, sure this time she has gotten
me. I plummet through the Black Emptiness. No rescue impedes. I will
evaporate, never again be. Already, some weird gravity pulls me apart.

As always after these beatings, there is another present. I don't want
her to be here. She is too good for this. I don't want her to see. I will save her
for the day when I get out. If she sees what is going on, she will be destroyed.
If she were here, if she did see, her anger and outrage would get me killed.
I will keep her away, until I am ready. I push hard, push her away.

It was okay for Mommy or Daddy or Evie or Kai to beat me in a
spontaneous explosion after a long period of denying their rage. After
all, these were decent people who went to church on Sunday. They
controlled themselves. They didn't sass bosses, give trouble to the law or
the state, annoy their friends. They worked the same factories, cleaned
the same houses, as the scary Colored people who were rioting; they
went home to the same state-issue surplus food and cold water, no hot.
They didn't react by causing trouble; they responded by working hard,
sending money home, closing sentences with "Sir," and "Ma'am." Sure,
they got frustrated sometimes. You'd only expect that. After the outburst
was over, it had to be ignored. It was not real life but a departure from it.
Because these were good people. Anybody who said otherwise was bad.

After a measured time they would approach me with sweet food. My
choice: abandon the grief and pain of that beaten five-year-old, because
all she is is pain, and venture out for some chocolate-covered peanuts, or
sit alone, immobile, brooding, with no solution.

Everyone let me know that it would have been selfish for a kid like
me to be allowed to be aware of my needs, never mind expect them to be
met. Mommy's immediate response to any expression of need from me
was, "Omigod. This is another person whose bottomless needs I can
never meet." "I need shoes," was a secret code for, "I'm an addict just like

Daddy and I'm here to eat your soul in my own doomed cannibalistic struggle to achieve human status."

Mommy could have been straightforward. She could have said, "Yes, I am your mother, and, yes, it is my duty to provide you with adequate shoes, but, no, I don't have money for them right now." I loved Mommy. I would have figured out a way to get the shoes myself. Mommy couldn't allow that. Not just Daddy, but I too was to be saved by her. So, if I wanted shoes, and she couldn't supply them, she needed to change the reality to, "You don't need shoes. Here, have some chocolate." Mommy could not allow my love for her, or my trucking for myself, because those would have endangered her status as martyr, and mine as dead weight. Me, Evie, and Kai: we were the nails that fixed Mommy to Daddy, her cross: "I have to stay with him. I need the money. I couldn't support you without him."

Since my parents gave to themselves and to us without any conviction that they or we were yet worthy to receive, giving was a painfully guilt-ridden act. After living hungry for weeks or months, my parents would explode, joylessly: a used Cadillac with no transmission sat in the driveway. An old lady's leather coat, expensive but too ugly to wear – "Ingrate!" – hung in the closet. A gargantuan feast was served, but nobody felt like eating. Splurge goods could bear no relation to what was really needed because any such correspondence would have made the expenditure of money real, the need real, us ready and deserving.

The addict is trained to hoard her needs, to live for a long time in deprivation as she watches and waits for the Monster's, her supplier and keeper's, defenses to fall. Then she caters to her Monster's worst self-condemnation. The Monster fears the needs of the addict because of the volcano of resentment the addict has stored up. Need is understood as scary, vengeful, shaming. The Monster only meets needs under duress. "Yes, Mommy, you have always been a lousy mother, and you should buy me that ice cream cake."

To keep faith with and protect my parents, I've incorporated several lies: my needs are scary and bottomless; my needs are unimportant, the only way to get my needs met is to completely sell out my dignity to someone else's drama; even I can't meet my own needs.

DEAR DIARY, AFTER being beaten, I lusted for suicide. I don't know if I've ever felt anything more thoroughly. I felt certain that the desire to erase myself was my signature emotion.

When they returned to their senses enough to feel guilty they sucked me back in from the void. My desire to stay alive was their tool to set me up to be used and hurt all over again. They lured me into their game by tricking me into enjoying life. They did this by being nice to me. I had no way of knowing whether across the street, in the next town, in a stranger's heart, there was any different reality. My family was life and power; feeling good about them meant feeling good about life. Enjoying life meant being a sucker and a fool; wanting to live meant playing their game and abandoning my own plan to save myself by keeping myself pure from becoming the kind of people they are.

I am intimidated by this suicidal five-year-old's determined, articulate urge not to be. Her singleness of purpose, refusal to buy into any message of hope, terrify me. She tears off my favorite mask, the one I most like presenting to the world, and to myself – spunky survivor. I am afraid of her because she has reason to direct fury at me. I abandoned and betrayed her. I took the deal. I smiled at them. I kissed Mommy. I ate the chocolate-covered peanuts. I tried being super nice to avoid abuse but when the abuse continued, I continued to agree to life on their terms.

To live I had to abandon the five-year-old. She was demanding, and the world could not meet my demands. She was selfish, and I was told I had no right to be. She was self-defined, and others controlled the script. She was impetuous, and I had to monitor every move. She hurt, and I could not show hurt, because hurt would incriminate every adult who ever saw, and did nothing. She was sensitive, and I knew I could not see or feel or hear or think and keep breathing.

Great. Fine. Terrific. So not only do I have to reform today's Miroswava Hudak, I also have to do – what – with this – what, what, completely separate five-year-old self? Of whom I'm scared to death and from whom I feel completely apart. Great. Fine. Terrific. Easy as pie.

Christ, what next.

DEAR DIARY, I was lying in bed. The phone rang. It was that Martha Streichert, the short blonde in the very bad car. "We're leaving for the Pine Barrens," she announced.

"What for?" I mumbled.

"Camping," she said.

"God, I'm jealous!"

"Wanna come?"

"Yeah! – But, camping? It's winter?"

"Winter's over, Miroswava. It's spring."

Now I'm sitting on the curb in front of my building, waiting for her to come pick me up. Apparently just by being paler than they I am entertaining the uniformed Soccer Spics who had been playing in the lot across the street. Now they're chanting, "Hey, Gringa! Gringa!" making kissing sounds, clapping their hands, and going "Woo woo." Eat my shit, amigos.

I'm scared. Martha has those three kids. Does she expect me to smile at them and buy little presents and make cooing sounds when they show me their special, boring toys? Will they come to call me "aunt" without my permission? I have to take a stand. Nip it in the bud. Even just kids' packaging scares me. Velvet, unscarred skins, so fine over their veins, thin arms empty of muscle: even if they lifted weights, they wouldn't have what it takes. Their outsize eyes are empty of story, empty of guile. They lack complex vocabulary. They're all sensation. If something feels good, it feels good. If it feels bad, no little speech makes it feel better. Kids can't translate pain into constructs like we can; they can't handily pocket and rationalize hurt away. When I stand next to a child, I always think, "How easy it would be to overwhelm this child. How much damage, with what minor exertion, could be done. How possible to skirt public censure." I can't stand these thoughts.

- Reminder: Learn how to say, "Eat my shit" in Spanish.

DEAR DIARY, MARTHA'S jalopy heaved up over the broken glass and the Soccer Spics whistled, hooted, clapped their hands, all the louder.

"Friends of yours?" she quipped.

"Can it," I growled. "Hey. With all that gear, you've got a full load."

"No problem. We have one of the kids sit in your lap," she announced.

And the fight began. "Last time!" and, "You promised!" and, "He always gets to!"

"Dexter, you're eight, remember? That's too big for a four-hour drive; now shut up. It's between Sparky and Shushu. I'm flipping a coin," barked drill sergeant Martha.

But I hadn't agreed to this. In fact, I hadn't even been consulted.

"Tails. You got it, Shush," Martha said, folding the front passenger seat forward and ushering Shushu out of the back. "I always use heads for Sparky," Martha explained, "because Sparky seems to have one. And I always use tails for Shushu, well, for obvious reasons," and with that, Martha walked round to the driver side, leaving me with Shushu.

Shushu was very pretty in a 1950's Vargas pin-up kind of way. "Tail," indeed. Blonde hair, ivory skin, eyes big and wide and blue. She was wearing jelly sandals, impregnated with little bits of multi-colored glitter, and she was sucking her thumb.

I squatted. I ventured, "Shushu?" She flung her arms around my neck. "Okay," I conceded. We entered the car as an inseparable unit.

"Want me to buzz your friends?" Martha asked.

"No!" I shouted, but then I said, "Go for it. And listen – do you know how to say 'Eat my shit' in Spanish?"

"Miroswava, I am shocked," Martha said. "Shocked at you. 'Eat my shit in Spanish' indeed. I'm sorry, but that is –" she was rolling down her window, "just so pedestrian." She targeted the car toward the Soccer Spics and hit the gas, hard.

I screamed, a little. Shushu patted my arm.

Martha drove straight up, bouncing over the curb, into the parking lot, straight at them, knocking down their orange cone goalposts. "*Eh, hijos de puta, vayanse a coger por el culo!*" she shouted.

"Well done," I laughed.

"You'd do no less for me." And we were on the road.

Mindful of my plan, I said, "Gosh. Three kids. And dad is not on the scene? You've got your hands full. Makes me realize how lucky I am." Dexter, Sparky and Shushu were pathetically easy targets. They look like welfare kids; they look cowed, as if they know they made their father fail them, and if they repeat their mistakes, the rest of the world will abandon them, too.

"Don't ever forget just how lucky you are, or you may yet end up like me," said Martha vehemently. My eyes grew wide. I clamped my arms tight around Shushu.

Shushu pressed herself insistently into my lap as if she were trying to glue herself there. Her silky blonde hair, not quite a solid, not quite a liquid, slid against my cheek, my chin. I brushed it away. She stroked the hairs on my arm, as if fascinated. I looked down and noticed that they form a grillwork of gold against pale freckled flesh. Before Shushu began touching them, if someone had put hands over my eyes and asked, I wouldn't have been able to report what color the hairs on my arms are.

I found myself throwing my arms around her every time the car came to a sudden stop, shielding her from strangers in gas stations, buying her bags of potato chips, after she resisted my offers for more healthful snacks like raisins and peanuts.

The kids are in their pup tents now. Martha's being a pain. She insisted on cooking dinner by herself so I could "Go off and have your adventure." She's doing the dinner dishes; she wouldn't let me help. I'm sitting on a log, next to our unambitious campfire.

We arrived this afternoon. With the immediate lift and acceleration of dragonflies, the children darted from the car. I surveyed a patch of scraggly pines in exceptionally filthy dirt, a site devoid of charm or wonder, and certainly nothing worth telling you about, Diary. Before I had unkinked myself from the ride, the kids discovered enough attractions of this campground to fill a hundred postcards home to grandpa. They exhibited dragonflies' sudden, frozen focus when stopped by bear claws in trees, Indian pottery shards, remnants of human skeletons, cobra holes, scats of some titanic struggle between something huge and ferocious and something beautiful and vulnerable, and fleeting but certain sightings of the Jersey Devil. "Shouldn't we report that to the Discovery Channel?" Dexter asked. They gathered as much of this bounty as they could and brought it to me, to inspect, to verify, to say, "Oooo, aaaaa."

All I wanted was to sit numbly for a while, to sip peppermint tea, to find the bathroom and stare in the mirror and reassure myself that I was the same person in this new place as I had been before the trek began. No longer at home, I couldn't rely on the couch or TV. I wanted to seek out what easy local fixes I could find. No such luck. Somebody had to say: "Yeah, that is a snakeskin, though maybe not actually a cobra. Why do snakes shed their skins? Who knows?" Sounding like Dr. Science on National Public Radio. In fact, none of them knew. What kind of elders do children have today? That they don't know these things? "Snakes shed their skins when they grow. After they finish, they're way bigger. Can you imagine what it would be like if you shed your skin every time you grew?"

"Yeah, my mother would get mad cause she'd hafta clean it up!" this from Sparky, the cute six year old, with Shushu's blonde hair, big eyes, and button nose, but a boy, and funny.

"Snakes don't have mothers," from Dexter, eight, thick, a bully. I don't like him. I mean, I like him in the abstract – small human male child – but in the particular, when I catch him kicking Shushu when no one is looking, I don't like him.

"Everybody has a mother," from me, Dr. Science.

"Look! Mira! Look what I found!" Shushu's "Mira" came out "Mewa," but I refuse to type that every time.

Shushu handed me a brown, brittle, gall-swelled oak leaf. Who was I to pass on to her my lack of wonder? To explain, "Shushu, brown, brittle, gall-swelled oak leaves aren't something we categorize as 'worth getting excited about.' See, there's a catalog of things worth getting excited about, like Billie Holiday's essential albums, but this is not one of them. What are they? Oh, you'll find out. Your knowing what they are will help others to decide whether *you're* worth getting excited about, and you'll find fewer and fewer of them as you age."

"Wow, Shushu. Wow!" I said, as if I were a five-year-old Vargas girl.

After I finished writing in you, Diary, while Martha was still doing dishes, I took out the John Bradshaw book I've been reading. It's obvious from its cover that the book promises self-help in recovery from childhood trauma.

Martha finished the dishes and came and sat across from me. I could sense her eyes on me, and on the book's cover. Finally, I asked, "Well?"

"Let me look at it," she said.

I passed the book to her. She flipped through it. "Oh, he's just one of those pitchmen on TV. 'Send us your money and all your problems will be solved.'"

I nodded, took the book back, and continued reading.

"No?" she finally asked.

"I don't think so," I began. "I attended one of his workshops in the city for free. I just called one of their eight hundred numbers and told them about losing my job. And he encouraged us to get local help, rather than to travel to his clinic in L.A."

I didn't return to reading. I figured I'd just wait. I filled in the time till she was ready by drawing in the dirt with a twig.

Then she said, "It's not for me like it was for you, Miroswava. In fact my father used to say that. That, yeah, we lived in Lenappi, but at least we weren't like them Hudaks. Look, I can talk to you like this, right? I'm straight. I'm a straight person. I lack charm."

I nodded. "Charm impairment. I've heard about it. And you're never going to change."

"Right. But I mean, everyone knew. I was ahead of you in school. I remember one day, looking at you, and just thinking – thinking your mother should be in jail, that's all. But, no. We were never beaten. Come Easter Sunday, I had entirely new outfits, from a new, flowered hat to lace-trimmed gloves, all the way down to new underwear."

"Yeah," I said.

"It's just that, in a way, I'm an orphan, and was raised by strangers, who couldn't bring themselves to love me. My mother disappeared when I was three. My aunts chipped in to do the mom thing on a time clock, punch in, punch out basis. My father was . . . Words don't come as easily to me as they do to you."

"Your father was what?"

"A German. Raised by two German immigrant parents. Been doing factory work since he was eleven years old." A long pause. "I don't know what you'd call it, what the name for it is."

"The name for what?"

"Like this. I heard some Mozart in school. 'The Magic Flute.' I liked it. I liked it so much the teacher noticed and gave me the record to take home, to play for a while. So I had it at home and was listening to it, and I didn't notice that he had come in. And he walked into my room, picked the needle up off the record, and said, 'This is not music for you. We are not the kind of people who listen to music like this.' What do you call that? Is that abuse? It's not abuse. But it's something. Sixteen years of that, before I finally left home.

"And then, it was like I was looking for a lifestyle that would fit. An attitude. We weren't poor. Not like you people. We lived in Lenappi, but up on a hill. So I met people like my husband, through him I knew Kai, worshipped Kai from afar, anyway. Did cocaine, hung out. But I couldn't even get addicted. I just did it for something to do. So I can't claim to be an addict, to be an abuse survivor. I have no name for it. You know," she said. "Parents always talk about how they want to give their kids something that they never had. At least I'll do that. At least my kids will have a name for it. 'Child of welfare mother.'"

I was watching her, listening, and occasionally asking questions. I suspect that at moments like this I may look wise. In fact, at moments like this I am clueless. I knew I'd be mulling over her words for days afterward. Meanwhile, I just kept looking at her, steadily, and nodding.

"It's just that," she said, "all my life, I've been thinking, I am somebody wrong, and if I could just be somebody else, I'd be right."

Okay. That sounded familiar. "You could read some of the books, attend some Twelve Step meetings," I suggested.

"And challenge everything I've done in my life so far? Do I have what it takes to handle that? Would it do any good? And do I want to know, in detail, how I've been fucked up? And how I'm fucking up my own kids?

"And, besides," she asked, pulling a pack of Marlboros out of her back jeans pocket, "How do you make it urgent? How do you get it so like it's a blackhead that you've just got to pop?

"Okay, that thing with my dad. Or even my marriage. I could work up a critical mass of despair over either one. And you think, 'Not another second. I can't stand it! Things have got to change,' and then the kid needs a frog costume sewn up for the school play, or we start bombing some other country. You're just hoping and praying that Sparky looks like a frog, not a six-year-old whose eccentric mother inexplicably decided to send him off to school in a green flannel jump suit. And yet not so real that some liberation band of radical frogs doesn't want to repatriate him as one of their lost changelings. So you're standing there at the sewing machine with three and a half yards of green flannel in one hand and a pair of pinking shears in the other and a mouthful of straight pins and you're watching CNN and American bombs dropping on some Third World country and hometown shots of yellow ribbons on oak trees for our boys over there. And you know, you know that under one of those bombs there was a mother making a frog costume for her little Abdul or Mohammed. How do you make yourself important in the face of that? Central to anything? It's just much easier to grab one of these . . . " she waved her cigarette.

"I'm desperate." I said. "My life stopped. Otherwise, I wouldn't be doing it, either."

It was quiet for a moment. Then Martha said, "You know something, Miroswava Hudak?"

"No, I guess I don't."

"You are the very first person from Lenappi I've ever allowed myself to use the word 'changeling' with."

I laughed. And then I said, "But you told me you've lived in Lenappi all your life?" I was just fact-checking, making sure I was correctly filing the stuff we'd told each other about ourselves during the long ride down. But I looked at Martha's eyes, and they were red, and wet. There were no teardrops on her face, which looked as small and mean as ever. Suddenly I regretted the question, or at least the casual tone I had used to ask it.

"Yes," she said. "All my life."

I wanted to say something enough to Martha, enough to honor the weight of everything she had just told me. But ever since this thing has begun my conception of the basics has wobbled. I thought of the difference between simple present tense, meant to convey an idea that is always true, and the present progressive, meant to communicate, only, that an action is taking place in present time. This tense does not commit; it takes no stand on permanence.

"Martha, I don't know what's permanent, and I don't know what I can commit to. So let me just say, right now, I am loving you."

She stood up, and so did I. Careful, more out of convention than any real threat, not to step into our sissy campfire, we hugged.

Oo oo oo oooo o. Great Horned Owl. Female.

D EAR DIARY, WHEN they hurt, they run to me, as if I were the solution. They plaster their delicate, insistent bodies against my calves and knees and thighs; I can feel their lungs rise and fall in spasms, can feel the fine films that encase them, the tender channels pulsing; their tentative life. Warm tears wet my skirt. Under my stroking they crumble; cooing renders them limp. They aren't finished yet! Their mortar hasn't yet hardened. And there's no guarantee that they'll make it, that they'll figure it out. I feel such awe for their work.

They teach me. I'm not inherently repulsive! There isn't some hidden nasty feel in my fat flesh, some unavoidable mistake revealed in the contours of my body! What I had often suspected is true. I feel good. Touch me; I *do.*

I went for a couple of long solo hikes. Martha smiled knowingly and chalked it up to my needing time away from the kids. That wasn't it at all. I needed time away from *me.* I wasn't used to this woman who cared about them, who got a kick out of them, who behaved responsibly and yet enthusiastically, with them.

The kids often fought. There was never anything sustained, but occasional outbursts of anger during which they'd do really awful things to each other. Dexter threw a bike at Sparky; Shushu demanded lap time and piggybacks even though her brothers never got any. Just as I had been shocked at their easy and uninhibited affection, I was shocked at their easy and uninhibited rage.

When we got back to Martha's, after Martha had tucked them in in their own rooms, they snuck out of bed and piled on top of each other on the floor, and slept that way. "They pull that every night," Martha said. "Like cattle."

DEAR DIARY, THE strangest dream last night. I've always rejected the cross as a symbol, not just for the brutality of what happened there. It was the form itself. I have no affinity for straight lines. On my school papers words and numbers lay where they fell, recording the logic of only a moment's inspiration, noodling about the page, like Martha's kids on the floor. The nuns would smack my knuckles hard with their wooden rulers. "Hudak! What do we have to do to get you to write on a straight line?" Demonic possession was implied. No one mentioned "dyslexia." An image of a crying angel was rubber-stamped to every page I handed in between first and fourth grade. These pages were hung on the wall especially for parent-teacher conferences, adding the humiliation of my parents in front of other parents to my humiliation in front of other kids. With this encouragement I learned to fight and fear my own idiosyncratic order.

Lines bisect. Lines arbitrarily hatchet continuums and put the rich over here, the poor over there, the worthy over here, the worthless over there, the possible over here, the dream over there. I saw life as a circle where what was wrong could circle back into what was right if you traveled far enough.

The cross, two lines come together, announced that there are impossibilities. It is the union of negation, in a symbol soaked with violence and tension: north, south, east, west, irreconcilables, pulling and meeting for one explosive moment of passionate union and conflict on one man's body, centered on one man's heart. The cross was the fruit of the church and state's collusion to kill Christ. It was the fate of a man who tried to live life well. He told us to pick up our crosses, and follow. He showed us what that looked like. He ended in a hole.

Circles included, said "Come on in," took no stand on the question of right and wrong. Always haunted by deja vu, I can't believe that time is a straight line. The cross pointed to divergent routes to take; it spoke of the pain of departure and the heightened emotion of arrival. The circle was mellow, a destination, it was safe, on target, at home.

Last light I dreamt that Shushu stood in front of me and held up a cross and said, "This, too, is the shape of love. We would have told you before, but you weren't ready."

DEAR DIARY, TODAY . . . Why today? Today wasn't such a bad day. Today the unexpected shadow on a stair, the irregularity in an otherwise blank wall – an exposed nail head, a squashed bug – out of the corner of the eye, moved. Today a voice out of the concoction of previously unnoticed background noise swirling around the empty apartment suddenly forms itself into: "Miroswava." An accusation, irrefutable, clearly in Mommy's voice, always ending in a period, the most final of punctuations, never a question mark, never an exclamation point, even screamed, because screaming implies the loss of control. I jump, but of course no one is there. And I am the one who is crazy.

Today my body was a comma. When I began jumping jacks, I felt something might crack. Why today? Could it be that some new clump of undigested past, more awful than what I've attended to and worked to describe here is about to be coughed up?

D EAR DIARY, SPRING dawns are so fresh, and pink, as if, for a moment, we inhabit a translucent seashell. Especially up where Martha lives; she found the only Section Eight house in the county, and it's hard by the reservoir. She was surprised to see me there at dawn but I remember her saying that she has insomnia, that she never sleeps.

"Miroswava, the buses don't run this early."

I couldn't talk at first. It took me a while to stop hyperventilating. The kids were still asleep. Luckily I hadn't disturbed them. We went out back, to the picnic table under a massive weeping willow just starting to green.

"That's a good, what, fifteen miles? You walked fifteen miles. Okay. You can't talk yet. You don't need CPR. Coffee? You don't drink coffee. I could get us some hash . . . "

"I had a dream. A really bad dream. It's Shushu. Her hair . . . "

I could see that Martha was trying to follow.

"When we were in the car. Shushu was sitting on my lap. Her hair kept brushing my cheek. It reminded me. I knew this, this, this person once. His name was Miles. Miles had a son. I used to play with the son, all the time. He had hair like Shushu's. Child hair. It reminded me. Last night I had a dream about this man, about Miles. I just need to tell someone about it."

"Tell."

"I dreamt that I found a way to open up his chest, and take out his heart, but to keep him alive. And then, I sat down in front of him, and while he was watching me, I put his heart on a plate, and, with a knife and fork, I ate it."

"You're angry at this Miles."

"No. No. You don't understand."

"So explain. I've got time. Welfare mothers don't have to punch in till the first tabloid talk show. That'll be Jerry Springer, and he doesn't come on till nine."

There. I had permission to talk. But how to begin? "It was when I was in the Peace Corps."

"Okay," said Martha. "This is something I've been meaning to ask you. How did you end up joining the Peace Corps, anyway?"

"How?" I asked.

"How, why," she said.

"Why? I wanted to save the world and get out of Lenappi. How? I saw a commercial on TV. They had an eight hundred number, so I called it and they sent me an application."

"An application."

"Yeah. It was a long application. Six pages. I had to get drunk before I could fill it out."

"I wish I'd seen that commercial before I met my husband," said Martha.

I didn't comment. I didn't want to play this game. I hate it when married women get cramps over it and blame the world, starting with single women. She spread her legs. She said, "I do." Nobody held a gun to her head. Deal with it. Single women aren't kissed by a different God; we aren't all Audrey Hepburn waiting for Cary Grant in the lobby of the Ritz in downtown Paris.

After a long, prickly silence, I went on.

"It took days to get there, Martha. Long enough that one guy from our group, a guy from Arkansas, lost his virginity in a Bangkok whorehouse. Others threw food to domesticated crocodiles. I overslept. I felt, I need to save my energy. I felt, something big's about to happen.

"Our plane landed in a valley, a valley so deep the height and pitch of the mountains terrified me. Think of that, Martha. Geography that terrorizes. This was a completely different *Earth* I'd landed on. Overhead were flying foxes – at first, with conviction, even if it was only the certainty of one second, I concluded that they were the flying minions of the Wicked Witch of the West from *The Wizard of Oz*. Reality explained by a fantasy movie. This was a completely different reality. But no, you see. They're bats with four-foot wingspans. The air was like a solid wall. Smells of every kind of shit. Monkey shit, human shit, buffalo shit. Incense. Bronze bells. Masks of elephants in red and purple. Terrific jet lag."

"They herded us onto a bus, to take us to the training site. Everything I owned in the world was in a duffel bag on its roof. Before I joined I was homeless, living here, there, hitchhiking coast to coast. We were all strangers to each other, but the ark instinct, I think, must be encoded in the genes. The other trainees had already paired off. Everyone had already met a best friend for life. Except me. I was sitting alone. And then he got on the bus. I don't know how else to say this to you, but for me, everything happened in that moment, the first moment I saw him. It doesn't make any more sense to me than it does to you. But for the next two years I measured time this way: how long till I see him again. How close will we get. How far till goodbye."

I dared to steal a glance at Martha. I loved her. She was allowing this. I went on:

"'Is this seat empty?' he asked. I looked at him, thinking, God, how could anyone be so oblivious?

"So I began the two years of pretending. Of acting like someone who doesn't believe, cause the world doesn't believe, and you don't want to stand out. 'Oh, you'll be our teacher? How nice.'

"'Yes.'"

"'Well, I'll sit with you, then.'"

"'How nice.' I was trying to talk like he talked. Here I am in Kathmandu, doing my best to fit in, by pretending to be an ethnically correct middle-class American.

"The bus rose to a pass in the mountains and then rolled down a road like spilled spaghetti. I couldn't stop. It was like the first conversation of my life. 'Look at that! The Himalaya! Look at that! That barefoot man, carrying a pack as big as he is! Look at that! That flock of cranes!'

"He knew everything! I wanted to know everything.

"The road followed a river. The river was chocolate brown, choppy and foamy from the recent monsoons. 'You should see these rivers in winter,' he said. 'They're blue-green.' Right then I began the wait for winter, his winter, his shade. And do you know, to this day, every time I see a river; every time I see that color; every time, every time . . . "

"Miroswava, do you need some tissues?"

I rushed on. "Another Peace Corps trainee came up to me and said: 'blah blah blah he's married blah blah blah' and I wanted to say, no, wrong, the subtitles are upside down. Somebody fix this, please.

"I don't know how or when what I saw in that first second, on the bus, became visible to others. But eventually the other trainees started pulling me aside. 'Don't you see that everyone is watching? Don't you think he feels it too? What in God's name are you going to do?' I never said anything. I think they concluded that I was playing it cool.

"Boy, were they wrong. I didn't say anything because I didn't have any words. I was dyslexic; I had been in remedial English classes till high school with kids who communicated with grunts and knives. That's part of why I diary so furiously now. I want my words. I'm convinced that the key is in them, somewhere. Every 'um.' Every pause. I had no package then for all these feelings. No currency to bank or to make change. I had no words.

"Life was not words. Life was sensations. Village women pulling down my sarong as I bathed at a bamboo tap channeling water from a stream. Them scrubbing my back with scratchy homegrown loofahs and brown soap bought in the bazaar. The hit of hill moonshine and the shock of the neighbors to see a woman drinking. Getting grabbed by a local Hindu and shoved up against a wall and not resisting, just because he was cute. The sensation of crossing a swift river lined with sharp stones. Struggling to remain vertical, and not topple, against the press of the current racing from 25,000 feet up down to sea-level in less than fifty miles, freezing water beating against my blue ankles as I balanced on sharp rocks. Of being out of Lenappi. The sensation of finally being free for the first time in my life, of begin treated as if I were no different from anybody else. Of having a body I could use. Sensations. There was no tomorrow. Poor people, powerless people, we don't learn tomorrow. There was no plan. Plans are for the rich, the powerful, the anal, like him, actually. His endless charts and graphs in class. So boring! I used to tease him so bad. Let's just cruise on to the next sensation.

"Training ended. Things end. You don't notice that unless things ending means losing something you can't bear to lose.

"We were walking along a road in the flat part of the country; the Gangetic plain, almost India. It was November, sunny and hot; the fields along the road were fuzzy, yellow with four-petaled flowers – mustard. I could hear, in the distance, someone whining out *qawwali*. Or maybe it was a tape. I did the best I could.

"'What if you really liked someone, and wanted to be their friend, but you loved them? How could you still stay friends with them?' He had all the answers to my questions, right? He heard everything I said, right? Not this time. He ran away. I looked up the hot, flat road, and there he was in front of me, fleeter of foot."

"C'mon on mommy's lap."

"I want to sit on Mira's lap." That's Shushu. The instincts of a coquette: use contact with your body to flatter the one farthest from you; withdraw contact to cause anxiety in the one closest to you.

"Miroswava is telling a story. She'll chop your head off the way she's waving those hands around. Dexter, get your mother some coffee. So he's just blown you off in the mustard fields. And sometime you'll get around to telling me what 'cow wowie' is."

"*Qawwali.* It's music, religious music. They say it's religious but if you look at what they're actually singing it's really all about sex. It sounds like – it sounds like there. Like cardamom tastes like there and crushed pine needles and ice crystals and a yak dung fire on a cold night smells like there and a silk sari, or an endless hill you're climbing with a heavy pack or sleeping deeply on a hard surface feels like there. So, back to the story. I ignored him for a while. A month, maybe."

"Did you think about trying to get him to talk about it again?"

"Never. Because if I did, if I ever forced the issue, I'd just be giving him a chance to tell me what I already knew: 'We regret to inform you, Miroswava, that a man like me could never love a mess like you.' As long as we didn't talk about it, I still could imagine I owned it. I had him, somehow. How? Always finding me and sitting next to me, and, when I became too attentive to the lecturer, I had his elbow in my ribs, and his little drawings in his notebook margins to amuse me and get my attention back on him.

"I had moments when I was doing nothing, nothing . . . nothing. At those moments suddenly I communicated to the gods, now, now I am worthy. I have hit upon the right prayer, and said it flawlessly. Now is the time to rescue me from nightmares and tension, to reward me with bliss, to make me feel, finally, okay. I wasn't even trying. I'd be standing on a flat roof and hanging my laundry against the Himalayan horizon. Nagging a sick friend into drinking her rehydration fluid. Teaching students how to play a game. Wearing a sari for the first time. Crying when my *ama* sacrificed the family goat. Flirting with Nepalis. Dancing alone. Sneaking out of the training house and going for a walk in the rice paddies under a full moon. I wouldn't even know he was watching. I wouldn't even know he was there. I wouldn't even be aware of what I was doing. And suddenly he'd be there, right behind me, or he'd wait till later, till I'd forgotten that moment, and he'd say something, something that cut right to the heart of me, to the essence of the moment, let me know he saw, he knew, he recorded, me. And suddenly, I – I didn't even own a camera – I, that moment of my life, was a beautiful picture, in a precious frame.

"It's thanks to Miles' eyes, and his reports back to me, that I discovered that I care for sick friends, that I cry over goats, that I flirt, that I dance, that I attend to lectures, and the moon."

"So I went back to pretending. For two years. Usually not in the same city, but, when in the same city, immediately in touch. Not knowing what it is, and arriving at his house, and just sitting there and waiting, maybe with his kid on my lap. Then he gets home, and seeing his face, and in that second, knowing that sensation. Sitting at his feet for hours, hours that became years, trying to memorize his very being, the color of his hair, the shadows he threw. What did he feel? I'll tell you. I didn't know then, and I don't care now. Anything for that sensation.

"So, finally my two years of Peace Corps service were completed. 'I'm leaving tomorrow,' I told him. 'Are you coming to the airport to say goodbye?'

"'No,' he said. 'I'm a Buddhist. I have renounced attachment.'

"'Okay, fine.' I could outdo his Buddhist cool with my hard Jersey ass any day in the week. I left his house, no looking back. And I think I could have taken it if that had been it. But it wasn't.

"The next morning I was at Kathmandu's toy airport with its little puddle-jumper planes. I scanned the mountains around this valley. I wasn't afraid of them any more; I was grief-stricken at the thought of leaving them and all they contained. But I felt that they, the mountains, had given me what strength I'd need to do it. But suddenly there he was. Unshaven, for the first time ever. Face red, wet. He grabbed me. He kissed me."

"And?"

"And then he ran away."

"Nothing since?"

"Nothing. I wrote once; he never wrote back. I've never even mentioned him to anyone I know. I never even mention him, not out loud, anyway, to myself.

"I did a search of the diaries I'd kept since then. Year after year, there was no mention, except for one stray sentence, repeated over and over. It appeared by itself, without exposition, like some stray particle shot from a distant interstellar accident to land in a cornfield. 'I still love him.' It wasn't until I started this experiment in dieting and writing and stuff that I wrote about him at all. The antidote for writing about the worst moments of my life was to project myself back into the best moments."

"You have to contact him."

"I can't."

"You have to."

"Forget it."

"You need – what's Oprah call it? It's her word of the week. 'Closure.' You need closure."

"I . . ."

"You wanna keep having nightmares that make you have to walk fifteen miles in the middle of the night? All right, look. I'm not going to twist your arm. You got the ball rolling, with this experiment you're trying. All this shit from your past is coming back up. And it's not going to let you alone, till you handle it."

DEAR DIARY, IT'S four a.m.
The Little Girl was lost in a forest, and Mommy was chasing her. Mommy's strong spine was stiff with anger because the Little Girl had shown weakness and fear. There was a huge, warty monster, pin-headed, fat-bottomed. It was Jabba the Hut, from *Star Wars*! Jabba was filled with a chocolate and peanut butter mixture. The Little Girl ran to Jabba for help. Jabba ate her, and the Little Girl turned into chocolate and peanut butter.

I'm shaking. I need to go out and look for a job. I need to decipher want-ads and impress strangers. I can't stop shaking. Hey, good morning, brand new day.

Later:

As it happens, I didn't do the job search thing today. I decided to clean the apartment, instead. The telephone and TV wires were snakes, conspiring to trip me. The carpet was pulling itself down, making itself too heavy to shake out. The couch spitefully scratched the veneer on the wood floor. I chewed them all out, knocked them around, showed them who was boss. I got the place clean in spite of them.

Damn! The past isn't going to earn me any money! It isn't going to get me into a better neighborhood! I want to be like the rest of the efficient people!

DEAR DIARY, I'M here in Martha's kitchen. It's bigger, but otherwise, just like Mommy's. Two fluorescent tube bulbs ping overhead. Leonardo's *Last Supper* is hung low enough over the dinner table for Judas to have collected a bit of macaroni and cheese on his nose. The necessaries are piled within reach: nested pots and pans, cereal in several flavors, lunch boxes starring cartoon heroes. The tablecloth's pattern is roses and daisies; the curtains are gingham; the wallpaper is a spirited salute to colonial days: muskets and drums, minutemen and maple leaves. And there's the overall cozy, warm aroma, just like in Mommy's kitchen.

Martha offered dinner as an incentive to help me complete the letter. I wondered what we'd have, what special treat she saves for guests. Was horrified to see her open some cans, dump them into a pot, and turn the heat on high. I screamed.

"What?" she challenged, hands on hip.

"Do you have to cook so assertively white trash? I bet you're disappointed that you have a stove. I bet you wish it were just one emptied-out coffee can over a wood fire."

"Oh, is that all." She shrugged, turning back to the stove.

As I type this, Shushu squirms in my lap. Every time the platen hits the end of a line and rings, she goes, "Whoopee!"

I had called Jake. Well, not only did Jake know Miles' current address, he knew something else, too. First Jake launched into one of those games of catch-up that former Peace Corps volunteers love so well. Years ago, when we had all just met, when we were idealistic kids saving the world in some Third World nation none of our family back home had ever heard of, we communicated purely and directly from the heart. Now, though, when we did communicate at all, we communicated solely in brags, having the kind of conversations we used to despise. "So, did you hear about so and so's cool new job as UN general secretary? And so and so's marrying TIME's man of the year? And so and so's discovering a cure for cancer? And so and so giving birth to the Messiah?" When I couldn't recite, "Wow, that's awesome," one more time, I cut to the chase: "Jake, I've been thinking of writing to Miles Aldrich. Do you have his current address, by any chance? Or any word on him?"

"Just about his divorce, that's all. I hear it was pretty nasty. They tried living in this country for a while and you know how that always ends up. But he can tell you about it. Here's his address. Got a pen?"

". . . his divorce." Hate. I hate him.

"Mira, marriage vows are just as final and binding for Buddhists as they are for Christians . . ." He had picked his bedroom, at night, the two of us in the same sleeping bag – it had been a cold night – for that little speech.

". . . his divorce." Want. I want him. Don't I? I have, always, haven't I? And if I don't at least try . . .

Crazy. I'll go crazy if I don't at least try.

I read to Martha the letter I composed to Miles. She didn't say anything for a long time. Finally I asked her what the hell was going through her head. She said, "I'm just trying to figure out how I would respond if I ever got a letter like that."

"Does that mean you don't like it? Should I not send it?"

"No," she said, and, "in fact, I'm now determined to live long enough to get a letter like that, from somebody, sometime, even if that means it's sent to my house by mistake."

So I guess that means she likes it.

Even though she didn't put me on the defensive, I defended myself.

"Martha, I don't know what else to do. I'm trying to re-parent myself, you know? So you think I'd get some thanks from my inner child, instead of all these endless demands. I feel like the parent who has worked the forty-hour week, bought the most popular Christmas present, and still the kid isn't satisfied."

"It's their job not to be satisfied," Martha said. "That's how they keep growing. So, what's different now?" she asked.

"What's different now," I repeated. "How about this? Saying this stuff out loud, or in this letter, anyway, finally forces me to side with my own feelings. Before, all that mattered was protecting him."

"I like it," she said. "Now, I want to show you something. Dexter, come stir this for me." She looked at me. "It's a very sensitive recipe. If you don't stir constantly, it just gets ruined."

I rolled my eyes. We went into the parlor. "Two things," she said, "about that other dream you told me about." She picked up a fat, dusty old dictionary. Opened it. Pointed to an entry and had me read it: "Cross: (Latin, crux, crucis, Indo European qreu, akin to curvus, Latin curve. See curve.)"

Then Martha opened to another page, and pointed out another entry: "Curve: (Latin, curvus, bent, Indo European base qer, to turn, bend, hense akin to Greek koronos, cor, circle)."

Then she said, "That's something, no? So crosses and circles are not as unconnected as your dream said. And, I once read this book by Buckminster Fuller. His favorite shape is the tetrahedron. It's three dimensional, but if you render it in a diagram, you get crosses."

I tensed. "I'm not good at math," I said.

"Yeah, well I am, but you don't have to be to get this."

"I'm not gonna get this," I warned.

"Just to spite me, eh?" she asked. "Don't worry about it. Thanks to tutoring at Tillman, I'm a regular Carl Sagan at translating difficult concepts to the unwashed masses. Look. Functioning things, from atoms to sails against the wind to crankshafts, come together at right angles so that movement is possible." She put her hands together in a cross shape to demonstrate a right angle.

"But Martha," I protested, "circles can move. Wheels roll."

"Yeah, but if you're inside that circle, you're always in the same place, no matter where you go."

D EAR DIARY, MY walk to the post office passes through an old Hungarian neighborhood. No living remnant remains, only signage ghosts. A massive red brick cube dominates the block. It is vacant now but it spitefully blots out the sun on this narrow side street bereft of Magyars. An Art Deco sign tells me that this used to be Kossuth school. The post office, uniformly staffed by African Americans, is on Bartok Avenue.

As I walked, some freelancer in my head reported, "You live without love, and because of this you are going to die. Don't mail this letter to Miles because loving him is the closest you will ever come to having love."

When I heard the letter hit the bottom of the box, I fainted. No big deal; in a minute a nice black guy had me out on the sidewalk, filling out some form attesting that no permanent damage had been done.

D EAR DIARY, GETTING braver. Had Mel over to dinner last night. I wanted to see if I could eat an abstinent meal in Mel's presence. And, I wanted something to distract me while I'm awaiting a reply to the letter.

I'd been shopping in Wayne so I met her at Tillman after her last class. I could see her through her students, who are barely younger than she, as she came toward me, smiling. She was wearing a sort of cute sailor suit, a navy skirt and white blouse with a little Navy tie, and Birkenstocks. I noticed, again, the combination of perky smile: "Isn't today just so *special?* Aren't we going to have an *intimate* time?" And her halting walk: "Am I doing this right? If not, I can go back and do it over." She looks so unthreatening. You'd think it was the result of practice.

Back here at my apartment, in spite of my many dropped hints, she actually tried to "help" me cook. She wanted to stir the egg whites into the soufflé, rather than fold them. She was ready to beat them when they weren't yet room temperature. She was ready to beat them with a wooden spoon, for God's sake! Everyone knows you need a wire whisk. It caught in my throat. It was like watching some clumsy virgin try to make love to an ex-husband.

After I definitely exiled her from the kitchen, I kept peeking at her. Mel is naturally thin. She has never been fat; she does not suffer to be thin. Claims she eats "like a horse!" Says, "If I keep this up, I'm going to have to go on a diet." In fact she fits into the package that was handed her at birth, and has had to perform no adjustments since.

"So," she said, startling me. "I decided against the California job."

"Because Chris didn't want to go. Because he knew he'd never get another academic job out there," I said.

"It's not that simple," she said.

I didn't bite.

If Jesus Christ got himself a really slick resume technician, and exaggerated a little, he could maybe have a resume like Mel's. She was in the swim team – *on* the swim team? Shit, I don't even know the prepositions – and can rescue a drowned child who has been clinically dead for minutes. She once swam faster than any other teenager in a ten-state radius. She has been published. She has marched and protested. She stands straight, her head all but flies off her body. She has kept her last name. And in all this training and self-discipline, no one taught her to do anything except ultimately defer to the man.

My silence didn't throw her at all. She sat in this chair, gazed out the window. She occasionally made some comment to me, "They look like Joshua trees."

"They're just plain old Jersey sumac," I replied. I studied her. I want to know what substance she has that I don't. What makes it possible for her to survive a day without using a drug of choice and makes it impossible for me to go without either using a drug of choice or obsessing on not using?

She was content sitting at this desk. Serene. She exhibited no need to do anything to augment her experience, or to justify her existence. That amazed me right away when I moved in with them. Chris would blow up, get drunk, act like an ass. She would never find anything to apologize for. I would, immediately. "I'm so sorry –" I'd quickly scout around for something I could identify as done wrong by me and correctable by me, in my clumsy efforts to defuse tension. Not Mel.

I've envied her in motion; now I envied her at rest. If I were simply sitting as she was, my mind would unreel: "Why am I doing nothing when the rest of the world is out there consuming, living, having a good time? Are these the optimum people I could be with? Couldn't I find others funnier, smarter, more creative? I got screwed again! Better enhance this experience fast, get some extra life, some *food* before it's too late. Don't I have some dirty laundry that needs doing? Some unanswered letters? Didn't I once want to learn archery? And I never did. So why am I sitting here doing nothing?"

"Mel, I need to talk."

"Mmm?"

"I need to talk about a guy I used to know. Can you listen to that?"

"I suppose."

As I was serving dinner, I sputtered out a truncated version of the Miles saga.

She said nothing.

"Talk, Mel."

"Well, I know exactly what's going on," she declared.

"What?" I asked.

"Sometimes I wonder if it does much good to tell you things. Do you ever listen?"

"Mel, what do you want me to do, plead with you to say something?"

She sighed, deeply. "Well, okay. Okay. There's a book I want you to look at. It's called, *Women Who Love Too Much*."

"Omigod."

"You knew he was married."

"This isn't like that!" I shouted.

"Like what? Like Max, who was raised by wolves and used to shoot heroin? Like Konrad, another married man? Like that hairy – lunatic Croatian who mentally never left Ellis Island? What was his name?"

"Bruno. He was processed at Kennedy. They don't process immigrants at Ellis Island any more."

"Didn't you tell me once that spending time with him was like screwing your own eyeballs out of your own head?"

"I never said I didn't love him."

"Mira, do you want to hear what I have to say or not? Weren't you just pleading with me to say something?"

"Yes. All right. Go ahead."

"Have you ever dated a single man who has a steady job? Men like that aren't so hard to find. Most men work for a living, Mira. I don't think you want to be treated with respect. If you demanded it, you'd get it. We do create our own realities."

Be my role model, I wanted to say. You have the currency, the body, the breeding, the youth, and what do you spend it on? Chris, a ba aging alkie. But I didn't say it. I picked up my fork and toyed with . food.

I slumped. Mel's head was thrown back as far as ever. I could never understand how she transports food to her mouth without splattering herself. She never looks down at her plate. She never inclines toward it.

I was flailing inside. Scared, adrift, omigosh, they've got me again. What can I do *fast* to reestablish my façade?

After a long silence, I said: "Konrad used to look at me as if I were Marilyn Monroe. And I didn't have to do the Marilyn to get that. No make-up, no squirming. No one had ever looked at me like that before, and no one has since. For you maybe it's annoying. Lots of men look at you that way. For me, it felt like something I had to experience once before I died.

"I cared about what made him sad. I really thought I had something to say to him that he'd never hear from anybody else. I miss him. I don't know. I miss the person I got to be with him. I miss being Marilyn Monroe. I miss being felt. Not just touched, like someone in the subway. I miss being felt. That has not come easy to me. Most of my life it has come not at all.

"It's never gonna be for me like it is for you. We women are never gonna be able to unite, to create any kind of real feminism, until we admit that to each other. That we are seen most importantly by men, and that their eyes divide us by assigning us to different nations."

"Well, I don't know why you asked me, then," she reprimanded.

"Have you ever needed to talk to me about anything that I haven't been there?" I protested.

"Don't be ridiculous, Mira. I *am* being there. Don't tell me you are the only one who's allowed an opinion. I just think you could benefit from this book. Don't tell me it's because you're fat. I see lots of fat women with men. It's you. You bring all this on yourself."

"I do not! How could you say that?" By that point, I was hanging half way across the table. I tried over and over to justify my loves to Mel. She seemed to enjoy being positioned as judge; she never resisted my handing her the chance to condemn and hang me.

"Have you got any Earl Grey?" she asked.

e." I got up and fixed the tea. I had bought some as
to the new place. I never drink it, but it is Mel's
lel hasn't done any work to earn love. Mel doesn't
are people out there doing such work. Mel's got no
ng. Even if I tried to explain it to her Mel'd never
understand. I am unapproachably less than Mel; I am unapproachably
higher.

I reached a point where I didn't want to let myself go crazy like this
any more. I had to do something to make it stop. As I fixed the tea, as I
brought it to her, as she sipped it, I fantasized an Academy Awards
ceremony. "And now, ladies and gentlemen, the award for the one nurse's
aid at the Lenappi Nursing Home who never fainted or vomited while
lancing a pus-filled bedsore or performing a manual extraction of
impacted feces! And the winner is, why, yes, it's Miroswava Hudak!" "Our
next award goes to the teacher whose students brought her the most
presents at the MidTown Adult Learning Center. And the winner is, no!
Again! It's Miroswava Hudak!"

I smiled ridiculously. The spell broke.

"Mel," I said.

"Mm? What now."

"I guess I've never told you this. I'm grateful to you. You're from a
different world than me, than I, and every time we get together, you allow
me into that world a little bit. That's one of the reasons I want to keep you
in my life, and why I'm glad we didn't – you know – bag each other, just
forget about each other, after I moved out. And another thing. You're
really beautiful. I enjoy that. Thanks."

Mel looked terribly surprised.

DEAR DIARY, I'M branching out. Except for Mommy's birthday,
which doesn't really count, I haven't eaten out yet. Decided to go
into the city to see if I could pull it off.

And I saw him. Konrad. I was watching from a passing bus. How
many times have I watched from a bus, yearning for the sight of him, as if
that were something timed, weighed, denied me by my empty pockets
and its excessive price? Even after I'd had him and had him and had
him and seen him naked, washed his hair, rubbed his back, his feet, I

still watched for him, eagerly, hungrily, from passing buses, as if I were some legend character, oddly cursed to yearning for what she already had.

And there he was. He was wearing a black coat whose tails swept along behind him, almost independent of him. He was with a woman. A girl. Maybe one of his students? But not for long. She was very pretty. Very small. Very obediently attentive. She was skipping to keep up with his giant strides. He looked completely bored. God bless him.

My God, but he is magnificent, in a late November sort of way. His is the limited palette of the inevitable colors exposed after summer's ostrich plumes and indigo bunting fly. He's metal. He's earth. His are the limited lines of wind-stripped geography. I pored over the exposed planes and sheer angles of his cheek and nose and Adam's apple. My God, I love him.

The bus was freed by a green light. I closed my eyes. I wanted to savor every living breath. He came again. He was very big, very solemn and authoritative. "I am here for your fantasy, Miroswava. I am here to put my arms around you and promise you that I will fight for you, forever."

But it just didn't work. "You can put your arms around me, Konrad, please do, but you can't fight for me. You don't feel my wounds. You don't burn my fire. And you don't know my words."

See that, Diary? I can't even fantasize right any more. And that scares me more than anything. Without a functional cooling system, it won't be too long before I blow my head gasket.

I got off the bus and went looking for an appropriate restaurant. I needed to use a bathroom and slipped into someplace fancy. Over the gleaming bathroom mirror, crinkled glass globes susurrated light. I walked back into the lobby on carpeting as sink-in-able as mud; a piano tucked behind a captive rain forest played Cole Porter; I sang along under my breath. People came and went, looking like they would get what they wanted today, but looking not to be in any hurry at all. A hostess asked me if I had come for the all-you-can-eat brunch.

"Excuse me," I asked. "Did you just say *all* I can eat?"

"Yes, ma'am."

"All *I* can eat?"

"Yeah."

I scanned the tables. The napkins were as big and plush as my bath towels. I stood, staring at her, for a long time.

"Here. Lay down on the couch. Don't touch anything. It's all very expensive, and they like everything in its place. Otherwise I could get fired. And while I'm upstairs, don't dare sneak into the kitchen and eat anything."

As soon as I hear the vacuum cleaner upstairs – mother ESP is confounded by the noise and electromagnetic field set up by an active vacuum cleaner – I have my fingers in some tiny jar that costs what they'll pay my mother for her day. I feel like I've found the pantry in Heaven. A tiny, unmissable bit of everything will coat my finger before I'm through. If it is a soft something, like premium ice cream, my scoop will mirror existing scoops; it will merely be deeper. If it is a chunky something, an English mandarin marmalade, my finger will reproduce the patterns of the chunks found before my pinkie arrived to sack and pillage. The remaining slices of very thin and pink, very salty ham will lay as they had lain before their neighbors were removed.

I know that if I take one smidgen more than an unmissable bit, my mother will be humiliated and dismissed. That weight presses into my shoulders as I struggle, through calculated fingerfuls, to get mine.

Not only do these people have more money than us, they've gotta shop in completely different stores. Why do so many rich foods taste like bar soap? Or smell like Daddy's socks? These foods are National Geographic material.

I want it all. I want to leave this divine pantry looking as if fifty thousand million hungry Mongol hoards had ridden through, forgetting their napkins. I want to stand there, in my pajamas, with the whooping cough that kept me out of St. Francis School this day, and confront the rich keepers of my mother's dignity.

"I ate your macadamia nuts. That's right; it was me. I have them in my tummy now and so you can't never have them in yours. I am now what you are supposed to be. Now fire my mother. Me and her are runnin away. She's gonna finish her high school, be a famous novelist and I'm

gonna support us by raiding rich people's kitchens. Whaddya think of that?"

"Phhhhhhhhheeeeiiiiooouugh." The sound of a vacuum cleaner revving down.

I've studied the labels; every can, carton, bag, is back in the exact position it had occupied. If the lid had been screwed on once not three times, I screw it back once. If the bag had been crimped down to the words, "Imported, sun dried . . ." I crimp it back to those words. If I have to wipe the counter, I wipe the whole counter, so no one part looks incriminatingly cleaner than the rest. I am extra careful with the wine.

I returned to the ladies' room to ponder. A spider-thin, silver-haired woman followed. I was sure she would demand my papers. She didn't; rather, she gave me an inclusive smile. It wasn't the smile you smile at the lady who is there to take your coat; it wasn't the smile you smile at someone who can charitably be assumed to be lost, but is suspected of being a parvenu. This smile's pronoun was "we." The lady had no way of knowing that this black skirt and puffy-sleeved white shirt were bought at the Salvation army, and stitched, starched, bleached and tucked in strategic places. She had no way of knowing that I glanced automatically at her shoes, and assessed her body shape and carriage, and concluded, based on this data, that her "we" was not one I could invest in. I smiled back, my teacher smile, which has never been challenged.

What emboldened me, what saddened me, was that the kind of quick glances these people give, the glances that ascertain whether or not there are any threats in their immediate environment, wouldn't expose me. Again, I wondered, was my desire to control my eating one last effort to become one of Them? Or one last effort to shake off what They had done to me?

The brunch was pretty good. And I stuck to my diet.

D EAR DIARY, WHEN we were still living together, Chris had demanded: "Tell me what you're writing about!" I refused. I didn't keep quiet because I thought he wouldn't understand. I kept quiet because I was certain he understood. At that point I wanted to figure it out for myself. When I finally broke down and tried to get Konrad to talk about my body, it's because I was tired of trying to figure it out myself. I wanted one of Them to give me the answer. I was making the same mistake the night I tried to talk to Mel. I thought she'd just have the answer ready and hand it to me and it would fit and work as neat as a key in a lock.

Because all humans are arranged on a ladder. The Hudaks are doing something wrong, and Those up above are doing it right. As funny as any Hudak is, as smart as curious, as strong, Those up above are that much funnier, smarter, deeper, stronger.

After a day of being perfectly thin, perfectly clean, and perfectly American, They go home to make spontaneous jokes of perfect wit, nurture perfect children perfectly, watch perfect TV programs which a Hudak antenna cannot draw, and make perfect love to the perfect spouse. On Sunday They pray to a better God and that God hears Them perfectly.

But I get it now, that I was wrong. Konrad didn't have the answer. Maybe he had no idea what was going on that night. Maybe he was scared. Maybe he was sad. Maybe that's why he was crying. Shit, I blew it by him! Because I didn't know. I didn't know that he has things he can't do, just like I have things I can't do. Just like Mel.

I was getting furious at Mel. I thought of the times I kept hot Earl Grey on her desk as she studied late nights, finishing her degree. I thought of the times I held her hand as she subtly ranted and whined about Chris. "Subtly" – key word. She never burst into my room in tears, and said, "I need you, Mira." No. That would be my style. Mel would put out careful feelers, send minimalist telegrams – a heavy sigh, a mopey, foreign movie facial expression – suggesting that her life was less than optimal. If I said, "Gosh. You sound sad. Let me give you a hug," she'd smack me right down. I had to decode her, support her, teach her, without ever letting on that that's what I was doing. And I did. And that's why she's kept me in her life.

Now here's something I've never written about, or talked about, because she implied that I ought not to, and so I never did. Her abortion. After it was all over, she slipped a store-bought card under my door. Matisse's "Red Room" was on the cover. In the blank inside Mel had written, "You have been the Great Mother to me in this."

She knows I'm Catholic. That doesn't mean I'm anti-abortion. It does mean it's harder to be pro-choice. And this: women's talk of how they feel about unwanted pregnancies is particularly painful for me. She never noted it. She never asked how I felt hiding it from Chris. She just, without self-consciousness, walked into my room and presented me with her need. She just, without anxiety, assumed that need would be filled. And I filled it. Because that's what you do. You note need. You respond to it. You do what you have to do. You don't quit, you don't walk until the other is okay.

So I was furious, I felt so shortchanged, the other night when she didn't do the same for me. Her words were lame. But my fury is misplaced. This day-and-night difference between us is not best attributed to meanness on Mel's part. She's not holding back anything that she has – compassion, complexity, humor, story. She just doesn't have any of those. I can do something that she can't.

O h   M y   G o d.

D EAR DIARY, I admit I approach you with some hesitation today. It has been weeks since I've last written.

I guess I've put it off at least partly because, before I write, it all seems so impossibly hard, so complex and forbidden. I feel that to write in you, Diary, to get it all down, I must be braver and stronger and smarter than I've ever known myself to be. And then, after I've gotten it down, and I go back and reread it, what I've girded my loins to say, what I've struggled to say, is so elemental, so kindergarten, that I can feel nothing but shame and amazement that I was ever such a freakishly oblivious person.

And, why? Why work so hard to write all this? I am the only one. The only speaker of this language in the whole world. I'm teaching it to you, Diary, word by word, episode by episode . . . Is that true?

I don't want to study this language. I resist. I say, "'But these are clean, white pages. Protect this niceness. Let me record something that wants to flourish, like a great tree, not something ugly, something that wants to be over." But force is exerted, and the alternate history is told. The question is, who exerts this force? Diary, do I force these words on your clean, white pages? Or are you the one exerting the force? Do you feel your clean whiteness less or incomplete without these difficult words? Do you tug transgressive words out of my gripped hands? Are we working with or against each other? And just what is the goal here? It seems less like what I thought it would be.

I don't know. But I do know that we are working together in one respect. We are both trying to find the something in all of this that wants to flourish like a great tree. And we have something else in common. You understand only as much as I do, and that is only as much as we have come to learn over this many pages, no more. For any more understanding than that, we must wait for the next entry.

DEAR DIARY, I told Martha I didn't want to be there when she called. I came a good hour after she was scheduled to call. "Okay, so tell me," I asked, as soon as I walked in the door and had Sparky, whose turn it was, firmly nestled in my lap, Shushu holding my hand and sucking her thumb by my side.

Martha took forever to get ready to talk. She had to make her cup of instant coffee. She had to give Dexter some liquid penicillin. She had to –

"Just tell me!"

"Impatient, aren't we?" she snapped, not warmly. "Okay. A man answered the phone. I asked, 'Is this the Aldrich residence?' The man replied in a stiff, kinda formal voice, 'Yes, this is the Aldrich residence.' I asked if I might please speak to Miles Aldrich. 'This is Miles Aldrich.' 'Hi,' I said. 'My name is Martha Streichert. I'm a friend of Miroswava Hudak. I'm calling because, well, Miroswava told me that some weeks ago she sent you a letter, and she asked that I telephone just to make sure that you received it.' There was a slight pause, and when he spoke again his voice was no longer so stiff or so formal, but . . . softer. Halting. 'Yes, I received the letter.' There was another pause. It was my turn now. 'Well, I guess that's about it, then.' I was trying to sound as chipper and nonchalant as possible. He spoke again, this time in a kind of soft monotone. 'You're a friend of Miroswava?' 'Yes,' I replied. There was a quiet, 'Oh,' and then an uncomfortable pause. 'Well,' I said. 'It was really nice talking to you.' Before he hung up he said, 'Tell her I said thank you.' So!" Martha banged the table. "That's it. You got closure."

I looked up at her, blinking. "Are you crazy?"

"No, are you? You told him you loved him. You asked him to reply. To say something, anything, to give you some closure. And what did he do? He completely ignored you. He's – what I've been expecting all along, actually – a wimp. He's not good enough for you, Miroswava. If he had any balls at all, he'd do something. He can't shit, and he can't get off the pot. Move on." Martha stood up and turned to her dishes in the sink.

"I'm going to see him."

"Oh yeah?" She didn't turn around.

"Yeah," I put Sparky down and shooed him into the parlor. "There's a conference for former Peace Corps Volunteers in the city next weekend. I know he's going because I called and asked. He's registered, anyway."

She turned around. She wore a poker face. "Do what you have to do." She turned back around.

I waited a long time. Finally, I said, "Well?"

"Well what?" She banged the sink top, spun around and stared at me. "What do you want me to say to you, Miroswava? That I'm worried about you? That you're being a fool? Will you listen? You won't." She turned back to her dishes.

"Worried. Why worried," I whispered, almost to myself. I didn't even realize I was speaking out loud till she muttered,

"Worried, of course, worried."

"He's a good man. He's the best person I know. You should see all he's done, and all he's doing now. I got the brochure from Peace Corps. He's doing great things. Third World development –"

Martha's back was still to me, but I could see her head swing side to side. She leaned into the sink; the heels of her hands pressed into either side of it. Her head was suspended low between her shoulders. "Yeah, yeah, yeah. But what he did to you – it doesn't matter. He will never lose cash, respect, affection, home, friends, sleep at night, over you. What do you think? That anyone who loves him or hires him or admires him or writes about him for little brochures would ever challenge him over how he treats someone like you? People who get called 'good people' in brochures are good because somebody's watching. People do good things not just to do good things but because somebody else is standing there with a camera and a notebook. When somebody like him is with somebody like you, nobody's watching. And he gets that, evidently. All that needs to happen is for you to get it, too, and move the fuck on. Closure."

"But, Martha, look. He –"

"Not another word about him. I don't want to hear it."

"Martha, c'mon. Listen. I –"

She began, humming, loudly, the theme song to the "Mr. Ed Show." Where did she come up with that?

"Martha . . . "

"Not another word. I will not listen to another word about him. Closure, Miroswava. Closure. Just, stop – just stop remembering. You can do that. Remembering is a conscious act. You can choose not to remember. That's what I do. You'll be a lot happier."

"This is my life, Martha."

She threw her sponge down. "It is *not* your life. Closure. I'm not going to support you in this. You did what you have to do, and I admire that. But now it's time to move on, and I'm not going to support you in this. Not any more. I will never listen to another word about this guy."

I could feel my face from the inside. I had just been slapped, and that is the face I was wearing, a face I know very well. I sat down at the table. Martha went back to her dishes.

I've thought and thought about this, and it doesn't make sense to me. He was always kind to me. To have been so kind to someone like me, he must have been the best man I have ever known. I just don't understand why he's being so strange, but I'll find out.

DEAR DIARY, I practiced the Scarlett O'Hara meditation. "Fiddle dee dee. I won't think about it now. I'll think about it tomorrow. Tomorrow is another day." At first tomorrow was next week, and then it was really tomorrow, and then it became the next hour I wasn't thinking about, and then the next half hour, the next five minutes. Eventually I was focused with military concentration on the next preparatory step as if that step were to a cliff edge, as if I had no life to consider after that step was complete.

I bathed for over an hour. Shaved legs right up over my butt. Took an old toothbrush and scoured out every last shred of toe cheese. Clipped toenails till they bled. Pumiced my heels. Filed my fingernails into ten perfect almonds, and polished them with clear. Tweezed brows, though they didn't need it. Washed hair in Pantene. Brushed teeth with Rembrandt. Brushed hair one hundred times. Steamed pores. Washed my black skirt and puffy-sleeved white blouse in Woolite, rinsed them with Downy, and ironed them with starch. Even bought new underwear. Felt like I was about to submit myself for inspection to The Centers for Disease Control in Atlanta.

The conference was held in the Museum of Natural History. There was a belly dancer and Third World hors d'oeuvres and tablers for Food First and the Sierra Club and Amnesty International. I met a heavily bearded, bear-like ex-vol in camouflage attire who had served in Zaire. He gave the name of "Rip." He knew all about the PCV named Captain Video and the witch in his village that turned herself into a giant pig. How did that story travel from one country to the next? Amazing.

And I knew I was passing as nice, as normal, right place, right person, right dialogue, especially when Rip gave me his number and invited me to the annual Fourth of July salsa contest and tofu barbecue at his place in Woodstock, New York. And I was some new physical particle that could be both stone and fire simultaneously. And then I knew I was looking right at him. Knew I was looking right at him, knew first rather than saw. Knew cause I registered what was happening to me. I was shuttling back into being a woman I've told myself I can't, under any circumstances, risk being ever again.

Several tables ahead of where Rip and I were standing. Just beyond Food First. The silhouette that that body, that soul, those movements, sounds, smells, those inhalations and exhalations, those memories, those stories, those idiosyncratic word choices, cut out of the surrounding, gratuitous nothing that is not just that. How that used to be bed when I was tired, home when I wandered, hot soup on a cold day, my favorite broken-in jeans, and the endless wonderful surprise of the very best ever Christmas morning.

But now, but now. What is the next detail? The next preparatory step I can focus on with military concentration? The next element I can survive by chanting, "Fiddle dee dee"?

"Man, them lucky bastards in Thailand didn't know how easy they had it," Rip declares. "Was there dengue at your post? You know what they say about dengue? It ain't fatal, but, when you got it, you wish it was. They don't call it breakbone fever for nothing."

"Dengue? Nah, no dengue. We had terrestrial leeches, though. Lots of 'em," I boast to Rip, smiling.

He's wearing a suit. A suit! Square shoulders. Solid navy blue. I remember tie-dye t-shirts, plaid sarongs, flip-flops. God, he looks handsome in a suit. And why not? It is the folk costume of his people. He glances toward Rip and me; his eyes keep moving. He doesn't see me. I don't know what he sees. He does nothing to indicate that he sees me. He does nothing to indicate that he sees anything of any consequence to him. He doesn't see me. And, like that first time, on the bus, I now know everything I need to know. There's the slam of that closure Martha had been talking about. But since I am who I am I take the next step.

"Rip, can you gimme a minute? I think I see somebody over there I used to know in country." 'I think I see somebody over there I used to know in country': how easily I slip into lying. Lying words, lying identity.

"Great. So can you make it on the Fourth? You've got me very intrigued with this talk of your grandma's horseradish salsa."

"I'll do my best, okay?"

"Great."

I take the next step. It is forward, over marble tile in the Museum of Natural History.

He looks less. Less than what? Did I really make it all up? Am I really that crazy? If so, then why about him? There are about five tables between us now. Gay Volunteers, Differently Abled Volunteers, Senior Volunteers.

A white woman in a red sari whose nametag reads "Graceless Shovelful" stops me. "You look familiar," she says.

"I often get that," I say, as I move on.

How many guys did I lay in those days, anyway? I start finger counting. Get confused about some names – Was Tom Tim or visa versa? – and quit. If I made it all up, why him? Why not any of the others? The mission doctor met in the dusty border town, the former gymnast who built bridges. The Marine who bought me off with a pound bag of peanut M&M's from the commissary I had no access to. "You could suck the chrome off a trailer hitch," he had told me. If it is just fantasy, then why *not* them? There are about four tables between us now. Springsteen's "Ramrod" comes on over the sound system.

A gray-haired man in a Nehru jacket sticks out his hand. "Hi. Rick Blick. I was among the first volunteers. I bet I'm old enough to be your father. I bet you didn't know that back in the old days, PCVs would play touch football with Jack Kennedy on the Grassy Knoll."

I promise, "Sure, but maybe later," and move on.

There's still four tables between us. He looks perturbed, distrustful, boring, white. And it hits me and I become the proverbial ton of bricks: I am so not in love with this person, with his distrust, his bored response to life, a life that has been pretty cushy. There are about three tables between us. The one to my left has some PETA pamphlets on vivisection. Pro? Con? I'm not sure, but I do sign their petition. I am close enough that if no one else were in this giant hall, and I spoke his name as softly as possible, he couldn't help but hear, and recognize the voice. He turns sideways. A pot belly! Say it isn't so! The man once elegantly slim as a fasting Buddha has a potbelly? And the chin. It was never much of a chin, always engaged in something of a holding action against the formidable gravitational pull of his bulky Adam's apple. The chin is being inexorably swallowed by the neck.

Martha was right. I did make it all up. There is nothing special about this man. Springsteen's "The Price you Pay" comes on over the sound system. Who decided to play the B-side of "The River"? Am I imagining this, too? If I have to imagine soundtrack, why not Sinatra's, "In The Wee Small Hours"? And if he is just what he looks to be to me right now, an unremarkable white man, then why am I shaking and unable to stop?

An older man, in an even more awe-inspiring suit than his, just came up to him and demanded something from Miles. Miles. I'm saying that name again, and it's in reference to an animate, full color, unpredictable solid outside of myself. This is no wispy phantasm inside my head that I can bend and twist and pose as I like, to which I can assign what lines of dialogue I choose. An older man in a suit of authority demands something from Miles that he hasn't yet gotten, and Miles looks at him and says nothing, but his face says, "This is all so silly; I'm just enduring." Oooo *yes.* I know that face! That pasty annoyance. So like a pouting boy he can be. A woman just smiled at him and he smiles back and his smile is sweet and vague.

I'd have a joke, a trick, and make his pique disappear, like a rabbit in a hat. I know his vague sweetness. It was my hard-won reward. Suddenly, he is not the point at all. Not the pale man in the blue suit, but me, Miroswava Therese Hudak. I had been powerful and beautiful, bubbling up laughter and sharp refreshment like a spring. He drew it out of me. I didn't know I had had it before him. It hasn't been asked for since. Suddenly I am that woman, and girl, I used to be. She has been held hostage by tragic narrative; this is now a rescue mission. I feel stone self-confident. And all the years in between disappear and I know more certainly than I've ever known anything that I must love this man.

You will be happy to know, Diary, that his hands have not changed. Time has claimed his trim profile, what chin he did have. His hands are exactly as they once were, exceptionally long, pale, translucent, with blunt tipped fingers that reach degrees of expressiveness that his mouth would never produce. I know because there were no more tables between us when my eyes met his hands.

I am a tall woman and when he turned toward me I felt, again, what I used to feel in the presence of this very tall man. My liberation from being, though a girl, and awkward, the tallest thing on the landscape. The kind of shadows he'll throw, the views he'll block, the aura and mythology society unthinkingly cedes a tall man.

I said nothing because I'd already surrendered to there being nothing I could say. I didn't walk away because I require the prods only the theater of the real can deliver. My one regret, right now, in writing this, is that I forgot to smell him. Subtly, so as not to be noticed, or obvious, just leaning in close, flinging nostrils wide, and, noisy as a vacuum cleaner, perpetrating sensual rape, letting any observer conclude whatever he needed to conclude. I remember, on that first bus ride, assessing his smell immediately, with approval. And time after time, resting in it as against a fireside recliner. But I can't remember what it was. I've been able to summon his face over the years, and his voice, but no hint of his smell. It's a terrible senility. You can't get it from a photo, or words on a page; there are some precious things for which we haven't yet mastered the appropriate preservative techniques. I wanted custody.

But in the speedy tension of the moment, I forgot to smell him. Just as well.

He looks down at me. I look the same. Even if I didn't look the same, a big, honking plastic nametag is hammered into my left boob. I doubt he's ever met another "Miroswava Hudak," in any form.

"Hon?" She looks just like him. Tall, thin, blonde, wholesome. Human müesli. Also in a suit. Her folk costume. "Oh, hi. Did you used to serve with Miles?"

He sees me. For less than a second. And then, though his face was turned in my direction, his eyes directed at me, he stopped seeing me.

"You were once my teacher," I said.

"My memory is not what it used to be," he muttered.

He was one table behind me now. The sound system was playing "Drive All Night." One of Springsteen's more incomprehensible songs, what with its references to having lost someone, and yet vows of eternal love. And that offer to drive all night in order to buy her some shoes, what's all that about? Jersey is not a shoe-deficit state. He could have just gone to the mall in Paramus.

I remembered his fingers in my flesh this way; sharp, almost pointed, like the talons of a bird, like a pencil run through a sharpener too many times, in the soft flesh of my upper arm. But they're not really pointed, just so thin and untutored at touch as to hurt. I am spun around.

"Do you realize how horribly unfair you're being to me?" he hisses into my face.

I look up at him, and acknowledge that I cannot rejoice, though I am this close. I acknowledge that it is now my job to exile myself, until he empties himself of the rage I unwittingly cause him, with my eagerness to please him as much as he pleases me. And just before I exile myself, running a fleeting glance across his pale, self-important face, I remember: when I was a kid, in Lenappi, this is the kind of person I pitied, and mocked. But I do not pay attention to that awareness; I am working too hard at exiling myself, so that I do not offend.

"You always had a very active imagination," the man asserts.

Wait. I'm going to stop working so hard at exiling myself, and I'm going to attend to this, to focus on it: "This is the kind of person I pitied, and mocked, when I was a kid, in Lenappi." Never obeyed. I have to say something. I have to get this right. This will be one of those moments where an *esprit d'escalier*, that regret that you feel for the wrongly said thing, or the unsaid right one, could kill.

"Yes," I agreed. "I am just now learning to credit myself with that." Because I did not want to be in this man's company any longer, I shook free from his hurtfully thin fingers and I exited through the giant hall's double doors.

When I got home to Paterson I changed into my jeans and bused north and took a very long hike with a panting Benjie through the thickest of tick-filthy swamps in back of St. Francis school.

DEAR DIARY, NOT much to report today. Went shopping, cleaned the place a bit, kept to my diet all day.

DEAR DIARY, JUST like yesterday. And checked out some want-ads. Mel tells me there's a help-wanted sign in a café near Tillman; says the students give good tips. I'll check it out.

DEAR DIARY, STILL haven't checked out the café job. I've never waitressed. Could I? I know it's not an easy job.

DEAR DIARY, CUT it out! What do you want from me? Why should I even bother?

Am I crazy? Are my memories fantasies? If so, maybe I really did have a good childhood! Mommy used to order me, before every parent-teacher conference: "Remember. I never hit you." My whole goal in writing here has been to tell the truth. What if I'm incapable of that? What if I'm just typing out lies and fantasies?

Last night – God forgive me. Last night I dug out my old diaries from them days and reread them all, cover to cover. I assumed the mindset I assume when reading any text. And *this* audience member was not unsure; rather, I was sure: "This is a love story." I put down the old notebook, fragrant, still, of the chai from the tea shop were I bought it, and the smoke of the guttering flame by which I wrote. I walked away. I tested the idea: "Miles loved me." The idea was so absurd it wasn't even interesting. I went back and picked up the old notebook. I began to read. And I was certain. Not about Miles. Not about me. But about these characters in this plot. This dialogue, incident, narrative drive, climax, are doing the work of telling a love story.

No, I wasn't trying to compose a love story when I was writing those diaries. I was no swooney Victorian lady novelist. I was an attention-deficit flibbertigibbet in Vibram rubber lug boots having the adventure of her life. At the ends of over-packed days, crowded up to the light of shared and puny lanterns, with rheumy, Third World ball point pens, I'd jot down details. I had no idea then that ten years on I'd be an archaeologist, scratching this narrative midden for evidence of anything.

"Miles was God and I was lucky to breathe his air": that's my story, and I'm sticking to it. "We never met, and nothing of consequence happened between us": that's Miles' alibi. "He's a creep, you were young, and you'd best forget him": so chants my Greek chorus of friends. The page is the surprise witness whose testimony rocks the court. The page records events no witness could deny. I don't deny them. Miles couldn't, either. Did he do that? Yes. Did he say that? Yes. And that. And that. And that: the accumulated impact of those events on the page changes a random cluster of individual droplets; they crest into a perfectly formed wave, a love story that I never suspected, and that Miles has denied, though it's never been told. The page remembers something that all humans concerned must forget.

And since the pen, the page, the fact on the page, narrative, are my boon companions, the spoon I'm relying on to dig myself out of my grave, the hammer I am confident can build me a new house, I am now crippled by the unacceptable transubstantiation these pages insist on working on the story, the substance, of my life.

It's just like how I felt when I imagined thieves breaking in and reading about my taking Mommy out to dinner. What I know is true is different from what the page tells me.

Martha had pounded me. "He was married! He was your teacher! He used you! Why can't you drum up enough outrage to flush this wimp out of your system for good!" She diagnosed, "He was bad!" And I'm supposed to conclude: "Yes! From now on, I'll love only good people, and I'll be safe!"

But he was kind to me. The first to be so. What does it say *about me* if the first person to see anything to be kind to in me was bad? Whatever it says, I can't bear to hear it. And how do I recognize these bad people in the future, to make sure I never again cause this pain, make this blunder? What is the sign? I read the story, and I look, I look, so hard, for the sign. Did Miles, like the fairy tale Bluebeard, ever hand me a key that couldn't stop bleeding? My parents did things to me that I would rather die than experience again and they are widely considered good.

When I read the story, I do not see Woman-Who-Loves-Too-Much throwing herself at Bluebeard. I see the Mira character off in her own little world, silent, absorbed in her task. She's writing a letter to Sita, her newfound sister. She's perched under a pipal tree on a row of boulders. Overhead the tinsmith bird works his delicate hammer of song. Mira suddenly learns she is not invisible; a man's voice calls her name: "It's good of you to write her. Keep in touch; she'll never forget her first contact with an American. Especially one like you."

I am disarmed. I have no defense to offer that Mira on the page, no defense to offer her against the sweetness she feels when this happens.

Because this is bad! This hurts! I did something wrong. I don't know what it is. I run my eyes like a vacuum cleaner over the text recording the sweetest moments of my life. I do not do this to savor my life. I do this to expose the dirt that makes my singular sweetness bad and wrong and impossible and never to be repeated in any circumstance on pain of death. What happened? What happened? What happened?

I seek The Moment. When she should have gotten it. That this Miles has the worst intentions. That she, Mira, does not possess the cards. That they are bad medicine. The moment hovers in the background, but only closely enough to engage the reader's involvement even more, to create exciting suspense. As in all the best love stories, the moment seems to be coming and then you are convinced that you hate and blame one character or the other – Miles! How could you run away! Mira! How could you ridicule him like that when he's trying so hard! And you think, why am I even investing my anticipation in this plot? There is so much darkness here there can never be light. And then she tries and he is present and you think, Aha, aha, like I said, they're going to find a way.

D EAR DIARY, I can't take it any more. I can't take it. I can't take it. I
must have something sweet.

*A red mud loft. Thatch roof overhead. In the story below, newly born
lambs feed in a manger. She is sitting on a wooden cot, her bed. He sits
beside her.*

"Mira," he says, gravely, indicating her ankles.

"Aw, c'mon, it's just you," she teases. "Not like it's anybody important."

*"I believe I've told you," he chides, his slender, pale finger still pointing,
"never to show your ankles in the presence of a man."*

*"Yeah, and you've told me to never be alone in a room with a man,
and here we are, and you've told me to never sit on a bed with a man, and
there you are."*

"Mira," he repeats, inflating the full boom of his deep voice.

*Oh, this is fun, she thinks. Pumping such a rich sound out of such a
skinny body.*

He knows she has to play; he knows he'll eventually win.

*"Oh, all right." Slowly, delicately, she lifts her sarong by its hem, lifts
it high up over her toes, ankles, calves, knees, thighs, to where the body
becomes singular, pauses; lets it drop, lets it flutter down. She looks at
him, smiling.*

*"Thank you. I think," he says. He holds a chart of letters in a foreign
alphabet. Her feet bounce on the floor. "Ready?" he asks.*

*She nods her head in every direction and pulls gum out of her mouth
and holds it in her hand. She smiles, big and broad. With a look-ma-no-
hands daredevil air, she never even glances at the chart. She begins: "Ka,
kha, ga, gha, nga." Her delivery is precise, practiced, but flush with
triumph. He studies her lips, her tongue, when and how they meet, when
and how they part. He monitors her breath, its production, its inhibition.
"Sha, sha, sa, ha." She completes the series of sounds and smiles again,
even more broadly, and then puts the gum back in her mouth.*

*He finally lets go of his reward for her, his smile. "That is the best
pronunciation of the Devanagari alphabet I've ever heard from a non-
native."*

"She." "Them." That used to be "me," "us." That used to be my
memory, my memory of doing something right in front of a teacher, not

just right, but *the best*. May I? Still keep that memory? Please? that I had mastered the best pronunciation of Devanagari, ever?

D EAR DIARY, "WELL, look who's arisen from the tomb," Martha clapped her hands. I didn't smile, or even look, at her. I just squatted down and spread my arms wide for Shushu, Sparky, and Dexter, who nearly knocked me over.

"Mewa! Mewa! We thought you died!"

"Pay no attention to Shu," barked Martha, in a voice that I suddenly remembered can be terribly harsh. "She's going through a death phase. The class hamster died." Martha pulled Shushu away from me and stroked her hair. "Hey, little girl. Did you know that when I was smaller than you are now my mommy died?" Shushu let out a muffled cry and wriggled her way back to me.

I moved into the parlor, sat on the couch, and grabbed the TV remote control. Martha stood in the doorway, staring at me. "So, over?" she asked, during the first commercial break.

"I don't know what you're talking about," I said, never looking at her.

"That's my girl," Martha said, turning back into the kitchen and her dishes. After a while, "I've got news for you," she said.

"Big excitement."

"If you like paying the rent it should be. I got you a job at Tillman."

"What?" I jumped up off the couch and went into the kitchen. "What? Janitorial? That pays the best."

She looked at me, said "Feh," shook her head. "You know, Miroswava, I have you on something of a pedestal, because you are so much smarter than I. But you're really a jerk about some things."

"Make a list," I said.

"What?" she asked.

"Make a list. Of the things I'm a jerk about. I'll go down the list, and fix them, one by one, until I get it right."

I started drying dishes and putting them away. The kids heard an ice cream truck and trooped outside, after Martha and I gave them all our change.

"You know what I did yesterday?" she asked.

"Let me think. Checked the blue book resale price on your kids?"

"I'm way ahead of you there," she said. "Nope. My brother-in-law handed me twenty bucks. So, that quick, I decided on pizza for dinner. Shush and Sparky were at Head Start, and Dexter was off expanding his rap sheet somewhere. So I had time. Do you realize how precious time is to a single mother?"

"I'm sure I don't."

"I hope you notice how I'm passing up on all these barbs you're sending my way, and I hope I'm earning some points. Time is very precious, very rare, to a single mother," she said. "So you know what I decided to do?"

"Haven't I been asked this already?"

"Good. You're paying attention."

What was up? Usually Martha was much more straightforward.

"I went in the backyard, Miroswava. I turned off Ricki Lake – not easy, by the way. The topic was 'My Mother's a Ho and She's Gotta Stop Bringing Her Trix' – spelled T, R, I, X – 'Home.' So I turned off that, got up off my fat ass and went in the back yard and tried to identify plants. Remember? From the camping trip? How you were teaching us all how to identify all the different plants? You may not even remember because it's so automatic for you. I could never do that. Here." She reached into her pocket, pulled out a tiny, new flower. Four petals; yellow. "This. It's a mustard, isn't it?"

"No." I said. "It's poison ivy."

"No, it's not," she said. "It's a mustard. I know because I bought this." She wiped her hands on her apron, reached up over the sink, pulled something down. She asked me, "Are your hands clean?" and then handed it to me before even checking to make sure. *The Peterson Guide Series. A Field Guide to Wildflowers of Northeastern and North Central North America.* "I had to run down to the mall and blow the twenty bucks on this. We never did have that pizza for dinner. Because of you. You're a natural born teacher, Miroswava."

I put down the dish I was drying and went into the living room and started to break off bits of spider plant and stick them into Dom Perignon's cage. "Let him out," said Martha. "I let him fly around when the kids aren't here." I reached up to open his cage, and then my hand dropped.

I walked back into the kitchen. "So with all that you never told me. What's the job?"

"I got you a job," Martha said. "Teaching. At Tillman."

My head jerked back. "You shouldn't have wasted your time! I only have a BA. You can't teach college –"

"This program you can. It's how I started out there. It's a special program for all the hard-case students. It's to give us what they call non-traditional students a chance to figure out how to do college. Remedial reading, writing, all that stuff. But what we basically need is how to act around white people. Napkins, bullshitting 101, you get the idea."

"I think you're wrong. You need at least an MA."

"I know. That's why they couldn't put my name on the curriculum packet she uses. I wrote it, but I don't even have my BA yet. But I talked to Dr. Rothenberg. She's in charge. This lady loves me, believe me. You know how bleeding heart liberals love to matronize a striving welfare mom. It's their favorite thing to do, after eating Brie and playing tennis. I told her about you and she wants you. I'm telling you, you've got the job if you want it. It's part time, so it'll give you time for your writing. And it's walking distance from where you live. Not walking distance for a normal person, but walking distance for you."

I had wandered back into the living room. "Well, what the hell, paying rent is nice," I said, sticking some more of the spider plant bits into Dom Perignon's cage.

D EAR DIARY, "MIRA! How funny. Your name means 'look' in Spanish. Do you speak any Spanish, hon? It's good to know some Spanish. Lots of these kids'll be coming from households where the L one is Spanish. You follow me? I don't want to weigh you down with the grad school jargon. 'L one.' It means, Language one. That's because, in some of these households, it's not like the households we grew up in, we Anglos grew up in, do you know that word? It means people like us. 'Anglos.' In some of these households, not everybody speaks English all the time. They had another language. But it says here your name is 'Miroswava.' So, 'Mira's' for short? Good idea. That's kind of a weird name. Were your parents hippies, or something? So it's good to know some Spanish. Can you promise me you'll learn some Spanish, dear? Although, I guess you already know one word. 'Mira!' It means 'look'!"

"*Hablo un poco español,*" I said.

"Hmm? Whaddya say? Now. Like I said. It's the beamer. I don't think there'll be too many other BMWs in the parking lot, you know what I mean?" Dr. Rothenberg held her car key high. The key chain dripped a small aluminum Buddha. "Oh, you're noticing my Buddha. Do you know the dharma? But you wear that crucifix. I've been studying Buddhism ever since the divorce. It has helped me tremendously. Get over the rage. And my abandonment issues. You know what I mean? Because it is all an illusion."

"I've heard that said. Dr. Rothenberg, I'm happy to get your bag, but, I was told that this was to be a teaching position."

Dr. Rothenberg was so tiny I could pick her up with one finger latched under the Bloomies label sticking out of her collar. But, from her big hair, dyed a radioactive shade of henna, to her spiked red heels, everything about her impressed me as a preemptive strike. I wondered how she saw me, without make-up, in cotton, my hair as God intended. To her I probably looked like a Dorothea Lange photograph of Depression-era migrant workers.

She stopped talking and stared at me, silently, for several moments. I had no idea what was coming next. I wondered if this were a management technique taught at Columbia Teachers College. Just stop what you're doing, stare at your underling, and give her no clue as to, when you speak again, whether you'll be Pol Pot, grandma, or some combination thereof. And then it occurred to me – maybe she was staring this long because she herself didn't know. Or maybe she's just contemplating the low cal frozen yogurt she'll get in the mall on the drive back to Hackensack.

"Mira, please. Take a seat." I did. "Mira, of course it's a teaching position. I know how it must be for you and the other girls. You girls have been teaching for years, and here you get this new Ph.D. fresh outta Columbia Teachers College. You're thinking, 'What kind of trendy academic techniques is she gonna force us to use? We've got our old tried and true methods.'"

"It's not that," I tried to say.

"Sh, sh. Give me a moment, Mira." Dr. Rothenberg looked out the window at Tillman's spacious green lawns. "It's that, Mira, isn't it? Clean, green, safe. We all want to make sure that our students can have equal access to that, the same as those of us born with better privileges."

"Fetching stuff from your car is not teaching," I cut in.

Dr. Rothenberg nodded. I thought I'd broken through. But, when she spoke again, she said, "Mira, I'm going to give you and the other girls as free of a hand as I can. Believe, me, I respect the old ways."

"Girls." And then, "the old ways." Dr. Rothenberg and I looked to be about the same age. First time I'd ever had a boss the same age as I. I could feel myself slipping backward. It was only a matter of time until I developed gills and fins.

"See this?" Dr. Rothenberg said, holding up her Buddha key chain. "I take this very seriously, Mira. I'm gonna tell you something. I've taken another name, Tara," she pronounced it "Tear uh," "After Green Tara, the Buddhist saint. I want to have the kind of relationship with you girls where we can call each other by our first names, when that's appropriate. Not on campus, of course, but –"

So this was the technique. To wear me down by prattling poppycock.

"You said it's a green BMW?"

"Now, Mira, I know how it may look. But it's not that way. After the divorce, well, Larry did MIS management for Smith Barney. If I was really that kind of a gold digger, I would have come away with more than a beamer, you know what I mean? But if I'm going to do this work, education work, I mean, I've thought about this ever since I was a little girl! You were just like me, I bet. The teacher's pet, right? Always assigned hall monitor? Taking home little pieces of chalk in your pockets so you could play school with your friends? This is so important to me, in an edge community like this, where you've got Paterson just at the bottom of that hill, I needed reliable transportation, you know what I mean?"

"And it was a leather briefcase? Monogrammed?"

"There. The bells are chiming the hour. Don't you just love that? It's so quaint. You hurry along, dear. I'll see you in class. Don't worry about being late. I'll come up with something to tell the students, trust me!" she winked, and dimpled.

And she was off, leaving me alone in her small but pleasant office, with its lush green view. "You could tell them I was playing fetch for their teacher, who managed to come to class on the first day without materials, but with candy corn fingernails, ten bucks a pop," I said, to no one.

I was taking the short cut to the parking lot. Walking not along the broad but slow sidewalk meandering across the green, choked, at this hour, with students, but behind Pitcher Hall. That route is faster, but few take it; a stream runs behind Pitcher and the path is narrow, rocky and steep and lined with slick moss, tick trefoil, and poison ivy.

There was a guy up ahead of me on the path, coming toward me. I walked faster, harder, chest full as a sail. I don't care, you bastard. I'm never going to forget what I've learned. That nothing I do makes me a person you'd even say excuse me to. Nobody else can see us here and if I have to knife you or get knifed, I am not moving to give you this trail. Well, at least I've got my Diamon Deb fingernail file and it is pretty sharp. After Miles, I am never going to be so stupid as to give another one so much as an inch.

And then, quick change, I realized, this isn't a Tillman student at all. He didn't have any books. His black hair was clipped close to his skull, like the ears on a Doberman. His head looked oval and small, in comparison to his body. His locomotion was not a walk but an exaggerated swagger. He had on a white shirt, opened low, and a black leather jacket, hanging open. His legs and hips had the tight slimness of youth. He looked tall, but, as he got closer, I realized he couldn't have been much taller than I.

Okay, so what's a kid like that doing on this campus in the middle of the day? Breaking into cars? Rape? I thought of those Spics who used to drive in from Paterson to work in Lenappi's factories. They'd pile eight to a car. The cars hung low, like the belly of a just-whelped bitch. The Spics would lean out the window, "Mira! Mira! Jou want to party?" Saliva pooled under my soft palate, as if in preparation to vomit. How did they know my name? At home Mommy, who worked with some of them, explained. "They don't know your name. It's just a word in their language." And that, somehow, made their casually brutal predation worse. Well, there's not a carful of you now, Jose. Or a parking lot full of soccer buddies. It's just one on one.

I walked faster, harder, as if I were a bullet, as if he were a target. Go for it, Jose. Cause me trouble. I calculated his best moves. I reviewed my best responses. God, this is such a rush. All that energy that has no place to go, that is just something you're supposed to get over, suddenly finds its appropriate application, when the fist hits another body and I can feel that body crumple beneath me. Finally, I get to play in the arena where, at least not since I left home, I never lose.

Yeah, I could scream. I am white, after all. At a Tillman wine and cheese it'd be the faded colors and haggard nap of my Salvation Army fabrics They'd notice, and I'd be no better than this Jose. A funding application committee, Dr. Rothenberg had assured me, wouldn't let a Jose get by without one of those special scholarships for Hispanics, while I'd get shafted. But behind a building, to a Tillman security guard, I'm a white woman, and he's a Spic.

But screaming would mean so much less fun. A knee in his balls, nails in his eyes; it's been too long since a good street fight. Last time – was it the time I was hitching through Texas and that scurvy fool in a cowboy hat had the bad judgment to pull a gun? How that ended was just so sweet. Him begging me to stop and me standing proud. Don't pull a gun if you can't keep it, I always say.

Go for it, Jose. Cause me trouble. Give me one excuse.

I could tell – he didn't want to give me the path, either. I kept walking, firmer, faster, chest fuller. Chanting in my head the spell that hardens your body into a weapon: "motherfucker cocksucker scumbag Spic." His eyes opened a bit wider; he looked confused. As well he should. As I passed this boy, as I cut through his attitude, as I ditched him in the poison ivy, I gave him a look. All of it, in one look. I could tell that we have enough in common that he knew exactly what that look meant. He could've transcribed it. Could've diagramed every sentence. And by standing there and taking that look, we both knew he lost. And then I got her bag and reported to my first class.

I stepped into the ladies' room in Wicke Hall for the necessary transformation. I went into a stall and took down my panties, though I had no need to pee. Stood up, ratcheted up my pantyhose, smoothed it. Took a deep breath. Walked out and faced the mirror, and saw what I'd hoped and expected to see. The teacher. Uncomplicated. Pink blouse, skirt with little flowers. All but invisible, small, gold earrings. Black pumps. A bit down at the heels, but pumps. Ran my comb through my already smooth hair. Smiled. It's so weird. That I can look this way, effortlessly. Even I, who knows what's behind it, would trust that smile.

I shamelessly scan new students like a shopper at a video store. I want sound effects, spectacle, insight, something I've never seen before and can't get at home on TV. The crew circled round Dr. Rothenberg – she would have them put the desks in a circle, first thing – this crew promised all that and more. I handed Dr. Rothenberg her briefcase.

"Thanks, hon. Students," she said, "This is Mira Hudak." I heard someone come in the door behind me. "She'll be co-teaching with me," I turned to smile at the students. Thanks to the practice session in the bathroom, and a few thousand others like it, I knew what I looked like to these kids: the teacher. I turned around the circle, took in their smiles, nods, or coolly blank faces. I circled fully to the door I'd just come in. And I thought, he's not all that tall. Maybe just a bit taller than I.

Diary, it was he. That kid from behind Pitcher Hall. And it was that moment I'd hoped I'd never have to face as a teacher. Exposure. He stared at me; he smiled. Showed some white teeth. It was a horrible smile: reptilian, cold, "Ha, ha, I win." I lowered my gaze, and took an empty chair in the circle. And I knew that by lowering my gaze, I had lost. I held my breath, hoping he wouldn't sit anywhere near me.

"Gabriel," 'Gah brree ail' God, Doctor Rothenberg pronounced it the most romantic way possible, "Please come and join us in the circle."

I looked down at my roster. Suarez, Gabriel. Age Nineteen. Puerto Rican. From Newark.

Suarez didn't say anything. He just stared at her, from the desk he had noisily scraped across the floor, and thrown against the back wall. Now, this was annoying. We were all ready for class, and here he was, stretched, lounging, playing chicken with Dr. Rothenberg. He stared at her for a moment; his stare was so blank, I wondered. Autistic? No English language skills at all? But then he stood up, and sauntered to an empty chair in the circle, thank God, across from me. But that's the thing with the circle arrangement. He sits the farthest away, and he's facing you.

Dr. Rothenberg opened her briefcase. Okay, what was the lesson plan I had to go fetch? "Students, I want to welcome you to Tillman

College and the Summer Session for Non-traditional Students, or SSNoS. Now, maybe we can get started by talking about what we mean by non-traditional students. Victor?"

Sweet looking, older – 24, Dominican. Shirt and tie. Dark. "Not like the usual college students. Maybe older, maybe first time anyone from family in college. Etta she has a kid. Anwar he from another country."

"Very good, Victor. Dave?"

Dave looked Polish to me. The ice colored eyes; something else I couldn't place. I looked down at the list. Yup. Dombrowski. "Like, some of these other students, they get to pay themselves. We need financial aid."

"Thank you, Dave. Lee?" An Asian-looking boy picked his head up off his desk. Before he could say anything, Suarez said, "They white. We not."

"Thank you, Gabriel. What about Dave? He's white."

"He na white. He a Polak. From Newark!"

"My man!" Dave called out. The kids laughed. Dr. Rothenberg put her hands out and gestured, palms down, toward the floor. "Okay, okay."

The exercise continued. At first, I thought, this is so lame. We all know the difference between these kids and not these kids. And then I tried to come up with the way I'd answer the question if I were one of them, and someone were asking me. There were plenty of African Americans and Hispanics on this campus, teachers and students both, who'd be offended to be associated with the SSNoS program. In our class of eleven, African Americans were a minority. Was the essence of their identity, then, poverty? Anwar didn't look poor at all, but he looked SSNoS. The kind of kid you'd feel guilty for turning loose on any American campus.

But then I got caught up in another question, a more urgent one. I realized I wasn't saying anything and I wasn't saying anything because I didn't have my teacher on. Suarez had seen me. He had brought my identity into this classroom. I worked away at it. How could I possibly teach with my identity in the same room with me?

A new exercise began. Students were asked to give examples of the epithets SSNoS student might encounter at Tillman. Black students, for example, might be called "Nigger," "colored," "coon." The words were written on the blackboard. At first some students started to take notes, but, looking confused, they eventually put their pens down. Indians might be called "dot-heads." Asians might be told to get some eyelids. And then Dr. Rothenberg asked for words that might be used against women.

I felt his eyes on me and I looked up. "Pussy whip," he said.

"Gabriel, thank you," Dr. Rothenberg said. "Pussy whip," she wrote on the blackboard.

"Cock tease. Disease carrier," he said.

"Hmm. I'd not heard that one. Is that right, Gabriel? Is that in common use?"

"Oh, yeah," called out Dave, supporting his Newark compatriot.

"Okay." She wrote "disease carrier" on the blackboard.

"Cunt, heifer, ho," Suarez said.

"My, Gabriel, you do have a lot to say on this topic. Give me a chance to get it all up."

He nodded graciously. She caught up, and he continued.

I couldn't say he was enthusiastic. His otherwise apparently human form exuded no warmth. His body jerked every time he spit out an even lower, meaner word for women. I watched him, my fascination overcoming my discomfort. My gaze became as unafraid as his was challenging. I thought about the taxpayer dollars that underwrite Suarez so he could sit in that chair and say those twisted things. He'll be able to get a professional job once he completes this program and his fully-funded college degree.

I've been looking for someone to hate. I think of how I've been hurt and how easy it would be if I could just hate other people. This Suarez, no matter how romantically pronounced, this is pure evil. I am allowed to hate this, and feel good about it.

DEAR DIARY, MORNINGS I "co-teach" with Dr. Rothenberg. Afternoons I staff the Writing Center, along with Martha and Monique. The Writing Center is big enough to accommodate a class of thirty at once. The walls are lined with computers and printers; in the middle are tables and chairs where we tutors can go over students' work. And for those inevitable moments when you need to take a minibreak, either as a student, from a clueless teacher, or, as a teacher, from a hopeless student, opposite the entry door there is a bank of windows with a fond view of one of Tillman's many grassy green swards. During our first staff training there Monique took notes in Italian. "Are you Italian?" I asked. She regarded me with a tragic bemusement. "No." Oh, okay. She didn't say, but reeked: "Yes, we all work the same no-benefit, part-time job, but, at the end of the day, you'll have no benefits and be *you*, whereas I'll have no benefits and be a thin blonde named 'Monique.'"

I was sitting in the Writing Center chewing over that question from class. How *do* we know? That the kid in front of us is SSNoS? The second we conclude, even unconsciously, that we are talking to a "non-traditional student," we are under orders to act as if we have a superior way to talk to professors, to dress, to budget time, to make life decisions, to relate to family. We must assume the tone of voice and vocabulary we use when talking to babies or growling dogs. Patiently, gently, ignoring any anger or racism or intelligence he might show. If we don't, we're being unkind. We're withholding vital guidance. Such withholding is an immoral, ungenerous act, a hoarding of cultural wealth among us, the few, a failure to disburse it among those many who may or may not feel its lack.

If we ever addressed a student who is not SSNoS the way we address SSNoS students, we'd make fools of ourselves. We'd insult the student we'd mistaken as SSNoS. And what is the defining essence of a student not in the SSNoS program, anyway? What is a "traditional" student? A kid who has a right to be here? A kid who's doing it right?

It was a slow afternoon. The kids' Writing Center hours are tallied at the end of the semester, so nobody came in the first day. I'll bet they'll all try to rack up all their hours the last week of the program. So, with the free time, I tried to discuss these questions with Martha.

"Give me a break, Miroswava. You know damn well the difference between Wayne and Paterson, and if you tell me you don't, just try walking down any street in Wayne after midnight, and any street in Paterson."

I was suddenly aware of the one kid we did have in the Center. Munal. He's seventeen, our youngest, with just a GED, no high school diploma. As thin and brittle as sun-dried paper. The only big thing about him is his hair, bristly as a Brillo pad and no color I can think of the name for. The fluorescent lights were particularly unkind to his blotchy skin. His body was the kind others find it necessary to protect, or punch in. He produces some effort at attitude. He is, after all, Palestinian. But he seemed to be getting it wrong. "I have paid my tuition and I am here to be tutored! If that's okay?" He is, after all, a boy. I told him Dr. Rothenberg hadn't left any work yet, but he insisted. He paid! He wouldn't be cheated! I dug through a file cabinet and came up with a sheaf of ancient mimeographs. Now he was sitting in a corner, reading five-hundred-word passages, one on the mighty force of nature that is a tornado, another on George Washington, military strategist, and answering multiple choice comprehension questions that asked him to select between A, B, and C. "George Washington was A: the Father of Our Country; B: The Designer of West Point, or C: The Architect of the Constitution." Munal didn't look like a threat to anyone. Munal lived in Paterson. I looked at him and then looked at Martha.

"Oh, give me a break," Martha snapped. "Look. These kids know the score better than we do. We're not helping them any by being phony politically correct." She stepped away.

I went to the door and took charge of entry and exit tabulations. Every time a student enters, we have to put a check next to his name, and, eventually, calculate the exact number of minutes per week each student has spent in the Writing Center.

A young guy centered in a sheen of imperious energy, his own spotlight, shot into the room. I had to look up and as I looked at him, I asked myself, why did I just have to look up? He *was* reasonably attractive but it was more than that. Someone could have his features – fuzzy blondish hair, a scaffolding of prominent, symmetrical bones, very good skin – but still be ugly. Something else. What? Sexiness? Like, "I've pleased women and I know it." Or, "I know I'm better than anything you can offer me"? Yes, that was it. Accustomed to being better than anything anyone in his milieu offers him.

I was lost in watching his attitude as a form of performance art, especially as it played to frayed Martha, foreign, teen Munal, and me. But, mindful of my new official capacity, "May I help you?" I asked.

"Is Dr. Rothenberg here?"

I gave up. That last line was just too funny. "Does anyone in here look like a Dr. Rothenberg? Maybe I can help."

"I have to speak to Dr. Rothenberg."

"She won't be here again till tomorrow morning. Want to leave a message?"

"Oh." And he left.

I was thinking, "You think I have nothing to offer you, but you are wrong. If you'd shake that imperious sheen like water off your coat, you'd see that I can give you what you want. Hey, no problem. Maybe you're a little different. But only a little. Maybe I don't have that much more than you. But I do have more." And in writing this I realize that that's one way I feel my status. When "hello" becomes a competition.

D EAR DIARY, WANDA got married today.
I gazed across the dimmed firehouse, through multi-colored crepe spiraling down from the ceiling, and silver ribbons holding up pink and white helium balloons, around the bulges of my uncles' muscles. I swayed back and forth to James Galway fluting "I will always love you." I reflected on my memories and my family.

Back at St. Francis, in response to popular demand, I used to let the other kids ogle my bruises. After six years of this, Sister Principal called me in to her office.

"Where do you get all those bruises, Hudak?"

I exhale. I can finally glimpse the dewy green fields beyond the barbed wire. God is acting on my prayers at last. My reward, all the greater for my dumb patience, comes now because I've played my role, nobly and humbly. Sister Principal is asking the question, but she knows the answer. It's my job to protect my parents. It's this nun's job to protect me. I'll lie, but she'd help, anyway, because I've been a patient Catholic girl, like Saint Therese the Little Flower, famous consumer of tubercular invalids' spit. Sister will help because I've protected my parents' honor, which is my first duty. Like Saint Therese, I have no duty to myself.

"Where do you get all those bruises, Hudak?"

"I fall down a lot, Sister."

"Oh. I see. You may go."

I turn and troop out of her office. It'll be a week before I allow myself to realize that that had been my chance, and I had blown it.

Every teacher I have ever had, every nurse, doctor, or dentist who laid sterilized hands on me and got paid to heal, every good friend who "really cared," every housemate who regarded me with a bemused superiority, every lover who liked to imagine that he touched me, every neighbor who toted over a casserole, every one is lined up against the ruled wall of a police station. I am wearing heels that click, and boxing gloves. I march down the lineup. I accuse, "It takes a village to destroy a child. You saw. You heard. You could have done something. One compassionate remark would absolve you now. A dime for me to call if it got bad. A cot in your basement. Directions to a shelter. If you had only squatted and whispered, 'What's happening is wrong. Get out as soon as you can. Never look back.' But, no. You did none of these things. You did nothing. 'The arc of the moral universe is long, but it bends toward justice.' And justice has teeth." Then I deliver punishment to the suspects in the police station line-up. It is the worst punishment I can imagine. I damn them to life as human beings among human beings, lived consciously.

Because They had the power. They had the knowledge. They were skinny; I was fat. They were rich; I was poor. They had x-ray eyes that saw the knives and forks beside the plate. So, so, They must have known. They must have known that the solution was to . . . was to . . . They must have known. They must still know. And They remain silent out of spite, because They like watching me eat with my hands. And because They'd never challenge power.

Everyone owes the bank. Not only Aunt Olga and Aunt Eva and the rest who grew up eating and going to school while Mommy worked and sent money home are indebted to her. Even newcomers are indebted. Every now and then some new, untutored in-law who would be nice to me. But eventually this kind and unusual person would need money, and Mommy would give. This kind and unusual person needed free childcare, and Mommy came through. This kind and unusual person wanted to feel some old country roots, and Mommy told a story. This was never artifice. Mommy would give until there was nothing left. That is her way.

I'm standing alone in front of my fifth grade class. Sister Principal directs the other students' attention to my old, holey, fake leather shoes.

"Those shoes aren't fit for a good Catholic girl! They are a disgrace to your uniform! Would St. Therese, the Little Flower, and the model for you young ladies, ever wear such shoes? Get out of this classroom. Stand completely still, in the hallway, until I tell you you can move."

I am standing alone when my better-shod classmates parade past to lunch, to recess, to the afternoon rosary, and, finally, as the tension rises, to home. They avert their eyes from me now, though I had been their entertainment earlier in the day. I am standing alone when the only sound coming from the playground is the ting, ting, ting of the grommets on the empty flag cord beating against the hollow aluminum pole. I am standing alone when the light on these black and white hallway tiles startles me. The sight is unfamiliar because, before today, I'd been an eight to three resident of this building. It's the yolky dust of sunset. I am standing alone, immobile and silent, when urine trickles down my leg. When Sister Principal, who had been filling in the time by flipping through a copy of LIFE magazine, views, with satisfaction, the little puddle around my shoes, she sends me home. My punishment continues as I walk down Lackawanna Avenue. Everyone I pass can conclude that one of Mrs. Hudak's bad seeds has busted loose again, shown the true colors, cause, look, she's just walking home now. It's six and she's still in her school uniform! That heavy smack of urine-wet tartan wool on the back of her calves tells the whole story you need to know about that clan.

Mommy packs me, still wet, into the car; while speeding to a liquor store, she says, "Remember; you have never been hit. Remember; you are on trial here, not me." We then drive to the nuns' home. I am amazed to see they live lower than we, in a trailer in the weedier part of town. Mommy is as gracious and beautiful as in the old photos from the forties; I can almost hear Glenn Miller's "In the Mood" every time she throws her head back and laughs. A large red jug is handed off to a beaming Sister. And Mommy is vowing: "I promise you; she'll never do it again." As we drive away, I catch appreciative nuns smiling in the rearview mirror. Mommy has just made herself some more allies. And in a black and white world, if you ally with one, you must condemn the other.

Recipients of Mommy's breathtaking material generosity needed to condemn me as the villain. "Here is a sad story," they thought. "An unhappy family. There must be a villain. The villain can't be this woman who works so hard and gives so much to us. The villain, then, must be that child. We have to take sides. It would be self-defeating to side with a child who can't give you anything." Their rudimentary misunderstanding of narrative was not their only comfort. There was also the simple chicken-shit fear that good people rationalize this way: "Why risk it? The kids will survive. Kids are resilient. And that kid is weird, anyway."

My family. The firehouse could have been backstage at a beauty pageant. Just gazing at the long, lean bodies, sharp, regular features, sets of hard muscles and crystalline blue eyes, gave me pleasure. It delighted me to remind myself that these were my blood. Sailors, drunks, telephone linemen. The firehouse was a salon; everyone had a story, and was telling it, true stories of the shore house haunted by a cranky old WASP, miracle cures from backyard herbs or a special Mary rosary from Yugoslavia, alien touchdowns. The firehouse was a gallery opening: duck decoys, long, illustrated letters passed hand to hand, Anna's embroidered shawl, Tonia's painted shoes. Why do years go by that I don't see my own people?

I felt ill at ease next to anyone else in the room. I could sense that my presence made others uncomfortable. I sat with Mommy and Evie. Like two carefree girls they were jabbering about my niece's christening, and all the folks who came. I felt myself falling – no – falling is exciting. It pumps adrenaline; hyper-alertness makes every detail vivid. I realized I was in the hole, without ever having fallen into it. I had no mouth, hands, legs, heart, mind. I got up, and I moved two seats down, next to cousin Witek's wife.

Jennifer turned her gaze from the dance floor to me. "Oh, Evie, is it?" she shouted, as if across a great distance. "No, no. You're – what is it? I can never get it right. It's something like Mary, but it's not –" she waved her plump and sturdy arms in their stiff and shiny homemade sleeves.

"Miroswava," I said, blinking, like one up from a long time down.

"Mira – what? Don't tell me."

"Around here it's usually just 'Mee,'" I said.

She laughed, for no reason apparent to me. "So, is this great, or what? Look at your cousin. I can't get him off the dance floor. You people really love to dance."

Jennifer and I talked. We didn't talk about family. We talked about anything else. "Where'd you find such fabulous rickrack for your dress?"

I asked. I can only do it if I talk about anything else. Evie and Mommy got up and moved to another table.

Jennifer began emphasizing anything we had in common. "Are you wearing 'Just My Size' pantyhose? You are? Me, too! They're the only brand for women like us. Although maybe you've lost a little weight since the last time I saw you? When was that? Yeah, I've been on a diet, too."

I'll let my bigotry show, and write: ethnically correct women laugh and smile mirthlessly. I've never seen a woman socialized as a Slav laugh unless she meant it. My housemates have commented on this. I am "grim" and "too serious." That assessment's mirror never occurs to them. That they are "shallow," and "frivolous."

And ethnically correct girls, when they're being nice, so often work to make new acquaintances into their identical twin. As we talked and as she tried to make us instant friends with everything in common I sized up this woman. I stationed her firmly in the hard-choice landscape of a Biblical parable. "Tell me, kind and decent cousin, tell me with finality and just this once. Reveal it in the way you talk about Uncle Rocky over there getting just too drunk, and the fear in his little daughter Leena's eyes; do you see that? Do you, like everyone else here, laugh at it? Tell me."

I do this all the time now. I meet a new person who seems kind and decent, who seems, simply, good. The interrogation begins. "Tell me, new person, new kind and decent person. Suppose you passed a girl child on the street. Suppose you had a young woman in your class. Suppose there were a new employee in your business. Suppose you picked someone up in a bar. Her eyes never leave the floor. Her mind and hands seem unconnected. She seems unaware that it is three a.m., and that she is alone in a dangerous neighborhood . . . She's alone; there are no witnesses. She's alone; she has no allies. She's exposing herself to you, without normal inhibition. She's giving herself to you, as no one else does. She defers to you in everything. 'Well, you know more about this than I do.' Would you not be just the slightest bit tempted to act the God? To forget any humility and decency you exercise when with 'normal' people? She never brakes you by saying, 'You've gone too far,' 'Don't be so full of yourself,' or even just 'Stop.' She seems unable to say these, in fact. In fact when you hurt her she cowers and trembles as if she'd done something wrong. Suppose suddenly you realize you've been stepping on her foot and yet she's never said a word. Would you get off her foot and move away? Or would you then make yourself even taller by stepping on her face? Or would you then, realizing that you had someone who would take whatever you put out, put it all out? All of it. There's nothing stopping you. And how kind and decent would you look if anyone besides a girl who keeps her gaze on the floor saw what you were doing?"

Wayne Hospital advertised a "Re-parenting Yourself" Support Group. I tried to talk about this there. I was called "hard." It was suggested that I think too much, certainly for a woman. I was called "cynical." I was told that what I really need is to get away from those bad people, my family, and spend time with good people. So I can experience what goodness is. So I can "learn" to "trust."

So I did some research. I took down the dictionary maintained by my society. I looked up this key word "good," that plays such a prominent role in others' prescriptions for my regeneration. The definition I found was this: "A good person is a person who keeps everybody's glass filled. A good person is a person who never risks one moment of discomfort in himself or in others, who never risks betraying his own weakness or anybody else's by confronting, or even talking about, evil. A good person is a person who knows that those who are hurting must not be seen. When he is with the invisible, he too becomes invisible. When with hurting, invisible people he exercises a separate, lesser, morality."

Alas, the folks at the support group had gotten it all wrong. They did not respond to pain by aiding or comforting the person in pain. They responded to pain by condemning and blaming their designated villain, the person whose badness lifted them up to moral superiority. I wanted to, metaphorically, of course, throw my body between them and Mommy. They would kill me before I ever let them hurt her. One measure of goodness can be arrived at this way. Subtract the pain you have passed on to others from the pain life has caused you. Compare the remainder to the good you have managed to do. By that measure, Mommy is a better person than any of the self-righteous ethical arrivistes at that meeting.

They became angry at, disappointed in, me. "Why did you tell us all this?" they demanded. I didn't tell them "all this" to reinforce cannibal hierarchies and their elites. I told them "all this," and I write about this, because I want to understand the machinery that destroys children, and the possibility, in that machinery, for expressions of love.

A family reunion of shoes and calves and knees. I am invisible, in the sun-dappled understory, on the floor; in the canopy above, grownups loudly make impossible claims, hug, throw fists. Suddenly, the indentation and abrupt popping of the delicate surface of a bubble. A woman squats and speaks.

"Well, would ya look at that! She makes her own doll clothes! Do you make your own doll clothes, honey?"

She isn't one of us. She is smiling and nice and her niceness is real, though her nails and hair and lip color are all marvelously obvious inventions.

"Look at this one. Such tiny stitches!" she says, fingering a tiny gown.

Her hair is blonder and shinier than the Breck girl's in the shampoo ad on the back of every women's magazine. I almost reach up to touch it, then draw back my hand. It's enough just to see. I don't want to test. She is wearing a tight dress that even my Barbie doll, for whom I will soon copy it, could not wear better.

"You make 'em yourself, don't ya, honey?"

How does she know? How can she see them? My doll dresses are invisible to everyone. Is she an angel? Yes, yes, she is. Since she is an angel, no one else can hear us.

"Yes, yes, I do. See this one? See how I sewed the black lace over the green satin? See how it's pleated? You know how to make that happen? You fold over the waist, every couple of, couple of, couple of feet or so. Isn't that something? How you can do that? And see this one that Midge is wearing, see the grapes on it? She only wears it when she drinks wine. I call it her wine-drinking dress. See?"

"Wow! How special! Good job, honey!"

I lived off memories of that encounter for years. I was so grateful for her nail polish, her aggressive smile, the unhesitating momentum with which she pierced my bubble. She saw me. She didn't address me by speaking through Mommy. She addressed me directly as if I had the same human capacity as anyone else she spoke to that day. Whenever I execute one of my periodic purges of memory, I never let myself let go of Aunt Grace.

"Uncle Stan's second wife is here, no, Jennifer?"

"Yeah, and Grace came, too."

She wouldn't remember me. And I wouldn't recognize her. Our brief encounter over doll clothes was some twenty-five years ago. But I began asking around. "Which one is Aunt Grace? Which one is Uncle Stanley's first wife, the mother of the bride?"

Aunt Eva finally pointed her out to me. I realized I could have spotted her. She was in a tight pink satin dress with a scooped back that even my Barbie doll could not wear better. Her cheeks and jaw were cut in facets like a diamond. She was quaffing champagne with her twenty-five-year-old date.

I wondered what she'd heard about me. I admired her from afar. I was grateful for her presence, for her existence, but I made no attempt to approach. I got up, and tried to dance.

I felt the indentation and the pop of a bubble. Someone grabbed my wrist and began to dance with me. How impossible that Aunt Grace could grasp my wrist.

We danced three dances together, a rock song, a polka, and a slow one. Just when I was ready to explain, "Aunt Grace, it's Mee. Remember? The fat one. The shy one. That's why I'm dancing so badly." She lifted her head off my shoulder and grabbed my jaw and said, "I wanted to dance with you, Miroswava, because you're not like the other people here. You're wild! It's obvious from the way you dance that you love life!"

- Reminder: Send one of those pamphlets from the Safety House shelter to Cousin Leena . . . What is her address? Gotta ask Mommy. No. No. I can look it up in the Carbonburgh phone book, at the Tillman College library reference desk.

DEAR DIARY, DR. Rothenberg was teaching. She's got some good moves. She uses a black ink Bic to correct spelling, grammar and punctuation, and then a purple ink fountain pen to compose lengthy personal notes. She must have gotten that pen from the Levenger's catalogue. The barrel is faux tortoise shell. I read on a paper of Sharifa's, "Dear Sharifa, I became aroused while reading this paragraph." At first I thought, God, the fool is setting herself up! – but then I realized – what could the kids say that would be richer than that? She's forbidden me from using my red pen on their papers. So, I make sure she won't be seeing papers after I've been at them. I need my red pen. "Miss, after you get done with our papers, they bleed!"

Dr. Rothenberg was introducing the kids to theories they'd be expected to know in college, like postmodernism. I was gazing dreamily at Anwar. I can't help it. He's so tall and luscious, you'd think somebody airbrushed him into our class. His whole body was flung back over his chair, over two chairs, over three, arms and legs and torso sprawled across the vast territory he claims before every class begins: his personal Manifest Destiny.

Are Arabs as lushly, satisfyingly beautiful to other people as they are to me? As beautiful to each other? If so, how can they keep their hands off of each other? How can they concentrate on their work? Maybe that's why they have that reputation. But then Dr. Rothenberg asks him a question, and he talks, and his missing tooth gapes, or the empty space where his tooth used to be, and handsome Anwar is exposed, once again, as SSNoS.

Yeah, but, Munal. Wow, was he at the back of the line when looks were handed out. Poor child. I can't dream up any intervention, no haircut, skin treatment, or exercise routine, that could turn that kid's "Before" into an "After."

"Kid": Dr. Rothenberg has warned me not to refer to SSNoS students that way. And she's right, especially when it comes to Abdullah. From behind, Abdullah looks like an adolescent wrestler. He's only about five six, with slim hips and bandy little legs. He flares out in his shoulders and upper arms; his long, bushy hair dangles in an incongruous ponytail between pit-bull shoulders. When I walk up to the front of the room and stand before the class, I am disarmed. Abdullah's older than I am, in his late thirties, with skin that nothing has been allowed to be kind to. I don't know what he does, but his face is a business card: "Trouble. Stopped and started." I want him to teach me.

Okay. So we were discussing postmodernism. Dr. Rothenberg asked, "What is truth? What is a fact? What is real? Anwar? What is real? What is real? Tell us."

Anwar shot up from his lounge and launched a rant on the Balfour Declaration, with Yassir Arafat serving as exclamation point. After an impassioned, but awkward while, Abdullah put his fingers around Anwar's wrist and pulled him down. Dr. Rothenberg nodded politely and returned to postmodernism. I puzzled over this strange series of events for some time before I realized, "What is real?" Anwar had heard as a question about Israel.

When I mentally rejoined the class, Dr. Rothenberg was discussing *My Antonia*. It came up that Willa Cather was a lesbian. Troy had been mentally absent the whole time. Of all of them, Troy scares me. He's big. Not just big, gift of Mother Nature, but hours and hours in Tony's Gym big. He and Dave Dombrowski both wear guinea tees that expose fully engorged biceps. You almost want to pass a law banning guns and guinea tees in this class.

Big Dave doesn't scare me. He's a Labrador pup. Dave's needs are fully satisfied by his girlfriend, proud of her mall clerk job, who even now, though they are the same age, looks like his mom in his prom wallet photo. Dave is satisfied by his burger and fries, never finished, satisfied by his sneakers, the hottest brand, whose two heels never touch the ground together.

Troy does scare me. I don't see him want anything. He doesn't look bad, or sadistic – a look that would communicate tastes and desires, and attendant vulnerability. He looks, punishingly, self-sufficient. He looks as if solitary confinement on bread and water would suit him just fine. He never takes notes; doesn't let anything in. It's not that he doesn't hear, or understand; for that we have Lee, whose head is always on his desk. It's that Troy doesn't need anything that he hears or sees. He never speaks; nothing gets out. Today, though, he was rumbling, a restive volcano. Finally, Dr. Rothenberg addressed it. "Troy? I'm sure the whole class would be grateful if you shared your reflections with us."

And Troy muttered, a bit louder, "I don't wanna hear about no faggot in this class."

"We went over this the first day, Troy," said Dr. Rothenberg, in a helpful tone, maybe either too naïve or too well-meaning to be scared. "Words like 'faggot,' like 'ho,' like 'nigger' –"

"Don't you disrespect me, woman," Troy said, and I've never sat up straighter in my life. Dr. Rothenberg, small, clueless, on those damn, faggoty, JAP, high-heel shoes she insists on wearing. I could run up there and – what? What could I throw against anything as hard and big, against anything as self-sufficient as Troy? I reached for my Diamon Deb and did some calculations involving his eyes and my speed, and whatever fallout I'd be risking. I'd be off this campus forever. I let the Diamon Deb go.

Dr. Rothenberg was truly gentle. "I meant no disrespect, Troy." She looked at him, unafraid, present. And she was smart enough to let it go at that, no more words. God bless her.

"Then I don't wanna hear the word 'nigger' in this class no more. Never again. You down with that?"

Sharifa broke in. "Don't you get it? You use the word 'faggot.' It's just like when somebody calls us 'nigger.'"

I got there first; Troy's hand made contact with my hand, not Sharifa's face. Sharifa screamed.

"This is what you get when you make us read faggots in school," explained Suarez dispassionately. Ten other kids reported their analyses simultaneously. Dr. Rothenberg called an SOS into a cellular phone. Campus security came. Dave flicked a paper football; Suarez flicked it back. Sharifa and Carolina laughed high and loud, a full brass section. Dr. Rothenberg gave the security guard a brief report. Troy left calmly and willingly. I was sure that after Troy told the guard his side of the story, the guard would commend him. Abdullah hunkered down on the radiators under the window. He, Anwar and Munal began what looked like universal dismissal in Arabic. Etta, the poor romantic fool, leaned into Supreme, feigning frightened femininity. Supreme is our Nation of Islam representative, always in a suit and a bow tie. Etta's told me that earnest, humorless Supreme would make the perfect father for her baby boy. Supreme, in a separate conversation, has told me he'd never date white. One day I will draw to Supreme's attention that Etta is, in fact, like all true redheads, speckled. I find myself annoyed at Supreme's race-based activism. I refuse to believe that the central fact of his life is his skin color. Rather, it's his beauty. Supreme is the kind of heir who need never give thought to the doors he'll open with his genetic inheritance. "Uh, Dr. Rothenberg, one more thing," said the security guard, poking his head in the door. She got up and left.

"Students!" I said, walking to the front of the class.

"More faggots?" inquired Suarez.

I made a face at him, all but stuck my tongue out, and then remembered that I was the teacher, endowed with more sophisticated weaponry with which to do battle against homophobic speech. I wondered what that weaponry might be.

"Students, please. There's been some disruption, but we do have work to do." The Palestinians returned from their exile on the radiators. But I didn't have the rest of the class. How to get them?

Abdullah loudly slammed the flat of his hand into his copy of *My Antonia*. He stared at the book. All the energy of the now silent room was sucked up, with Abdullah's hand the center of the cyclone. Then he looked at me, giving that energy to me. I nodded a quick thank you.

"Victor!" I said, choosing my likeliest ally. "You had been saying something about the differences between the Czech immigration earlier in this century, and the Dominican experience today." "The Dominican Experience Today." A perfect title for one of those five-hundred-word excerpts Munal is ever reading. Did I want Victor to choose A, B, or C? Something had just happened. Something is real. We should have been talking about that. But Victor had taken the ball and was running with it. Carolina and Sharifa put down their combs. Supreme brushed Etta off his jacket like dandruff. Great. I was passing. And I was dragging them all down with me.

I jerked toward Suarez. He was drumming his pointy-toed boots against the empty metal cage under his desk, where students are meant to put their books. Drumming as if counting out time, the allotted time until something happened. I met his eyes with my eyes. I swung my head, by way of an apology.

* * *

Mao Tse-tung? Yeah. I think mostly just because he was so fat, and he had rotten teeth.

Krushchev: him, too, yes; Stalin: absolutely, yes. All Russians? No. Not the Czar, the czarina, nor their little czarlings.

No American presidents. Not a single one.

Is it a matter of being American? No. Jawaharlal Nehru would never have been one. His daughter, Indira Gandhi, wouldn't have been one, either.

Is it a matter of dynasty, then? Inherited status?

Nope. Evita Peron would never have been one. And she came from one trashy background.

Nelson Mandela, who *is* from royalty, *would* be one, but he'd be the teacher's pet.

How about fictional characters?

Tom Joad, from *The Grapes of Wrath*, yes.

No one from Shakespeare – it's the iambic pentameter. And the British accent.

Eliza Doolittle? Not her, either. Cockney's fine; anything British.

No one from *Gone with the Wind*, not even the slaves. That mindset of aristocracy in the American South would transfer perfectly to the here and now.

But, Count Dracula, yes, Eastern European aristocracy is just too weirdly foreign.

Dostoyevsky's characters? Don't even think about it, yes, yes, but they'd all be kicked out for fighting and drinking and just generally being too morose.

Madame Bovary, yes, but she would marry her teacher and move to the suburbs.

* * *

I was putting in my hours in the Writing Center. Munal's five-hundred-word excerpt for the day was "Old Ironsides, America's Most Beloved Frigate." He picked A, C, A. Had to tell him it was really C, B, C.

While Munal was reading the next excerpt, I was killing time by making the above list. Suppose a world leader, or a fictional character, applied to Tillman. Would he or she be assigned to us? I thought maybe this would offer me some insight as to what decisive factor determines who is SSNoS and who is not. Martha and Monique were off on an extended coffee break. Sharifa came in and interrupted my list-making.

"Dr. Hudak, you got some time to look at somethin I wrote?"

"Dr. Rothenberg's the doctor, Sharifa. I'm just Ms. Hudak, or Mira, if you want."

"Oh," Sharifa said, and she quietly turned and walked out the door.

Stuck up bitch, I thought, doesn't want someone with just a BA looking at her work. Okay, fine, she doesn't think I'm good enough because I don't have a Ph.D. – wait, I'm crazy. I ran out the door. "Sharifa! Wait up." She stopped, looked down, looked guilty. "Sharifa, do you know why Dr. Rothenberg is called 'doctor' and why I'm not?"

"Cause she got some medical background you ain't?"

"Actually, no. It just means that she has been in school longer than I. But I am a certified teacher, and I'd be happy to look at your paper, if that's all right with you," I said.

We returned to the Center. As I read her paper, I compared the Sharifa sitting next to me to the invoice inside my head. All Sharifa would have to do to scare the shit out of some Wayne residents would be to walk down their street. But the girl sitting next to me wasn't displaying any of the shibboleths assigned to the frightening stereotype. No knife, no needle tracks, no arrogant swagger. In fact from what I could see, Sharifa was average. Average height; about five five. Average weight; maybe 130. Short hair, tightly curled in what looked to be a salon hairdo. She wasn't wearing the big brassy earrings that every other black girl her age in Paterson is wearing now, but pinkie-circumference silver hoops, and a single, slender, silver chain. She wore a black blouse and gray plaid pants. Her clothes were pristine. In fact, all our kids are. They all look as if, every morning, before they came to campus, they go through the kind of ablutions I went through before my reunion with Miles.

But Sharifa talked loud; loud for whites. She laughed loud and high-pitched. And, she was a young, black, woman.

So that's it. Being black. That's what makes her SSNoS.

Bullshit. Esther Hemings is a black woman, and she's got a six-figure job. She gets her name in the paper regularly. She lives in Wayne. What's more, she's big and fat and ugly, and she likes to make her point to local politicos by switching to Black English.

So I still don't know. And as long as I don't know, I have nothing to teach these kids. You're losing focus, Miroswava Hudak. Stick to what you can do; stick to what you know; stick to now. That's the only way to serve.

Sharifa's paper was a brief bio of Willa Cather. It looked fine, except for the predictable lapses into Black English, all of which I circled with my red pen. As I did so I heard echoes of a dozen lectures I'd sat through. Black English is a rule-governed language, I'd been taught. Black English is as complex and expressive as Standard English, I'd been taught. Most importantly, use of Black English is no reflection on the intelligence of its user, any more than use of Standard English is, I'd been taught. Taught well enough that I could be woken from a sound sleep and write all that down into a blue examination booklet.

I tried to sound as casual and politically neutral as possible. I struggled to point out Sharifa's departures from Standard English without patronizing her. Buddy to buddy, I said, "This looks fine, Sharifa, if a bit flowery. I wasn't aware that Cather was up for sainthood." I assumed that Sharifa was praising Cather so enthusiastically in order to earn points with me or Dr. Rothenberg. "What you've got to watch out for is the usual. You know, when you've got a third person singular noun, you've got to have an 's' on the verb in the simple present tense. Not 'Cather write,' but 'Cather writes.' You know that, right? It's okay to use these forms in day to day life, but on an academic paper, it just won't fly."

"Well, yeah."

"Okay, anything else?"

"No, I gotta get my bus."

"You take the 86?"

"Yeah."

"I walk that route home. Wave to me from the window sometime," I said.

"Cool," she said.

Sharifa left. Munal resisted my prodding to get him to try something besides his five-hundred-word excerpts, which I wish I had never found.

Martha and Monique returned, gabbing and laughing in an impenetrable conspiracy. I went outside to enjoy the weather. I found Sharifa crying in some lilacs. I grabbed her arm.

"Honey, what did I do?"

"Is not you, Ms. Hudak. It's me. I so stupid I hate myself!"

Suarez and Dave cruised by. I nodded a casual hello, hoping they'd move on. After the requisite reconnaissance, which let me know that they were watching me, they did.

"Sharifa, let's sit down somewhere, okay?" We went behind Wicke Hall and sat knee-high in some bright, blooming dandelions.

"I don't know what it is. I don't know. It's like I can't help myself. I do that all the time."

"Do what, honey?"

"Like you said. Here." She waved the red-stained sheet at me.

"Sharifa, I'm not following you."

"Writing wrong. I try so hard to write good and I can't. Every paper it's like this. It always has been. I can't. I can't."

"Honey, I'm not following you. What's the problem?"

"All this! You see it! I can't write right!"

Omigod. Oh my God. Sharifa has never heard of Black English. All those high-minded lectures they gave me about its acceptability, all those careful debates about whether it should be called Black English, Urban English, Ebonics or B.V.E.; all those alerts about the recognition of forms and how to standardize them, had passed Sharifa right by. No one had brought this good news to Sharifa's neighborhood to proselytize there. Sharifa, a girl, a pretty girl, a girl trying hard, was taking it all on herself. It was all bad, and all her fault. She had no idea of third person singulars and invisible 's's. She just saw a field of red scribbles evidencing her own mysterious, inescapable, inadequacy.

After a while I brought Sharifa to Dr. Hemings' office. When I got back to the Center, I tried to talk about it with Martha.

"What the hell is she doing here?" Martha asked.

I couldn't reply.

"Don't give me that look," she said. "It's not doing these kids any good to put them someplace they're not ready to be. And what about students like me? I *am* ready. I worked damn hard to get ready. I'm not getting any younger and I don't have the time to waste. In one of my classes, we're reading a book by Martin Buber. I'm struggling to understand this guy's love philosophy, to get my brain around 'I and thou' relationships. And some kid – a white kid, this time – raises his hand, and says, 'Excuse me, what's the Holocaust?' That kid's not ready. I am. He's holding me back. I have no patience."

"Great," I said. "Look. Isn't it a given that every class is gonna contain students bringing different gifts? Blame the institution, the methods of teaching. Blame the professors who just read from their notes as if students were universal parts, rather than individuals."

"Explain, please," she said.

"Okay," I said. "Let's turn it around. We need teachers who are more than we. Does anybody on this campus with any kind of power know what Sharifa knows? She wasn't brain dead all the years she lived before she came here. She was figuring out how to handle it when a woman's pushing you on an elevator, or a store clerk's shortchanging you, or even a dog's growling at you could be just an accident, or could be because she's black. I bet she knows how to handle it when the bus is late again in the snow or rain; do any of our Ph.D. doctors know that?"

Monique cut in. "Mira – is that what I should call you, 'Mira'? Your first name is just too – colorful. I was talking to one of your students, Troy. He's nineteen years old, Mira, and he's never heard of Vietnam."

"And?" I challenged.

"That's what they're here for. To learn these things."

"Monique, Troy has been in schools for thirteen years of his life. If he doesn't know about the Vietnam War, should we really take that as a sign that he needs more conventional schooling?"

"So what are you gonna do, Miroswava, let them run in the streets?" asked Martha.

"Martha, I watch Dr. Rothenberg try, with full heart, to teach these kids. And then I look at them. I see knees jumping up and down, heads hitting desks, shoulders slumping. I see faces struggling not to look desperate. They don't get a word she's saying, Martha. What does that do to their faith in words as currency? They're desperate. She's desperate. A kid is trying to say, 'We must end discrimination now.' Does he say that?

Does he have any kind of faith left in words? Not after the jumble of class. He has faith in sounding incomprehensible. Here's something I heard Victor say today, I swear: 'An immediate look at the potential applicants for working toward and increasing black white tension is my goal in this discussion of multiculturalism.' So Dr. Rothenberg says, '"Multiculturalism." That's good.'"

"What's good? Multiculturalism? I'm for it. Where do I vote?" It was Toph, that kid with the "always-better-than-what-I'm-offered" attitude who had come into the Center looking for Dr. Rothenberg. Turns out he's one of us. We now had a ratio of four tutors to our one student, who was perfectly happy reading five-hundred-word excerpts all by himself. Toph's name is really Christopher, but, being from Ridgewood, New Jersey's showroom suburb, he goes by "Toph." He's trying to act like one of us now. But as soon as he arrived, we scattered like balls hit by a cue, and the conversation died.

D EAR DIARY, NO one talks to the children of the elite about faith and humility. To our kids it's okay to say, "You're learning to be a fish now, and in three months we're going to toss you into the ocean and you're going to swim all day, never speak, and operate without breathing air." At the threshold of adulthood, when mainstream students are allowed to feel at the top of their powers, SSNoS students must become infants. They must find a trustworthy guide as reliable and selfless as a mother. They must stop to question every automatic reflex they have, and abandon many, including their natural language, their sense of humor, their significant gestures, their ways of interacting, before we will accept them, before we will label them "successful."

Okay, Diary. I take your point. Why *am* I using the pronoun "they"? Why don't I just say what I mean: "we"?

We must always see ourselves, not as persons, but as old jalopies in the driveway, hood up, engine scattered in pieces on the lawn, the ankles of a befuddled learn-as-you-go mechanic sticking out from underneath. Always not yet ready to be taken on the road, while the lucky speed past.

I'm reading a book about incest survivors. The book pisses me off. Of course the topic outrages me. But the book itself pisses me off. The authors make the same kinds of promises that the Wizard of Oz made.

Somewhere over the rainbow there are backrubs in Santa Cruz, carrot cake in Boston, joyful communities of affirming women in Boulder.

Do I have to travel three thousand miles and live in a stuck-up university town in an earthquake zone, where the only job somebody like me can get is cleaning houses, to "recover?" And given what I know about how women are to each other, why should I be more comfortable in a strictly estrogenic community? No thanks. I'll be true to my lust and stick it out in a mixed-gender world. The women who told their stories in the book had names like "SparkleFreedomSunshine" and "Taupe." I do not have an Anglo-Saxon word for a first name, nor a pastel color for a last name. I have a Slavic name, a Slavic peasant's name. I will not change my name. "Recovery" will not be to me what Ellis Island was to my parents. If I break with my past what do I break into? A world that doesn't remember what I remember. If I, newly christened Flushglowmantle Banananutbread, walk into a cafe in Santa Cruz, and submit to Japanese massage and Yemeni hors d'oeuvres and folk songs sung by a Jewish former New Yorker wearing a serape and if I spend the rest of my life there, where being ethnically correct or a "Woman of Color" are the only two options available in the all-powerful identity check-off boxes, what will I have gained? To me that life is measured in terms of what I have lost.

We do it to ourselves. We shove ourselves to the margins and insist that only what They have is worthy.

Surrounding the cash register at Milt's, the candy, cigarette and periodical shop where I buy the Sunday *Times*, are hundreds of magical, get-rich-quick gimmicks and gadgets. "Pick your very own special magic lottery numbers!" "Interpret your dreams for cash and romance!" "Discover your lucky day!" Scattered, gaudy booklets, candles, amulets. Daddy used to bring stuff like this home. Up on the hill, in Wayne, shoppers would be embarrassed by them.

I can imagine someone like Toph shuddering in contempt at these quaint alien people who require lucky lottery numbers to make it through the day, who, naïve and desperate, buy a book published by some unscrupulous sharpie in Queens and bend over it, interpreting their dreams. But our naïveté and desperation are not alien at all. We're hand in hand with that comfortable white boy; without us, his life would not exist. Somebody had to be made desperate, afraid, uneducated, so we somebodies would be willing to clean his toilet, work his factories, lose his contests.

Bravely arguing for failure, Monique said something like, "Isn't constant anxiety about her language a small price for Sharifa to pay for a mall clerk job? Isn't that better than anything Paterson can offer her? And, if you want 'A's, you have to have 'F's. Placement on some continuum is inescapable."

Maybe so. But there won't be any 'F's for these kids. Not if I have anything to say about it.

But how can I give them anything? I don't even fall on the continuum. Sharifa may be doing it wrong on an academic paper, but when she says "He go" at home in Paterson, she's doing it absolutely right. I am always alone. I am never okay. I never think or feel what the people around me are thinking or feeling. I always laugh in the wrong places. No group is invested in preserving, past my death, the way I see. No tribe is enriched by my visions. My survival depends on the efficiency of my camouflage. Everything I say is misunderstood, because no one has any idea of where I've been. Is this right? Am I being brutally honest or simply insane?

You know what? I don't care. I don't care if I'm crazy. I don't care if Suarez is evil. I'm gonna do this, if it's the last thing I do. The question is, how?

I used to wonder about this as a kid. Who gets to decide who plays the monster? If you told the story from the point of view of the trolls, wouldn't those billy goats look much different? Words. It's gotta be words. If it's just a question of telling a story, let's get the story from the trolls, just like I'm trying to do here with you, Diary. The billy goats want gratitude? I'll show Them gratitude.

I cannot help but think, or maybe feel, that it would be so easy, sweet, pleasurable and good, to give myself Miles right now.

I just tried. Even my imaginary Miles had no idea what I was talking about. Is that because of what happened at the Peace Corps reunion, or was it something else?

DEAR DIARY, WENT to bed early; slept nine hours; dreamt. Hooped, canvas roofs trembled like clothes on an overburdened, storm-tossed line; they took in air and billowed against their scaffolds.

Wagon beds, loosely fit, splintering planks, rattled. Village-wright-hewn wheels dragged over mud into a sodden refugee camp. Careworn camp directors, clipboards gripped in fists, catalogued incoming refugees and their varied traumata. Everyone in the dream – the directors, their hair up in buns, and all of the refugees: aloof and intellectual Jews, ox-like Polish Peasants, Gypsies, hiding a forbidden world behind the beaded curtain of their cimbalom, Tarot cards and smiles – everyone in the dream was my twin.

When the directors concluded that the camp couldn't house any more, that relief agencies wouldn't feed anymore, the last straggler squeezed past. She was a girl, the youngest of all. She was all alone. She could barely stand. She was the Most Fragile Refugee.

The directors tossed Most Fragile into a therapeutically heated pool to get her used to moving again; air and earth were much too harsh. Bits of Most Fragile dissolved. The directors, heavily, sadly, shook their heads and wrote her off as dead. They were secretly satisfied. They knew they lacked the life force, the starch, counsel, or straw mattress ticking, to transfuse Most Fragile. Better, they thought, that the powdered milk and tinned meat feed someone with some chance of making it. The directors walked away from this triage, turning their tunnel vision back to their hoarded catalogues.

Most Fragile wormed her way out of the pool. She solidified what was left of herself, geared it up, and then continued on her quest. Apparently she had not been lured here by the charms of a refugee camp, after all. Apparently she was tracking someone down. Why Most Fragile stalked this particular target, I do not know, but her target was not hard to spot. Designer attire, Hermès scarves, and Gauloises cigarettes can be so punishingly rare in refugee camps. This lone Hungarian woman was mighty soignée for an aid recipient. In spite of her being just as homeless and war-ravaged as anyone else there, her very body articulated: she was different. She was an aristocrat. She was a Countess.

"Some of these people; you'll forgive me, but it's just so obviously genetic. Born to end up in a place like this. Sure, you have some setbacks. But what do you do? Life never promised you a rose garden. I'm off to the city. I can't go wrong in this dog-eat-dog world; those rules suit me fine. Simple and uncomplicated. Let the cream rise to the top and devil take the hindmost. Of course I won't forget you, my little refugees. I'm a deeply sentimental woman. When I make it really big, I'll donate some proper lingerie. I give you my word." The Hungarian Countess was at the edge of the camp; her fetchingly shod heel skewered the mud road.

Most Fragile stopped her. "We will travel together."

The Countess kind of laughed. It was a dry sound, crackling cigarette paper, or catgut on violin wire before music is made. "No. You don't understand. I don't feel much. I remember nothing beyond my last good meal, lay, and massage. I can and will make it. I don't fit in here."

Most Fragile spoke again. "We will travel together."

The Countess deigned a wry and rueful gaze to Most Fragile. "So, you're a slow learner, eh? That's okay. It takes all kinds. I'll explain again."

"No," said Most Fragile. "I do understand. You're hankering to go to where the people who accept themselves are. You envy them and want to abandon us. Well enough. But we *will* travel together."

Again, the dry laugh. Perhaps nothing did get to this woman. "Let's get real, *mon petit chou*, shall we? Your muscles dissolved in the pool. I can't carry you. I get this twinge in my shoulder. I cannot, at this juncture, alas, hire transport. The jewels in my girdle are reserved capital. You're not continent. You'd burp and fart, and lose me trade. Attempting to save you would drown us both. It just wouldn't be humane."

To which Most Fragile replied, "We will travel together."

That was it. I woke up.

D EAR DIARY, DR. Rothenberg needs a rest, I explained. She's teaching these kids five hours a day, five days a week, chairing staff development sessions, overseeing the Writing Center. "Gee, Dr. Rothenberg, why don't you take one day a week where you address all that paperwork that's been building up and let me take the ki—students? Oh, yeah, I'm sure. No, it won't be asking too much of me." It was that easy.

A class looks different when you look at it as a teacher. Perspective changes. They're farther away. Even so, you feel more exposed. "Students, Dr. Rothenberg will be devoting Fridays to paperwork from now on," I announced. "I'll be your teacher on Fridays." Not a ripple. No smiles; no frowns. Not good.

"Do we gotta buy another book?" asked Dave.

"No," I said. "There will be no required textbook for this course."

"We gonna sit in a circle and talk about our feelings?" from Suarez.

"Maybe," I said. "But you're also going to write."

"About our feelings?" also Suarez.

"Sometimes," I said.

"Easy A," Suarez.

"In your dreams," I said. Okay. A ripple. "You kids are taking tennis, aren't you?" I glanced at Abdullah, his countenance as old as Genesis. "I mean, you students?" Yeah, they nodded. "Okay. Then you know about nets. We're gonna play in here, but we're gonna play to the net. If you can hit the ball fair, while you talk about your feelings, Suarez, you get your easy A. I'm gonna tell you everything I know about where the net is, and you're gonna listen. You'll listen because every time you hit the ball foul the other students will correct you. That'll be half the class. The other half will be what you give to me. You have something, and I want it."

"I ready," Suarez thrust his hips forward.

"I wish," I said. A laugh. Even better than a ripple. "Look. A lot of teachers on this campus don't know anything about you kids. They assume you're all –"

"Terrorists!" piped Munal.

"You, they assume you're a terrorist, Munal. They assume Troy is –"

"A nigger," said Sharifa, defiant to the last.

"And we all carry switch blades," said Suarez.

"Yeah, could I borrow yours? I've got this hangnail," I asked. The best laugh so far. *All right!* "Kids, students, listen. That's what I want from you. I want the truth of your lives. In writing, an essay of at least five hundred words, every week." A groan. Very good. "My only rule is that you hit the ball fair. You can even write fiction, if you want. But you won't hit the ball over the net, unless you believe in what you write. Don't tell me a real or even fictional character hates women and then have him refer to women as 'ladies.' I wanna hear him calling them 'bitches'." The students gasped. Great! "English has a very rich vocabulary," The students gasped again. Very bad. "What's up?"

"They think you use that word again," Suarez reported.

"No, no," I protested, "I use that word only once a semester." I was still looking at him, and he at me; we were the only two laughing. Very, very bad.

"You kids are just too used to letting what the teacher says go right over your heads," I said, not sure if it was to myself or not. "Okay." I opened my backpack. "Do you know what these are?" I dumped their meal tickets on the desk. "That's right, children, lunch. We're going to play a game. The game is called 'Jeopardy.' We're gonna play for your meal tickets. You win; you get your cafeteria lunch and you get to sell somebody else his lunch, for whatever the market will bear. You lose, you have my sympathy."

"Hey, man! That's not fair!" called out Munal.

"Deal with it; life's not fair," I said, but then I bit my tongue. I was talking to a Palestinian.

I had made the game myself. The categories were things they would know: "Bus Lines Between Tillman College and Newark, Paterson, and Jersey City," "Jackie Chan Movies," "Rap Lyrics," etc. I composed the questions in basic English. I didn't want it to be hard. I want them to put some value on words, and to discover that there's a price to be paid if they say the wrong one.

Lunch at stake, the kids learned this quickly enough. And I learned something, too. There was a category, "Famous Women in History." "She was the queen of Egypt," the answer. Anwar again raised his hand, his whole body; he nearly jumped out of his chair. "Carolina!" he shouted, with a Huck Finn awe and enthusiasm. Then he slapped his hand over his mouth and recoiled. Abdullah helped him down.

And Carolina, a tall and beautiful Salvadoran model with tall and beautiful black hair, the only one in class who never got the point of the game, did not so much as flicker. How do I get to her, if neither lunch, nor a crush from a stud like Anwar, can?

DEAR DIARY, I haven't written in a while. I'm sorry. But a lot's been going on. I'm trying to better manage time so I can more regularly keep my rendezvous here with you, Diary. I bought an engagement calendar. As my pen hovered above the crisp, virginal opening page, I considered:

My country has deployed tens of thousands of troops overseas, their weapons sci-fi, horrific.

There is a recession on and I have no skills that guarantee employment.

I need love, community, companionship, desperately, urgently, now.

I just paid Dr. Slimak hundreds of dollars for root canal, there are more bills to come, and I haven't adequate cash inflow to meet them.

I have no pension.

Etta is intellectual Teflon. Supreme stubbornly refuses to love Etta. Dave's so content in boyish oblivion; why waken him? Do I or the academic canon have anything better to offer than twilight softball and the corner bar? Carolina wastes away, pining for El Salvador. And, "Miss, Anwar, he call me up, and he tol me he in lub wi me!" I lectured her: "Be kind; a beautiful woman is as powerful as a strong man. Be responsible. Anwar may seem cocky, but he is truly vulnerable." I resist urging, "Do it, do it, do it for me! And describe it to me later."

Sharifa recounts, to anyone stationary beside her long enough to hear, the progress of her diabetes. I can't decide if this is a SSNoS trait, and I must break her of it, or if it's her personal idiosyncrasy, and I must just move faster when around her. Munal's acne. Troy's attitude. Carolina's beauty. She's like all the wonderful witches I drew as a child. Glossy black hair defies what hair can do and plunges past her shoulders, with no sacrifice in density. Her skin is creamy, unexpected, like the underlining of a duck's wing. Cantilevered brows rise to Vivien Leigh heights above slanted green eyes. Cleft chin. And I always save him for last. Suarez. The test I keep failing to pass.

I haven't eaten lunch and I'm hungry.

I'm trying to schedule these things according to the appropriate priorities.

A voice says, "You've put it off too long! You've got to do it now!

"Old age is coming. Sell your soul to the highest bidder. Put those pennies against other pennies for when you're wetting your pants again.

"The world is about to blow up. It's about time you joined the club of elites invited to the underground shelters equipped to ensure post-Armageddon survival.

"Be somebody else. Do something else. Go somewhere with no holes in the ozone or toxic waste or high rape rates or radon. Time is passing. Make more money. Learn what to do with it. Buy a house. Take in boarders. Be more practical. Stop getting old. Stop needing poetry. Don't cry over newspaper headlines. Make it right for your parents and your grandparents who left everything they knew and with nothing but a feather quilt they came to America. Redeem all those hours of backbreak Babka and Tetka and Mamma sweat over sugar beets in the vast, hot fields under the lash of those effete Hungarian *aristos*. Be wise and strong and simple so you don't betray them. Be rich and successful so you fulfill them. Have more energy. Invest in sure things. Save the world."

I crawl inside to some deeper, more hidden place. I know it'll be another decade before I can buy another spiffy new Mary Engelbreit engagement calendar.

As an active addict I underwrote such manic drive with deficit funding. I can't do that any more. I can't afford to put my libido on hold in anticipation of being alone with a gallon of ice cream at the end of the day. I now require minute-by-minute involvement and satisfaction. Rather than the Scarlett O'Hara meditation, "Fiddle dee dee; tomorrow is another day," every now and then I pull myself into life. "Miroswava, you are seeing this; it is your sight; see it. You are thinking this; it is your thought; think it. You are feeling this; it is your feeling; feel it. You are doing this; it is your deed; do it. You are experiencing this; it is your experience; experience it."

I draw back my hand, the flame is so bright and hot and flush. I mean, little things: the shadow Benjie casts on a Lenappi sidewalk as he strains at his leash. Even in that pebbled black and gray silhouette his eagerness is unmistakable, in the taut creaseless rope, his delicate panting tongue, the quick tap of his paw, its quick withdrawal, its quick tap down again, no lingering. His eagerness is visible in my extended stride, in my striving to keep up. He's a tugboat. I'm an ocean liner. This twelve-pound dog is walking me, the shadow tells. Little things. Suddenly the idea that I'd need to eat cookie dough to enhance life seems patently grandiose and infantile. As if I were camped on the surface of the sun and obsessed with the cleverness and indispensability of my pocket lighter.

As soon as I feel secure in being this new woman with time, I panic. What if all those well-meaning world leaders blow us up? What if the only man in America who could ever possibly love me gets married two seconds before I'm ready to get out there and find him? What if my parents die before I do anything worthy? What if radioactive interstellar locusts –

I matter now. I matter now. I matter now. I matter now. No matter what happens, I'll stick with me. In any world, that's the only way I can survive. For now, I will not, even in my imagination, write, "Sit down with Sadaam and get this thing straightened out," in my brand new, Mary Engelbreit engagement calendar.

Last night the very high walls of my loft echoed around me, surgically bare. This morning I called Martha. She came over with the kids and a ladder. I got my posters out of storage.

"How does this look here? Lower? To the right?"

"It would look great above the bathroom door," I replied.

She wasn't happy. "I could never reach that high."

"How about if you stand on my shoulders?"

"You'd never be able to lift me."

"Martha, I can carry a lot, believe me."

"Aaaaa! This isn't fun!"

"Why? I'm enjoying it."

"Put me down. What do you think I brought the ladder for?"

"Awww. Must you be so practical?"

"Gone with the Wind" now hangs above the bathroom door. As an antidote to the heaving bosom and burning Atlanta of that poster, I've got "The Age of Giant Reptiles" hanging next to it. There's a gorgeous print above the couch: eucalyptus leaves drooping under the weight of that patented Northern California sunset gold.

Martha and I went to a garage sale. I saw a full length mirror. I've had over twenty addresses. In none of them have I ever hung a mirror.

"How much?" I asked.

"Seven dollars," the garage salesman replied.

"I'll take it," I said.

"Fool. You're supposed to bargain," chided Martha.

When I enter the apartment now, formerly so stark, I have an eerie feeling. "Wait a minute. Someone's been here." And I have to remind myself, to reassure myself. "It's okay; it's *me.*"

Toph is after me now. It has to do with – But first I have to talk about the Palestinians, and Abdullah's essay. I never thought I'd have to completely rearrange my politics in order to grade a student's paper.

When I spotted the first kaffiyeh on a student, "Teaching isn't political," I promised myself. But one day Dr. Rothenberg was conducting a discussion on "The Media in My Country Compared to the Media in the U.S." She called on Munal. He said, "Actually, I don't have a country."

Victor challenged this immediately. "What do you mean you don't have a country?"

"I just don't have a country." God help him, Munal looked like he always looks when he's delivering one of his eternal apologies. "Miss Hudak, I am so sorry, I got this wrong. Miss Hudak, I am so sorry, this will not be my best homeworks, because I had to work very late in my cousin's shop. Miss Hudak, please forgive me, I don't have a country."

Carolina asked, "You have no country how long?" And I thought, Aha, the ideal opportunity to teach the present perfect. I sprang up and began writing on the blackboard behind Dr. Rothenberg, "How long have you been without a country?" I stood back and looked at that sentence. I thought of Daddy born in an empire called, "Russia," and those horrible maps of Poland's bloody partitions.

No, I'm not saying this straight. Even in a reflective diary like this, sometimes you just gotta cut to the chase. I was scared when I saw that I'd be teaching Palestinians. I thought they'd be like some perverse G.I. Joe dolls; that they'd come equipped with slots in their abdomens for unobtrusive smuggling of suicide bombs.

Monsters or not, I knew I had to teach them, and I saw that a prescriptive method wouldn't work. Even something as minimally prescriptive as that media question coerced their round peg of experience into square expectations.

I wanted them to have their own words in their mouths, before we tried to jam anybody else's in there, including mine. Just like I promised, there's no textbook. More often than not, I give one word assignments: "love," "family," "forgiveness." At first it came hard to some of the kids. Abdullah got all stopped up cause he just didn't have the words in English. So I took away his bilingual dictionary and made him describe it all to me, using what words he did have. Then I had him write it all down, for the assignment, "Work."

"I make the artificial body part, dog or human," he began. "Hips, for example." I know few writers who could avoid mining a job description like that for every colorful anecdote imaginable. Not him. Not one anecdote. We all, the students and I, laughed. Abdullah didn't. He never explained why he makes body parts, or who uses those body parts. But I had hammered home to him: the use of too many words is as bad as too few. I guess the dog and human hips' ultimate purpose doesn't matter to him. Reading a few spare sentences more, he swept us away from Tillman's campus, into a wadi where one might encounter Joseph in his coat of many colors around a tan, greenless bend. "That is my job here. My job at home was different. I had to do many things. I started doing this work as a young boy. One day my friends and I went into the hills. We camped for three days, following the track of a herd of deer. We know this path because our ancestors made it. We can name many of those ancestors, but not all. But we respect them all. Finally, we found the deer. We sat in the brush and watched them, so quiet you couldn't believe, and for so long. When they lay down to sleep we sneaked up behind them and tied them up and brought them home. My mother cooked a special dish that takes three hours to prepare. She had to grind the spice, and take out special food we keep in storage. She slices the apricots very thin. She never wastes. I was so hungry from hunting, I thought I would die while she cooked, but when she served the food, it was so delicious, I almost ate my fingers. There is no food like that in America. That is why Americans are so fat. The food is fast and it tastes like nothing. Now I am an adult. In America I earn a thousand dollars a week, but I feel like I am in prison. I wish I could return to the days of my childhood."

As soon as Abdullah was done reading, I glanced at Suarez. "See? See?" I thought. "Wasn't that fantastic? Isn't this working, after all?" But, for once, he wasn't looking at me. He was looking at the floor. I kept him after.

"Suarez! What's up? Everybody loved Abdullah's piece, but you didn't say a word."

"Nothing," he said.

Someone whispered his name from the hall. He jerked his head toward the sound. He hissed to a girl standing outside. I peeked at her. She looked brassy and damned stupid; she looked the type to never fully open her eyes or close her mouth. Or her legs either, I'll wager. I looked back at him, my lips pressed together. "Okay. You may go," I said, hoping he'd find a reason to stay. He didn't.

The next Friday, you can bet that I made sure to nag some more. "Okay, Suarez. No free ride in this class. You been sitting back listening to everybody else, and you been kind enough to point out every double subject from Victor and every drop of the third person 's' from Sharifa. Now you thrill us. And give us a chance to get right back at you."

"Naaa. I screw up."

At this point I don't have to say anything. The kids started chanting "Show us show us show us."

"All's I got is a rough draf."

The kids whined.

"Aw right. Shut up. Here it is." He began to read. "So, in this class we're taking, Abdullah wrote about home. The assignment was 'Work,' but really he wrote about home. I live in Newark. My mother is from Puerto Rico. I was born there but I don't remember it good, not like Abdullah. Sometimes I wonder whether I'm remembering something, or if I'm making it up, or getting it from TV or movies.

"What kind of chairs did they sit in? Were the chairs made out of wood or plastic? How did they sit? How did they feel when they were there? When did they go to bed? When did they get up? What woke them up? Alarm clocks? Roosters?

"I don't even know the name of the town. I want to go back sometime but I have to find that out first. Speaking Spanish is bad. I ask my mother sometimes. She don't talk. What kind of floor did my grandmother walk on? Was she a Catholic or did she do Santeria? Did she talk to God with rosary beds, or with colored candles? Was her name Sophia, Maria, Lourdes or what?

"Do they eat beans and rice every day? Do they have bathrooms inside? Tell me the color of the sky in Puerto Rico. When do you notice it over your head? I notice it in bed, when I'm most asleep, and there's a full moon. I bet you see palms around your moon. You come here to Newark and I'll show you something different. You can tell me if it looks the same.

"People call me stubborn. People call me tough. I am curious. I have moods. I am a lover. How about you? And what would it be like if I did these things there? Would it be more different, or more the same? Were there any eyes like mine before mine? How did they see what they saw? What's this got to do with Newark? What were we before we were American?" And then he stopped reading. No final flourish; just stopping, putting the paper down. He rolled his head around on his neck but kept his eyes down.

"That's it?" I asked.

"That's it," he said, rolling his eyes up for a brief glimpse, but keeping his head low.

"Suarez, I've been teaching ten years; in ten years I've been trying to get students to ask questions like that. Suarez, not just anybody could come up with questions like that."

"Yeah, but, I don know. Abdullah, he got –"

"Double subject!" from Victor.

"No 's'!" from Sharifa.

"Abdullah gots the story. He knows. I'm just asking. I figure I can go to the encyclopedia –"

"Not for this class, Suarez. No encyclopedia. We're gonna even that one out, work on its symmetry – don't give me that look. You'll get a dictionary and you'll look it up. 'Symmetry.' There are no permanent mysteries, not in this class. You'll work on its symmetry and it'll be your first easy A."

Pause. Even the other students' silence suggested that they were acknowledging that I hadn't said enough yet to honor his piece. How to do that? I wanted to say, I wanted to notice, the unexpected beauty of his sound caged in his shyness-strangled muscles. I caught myself, in the linoleum room under humming artificial light. People don't say things like that. I caught myself. Am I people or am I me? Am I demanding that these kids be people or that they be themselves?

"And –" Say it. Just remember where the net is. "Suarez, the way you read it. You read really well. You should record yourself; cults of teenage girls would listen over and over, and apply great meaning to every hesitation. Your voice is – your *reading* voice – it's beautiful, Suarez. I mean, as a tool, for making words, sounds. As a tool for expressing what you – the very good stuff you wrote. We'd be lying if we didn't add that part."

The boy couldn't hide looking pleased, and stunned. It was one of those great moments teaching offers. "You bullshittin me," he said.

I smiled. "I think the word you want is 'flatter.'"

"You flatterin me."

"No," I said. "I never flatter."

I looked to the others for backup. They nodded. Sharifa said, "She right, Gabriel." I gave her a look. "She *rights*, Gabriel. We all think so."

Suarez smiled, relieved, but quizzical.

So now they're all saying, all over campus, that somehow the plan to group the students heterogeneously was undermined, and I got the best, that it's not fair, or maybe I write their papers for them. Those pathetic cocksuckers. They wish.

Toph started sniffing around after that but he really changed after he heard Martha ask me when I was gonna enter the writing contest. "Oh, you write, too?" he asked, suddenly lathering me with the deference he'd heretofore reserved for Dr. Rothenberg. "Oh, you write, too?" I mean, look. Since Toph first met me he has seen me, or heard rumors of me, in the Writing Center, after hours, until midnight, with my walk home to Paterson still ahead of me; before dawn, before the place opens, cozying up to the janitor to be let in, and, eventually, getting the janitor's key and having a bootleg copy made, so I could get in here, so I could use Tillman's computers, and any spare time I have, to write. "Oh, you write, too?" Give me a break. I have to wonder what "writing" means to him. Pumping out derivative little poems and papers that remind his profs of themselves, when they were lads, and help him to get published? Get published in derivative little journals that have taken upon themselves the heroic task of reminding the reader what the world looks like to privileged, ethnically correct slackers and pre-dead white males? Which publish, too, no doubt, the works of persons of color and the poor and lesbians, all of whom buy the right to publish by playacting their role of the persons of color and poor and lesbians in the imagination of the privileged and the ethnically correct? "Oh, you write, too." *Feh!* But I do enjoy Toph. I allow myself to.

Today Martha and I were talking and laughing and he watched us. I watched him watching us. Neither one of us wanted to get caught. Neither one of us wanted to stop. It was like a game of tag we played with our gaze. I was happy for eye candy I'm allowed. There's so many men you're not allowed to look at. Married men, jail bait, priests, strangers who might turn out to be perverts. Here was maleness allowed my eyes: the broad shoulders, tapering to narrow waist and hips, the mobile puzzle of muscles and bones in his back, the territorial stance assumed in the plastic chair.

DEAR DIARY, TOPH reported to the Writing Center this morning an hour late – nothing new, and he never gets docked. He hung up his bag, and came and sat next to me as if that were his assignment. "I'd like to learn more about this work you've been doing with Munal." I almost spit out my peppermint tea. The topic changed quickly. At a certain point I think we actually talked about the weather.

As we chatted, he fanned out his plumage. "I try to get plenty of exercise," he announced. "I'll probably go swimming after work." He was wearing a "Save the Rainforests" T-shirt. He sat with his bicep-heavy arms thrown wide, and leaned over the table toward me.

It was so poignant and so absurd. I was wearing a sweater I'd found bunched up on Broadway one morning while walking to work, a skirt I filched out of a care package Mommy was mailing to Slovakia. I work in pumps, but I carry my walking-to-work sneakers in my backpack, like some garlic shoved in for a trip through Transylvania. I don't know if others notice that old sneaker scent. All I could smell was Suarez's bodega cologne on my cuff. I'd been scribbling on one of his papers, I think I had borrowed his pen, and just from that, or running my hand over his page, my wrist had been baptized. In any case, I know I didn't smell like a Ridgewood girl. I wanted to adjure Toph, "Stop! I am not a woman to be bragged to!" I wanted to rescue him from social embarrassment and existential futility, like those horny male creatures on nature shows risk when they attempt to mate with the papier-mâché female the biologists have set up.

DEAR DIARY, I had hoped that we could just keep playing with it as if it were a beach ball. That it would be this big, buoyant thing that floats back and forth between us. That each of us would do our part, tap it toward the other in turn, ensuring that it remained airborne, that it never fell to earth, indefinitely. And why not? Men and women can maintain unfulfilled sexual tension on sitcoms for years. Will they? Won't they? He never gets angry and frustrated. She never demands a ring. It produces witty one-liners, and the audience keeps coming back. But I'm getting the sense that Toph wants more.

I had just walked, top speed, uphill several miles from Paterson. Suarez, of all people, said once, seeing me just after my walk, "You look so ready." I guess he was using English the way people for whom it's a second language do. But I liked that phrase and I've held on to it. I feel ready, and not at all apologetic, after my walk.

"So, Mystery Woman, did you enter the writing contest?" Toph asked.

"No mystery. Yes," I said.

"Well, that's cool. Everybody else has been whining about their entries ever since the first announcement. Everybody's in here having all of us read their entries and edit them and rewrite them. Martha's rewritten hers so many times; it started out being about the chief exports of Brazil and now it's about little Shushu. You just slip yours in over the transom with no docudrama at all. Did you have anybody read it? Did you even edit? I bet not. I bet you just sat down, wrote something, and handed it in twenty minutes later."

I shrugged. I was waiting for him to repeat that thing where he sits with his fists together and yawns and throws out his shoulders, thus emphasizing his biceps. "Wait a minute," I said. "What do you mean calling her, 'Shushu?' Her name is Susan."

"Yeah, but – everybody calls her 'Shushu,'" Toph said.

"Since when are you everybody?" I asked.

Munal came up to return the dictionary; I put it away, and then gave my attention to him.

"So, Munal, did you leave any words in there for anybody else to use?"

"What, Miss Hudak, I mean, Mira? Words for anybody – oh. You are making another joke on me."

"No way. You know you have to pay the rental."

"What?"

"The rental. For every word you used."

"No way!" I love it when they learn Americanisms and then deploy them successfully.

"Way."

"What?"

"Way. Pay up. How many words did you use?"

"Miss Hudak – I mean, Mira!"

"Let me look at your work."

"I don't know. Many of the words I looked up aren't in the dictionary."

"They're in there. Believe me."

"No. I looked very hard."

"That was your mistake. You should have looked easily."

Munal looked down at his crumpled plastic shoes. "You are always picking on me."

"Yeah, but don't worry. The other students are controlling their envy admirably. Listen, lemme get the dictionary and go over your paper with you, okay?"

"No! There are too many mistakes."

"So what are you gonna do? Hide out in some cave somewhere until you're ready to speak academic English perfectly?"

"Maybe."

"I got news for you, Munal. You ain't gonna get ready to speak no academic English perfectly hanging out in no cave. Go sit down. I'll get the dictionary again and I'll show you some tricks to find words you don't know how to spell yet, okay? Kay. Way. Sit." I crouched on the floor and leaned into the squat, black cabinet, reaching back for the heavy book. And Toph, from above, said, "Even though I may not be everybody, I'd like to see some of your writing, sometime."

I just squatted there, staring into the black cabinet. "My writing," I whispered. "I see." It wasn't the reply he might have expected. I didn't try to explain. No explanation would have made Toph do that thing where he puts his fists together and yawns.

I walked over to Munal. In that seven-second walk, I put on the teacher persona. It normally takes at least a visit to the ladies' room to do that. "So. Munal. 'Philosopher.' Tell me how it's spelled."

"F I," he began.

"Nope. Can you think of another way?" I could feel Toph's eyes on my back. Martha barged in the door. Can you barge into your own workplace, a place you have every right to be? Martha can. "So, Miss Prim didn't even tell us she entered," Martha said to Toph.

Munal wasn't sure if he should attend to me or to Martha. She was so obviously performing to the whole room. I tapped Munal's arm. "Hmm? Any other way to spell the 'f' sound?"

"She didn't tell me," Toph said. "I thought at least she might have told you." This was too rich. That Martha, who, to me, refers to Toph as "that faggy stuck-up kid from Ridgewood," and Toph, who, to me, refers to Martha as "the welfare witch, enough to turn a man into a Republican" were now bonding strategically.

"Munal, what do you call the rulers in ancient Egypt?"

"Pharaoh."

"Well, I guess neither one of us is good enough for her, then. She probably wouldn't have told us *this*, either," said Martha, slapping today's campus newspaper with the back of her hand. "Says here that our little Miss Prim won first prize. She's going to be reading it at the awards ceremony. She's going to be reading to Tillman's president and Esther Hemings and a bunch of professors. So maybe then we peons can finally get to see what she's always writing about all the time."

I showed Munal "pharaoh" written out on a page, and then I wrote out "philosopher." I panicked. I won. I panicked. I had to read something I wrote in front of Them. Would the prize money compensate for the nightmare, prize money I had already budgeted to Dr. Slimak?

"Oh," he said. "I get it. You spell 'f' like 'ph.'"

No, Miroswava, no. It's a safe piece You wrote it especially for the contest, remember? "Sometimes, Munal. Let's visit that part of the dictionary, and find some more examples. And let's see if we can see an obvious difference between words like 'philosopher,' 'pharaoh,' 'philanthropy,' and words like 'fish,' 'foot,' 'far.' That way we'll know when to use 'ph,' and when to use 'f.' Okay? Kay." Oh, okay then. I can do that. I looked up at Toph, who was staring at me and seemed to be concentrating hard, and Martha, glowering, nothing new. I smiled.

D EAR DIARY, IT was raining. Raining and raining. Weather transforms my commute. I step with the urgency of Noah hammering; I feel myself Captain Ahab; Robinson Crusoe washed up on some soggy tropical isle. I want to spout, "Avast ye!" Because all I can make out from the drawstringed hole in the plastic hood around my face is water, green, and the surf-like slosh of passing vehicles.

I've seen how much good one-on-one teacher-student conferences can do, but teachers always save them for the end of the semester. I want the benefits now, so I'm sprinkling the conferences throughout the duration of SSNoS. Triage determined who'd get the first invites. I have not yet hit upon whatever it is I have to offer Carolina, Troy, or Lee. Lee keeps his head down on the desk so much I've forgotten what he looks like. Abdullah, Sharifa, Victor and Dave are cruising along just fine. Etta was a likely candidate for early intervention.

"Etta, I'd like to meet with you."

"Ms. Hudak, I don't wanna meet with you." And she walked away. If she had seemed angry I could have addressed it, but there wasn't any anger. Okay. I need to think about that some more.

Anwar is a major worry. One day, flung across several chairs, his concentration visibly skipping across the rooftops of the Tillman campus outside our window, he suddenly made a guest appearance in class. Completely ignoring the topic of the day's lesson, he interjected, "Ms. Hudak, tell me truly. What do you think of Islam?"

I didn't want to lose this opportunity. "Well, it's an interesting religion," I began, trying to sound like the teachers I read about, and despise, in liberal paperbacks from the nineteen-sixties.

"You guys can have four wives, right?" Dave cut to the chase.

"Hey," says Anwar, the picture of the magnanimous sheik, cascading his body over even more classroom furniture. "If I could, I would have ten wives."

From where Anwar was sitting, all he could see, if he had looked, and he hadn't, was the great black tower of Carolina's hair. *I* saw her face. She looked like she had just swallowed a spiny caterpillar. But her head never moved; her horror would not be appreciable from behind.

Anwar expounded, "Any woman, she not human, she crazy, if she not want any man, and every man, he want more than one woman. Our religion, it take care of that. Tsbeautiful." And with that, Anwar checked out again, off across the rooftops of Tillman College.

Carolina has not been so exalted around him ever since, has been less divine. But I can't imagine that Anwar likes the cowed, slightly shrewish understudy who has been taking the Carolina role in the goddess' place.

I want to get *to* the students *through* them. In their cafeteria debates that frighten our ethnically correct kids and enthrall me, the Arabs exercise a passionate involvement with words. Hyperbole, stretching: they make a mess. But they keep doing that until they hit upon sentences that are truly beautiful. And then they do it some more. In their fluid papers they sway verb tenses into sophisticated positions someone less intimate with language would never attempt. They're always the first to incorporate new words. They arouse Arabic envy in me. I've no idea of their language; can't even say "Hello, my name is," although I have been gigglingly instructed in "Let's have sex," "Fuck your God" "Lick my ass" and other conversational stoppers and starters. I'll keep these handy in case that certain rhetorical opportunity should ever present itself. In any case, the Arabs debate by setting question traps that funnel the one who answers into an unavoidable conclusion. I decided to try this with Anwar.

He arrived early, a bit moist. He pressed his cool planed cheek to mine.

"Anwar, you have no coat and no umbrella . . . "

"Ms. Hudak, I tell you truly, I have only my special work coat with me, so I left it in the car."

"Anwar, I promise you. I will never judge you, in any way, by the quality of the coat you are wearing."

He smiled, a ripe smile that generously allowed his epic features their full glory. "I know. I just don wan disrespect you."

I shook my head. After the unavoidable niceties – does even saying "Hello" in any Arab country ever take less than fifteen minutes? I took my plunge into rhetorical inquiry. "Anwar, I have a question for you."

My bet paid off. He looked to be at home. "Ask."

"Have you ever danced with a girl? I don't mean Arab dancing like you guys showed us in class, a bunch of men in a line. American style dancing where it's you and a girl face to face?"

"Yeah, of course," he said, waiting for the point.

"And have you ever danced with a girl whose body was like this?" I went rag-doll limp and sprawled all over my desk.

He laughed. "Oh, yeah!"

"Is it easy?"

"Impossible."

"Well, that's what it's like teaching you, Anwar. When are you going to do your part in the dance?"

He laughed; ah, there's that space where his tooth used to be. "Very good, my teacher!" he said.

So we talked a bit, but it didn't seem to go anywhere. Finally he banged the desk and demanded, "Teacher, tell me truly. How do you feel about Mohammed?"

"What does that matter?"

"That's all I care about."

"Mohammed and having ten wives, eh?" I sighed. "So how goes it with her?"

"Who her?" he asked, his chin high, his head thrown back, his mouth turned down.

"Don't be ridiculous," I said, impatient. "You telegraph the antecedent of that pronoun like any man in love. Maybe you'll have four wives someday, Anwar, or even ten, but right now when someone asks you about *her*, we all know who it is we're referring to. The queen of Egypt."

Ah, that bad, eh? I regretted my flippancy. "You have my condolences," I said. "Listen, was that sweater knit by Chinese prison workers?"

"Excuse me?" he asked.

"Red and green stripes on an itchy-looking polyester weave does nothing for you, Anwar. You're a very handsome man. Work with what Allah gave you. Have you ever worn pearl gray silk? Or, maybe silk is too much for class. But think, pearl gray. Red accents. But the right shade of red. Like, like this," I pulled a magazine out of my bag and flipped around till I found a rich, ember red in a lipstick ad. "Here. I'll tear it out for you. Take it shopping. Talk about your sports accomplishments. Anwar, forgive me for this, but, what is it about Carolina? I mean, I know she's beautiful, but a man as handsome as you –"

" – could have any woman," he acknowledged.

We both nodded. "So?" I finally asked.

"My teacher," he said, obviously struggling for words. "She is –
Carolina is – so – impossible. So hard. She never even looks at me, or at
any man."

"Untouched?"

"No," he said, frustrated. "That's not it."

"Inaccessible?"

"Yes! Yes, that's it. Inaccessible. That's it. Carolina is *inaccessible.*"
He enunciated slowly, carefully, perhaps taking pleasure in saying the
word that summed up his love, the word he finally had. At least I could
do that much for him.

We chatted some more. I don't know if I got anywhere. I guess time
will tell. I just wish I could lure Anwar out further from shore, into the
currents he could ride in the wider culture. There's so much going
on now in academia with Islam and multiculturalism. Conferences,
curriculum debates, publications, Edward Said's work . . . but Anwar
doesn't care. He doesn't care about any experience once removed.
A conference, a curriculum debate, a theory, is just the noise of
people not like him; it is not the dry dirt of Palestine, or a beautiful
woman, or God. Anwar cares about face-to-face. He doesn't care for what
gets written up in *The New York Times,* even if it's an article about his
home village. He cares about what the woman in front of him thinks of
Mohammed.

Just like Mommy and Daddy. The stuffed cabbage, the songs, life in
America as a cursed exile. But they couldn't bring themselves to the city
to catch one documentary film about Solidarity; they couldn't write a
one-page letter to Congressman Roe about economic aid for Poland.

Is that so bad? Tillman's mainstream students, Tillman's A students,
don't read *The New York Times* or write letters to politicians, either. For
them, the immediate politics of face-to-face is primary, too. They can't
make the leap to an experience once removed, either. But the majority
culture represents them. It is theirs. It is they.

I fear. Anwar will get more and more practiced, and comfortable,
absenting himself from class. He'll refuse to tap into newspapers and
public debates. He'll remain unable to make the kind of leaps that
come so easily to Victor. Victor can do this: "*My Antonia* is an old book
about Czechs and a woman, but it is also a book about immigrants. I am a

young Dominican man, but I am an immigrant; therefore, *My Antonia* is a book about me." I fear that Anwar's only significant contact outside of his subculture will continue to be stolen conversations about Mohammed with politely disinterested Americans and late-night love confessions to shocked indifferents like Carolina. And this is what I fear: he'll end up like my parents. Buried in a practiced self-exile.

Or maybe Anwar's immunity to scholarly writing about Palestine and Islam is not evidence of stubborn self-exile at all, but of a different process. You're in a crowded place, a public street, a shopping mall. You hear your name, called out. You immediately sense whether that call is directed at you or not. There is something in a voice that can immediately and unquestionably include, invite, or that can immediately and unquestionably pass you by, or uncategorically exclude. If the voice calls to you, you are gathered in by sound. You are altered from firm isolate to porous participant. You turn and enter a circle that telegraphs your worth, a circle of sound sharing meaning, meaning you help to create. If the voice has excluded you, the sound around you remains inert. You barely register it as you keep moving.

When a scholar composes a paper for a journal, his voice does not call to Anwar. No, I would bet that that scholar takes pains to make it understood that his voice is not calling to any spontaneous street stud who leads with his heart and his God, not at all. Anwar does not recognize sound sharing meaning with him. Anwar does not recognize this voice as an invitation to participate in shaping meaning through sound. Were he to respond to this voice no language would ensue, but only a forced, awkward encounter with no shared meaning. The only sound would be the reinforcement of exclusions through apologies and excuses. Anwar is too gracious for that. So, when he is exposed to this scholarly sound, it remains inert, as does he, and, rightly, he keeps moving.

I never fret over Troy this way. Troy who wants nothing. That lack of evident desire, that absence of visible dreams and curiosities, will serve Troy well, will take Troy far. Dead Troy is our class's most likely to succeed. Not Anwar, with his religious drives, Suarez with his questions, Etta of the romantic dreams that transport her far beyond Paterson. They, politicians, school administrators, They tell such lies, such damn lies: "What these kids need is some imagination! Some ambition! Some focus outside of the street!" But it's their very ambition, their very dreams, and questions that will crucify.

Evie told me this story. Once, many years ago, when Mommy was in repose, as she is wont to do, she surrounded herself with family photos, and meditated on them. She took up one of Kai, in his silver confirmation gown, posed before the Norway spruce in the front yard. Mommy noticed, with a sudden, all over chill, that somehow the camera had captured something impossible. In a snapshot from Lenappi you have to have a mess of kids, who knows whose kids, and dogs and even just a stray neighbor netted in the lens. But in this little white-framed square was just Kai and the tree. His silver confirmation gown fell straight to earth like the robes of an angel; he held his hands together, in the classic gesture of prayer, or supplication. And at that moment, the little voice informed Mommy, "This one's too good for this world. He's not going to make it." For her, then, it was just the quiet, terrible business of not mentioning this news to anyone, and holding it within her like a rust-blunted nail that through some accident had found its way to her most intimate interior. She had no opportunity of complaint; she just waited for the screaming headlines that so far only she had seen.

My big brother Kaiyetan could, with a quickly and well-broken bottle, slice off much of a combatant's face in a bar. Down the woods up slopes so steep you'd puke to keep up, where you saw nothing but bare dirt he found arrowheads, fossils, and flint. He'd give you some to keep, too. He'd tell you all the stories of how they came to be. You'd learn words like "cretaceous," "fool's gold," "manitou." When he felt like being that way, that's when he was Kaitoosh. He could do all these things I couldn't, nobody else could. He couldn't defeat fate.

The dreams of the lucky and the few become movies, paintings, the apotheosis of our species. The dreams of a man like Kai are embarrassments he survives if he's lucky. They're handicaps that get in the way of digging coal, shipping boxes, driving trucks, taking tickets at the Ten-Plex in Paramus.

"Don't take it to heart, Miroswava . . . "

Is that what Miles would say?

"Have humility, have faith . . . blah, blah, blah. It's enough that you care."

Don't tell me it's enough that I care. What did my care do for Kai? Care can't stop a cop's bullet in the back of your brother's head.

Suarez was next.

I'd been telling myself: I can do this; I don't have to be afraid. Suarez is not so tough. Troy scares me, and I decided that that's because I can't see him want anything. That day, behind Pitcher Hall, Suarez didn't scare me. I decided that that was because I could see that he was a person who wanted things, and it's through desire that you get to people. But where does he reveal his want? He can look so reptilian. I need to focus on the showcase of his want, so the snake face doesn't fool me into bargaining with it. I need to find out who's really in charge.

It's his nostrils, I decided. His nostrils are like other people's eyes; they reveal. They distend and quiver and lay flat. I tried to make a joke to calm myself: "You'll get to Anwar through questions, and to Suarez through his nostrils."

But I wasn't calm. My palms were wet though I'd been in out of the rain for some time. And, I asked myself, why is it that you call all the other kids by their first names, but he is always "Suarez?" Realizing that this was the time and he'd be here soon, I struggled to find the right prayer. When I heard his boots approach I whispered something I've since forgotten – oh, yeah. It was, "Let me be Jesus for him."

And there he was, in a long, black, fake leather trench coat.

I was seated at my desk, almost flush against the blackboard. The door the students were walking in is far from the teacher's desk, in back of the room, to my right. The seat I had set aside for conferring students was to my left. There was a big, empty space in front of my desk; the students walked in the back door and across this big empty space to that seat.

"Good afternoon. Come in. Sit down," I said, noting my own clipped words. None of the casual play, as with others.

Suarez approached me. Right at me. Walking continuously toward me. Me, wondering what was going on. Me, making unbroken eye contact; didn't think to look down to read his nostrils. Me, resolving: whatever you're gonna put out, kid, I'm gonna meet it and raise you. Wondering, what next? Waiting for him to veer left at the last second. His never veering left. He was upon me, next to me, brushing against me, which would have made common sense were this a packed subway, not an all but empty classroom. And then he walked behind me, through the breath of space between me and the blackboard, around to the empty seat to my left.

Okay, fine. You thought that would scare me or make me do something silly? Nope. Here I go: "Suarez, as I've already indicated, I'm very satisfied with your performance in class. Very satisfied. You're right on track, and going in the right direction." I noticed that I wasn't looking at him. Rather, I was sweeping my eyes from side to side of my attendance book. All my records on these kids are on scattered bits of paper, napkins after cafeteria talks, envelopes when I was crazy to scribble something down and had just gotten home with mail in hand. I'd hoped to someday enter these scraplets into the attendance book, which was as yet as virginally blank as it had been the day Dr. Rothenberg handed it to me, along with an inspirational lecture about how, if the school is burning, the first and last object a true teacher rescues is her attendance book. I kept sweeping my eyes over it, side to side, as if trying to learn from it, immediately and by osmosis, how red and blue and green lines, single lines and double lines, can do what I found myself floundering at, can create order, and meaning.

"Da mean wha gra?"

"Well, it depends on whether I grade you on effort or performance."

"Wha da mean?"

I shot my head up. His hair was wet. Combed with rain. I could see the troughs in his thick, black hair. "Care to ask me that question in a common language?"

"What does that mean?"

"Thanks for the demonstration," I snapped. "Suarez, Do you know how annoying it is for me, someone who loves the English language, every time you drop those final consonants and auxiliaries? And what is this shit you always cut Dr. Rothenberg's class?"

"I always attend your class. I always attend your hours in the Writing Center. Dr. Rothenberg, she don't do what you do." He was speaking in this terribly gentle, quiet voice. His sentences ended with a subtle rise in inflection, as if they were questions. I decided that this was a cultural thing; that this is how Puerto Rican males talk when they want to sound tough and intimidating. Not to be outdone, I cranked myself up harder.

"Don't bullshit me, Suarez."

"I think the word you want is 'flatter,'" he murmured.

I didn't stop even to breathe. "Suarez, you know your class attendance will be factored into your final grade! Dr. Rothenberg hammered that into you guys from the first day. Even Lee can get his butt in there, if not his brains, but it's too good for Gabriel Suarez?" There. His first name. And there really is no other way for someone named "Miroswava" to say it. You have to pronounce it in the most romantic way possible: Ga brree ail. "Give me a break. From here it doesn't look like lack of aptitude; that you've got plenty. From where I stand it just looks like emotional immaturity. Please grow up. I'm too young to be your mother."

It's a safe guess that you've said the wrong thing when you begin to study the white noise in a room. Robins, house sparrows and cardinals? A lawn mower? Yes. It had stopped raining.

My words hit his face like mud splattered on a watercolor. He lost definition; he hung his head. "Don't take this from a teacher," I wanted to shout. "Come home with your shield or on it!"

His hands were folded on the desk in front of him. He was looking at those hands. His breaths were loud and discrete. I began to count them. I had counted to seven when he spoke.

"I guess I have something of a problem when it comes to this idea of school," he said.

"You wanna tell me about it, or should we just sit here in silent meditation?" I snapped. "I get paid one way or the other, whether you decide to let yourself pass, or you make yourself fail. And if you fail this course, Suarez, forget it, no college for you. And that's gotta hurt some people you care about." What the hell was I doing?

"It start in fifth grade," he said, loud, finally defiant. "We been in this country for what – three years, maybe, four, something like that. We move a lot. Finally I got settle in school. In fifth grade we had this teacher who, ya know, everyday, he made us all line up. And he walk up and down the line, ya know, and then, wham!" Suarez's fist met his palm. "He'd clock one of us, right in the gut. And, ya know, somehow, he did this every day, but somehow, ya know, he always manage to pick the one who wasn ready. And so one day I punch him first. They put me in jubie after tha. I was hyperactive, ya know. They gimme some drugs, but them didn work too well. So they usta hafta make me drop my pants and beat me, ya know, on my bare ass. In front of the other kids. Then, ya know, I had ta fight the other kids to earn back tha respect. Then they sent me back to regular school. We had this teacher who usta swig outta vodka bottle in class. It was like this, word, 'Students'" swig, "'Today'" swig, "'We will do lesson'" swig, "'number nine.'" Swig. "Every other sentence. Just like that. He usta feel up the girls. You could see the girls want to stop it, you could see them cringe, but they couldn do nothin, cause the teachers could screw them over if they did. I want to do somethin, ya know, to protec those girls. But I didn wanna go back to jubie.

"I don know. You trying to teach us about somethin else. I can see that. But I ride home on the bus and I look 'Have you kill a nigger today?' spray paint on the overpass. You got us talkin nice in class, but that's still there. We got the Dot Busters in Newark. They beat the immigrants from India. They already kill one guy. At leas one guy. You think anything I learn here can make it different? My dad he work hard. Save up the money and he try to buy a house in a white neighborhood. Use a different name, said we was Italian. Seller found out we was Puerto Rican, not Italian, forget it. I can be one thing in your class and gotta go home on the bus every day and be somethin else. I look at Victor; I don see how he do it."

As he spoke, he kept his feet on the ground and wide apart, like a boxer. His voice was firm, loud, male, declarative, in control. And the entire time he spoke, under his breath, in between the words, he made tiny panting noises, "eh, eh, eh, eh, eh, eh," high, wet, like some small animal being killed.

While Suarez was talking, I memorized the grid of red, green, blue, single and double lines in my attendance book, in spite of how blurry they progressively became.

What do I do now what do I do now what do I do now. I've been such an idiot! Let me be Jesus for him. Miles! What do I do now? Miles, all I wanted from you, was that feeling, that you saw me. Against my own better judgment, I lifted my head.

Suarez looked utterly surprised. So surprised he looked like a teenage boy, which is what he is. He got up from the chair and walked toward me. I just kept looking at him. He raised his hand; I didn't flinch. He ran the tip of his forefinger across my cheek, collecting some of the tears. He looked at his wet finger, and then back at me. "Thank you," he said. I gasped.

The center of authority in the room had easily shifted from me to him. Suarez grew straight, his face, solemn. I remembered a phrase, maybe from high school Spanish, or maybe I learned this from Arnulfo Baca: "The ideal man is *feo, fuerte, y formal.*" Suarez looked out the window. I looked at him, ready to follow his lead.

"You know," he finally said, after a long pause. He seemed to be measuring every word before delivery. "Some of these kids, Troy, anyway, he don stand you. And I tell him, 'I stand everything she say.'" He looked at me, and smiled. Then he left.

I had a vague sensation that there was something else going on. A destination where I was supposed to punch-in, an assigned task I was to perform, an audience awaited. But I could not summon my exact itinerary. The nagging informed me that what I was doing now was self-indulgent and quietly wrong.

What I was doing now was sitting on the radiators next to the windows, the very windows that he had just been peering out of, and I was piecing together his words. I was also watching erect, discreet thunderclouds sail to the east, surrendering to brilliant blue sky. After I had arrived this morning, I had been tinkering with these radiators trying to get the heat to come on. The storm clouds' dramatic retreat was pushing that claustrophobic morning into the distant past. The hooded, conspiratorial figures of morning, dashing between doorways as if eluding capture, were now extinct. A new species thrived: bare-armed, laughing girls; flush, smug boys sauntered slowly as summer sun moves from east to west.

All I wanted to do was sit in this room for as long as I could feel Gabriel Suarez's former presence in it. All I wanted to do was look out this window, which he had just looked out.

"So, Mee, you want to be a writer when you grow up? What makes you think you can write?"

What has this got to do with Gabriel Suarez? What has this got to do with my joy or my paralysis?

I hang my head. I can't understand how Aunt Olga can be so smart, and yet not understand any of the rules. You just don't talk to me in this house; you say nothing that might be construed as positive. You can direct a mocking sentence to Mommy about me, which she will answer. That's it.

Mommy exhales smoke; she is ready.

Aunt Olga is giving me the indulgent look you give a drunk. "Can't you talk? How ya gonna write if ya can't talk?"

"Maybe she feels shy, Aunt Olga," *protests Evie, sure she is doing the right thing, sure she is coming to my rescue. She rinses out her coffee cup in the sink.* "Leave her alone."

I can't stand being rescued by my jailers, in an allowable way that never challenges the jail. I raise my head. "I've published some things."

"Oooooo," *sings Aunt Olga.*

"Oh, yeah?" *says Evie, displaying the feigned, exaggerated interest that will take her so far in life. It never fails to amaze me that They don't see, underneath, Evie's universal contempt.* "For money?"

"No. Small things. In small papers. People have read them." "People." *It would never get more precise; if it did it would be spoiled. Not "our people in Bayonne," or the Bacas or anyone's cousin. That someone I would never meet, whose car Uncle Stanley would never service, about whom Uncle Rocko would have no war story, held words in an order first arranged on my tongue on their tongue; their brain cells had fired thoughts conceived in mine. I didn't care whether they liked it or not, they had it, my thoughts were a cold I'd sneezed on them.*

"What do they say?" *Aunt Olga asks. And in those words I hear that she understands. Not, what did "he" say or "she" say – what was the reaction of someone in my village who might be able to get me a job. But I really don't know, I never know, if she really cares, or is making fun. I guess it's a little of both.*

"Why don't you read them and find out for yourself?" *Where do I get the courage to say this? From the hunger, over and over, to throw myself against my family, to vanquish them or finally be loved by them.*

"Get 'em," *she says, and plunges into a big slurp.*

I snake under the bed, on my belly, sneezing up dust, reaching. I find the folder in which I keep everything I have ever written, besides my diaries, for which I have a special hiding place. I pick out the stuff that's been published, and run to the kitchen, past my father in his easy chair, as if past a sentry training his hair trigger on me. I spread them on the table: photocopied newsletters friends have sold for change or given away.

"It's time to go." *Mommy said that. My stomach curls against my spine. I show no sign.*

"Yeah, wait." *Aunt Olga picks up a newsletter.*

"Give me one," *says Evie, folding her coltish frame against her creaking wooden chair.*

"I'm not gonna be waiting for you guys if Tessie comes."

Aunt Olga puts down what she is reading. "Sestra," *loud, exasperated.* "Sister." "We've got over an hour."

"She said she'd be here at quarter to three."

"She did not. She said three thirty."

"Quarter to three."

"Little Evie," *Aunt Olga says,* "Did you hear your mother say quarter to three when she told us to get ready, or three thirty?"

Evie puts down what she is reading. "What?"

"You don't know, sestra, and don't you 'sestra' me. Don't you talk to me like I'm some dumb immigrant just because you were born in America. You don't know you're so damn smart with your school book learning, which you never would have gotten if I didn't get out and work, while your precious silly skinny American ass was still in school, you don't know. Tessie says three thirty when she means quarter to three. She's been my friend for years. You hardly know her! You just know her cause I introduced you cause you're lousy at making friends, and you always have been, sestra!"

"This is beautiful," *Evie whispers. Her face is powdery, like dusk.* "You wrote this? Really? When, for heaven's sake? And not for school, or anything?" *She sucks in a breath.* "Ma," *she says, suddenly loud, calling on all of her privilege.* "Ma, read this."

"Goddamnit! I don't have time to read! Now are you coming with me or not?"

See? Evie thinks, because she is a relatively favored prisoner, that she is not in jail. She has been fooled into believing that because she receives special rations, she has a latent ability to change things. That's an illusion I'll never have to suffer losing.

"Mee," says Aunt Olga. "This one is funny. Have you tried to get it published? I mean, in a real – a real thing. You could make a lot of money. Really. Sestra, read what your daughter is writing."

"My daughter is a secretary," Mommy says, clamping her knotted hands into Evie's shoulders. Her fingers spread, equidistant, like the bars of a cage. "She makes a lot of money and bought me flowers for Mother's Day. We took a picture of the bouquet. Where is that picture – dcera," daughter "have you got it? Have you got that picture? Wait, wait, I've got it. I've got a copy in my purse. I can find it. Wait. Let me fish it out and show you. See?" All very sweet, like the honey that is used to catch flies. "Now let's go, dammit! I hear a car! She's gonna drive right by if we're not out there, and you jerks will still be sitting here."

"Stuff not hardly as good gets published. Really! There's some money in writing, if you know the right people," says Aunt Olga.

The center of gravity is not these women's pleasure in my words, but Mommy's reactions. I cast her a weather eye and see fear. It is frightening to see Mommy afraid.

"All right! All right! You didn't want to go shopping with me. Tessie's probably already driven past! I could have done my ironing this afternoon, but no, you said you wanted to go shopping! Well, shit on all of you, just like you shit on me!" They look at her as if she is an outsider, not essential to the process. Mommy stomps out of the kitchen, slams the door, stands at the edge of the driveway, smoking. She stands there for an hour until Tessie comes.

A few days later I am again snaking under the bed, looking for a poem I'd written about Bill, the boy I have loved, with some additions and subtractions, since for as long as I can remember. There are some revisions I need to make. But the poem is not there. Nothing is there.

I struggle against panic long enough to pick up this bed, turn it over, and rake a flashlight across its bottom, across the floor. I empty every closet in the house, even though I know.

Even though I know, still, today, I still dream of overturning a bed, cleaning out a closet, and finding everything I had written before that day.

Mommy, of course, it never occurs to me even to question, Mommy.

But then one day Evie says to me, "Mee. I'm so sorry. I don't know why I did it. Mee." I stare at her blankly. I do not forgive her, or tear into her, or squirt cleaning fluid at her face, or do anything else I've done in the past. All I do is I think, "Okay, I get it, now; now I get it. Okay."

And one day I come home to find the latest thing in expensive, electric typewriters on a new typing table in my room, a pretty bow on the top, and a box of fresh, clean, Eaton brand typing paper. Something like this would cost a week's salary, with the desk, even more. Not even Kaitek has ever had something like this. Evie, I understand; of course, Evie. And the world is repaired for me, a little bit.

As is the way here, I never mention the typewriter's appearance, any more than I mentioned the disappearance of my writing. I merely use the typewriter, day after day, late into night. I empty the pack of Eaton sheets and walk an hour to the typewriter store in Pompton Lakes to buy more.

"Do you like it?" asks the store's owner from behind the counter.

"Of course," I smile.

"It's one of our best," he beams. "She said she wanted the best, though I showed her more popularly priced brands. But your mom wanted the best for her daughter, she said, and she's still making payments on it."

For reasons I can't explain, the world hurts more than ever.

"Miroswava."

My head turned slowly. "Mmm?" was all I could say, although Martha had said my name with the kind of voice that demands a reply of "Seig heil!"

"We were supposed to meet at the Center, remember?"

"Now that you remind me."

"I remembered that you were meeting with students up here, but that was an hour ago. What's up? Did one of 'em pull a knife on you?"

"Of course."

"And? Do we call the police?"

"Why bring those pussies into it? I offed the kid with my Diamon Deb and he's stashed in the radiator."

"That's my girl. Is that what you're wearing to the reading?"

The Reading. Damn. That was the thing I had to do that I was trying to remember. I had won a contest, and I was expected to read.

"Hadn't planned on it." I fingered myself. "And my jeans are still wet. Let's make a quick stop in Paterson."

"It's almost time."

"Baby, they'll wait. I'm the star."

I starched and ironed the white blouse with the puffy sleeves. I slipped stockinged legs into the black skirt, and wrapped the fringed and flowered Polish shawl about my hips.

"Woo, woo," Martha said as I stepped down from the loft. "You really do look great, Miroswava. Now can we please get on the road? We are already fashionably late."

I had considered trying to get Dr. Rothenberg or Monique to read it. But then I saw the words through their eyes. "*Slivovica*," they'd pronounce all wrong. Even Bora's name; would they grant her the quickly rolled "r" and full "a" she deserved? No way. I had to read it.

I was last. As the runners-up read their entries, their grammatical errors, worse, their insensitivity to audience, to context, to pace and connotation, made me itch for my red pen. Suddenly I realized: "Aunt Bora" stuck out. A hurtful jerk against my ribcage: the familiar sense of being yanked out of place: "You're the one who's different here." This time not only was I doing it wrong, but my story was.

They announced my name. I took the podium. I looked at the suits. At Tillman's president, a bunch of profs, Esther Hemings. People who hold the SSNoS kids in the palms of their hands. I thought of Bora, my blood, who fed eleven kids on five acres and raised them in a two-room house. She had one of the old style Slavic houses, with a "black kitchen," warm but sooty, and a "clean room," bright but cold. She never traveled farther than a half-day's walk from her village. I have learned to live with doing it wrong for me. I will not do it wrong for Bora, or for the SSNoS kids.

I dropped my head. I read. I discovered my tongue, teeth and palate, my breath, making love to every word. These words were not resisting my love. They embraced me. Love flowed from me as if I had been receiving love all my life, as if I were a reservoir and could now distribute it, profligately. There was a confidence, as if it had been apprenticed to the proper teachers. Though my head was down, so I could read, I could feel my listeners claim my words, as earth claims cast seed. They would now remember Bora, too. When the applause came, I also knew.

But then it was over. The clock struck twelve. I was a pumpkin, a weird girl who, without adequate excuse, had wrapped a foreign shawl about her hips in suburban New Jersey. I bolted for the door. Toph's body was in my way. He was stronger.

"That was good," he said, as if at the end of a long tunnel. "Now why don't you come back and let people tell you?" I took his hand and followed because to do otherwise would draw attention. In the crowded lounge of wine and cheese I took up my allotment of wine and cheese, resisting the instinct to shove my pockets full. I stood as suave as Frankenstein's monster.

"Young lady!" boomed a pleasant looking woman whom I focused on and recognized as my old Professor Mack. "As soon as I heard the words 'goose poop' in your first sentence, I knew you were writing about Slovakia. Wonderful. Congratulations. So, where do you come from? What do you do on this campus? You can't be just a *tutor* in the *SSNoS program.* What's your *real* story, huh?" Her questions figured me as some kind of conspirator. She insistently didn't recognize me.

I shook her proffered hand and asked, "How do you know about goose poop?"

"Because I'm Slovak," she said.

"But your name."

"Remove the 'c,'" she said.

I did. "'Mak!' That's a Slovak name!"

She winked at me and moved on, making room for the next congratulator. I wanted to follow her. Oh yeah? Remove the 'c' yourself, I wanted to say. I was your student years ago on this campus, I wanted to say. Your handshake, and your name, would have meant more to me then. But I remained flush with the wall. I was trying to work out the fewer, as well as more, words one can say as a prizewinner, as opposed to an invisible working class student, and which of those things had any chance of ending up getting heard.

As soon as I sensed the pressure relenting, I made for the door. I walked toward the Writing Center, cause that's my route home. I couldn't help but notice that Toph was walking beside me. He asked if I wanted a ride. I stared at him as if I had just been released from solitary and was not eager to reveal that I hadn't yet mastered the new lingo that had come into fashion since my sentencing. Following the path of least resistance, I walked with Toph back to the library, where he'd parked his car. I thought, why did he follow me all the way down here, if his car is up there? He drove me home; I was distracted; he mentioned calling me to do some hiking. I said, "Uh huh."

I changed into cut-off jeans and walked back uphill to Wayne, where I flagged down a bus to Pompton Lakes. Walking the weedy shoulderless miles to Lenappi, I chanted the name of each flower as it brushed my calves: chicory, Queen Anne's lace, day lily. When I got to Saint Francis I didn't turn into Lenappi. I just kept walking. I reached the reservoir. The full moon was rising higher in a sky momentarily sapphire. I heard as well as felt the subdued thunder of deer hooves. Mosquitoes pricked my legs.

A cop stopped. "Excuse me, Miss. Do you need help?"

"No," I said. "I'm just walking."

"Well, you know, Miss," he said. "it's late, and dark, and there isn't much of a shoulder here. Maybe it's time to get back home. Your folks are probably worried."

He thought I was a runaway. But he was mistaken. I am a prizewinner. I tried to act moved and grateful and turned back towards Lenappi. Past the swamp and the eighteenth-century cemetery, past Arnulfo Baca's and the Bellochio's and the Krawczuk's. And I walked in the never-locked back door.

Benjie didn't jump up, bark, paw my knees, didn't demand love, adventure, excitement, a walk. He is getting old. I squatted down beside him and whispered as loudly as I could: "Benjie." Not even a twitch. Finally I circled him in my arms and carried him outside.

I went to the bathroom and when I returned, I saw him sitting in the rectangle of yellow light outside the screen door, staring up at it, waiting to be let back in to his comfy pension under the kitchen table. "Oh, Benj." I grabbed his spiral rag rug and lay it out on the stoop for him. We watched the full moon progress over the ridge in front of the house. The sky was drenched with moon juice wrung through clouds. Mommy opened the front door, leaned out of it, and said, "You'd just better make sure that that big, fat, rabid raccoon doesn't come around." She withdrew back into the house and slammed both the screen door and the wooden one shut tight.

"Mom," I said. "I just read a story about your village to a bunch of rich and important suits. They probably hadn't ever heard of Slovakia before. You were in the story, mom, and you were a hero."

I smiled. "C'mon, honey." I scooped Benjie up and brought him inside. I made him get into bed with me. I could hear Mommy through the sliding plastic door. I remembered when I was a kid, and we slept in the same bed together, and we spooned into each other, sometimes. I remember sometimes waking up in the night and wanting to fall back to sleep and lulling myself with her breaths, riding them as if they were a swing and could support my weight, and transport me, or chasing in and out of them, until I dropped off.

When I heard Mommy's last breaths, nasal clearings, rumblings, evening out into sleep, I curled around Benjie. I confessed to him, confessing this for the first time, that the only person I care about, the only person I have ever cared about, the only person I could easily show genuine tenderness or respect, was the person I saw today in Gabriel Suarez.

DEAR DIARY, I was lying in bed Sunday morning when he called. "Hello?" Pleasant but officious. At least I've perfected my Mary Tyler Moore over the telephone.

"Mira?"

"Who is this, please?" Really, I wasn't being coy; couldn't be sure who it might be.

"It's Toph. Sorry to wake you."

"No, no, I was awake." Whenever I'm awakened by a phone call I'm always convinced that I'd been awake previous to it. It's an odd sensation that fades as the call progresses and I feel more groggy and in dreamland, worried that I've been saying things like, "Rubber phosphorescent monkeys raided my garbage on Tuesday."

"It's a beautiful day," Toph asserted.

"Is it?"

"You haven't even looked out the window yet, have you? Want to go hiking?" he asked.

"I always want to go hiking. When? Where?"

"I'll be there in about twenty minutes, and then we can figure it out."

There was a silence.

"Okay?" he asked, sounding, for the first time, a bit unsure. Suddenly I realized that he wasn't giving orders, and that it was my job to say "Okay," or something. That I had a hand in letting this happen, in making this happen. That I could withhold the word "Okay." Was there any reason for me to do so?

"Okay," I said.

"You sure? You sounded a bit weak, there."

Oh, so he would demand enthusiasm. "Like I said," I said, suddenly sounding mean, though I had no such intention. "I always want to go hiking."

"Oh," he said, suddenly more reserved. "I see. Well then, we'll see what we can do to get the girl some hiking. Twenty minutes."

I got out of bed and walked, naked, up to the full-length mirror. I've been dieting for months, but I'm still fat. Not as fat as before, but fat. I've been studying myself in the mirror intently. Confronted with Toph's imminent arrival, I realized why. I'm looking for that new woman to appear – the slim one – the one worthy of love, investment and hope.

Excuse me.

I'm back. Just took a break to stand before the mirror and say, "You, right now, are worthy of love, investment and hope." Yes, it felt silly, but one has to do these things.

When he arrived we were suddenly formal with each other. As is right. We have been Mira and Toph on-campus. We were now two people newly introduced: Mira and Toph off-campus.

"Do you have any idea as to where you'd like to go?" he asked, after I got into his cute little car.

"Can you take me far away?" I pleaded. "Some place different, some place new, some place I've never been?"

He looked humbled, full of thought, and I think he liked that, being asked more than he expected to be asked. "Will ten dollars be enough?"

"Always."

"Would you like to go to the Palisades?" The Palisades sounded distant and hard, the kind of place I'd get carsick going to.

"Oh, yes."

I grew up an hour's drive from them, and until I got out of Toph's car, I didn't know what the Palisades were. I can recover from attraction to a man, but I can never conquer gratitude to, or forget crediting, a man who shows me a new wonderful thing. These Palisades were a new wonderful thing and they will always be Toph's. They're cliffs. They drop into the Hudson River, a full ten times further down than any drops I thought we had in Jersey.

I felt some affront in the face of these snotty, challenging rocks, so abruptly vertical. I compared the Palisades to the more horizontal rocks in my hometown. In Lenappi a glacial moraine rises from the forest floor. Like very slow whales boulders emerge from the earth. Lenappi boulders, basking all day as they do, are sun-warmed, soft with moss, sweet with berries. We rode them like elders' backs; we felt so hardy when we fell ten feet and didn't break anything. You couldn't fall off these Palisades and not break anything.

Toph bounced over a guardrail and perched on a neat drop of cliff. I sat way back and could feel my thighs clench to create some suction onto the slab of rock beneath me. I watched his back to me against the sky and thought, what abundant faith he has in his ability to spring. A too strong wind or the wing of a veering falcon could tip him into a demonstration of gravity. I am dense; my overtaxed springs are compressed. That is why I am so decidedly where I am when I am there, these days.

"Do you know," he called back to me, "once I got a deer with the first arrow I drew from my quiver that morning."

My mind raced. I wondered if I'd ever accomplished anything. Suddenly I remembered that I was the girl and not to brag, but to admire.

I was trying to say "Ooo." Instead, I said, "Awww."

He looked back at me holding on by my fingernails.

"You don't like hunting, do you?"

"Don't get me wrong. All the men in my family hunt. Kai made me eat his venison –"

"Made you."

"Yeah. To make me stronger –"

"That must have been fun."

He looked back towards Manhattan's skyline and I craved to be more compelling.

"Mira," sounding casual, "I want to confess to you all the animals I killed when I was a hunter, so you can forgive me. Deer. Lots of deer. Squirrels. Maybe five? A sparrow –"

"Ahh!"

"What?"

"Nothing."

"I guess that makes it an even hundred," he said.

"Hmm?"

"An even hundred times that you've said 'Ah,' or 'Oh,' or made a face or showed some other strong reaction to something and when I asked you what was going on you said, 'Nothing.' It's just like when I asked to see your writing, some time."

"Oh," I said.

Toph laughed raucously. But he went on: "A muskrat; I was thinking fur, that time, not food. A –"

"I'm sorry," I said.

"For?"

"For all the 'nothings.' It's just that, I wouldn't, no matter how hungry I was, ever kill a bird. They're so beautiful, and they can fly."

He laughed. "Mira Hudak, I don't kill because I'm hungry. I don't know if I've ever been hungry. That kind of hungry, anyway."

I was so frustrated. I had been trying so hard. To be present. Not to be too present. To answer the question that had been asked. Not to answer the question that hadn't been asked. But I was only amusing. Something about him is peeled from me. I struggled to compose the story in my head, because maintaining his distance, he wasn't writing it with me.

"Look," he said. "I don't want you to conclude that I'm some kind of macho Neanderthal just because I used to hunt. Mira, do you know that I am a gourmet chef of rare and precious cuisines?"

Is that what he said? Did he even ever say the words "gourmet," "chef," "cuisine"? I don't know. I don't remember how he said it. All I know is that the words he deployed conveyed the ideas that he can cook, that he can cook exclusive dishes mastered by few, that what he does with food elevates him from simple people. And that when I heard whatever words he did use, I felt intimidated, and a nut of rage. So I type those words I typed above, to recreate my reaction. But the thing is, my typing has not recreated my reaction. The tools I have at hand are too blunt: "gourmet," "chef," "cuisine." Toph's statement wasn't blunt. It was surgical. Enough to identify himself as member of an elite without sounding like a laughable, bigoted old fart. Just, simply, better. And I can't transcribe his words because those words, that style, are beyond my vocabulary.

He talked more. He used verbs that are not part of what it has occurred to me to do to food. "Braising fennel." I have never used the verb "to braise." I knew that as soon as I got home I could look it up in the dictionary for an adequate definition, and I knew that that dictionary definition would leave me only marginally more empowered.

He began to talk of hole-in-the-wall restaurants in Paterson where he'd drunk *chicha* and eaten heart. Waiters and cooks named "Maria" and "Tony." Not the names of relatives one respected, but of exotics who knew their place: producing heavy plates of hot food for him to eat, and then to glow warmly when told how well they cook. No, their place was not staying up late, struggling for words to record their heart's politics.

I can transcribe this part; I memorized it phonetically as he spoke: "We wade-fished off the East End that Sunday afternoon, and off the t-head at the Flagship. We were going after ling, but we got some Spanish mackerel, nature's most nearly perfect fish. We grilled them over a hot, fast mesquite fire –"

He turned, and glanced at me. "Omigod. What did I say?"

"Nothing," I replied. "Why?"

"You're giving me such a look," he said.

"I don't know what 'ling' means. Or 'mesquite,' either."

"Oh," he said. "Is that it. Ling is –"

"And I have no immediate desire to find out what ling is."

He shook his head, looked down. "Guess I've been talking to myself, here . . . look, I just wanted you to know, I mean, after I told you about hunting . . . I just wanted you to know that I'm not one of those macho guys. That I cook and . . . I just wanted you to know that I'm not like those SSNoS guys."

"What do you mean by that?"

"I mean I'm not like the SSNoS guys. All muscles, guinea Ts and swagger."

"How do you know that that's what they're like? You ever spend any time with them? I don't see you doing any more than the bare minimum. You're just there, half the time, to play with yourself on the computers. Chess, I mean."

"Where's this coming from?" he protested.

"You think just because you put an apron on occasionally – I don't know; do people wear aprons when they're cooking their mesquite? Just because you put on an apron occasionally doesn't mean you get to avoid responsibility for what you've got underneath it. Those SSNoS guys know what it means to take responsibility for being a man."

"I don't see why you have to get so upset –"

"Because those SSNoS kids are my people."

"How romantic," he said.

"Fuck you romantic," I said. "I'm just like those kids."

"You are nothing like those kids, Mira. You're nothing like Martha, either. How a woman like you can be friends –"

"What do you know about Martha?"

"And why do we call it 'SSNoS' anyway? It's as if we're supposed to not mention that the correct acronym would be SSNoTS. Snots. That's what these kids are. Snots."

"That joke is so unfunny that no one tells it!" I spit.

Toph sighed. "I'm going to take a time-out from this conversation," he said. He turned back towards the skyline.

During the ride home, thinking I was being driven to Paterson, I was shaken out of this obliviousness by a realization: the streets over which we rode were eggshell-smooth. I suddenly found myself being told, "And that's the high school I went to," "That's where we used to play spin the bottle at night." Well, at long last, I was in Ridgewood. I was surprised that I had entered without a check of my papers at the border crossing. Everything looked cozy and sterile. I know "cozy" and "sterile" contradict each other. Someday I'll have that word, and when I have it, I will defuse a lot of this yearning.

Suddenly found myself being told, "And there's my dad, working on the car." Why do I ask so politely and far in advance if men would like to meet Mommy and Daddy and expect it, nod meekly, when they say no? What did my last ethnically correct date say? "They're liable to feed me something made out of a pig's head." But I was supposed to be born ready for Ridgewood. Dad working on one car of many in multi-car garage. Sterile elf house adjacent to multi-car garage. Handsome, tall, slim dad, doing handiwork in his neatly stacked, well-appointed workshop. Pleasant dad. Maybe even sane. "Sane dad" always seemed like an oxymoron.

Toph's car stopped. Toph got out. He didn't pause. I was supposed to get out, too. I wasn't a fish encased in a wheeled fishbowl being driven through by Daddy to ogle Christmas and Hanukkah lights, I would be a real, interacting human.

"Hi, dad!"

"Hi, son." No. He didn't really say "son." He said, "With a couple more hours' work, I think I can get this back on the road. Oh, hi. Are you a friend of Christopher's?" He pulled his head out of the car hood. I noticed the Amnesty International sticker on the windshield.

"Yes, I'm –"

"Dad, this is Mira Hudak, that girl at work I've told you about."

"It's nice to meet you, Mr. Barnes," I said, sticking out my hand.

"Oh, please, call me 'John,'" he said, wiping his hands on a rag. He had a crisp, firm grip. "So this is she. I've heard a lot about you, young lady."

I kind of smiled.

Then there was this silence. And then I realized that the silence had been agreed to by Toph and Mr. Barnes; that I was the odd man out. The two of them were waiting for something. When it wasn't forthcoming, Toph punched my shoulder lightly and urged, "Say something amazing."

"Say something common," I replied.

D EAR DIARY, ABDULLAH was reading. "Married life is the most beautiful life there is. With marriage you have responsibility, and without responsibility, you are nothing." We all nodded snuggly. This is the kind of affirmation of Norman Rockwell values we've come to expect from Abdullah. Then he read, in the same voice he uses to describe the creation of a dog hip, "Our system is clear. If, as returning to Palestine, I found out that my wife had been with another man, even if he forced her, I would have to kill her."

"'*On* returning,' Abdullah," was all I could say. "'If, *on* returning to Palestine, I found out that my wife had been with another man' – good use of the past perfect, there. 'I would kill her.' And good use of the conditional."

He thanked me, bent over his paper to correct it.

"Thas okay wit you?" – Suarez.

His leather was gone. Suarez had made a grand entrance this morning in a pink button down shirt and neatly pressed, olive slacks. A big wad dropped at the mall for that outfit. He had carried himself into class with a new purposefulness, taut but fluid as a plumb line, a matador of academic inquiry, and wearing horn rim glasses. I'd asked, "Do you need those glasses?" He giggled. "Nah." But he kept them on.

He usually sits near the door; this morning he came and sat next to me, giving me a look as he sat down that I haven't seen before. I couldn't believe that that same face had ever looked reptilian. That face now confused and expectant. I could see this. And feel – I immediately felt what I feel around children. But I didn't have time to . . . Time. It wasn't time. I don't know. I was tense. I've got a lot on my mind.

"It's not okay," I said. "There's a 't' at the end of the word 'that.'"

"Thank you," Suarez said. "That t t t t t's okay. You kill your wife that's okay, Abdullah, as long as you put the 't' on the end of 'that's.' And, remember, the good use of the past perfect."

I had had it. Really had it. He'd been doing stuff like this all day. Fanning my face, peeking over at me. I'd been responding by concentrating all the harder on the lesson.

Nowhere near as winded as he had gotten me, he said, "You know, I gotta say, you Arabs, you crazy. I never kill a woman," he looked at me, "We Puerto Ricans, we like the *caña* just too much."

"'*Caña*,' what's that?" I asked, and as soon as the question tripped off my tongue I knew I had gone *splat*.

Suarez pumped his hips back and forth so vigorously his chair squeaked and inched forward over the tile. "You know. Cane. The sugar cane."

I turned bright red. The students cracked up. An impromptu contest began to see who could be the most outrageous, to turn me reddest. Suddenly Suarez was the comfortable and confident ringmaster. He laughed. He laughed so hard at all the double entendres tears filled his eyes. Finally I softly threatened to throw him and his worst accomplices out.

"I ain't taking this shit!" Troy asserted. He snorted, half-rose as if to come toward me, to settle this with a punch. Abdullah looked ready to silence everyone by slamming his hand on his book. I reached over and seized Abdullah's book.

"Class," I said, in a voice I had never heard come out of my body before. I immediately knew whose voice it was. As long as I had it, I was going to use it. "Lee! Can I just once have the very special privilege of seeing your *face*?" Damn if he didn't pick his head up off his desk and look at me. I thoroughly enjoyed the power of Mommy voice. "School's scary so what do you do? You make it something familiar, something you can never lose at. But there's a problem." I grabbed Carolina's copy of *Cosmopolitan*. "She's the one you want, right?" I opened at random to a Cosmo girl. "Or maybe, you want him," I pointed to a Cosmo guy. "You know what would be the most boring lay in the world for this girl, for this guy? It would be sex with –" I didn't say "someone like you." I said, "an uneducated person, who doesn't even know how to behave in a college classroom, or a business setting. Yes, someone who doesn't know how to use the past perfect tense. You can be as gorgeous and as young and as 'all-that' as a human being can possibly be. If you want the cane with the man or woman of your dreams, eventually, you're going to have to open your mouth and, the way you use language is going to help decide whom you get to screw, and who screws you. Get to work on your final drafts. I want them by the end of the hour."

"I ain't taking this from no woman," Troy said, but his head was down, and he was already correcting his work. In seconds, the whole class was silent. How quickly they became cowed. Fighting my sadness, fighting to remain poised, I turned to Carolina and began to pay her work my full attention.

Suarez was still watching. Watching me, watching my words as if they were visible, as if the air they fell into were a scale, weighing each. Watching the other students, their shrugs, aborted protests, surrender. Watching as if talking were a blood sport and any false move would result in important advantage gained or lost. Quietly, apart from his accomplices, he took out his pen, and set to work, saying nothing more. I spent much of the next hour trying to tune out his silence.

Later I was in the Writing Center. Toph came in. He hung up his bag. "I'm hanging up my bag," he said. I said what you say when someone announces to you that they're hanging up their bag. "Oh, okay." Then Toph reached round me to get a pen out of the jar behind me. To get a dictionary out of the file cabinet next to my legs. To use the wall phone above me. To put a fruit yogurt down on the desk beside the notebook I was scribbling in. Never once looking at the pens, the file cabinet, the phone, or the yogurt, but at me.

Yeah, Miles used to circle me, too, and look at me, too, and Konrad, too.

I focused on preparing next week's lesson. I want to figure out some exercise that will get the kids to put to work their natural ability to juggle voice and audience. They can do that while talking, some of them can. Munal can do a parrot-perfect impersonation of Esther Hemings haranguing Tillman's president in Black English. Then Munal replies as Tillman's president, and he gets that voice exactly right, too: grandson-of-a-butcher- "It-Pays-to-Increase-Your-Word-Power"-Standard-English. Now why can't these students do that on paper?

"I have something I'd like you to read," Toph said.

"I'm working on class for next week," I replied. "Tell me what you think of this. I give the kids a schematic diagram. A man looking tough. A woman crying. Some kids, a boy and a girl, watching. The students have to describe the event in the voice of each of the characters. Like, first, they would speak as the man talking to the woman, then to the kids, his cronies, a lawyer, a cop, a judge. Then they have to describe the same event in the voice of one of the kids talking to the other, talking to friends at school, talking to a teacher, a counselor, etc. Think that will get them thinking about voice, and audience?"

"It's my application for grad school."

"Grad school? Oh," I said. And I didn't say, "What exactly *is* that?" though I'd always been curious. "So," I said. "This is your application, eh?"

"No," he said, and he was speaking to me as if I were a teacher or his boss. He was a bit rigid, a little afraid, determined to do it right. "This is a sample of my criticism. It's a critical essay I wrote about intertextuality in the poetry of Ted Hughes and Slyvia Plath. They want to see a sample of my criticism."

I was somehow supposed to react; I could tell by the slow, grave look he was giving me. "And you want me to correct it?" I guessed.

"Well, it wouldn't hurt for another pair of eyes to look over it before it goes out. Dr. Rothenberg has urged me to publish it. And I thought you might like to read it. You are a Plath fan, aren't you?"

"Great. But you'll fix this error in the first sentence before you do that, right?"

"There's no error in the first sentence."

"Oh, really? Great." I handed it back to him. "I'm no Plath fan," I shrugged. I know she's some white lady who offed herself, but more than that I don't feel any need to know.

He studied the paper quizzically. "Most of Tillman's English faculty has been over this paper."

I laughed out loud. "One of my students could have caught it, Toph. You want I should get Abdullah up here? He could have corrected that in his sleep." The students were watching, listening. Suarez was there. He wasn't missing a thing.

"No! That won't be – what exactly is this error you're proposing?"

"Toph," I said, "look at this," I circled it with my red pen. "The object of a preposition can never be the subject of a sentence."

"Oh my God, you're right. But it can't be –"

"Toph, don't take it to heart. Converts are always the most zealous."

"Huh?"

"Gimme the paper. I'll finish it." I read the thing.

Toph stood behind me. His finger was in his mouth. His energy was on hold. So, this is why women like it. This is the payoff they get for nurturing men and coddling them but holding themselves back. Suddenly the woman's grip is on the leash. I did not find the experience terminally compelling. Once again I was a disappointment as a woman, or, women's satisfactions had disappointed me. I circled some more errors; handed the paper back to Toph.

"And?" he asked.

"And what?" I demanded.

"The content. Plath, Hughes," he protested, wounded for them.

"Rich people with made-up problems. A guy who wants more pussy than he can handle. Is that news? Give me poetry about real people," I didn't feel any need to be so bored and brusque, but I was.

"Springsteen?"

"Why not?"

"Wait a minute. They weren't rich."

"Oh, yeah? And you're gonna get into grad school writing about poor people? I don't think so. I gotta go. I've put in my hours for the week."

He put his feet up on the desk. "Fine." He grabbed his fruit yogurt and began spooning it into his mouth.

I paused in the doorway, staring at him intently. I only realized that that's what I was doing when he pointed his chin at me, tilted his head, and half closed his eyes. Omigod, he thinks I'm flirting. "Toph."

"Yes, Ms. Hudak?"

"Can I call you sometime, to ask about –"

"Yes?"

I wanted to ask him about grad school. Thing is, I wouldn't even know the first word of the first question. That's it; you have to know something before you can know anything. I decided to hit the reference library instead. "Never mind. Bye."

I was walking out the door when I heard, "Ms. Hudak," the first time he's ever called me that. I guess before that, Suarez hadn't called me anything. I turned round. "Yes?"

"We got any homework?"

"Suarez, you and I have got to set some time aside to work on auxiliaries."

"Any time," he said, with a sweeping magnanimity.

"And *why* don't you know about homework?" I chided.

"I don't know," he said. "Maybe it's because I am – what did you say I was? 'Immature?'"

My head jerked back. "I'm going to be late for my bus," I announced, to a roomful of people who see me walk everywhere. "Abdullah, do you have the assignment? Could you pass it on to Suarez? Thank you much."

It's around eight now. Just finished dinner.

I can't help feeling that I blew it. It's the first time we've seen each other since . . . But I'm supposed to be his teacher, right? That's what I'm supposed to be. Whatever he's gonna get from me, he's gonna get because I mastered what I came to teach, and taught it well. Cause I kept focused. I can't, I won't, do to Suarez or anybody else what Miles did to me.

But something about what happened today, or what didn't happen, and what happened with Toph, or what didn't happen, weighs on my body like lead sinkers. Did I disappoint Suarez? It's not my job. It's not my job to make him happy. My job is to teach English. Don't lose the trail.

I remember when Toph made his first appearance in the Writing Center. I thought we'd have so much fun with him, cutting him down to size. He's been a letdown; he treats me with deference. Martha says, "He's impressed by you." But why? At first I thought it was because my students were doing so well, but things shifted in a big way after I won the writing contest.

Jesus, could it be I impress him because I write? That's just too weird.

I've always regarded what writing I do as a particularly pernicious, particularly disabling form of Tourette's syndrome. A sufferer of classic Tourette's might spend seconds or minutes each day compulsively yelping out inappropriate, disruptive syllables. I spend hours in you, Diary, doing the same thing. Between us, who is more likely to hold down a job? To receive social sympathy? Know-it-all busybodies see me write and mistakenly conclude that I'm making a lifestyle choice. If only I did something wiser with my time I could taste all that now eludes me:

money, popularity, health insurance. But it's not a lifestyle choice. It's a compulsion.

You know, it was just in hearing those other entries at the reading, including Martha's – I mean, I don't think anyone is smarter than Martha. But it was only then that it occurred to me that not everyone does this, or can.

That sounds so fundamental. Why am I just figuring it out now? When did I decide that writing is one of the easy skills, that everyone has, and that therefore it has no value? Why do I always ignore what comes naturally to me, and dive into futile efforts at mastering what I find foreign – like Math, sports, being a submissive female, money, braising fennel?

- Reminder: spend tomorrow afternoon at Wayne public library, finding out exactly what grad school is, how one enters it, and what one can expect from it. Be sure to find out if there is any record of people like us going to grad school, not just Them. Look at last names of those who've done it.

My body hurts. I don't know how else to put it. I'm supposed to write out what's true here, not get caught up in judging whether it makes sense or fits or proves anything. My body hurts. Does it help to report that?

I keep saying "body." It's not "body." I could be more specific.

All right, I'll say it. My privates hurt. Labia, vagina, cervix. Feels like some caustic chemical is being rubbed in down there. Hurts so bad I couldn't stand while cooking supper. Had to drag a chair over to the kitchen and cook from a seated position. After dinner I washed and put some Vaseline on there and that didn't help. Inspected with a mirror; couldn't see anything. As I was looking at myself, thought, "You're so weird. So disgusting. Only you would have such a weird pain in such a disgusting place."

The setting sun is stenciling rose light in accordion folds on my stairwell. Why can't I enter that sweetness? Let it flood me? Wash away everything bad? Why, no matter how hard I try, do I still wake up, every morning, Miroswava Hudak?

I'd bring these questions to Miles like an apron full of apples. I'd spill everything out. I wouldn't tell him about the pain down you-know-where. But I'd talk around it somehow, just rush it all out.

I'd be ready to hear Miles say, "But, of course, your duty is to teach Gabriel, first and foremost. Any benefit you do him comes from mastery of the material at hand. You mustn't let emotions, if there are any, corrupt that service." I'd be ready to hear Miles say, "Toph seems a nice lad. You helped him by correcting his paper. If he has other upsets with you, how your hiking together ended, the silent ride back to Paterson, the petulant 'See ya,' spoken as he stared straight ahead and did not leave the car, he can bring them up, in his own good time. You just relax." I'd be ready to hear Miles say, "Whatever health concerns you've having, there is a professional out there who can address them. If you like, I'll drive you to the mission hospital. I'll be waiting for you till you're done. Just like that night in Kathmandu, I'll sit on the foot of your sick bed; I'll be there when you fall asleep; I'll be there when you wake again. My clownish play will make you laugh, and forget that you are hurting and speed healing."

And I'd nod and say, "Of course, Miles, you're so right, but I have this last nagging worry," and just his presence would draw out of me questions I had never articulated, not even to myself, before.

"What's the question tonight, Miroswava?"

"Still the same kid. He's good. The world needs folks with eyes like, with nostrils like, his. He takes in. Since I am so new, since I'm just testing it out myself, can I be sure that what he takes in from me is any good? He puts my words in the place where his words used to be. 'Immature.' Why did I say that? Why couldn't I say what I was feeling? And what was I feeling?"

"What were you feeling, Miroswava?" See, he would *ask*. Miles would always *ask*. And it would be a real question, the question of a child, with no narrative coercion, no agenda, behind it. He didn't ask like Toph asks, seeking that one last little elusive piece of his imaginary jigsaw puzzle he just knows he's already masterfully assembled.

"Oh, I don't know . . . Miles, as we change, as we become more adult, more efficient, more admirable, as we act less on instinct, on our bad, bad, working-class, street-rule upbringings, do we betray our hearts?"

"A good question. Let's see –" and at this point Miles would say something that I could never have predicted, and that's the wonder part, the border between what was my imagination and what was truly him.

Don't know if I've resolved anything, but that's a nice sweetness with which to sign off. Good night.

A monster stomps closer and closer on Lackawanna Avenue. He is blood hungry as a vampire. He's blank as Frankenstein. He's a giant like King Kong; like King Kong, his body is crawling with black hairs. He's hulky and he's clumsy but, just like an arrow, he's coming straight for me. I'm curled in my flannel p.j.s in the trundle bed near the window. I gotta find the best hiding place. I run to our snug hall closet. Its back wall folds like an accordion, the reverse of the stairs behind. The unpainted wood smells sweet. I show my friends the light wink through little knotholes; Mommy sends me here to fetch the bread pan for family-reunion recipes. I yank open the door. Aaa! There's a jungle inside. A thick green snake is hanging from the coat rack. He's been waiting for me. He wants to tangle me up worse than double Dutch ropes. He wants to choke me worse than my brother when he's really mad. He wants to get inside of me and erase me and replace me with some kind of snakey goo. I can't beat this snake. He knows it. I slam the closet door.

Everyone else has been erased already, or maybe I already have been erased just like a wrong answer. I'm in this different time and place where no one sees me, no one hears me, no one touches me. This place is our regular house, but our house has never been so empty. I race through it clean alone; it's only me and the monster coming. The sun doesn't move; nothing casts a shadow; the only thing happening is the monster coming. Maybe Mommy and Evie and Kai and even Mrs. Horthy are here, cleaning house, playing records, drinking coffee, but they can't see me or hear me or even the snake and I can't see them or hear them. The monster's coming.

I run into the parlor, scratch up the carpet with my nails, dig holes in the floor; bedrock brakes me like when I'm helping in the backyard garden. The Monster is coming. I run upstairs, trip over my nightgown hem, pick myself up, run, burrow through the crawlspace under the eaves. The whiff of stirred up mothballs stings my nose. Woolen coats punch through dry-cleaner plastic, flimsy as a bubble, and scratch my sleeping cheeks. I crawl under a stored folk custom from Czechoslovakia. The stomps are getting louder; the monster's coming. The earth is moaning, the monster's coming. The house frame is shuddering, like before a big storm. I can't beat this. Nothing can. No matter how deep I dig, he's gonna find me, he's gonna get me, he's gonna he's gonna he's gonna – The monster's coming. He is at the door. I can't beat this. I can't. I can't. I can't. I can't beat this. I gotta fight.

It's five a.m. now. At four a woman's panicked scream pitched me out of sound sleep. It was my scream. When I woke I found my hands gripping my blanket and sheet around my chin; shreds of fabric were in my mouth; the blanket and sheet were wet and mangled. Thank God there are no calories in wool.

I had that nightmare over and over between kindergarten and second grade. Now it's back. Will it be like it was in those days? Eczema erupted from the tips of my fingers up to my elbows, and remained, for two years. My skin cracked, bled, and itched ferociously. I'd wake in the middle of the night with small clumps of flesh under my nails. Evie dubbed me "Rash Rot." My teachers, suspicious of me, anyway, took it as proof. Well, hello. Here it is. The eczema has returned. It's right where it used to start, on the pointer finger of my right hand. It's just the diameter of a pencil eraser. For now.

How can I be perfectly abstinent all this while and learn nothing, advance not one inch? Haven't I dealt with enough already? Do I have to do this, too? When do I get a day off? I'm writing right now, but all I want to do, really, all that feels real, is to eat. Evie's right. Mommy's right. *"Yer weak, like your father. You need a crutch. Me, I don't need any crutch."*

Since beginning this diet, I have not had one satisfying night of sleep. In lieu of sleep, I lie in bed and review, over and over, the details of an imaginary security system. Window bars imbedded in cement: I have heard that they are illegal because they make emergency exit, during fires, for example, impossible. No matter, for my fantasy system, I bribe the city inspectors, and I have bars. Because an intruder could shoot or poison Dobermans, my Dobermans are inside, and trained to pounce silently. I also have a lap dog, not just to cuddle, but because it can sleep beside me and yap whenever there is a suspicious sound, thus preparing me. There are motion sensors and light sensors, but the system doesn't depend on high tech. High tech can be disabled with one power outage. A simple bar imbedded in a well in the floor and fixed under the doorknob makes entry impossible. Anyone could unscrew hinges and remove a door from its frame, thus rendering impotent any lock. I have a good metal frame encasing my hinges. Finally, there is the gun under my pillow. I hope the man makes it through all the barriers, because I want an excuse to shoot him dead with my own hand. When you think about all the precautions one can take, and that I one day will take, you realize that women who do get assaulted in their own homes have only themselves to blame.

Since I don't have the security system in place yet, every shadow, though obviously transparent, is a challenge; every scrape of shade against roughly painted sill a voice alerting me to be ready and quick enough, to be brave enough, to be strong enough. This demand's prerequisite for sleep is that I imagine the worst: waking up, feeling a man raping me. I wrap crocodile scales, the bark of a tree, around my anesthetized body. Then I picture waiting for however long it took, and kneecapping, mutilating, and eventually killing the man.

Come dawn, when the black is melting to gray, when I can hear commuter neighbors' cars rev, when the immigrant family's rooster crows, I know that whatever I've done to keep myself alive was enough for another night. I can reward myself. I relax and collapse and it's luscious. Now I can know what it feels like to sleep, and to dream.

If I tried to talk about this to anyone, I suspect they would insist on labeling it "incest;" tell me to "get help." But, no. Because nothing that bad happened to me at home. If something that bad had happened, I would have ended up in the hospital. But you did end up in the hospital. Yeah, but, if something that bad had happened, I would be a crisis, something you have to pay attention to. I would be one of those characters you feel sorry for on the six o'clock news. Nobody feels sorry for me. I'm not urgent. And it *is* a system, after all, not one man, so there really is no "place" to go for "help." If I just keep working away at it, crafting a passable Mary Tyler Moore I can slip into, it will all work out okay, one day.

Just made myself some peppermint tea. Stared into space for twenty minutes, then made myself some peppermint tea. Unpacked old photos of Daddy. I am confronted by my own dimples diving, my own chin pointing, my eyes sparkling with my special light, my features alive before I ever saw life. Daddy, you really were my own, personal, Gothic hero, in all those novels where the sweet young heroine wonders if her master is mad or merely unconventional.

It's as if I had two fathers. Everything changed after that hallucinatory fever I had in kindergarten. It lasted for days.

No one knows what's happening to me. I flop to and fro. I twitch. The wooden frame of the canvas cot creaks. I gotta get away from this heat. But I'm still burning. I try to get up. Those creatures with all the arms pull me back, so that the skeletons can come and get me and do bad horrible things to me. I open my mouth. I think I'm gonna scream. Some big hard thing crushes down my throat, crushes my tongue, flat. I am as dumb as a runned-over dog on the side of the road. No matter what I try, I can't bring any kind hands to touch me. All I am is bait for skeletons. They're coming; I can't run. They're here, on me, they jerk me back by my hair. Roads are twisted. Sense is rubber. Every word is a lie. I know I will lose. I know I am alone. I know I can't beat this. I gotta fight.

Daddy's coming down the hall. But he's not Daddy any more. He's really one of them, the skeletons, coming to get me. Oh, please, please! Don't send him in here! You don't know! He's one of the skeletons! He's coming . . . All I am left is bugged-out eyes, burning, dried up, opened wide.

I didn't even bathe alone. I didn't feel that anyone would hear, or would help – not even Mary, not even God.

I don't want to write about this. I want to eat turtles. Those wads of pecans and caramel covered with milk chocolate. This is odd. Usually the urge to eat fades as I write in greater and greater detail, as I get closer and closer to the strong feeling, no matter what the strong feeling is.

The closer I get to this little girl, the farther away I want to be. She's just a negligible bundle of fat and fear. No muscles define her. There's nothing cute about her. I can't advertise my stock of virtue by reducing her to a sticker affixed to a bumper. I can't join in; she sings no catchy anthem. There'd be no advantage to be gained from posing for a photo with her, and everything to be lost. Through the hard work of forgetting and forgetting and replacing one bit of me after another with Their qualities, I am not she, not like I used to be. I pass well enough that I can exercise some power – as long as I look like I'm doing what They want. I've studied the language long enough that I am now heard, as long as I manage to speak what They want to hear.

She sees the world differently than I can afford to see it. She has nothing to lose in concluding that it happened to her so that it wouldn't have to happen to Them. In concluding that the sacrifice of female bodies is an essential rite of Their reality.

The only place They have for her is naked and splayed on a theater marquee, or on the cover of a magazine They buy in the bad part of town. She's the star of movies and other narratives nice people do not mention. She is as grimy as the sidewalks in front of the store They buy her image in. No matter how clean and big and competent she someday becomes, if she ever identifies herself, she earns a smirk. The next one is ready to pull her into the dark. No one will protest, any more than They did the first time, because, to keep Themselves sane, They've already shut their eyes, relegating her to the dark. The sacrificed female: They demand that she be exposed; They forbid that she be seen.

As long as the girl agrees to be tainted, to be enfeebled in some way, she is allowed. As soon as she reveals that she feels, thinks, and functions, as They, They must erase her even more thoroughly than They had the first time, when she was being actively sacrificed. They can't admit that it happened to her merely by chance, and not because she really is somehow dirtier and baser and crummier – more deserving of sacrifice – than anyone else. They can't admit that someone they need to see as definitively other, could grow up to pass as one of Them.

I don't want to be her today because the world can't contain the woman who was once her and who can now teach. They would never let her do anything good for the SSNoS kids. They would never let her correct errors in Toph's papers, know something Toph doesn't know. They would never allow her words to win prizes. She can't see anything or say anything about Mel or Jim's supply closet antics or the US government in Iraq. They'd be forced to say: "On the one hand, since she makes claims about things that we must never admit happen, we must denounce everything she says as irrational. On the other hand, we know what she says is true, so we deny everything she says in this way: 'Given the trauma the poor thing has lived through, we can't take anything she says seriously.' We must put her stories out, as we put her eyes out, as we put her out."

Before I can put down this pen, before I can stand up from this desk, before I can do this day, I need a hero. I need to fit my feet into the footprints of the someone who has walked this way before. I require a model to work with or against, a weathered, proven skin to slip into when mine is too fragile to soldier on, the dog-eared log of an explorer's voyage. I'm starving for a compelling narrative, a folk tale, a paperback, a five star movie, that will make me laugh and cry and hold my breath and never forget.

No. I want no case studies. Case studies of the sacrificed female are a dime a dozen; they are the good man's porn. The hero of the case study is the psychiatrist who makes his and breaks his elder's careers with his innovative approach. The psychiatrist is compassionate yet daring. He is a hero.

The hero of the case study is its reader, the innocent bystander, the neighbor whose dinner is interrupted by a child's cry, the friend who casually asks, "Why are you afraid of the dark?" and is burdened with an unexpectedly honest reply. The only prerequisite for the reader's heroism, besides his propinquity to disaster, is his pity. He doesn't have to chance a trip to the rough side of town to throw a rock through a kiddie porn bookstore window. He doesn't have to teach anyone how to open a checking account or operate a washing machine. As long as the sacrificed female remains a silent lump, his passive pity looks heroic. This is why readers must break with the girl if she quickens. The quickening girl mutters about throwing rocks throw windows, about learning how to operate a bank account, or a washing machine; eventually she articulates something clearly: "Where was everybody when this was going on?" The ingrate girl defames the reader's heroism, just revealing what a bad seed she really was, all along.

The anti-hero of the case study is the perpetrator. As if he were the charmer's dancing snake, the reader's eyes never leave the perpetrator. The reader asks: "Why should he do that to a child?" "How could such terrible things happen?" "What must we do?" Surely the answers are to be gained through unbroken attention to this id-driven trickster, who performs acts readers only fantasize. Such attention demands a perpetrator who is complex, fascinating, who has interior life, motive and agency. A perpetrator probably much smarter than you or I, the typical brilliant criminal, and more handsome, too. A perpetrator who is saved or destroyed by the heroic psychiatrist and reader.

Everyone knows the names Jack the Ripper, the Boston Strangler; few know the names of their victims. The sacrificed female is never the hero of the case study. Rather, as she was in the hands of her abuser, in the case study she is, again, an object, there to make others feel big. Her sacrifice exists only to make the psychiatrist and the reader heroic, the perpetrator, fascinating.

No. I want no case studies, thank you very much. The demand is for the power, the truth, exclusive to story.

To shake myself out of paralytic despair and into action, I read inspirational biographies. I love movie heroes, like Gary Cooper. He was Lou Gehrig, Pride of the Yankees, the Iron Horse who set the record for number of consecutive baseball games played, in spite of a disease so horrible no one can even spell it, so it's just called "Lou Gehrig's disease." St. Francis school promoted saints. Holy cards of St. Therese the Little Flower were a hot commodity. The cards were stiff with rippled, cream-colored edges. St. Therese was untouched and rosier than any *Seventeen* magazine cover model. She was never folded. Cards were disbursed to teachers' pets for jobs well done, and later traded in a black market of real threats, false promises, and candy. My little girl fists, teeth and nails earned me a respectable collection. I hated St. Therese, God's little pet, but, she was my hero. Had to be.

In all the hero tales I've heard, read, or watched the crystal-clear distinction between good guy and enemy was breathtakingly thrilling. There could be team uniforms. I am always gratified that such courage and generosity breathe in the world. And my way is just as dark. And I am just as trapped. And I still cannot move.

I have tried, as best as I could, to reenact my heroes' struggles. I've taken every dare, and, when no one was around to do so, I've dared myself. Alone, I hiked through Asian tiger jungle, rode a moped across an African country at war, hitchhiked the breadth of the United States, climbed, carrying my own pack, to eighteen thousand feet. I worked for years in hospitals for the dying. With the Sisters of Charity in Calcutta, I hand-washed lice out of lepers' clothing. I've leafleted, picketed, been fire-hosed and tear-gassed. I've been seeking the courage, the most difficult courage that would change my life. If acts like these worked for my heroes, surely they would work for me. I would finally find the courage that would make it possible for me to function the day after having one of those nightmares. I have never found it.

My heroes lay beside me on the floor, crumpled up like yesterday's newspaper.

I need a hero whose heroism has been censored from the language of the heroic: Nobel, grand slam, "I want to thank the members of the Academy," "One small step for man." She will never find the vocabulary she requires in that lexicon. The shelf holding up the great books sags but you won't find her story in the Bible or the Declaration of Independence or the Odyssey. I need a body that has been penetrated and filled with filth, for no good reason, in the name of no cause. I need a hero whose heroism reminds me that uniforms are for games, and that cruelty and virtue are not distributed by team. I need a hero who has resurrected from societal blindness and deafness darker than any Good Friday tomb, muter than any tomb-sealing boulder.

And not just that. I require a hero who has been stupid. I need a hero who has done worse to herself, for longer, than the initial perpetrator did to her. I need a hero who has squandered her best time and energy frantically auditioning to play handmaid to those who destroy her. I need a good share of her memories to be simple shame and charring regret.

I'll recognize her heroism. She will not boast an impressive weapons cache, monument, or adoring fans. My hero will function. My hero will groom herself. My hero will tell the truth. My hero will be kind, even to men. My hero will keep trying. And she will never do to anyone else what They did to her.

But I lack her. And I feel her lack. I can't light this way myself. I can only stumble, and fall, and play the clown, the buzzing annoyance, the one who's always getting it wrong.

DEAR DIARY, SO, I had three good reasons to blow off work today. Dr. Rothenberg couldn't make it in yesterday – her divorce thing – which is why I was teaching, though it was Monday – so I had a day off coming to me!!! Actually, Dr. Rothenberg has been M.I.A. a lot lately, and I've been taking over more and more. Sometimes I get a phone call in advance. Sometimes it's as quick as her nodding to me and winking and just walking out the door and never making it back in. And, after that nightmare, my knees were water and I was a mess. And, I've been dying to go to this poetry festival.

I've been fingering the program, charting which poets I'd hear, dreaming up scenarios in which I have the nerve to actually speak, scripting what I'd say – ah, the wit, the truth, the passion! But I needed a ride and wasn't sure Martha would go for it. "Maybe," was all she'd say. "But it doesn't look good. Should we take the time off from work? How could I find anyone to sit the kids? And Dexter has to go to his soccer game."

"Bring the kids."

"Yeah, right."

"Martha, it's in a park, in Sussex County. They'll like it; kids are always so entertained by the sight of a cow. And why does Dexter need soccer, anyway?"

Martha chauffeurs her kids to soccer practice, McDonald's, St. Francis. She won't eat at McDonald's. She doesn't believe in God. She condemns organized sports as the cookie press that molds innocent boys into the kind of blindly aggressive, grandstanding bullies who tormented her when she was a little girl geek.

My parents really were different. They came from other countries. They could have taught me their languages, their dances, their customs; they didn't. I had always assumed that they did that out of some harsh yet accurate assessment of me: "We could milk goats and dance for days and survive on wild mushrooms; you cannot and do not deserve our secrets." Without the Atlantic Ocean as an excuse, Martha tends her own gap between herself and her kids. At least she can make them be right, be less like she is.

I've been arm-twisting for about a month now. She called this morning.

"Well, I'm glad to see that you still pick up the phone when I call," Martha said, in lieu of "Hello."

"First of all, I have no way of knowing who it is by the way the phone rings, and second of all, what the heck are you talking about, Martha?"

I could hear her take a drag on her cigarette. "You know, Monique is one of the people I'd pass on my way up the aisle in class. As I passed and she ignored me, I'd think, 'And fuck you, too.' Suddenly she sees me talking to you, and I'm in the club, I'm okay to talk to."

"Are you ever gonna make a point here?"

"You're a prize winner –"

"Sounds like you're pushing for some kind of prize yourself, Martha."

"The kids have missed you."

"They can talk to me. They have my number. Is there anything you want to say to me for yourself?"

"I'm drawing a blank," she said.

"Great. Talk to you later," I said.

She kept talking. "So, what does a woman do when she goes out on a date with someone like Toph? I was trying to picture this. Last time I went on a date, the guy copping a feel of your tits, under your bra, was the centerpiece of the evening. I can't see Toph doing that, not at all. So what do you two do? Read sonnets to each other? Gaze at the sunset? Savor the moment?"

"Have you made up your mind about the festival? I don't want to go to work today and neither do you. Take my word for it."

"I'm not taking these kids if it's gonna rain."

"I'm sorry to learn that your kids are water-soluble. Once again you've been gypped, Martha; most kids come with Scotch guard."

"All right. All right. We'll go. But if it rains . . . "

"We build an ark."

The first session was held in front of a bank of brassy day lilies. It was the day lilies that made it real. I know them. I've worn them in my hair while playing dress-up, eaten lily fritters, measured the year's progress by their high summer blossoming. They hit true as the arms on the best clock. Full sun roasting the back of my head struck the day lilies and released a glow from them as from stained glass. I squinted into each poet's eyes and when their eyes met mine, they struck from my lips an old-friend smile. The smile settled comfortable and familiar, though I don't remember the last time I wore it, or if I ever have. I often knew what the poets were going to say before they said it. It was like someone cracking open my head like a piñata and spilling its contents on the ground for everyone to finger and fuss over.

I realized I didn't want to go home. Or I realized: I don't want to get into the car and drive away from this and drive back to the center of gravity I've been living in surrender to. I want this day to be the hinge, the point demarcating before and after. A language is being allowed here that I crave to speak, and never stop speaking. The poets' speech is opening a door that I have never seen, though I've spent my whole life outside it, mourning its lack. I want to march up to these people and grasp their hands and say, "I will sit on the floor, and you will teach." They would say, "Yes." The only thing that prevents me from hearing their "yes" is my shy not asking. But I'll overcome that shyness one day and it will happen. Most importantly, because someone has given these poets a raised platform, placed folding aluminum chairs in front of them, printed up and distributed an official program, because this has been advertised in the local press, radio, and the vestibule of the PathMark supermarket, I am being assured that I am not insane, random, impotent, and useless in the ways that I have resigned myself to being.

I cranked Martha's arm. "Isn't this wonderful? I mean, really wonderful? And really worth coming for, worth Dexter's missing one game in the season?"

"I'm afraid, Miroswava," Martha said, looking angrier than usual, "that somebody's gonna come up to me and say, 'Get out. You don't belong here among all these deep, creative, people.'"

"Great. You be afraid. I wanted to enjoy this with you; I'll be damned if I'm going to suffer it with you. I'm going to attend the next one by myself." I walked away. Shushu ran after.

"Shushu, go with your mommy."

"I don't want to go with my mommy," she said, sounding a little desperate.

"Why?" I asked, buying time, looking for an out.

"My mommy locks me in my room all the time." I squatted down, opened my arms. Shushu smacked into my body. I looked toward Martha; her back was turned to us, and she was walking away.

Shushu's vacant stare brings to mind Marilyn Monroe, hardly any hero of *mine*, or Suarez's tacky tramp. Unlike the boys, she rarely runs to me to issue reports of adventures in the back woods. She runs up to me to be hugged. She's always orchestrating some plot which may result in what we'd call mean behavior or what we'd call nice behavior but whose only goal is to get attention.

So that tugging a dawdling child wouldn't slow me down – why, when you are in a hurry to get somewhere, do children always seemed glued to some invisible, dismissible place, moment, or posture? – I perched Shushu in piggyback position on my shoulders and marched toward the tent for the next event. She was no burden; Shu weighs less than my backpack after shopping, and her body lacks the punishing contours of a quart of canned kraut. We took a seat in the aluminum folding chairs. I hoped Shushu would want to be let down, but she cuddled in my lap. I was stuck with her.

I rationalized: this was just fifty-five minutes out of Shushu's life. I couldn't make a difference, and I didn't want to be drawn into the pain. And then I remembered Aunt Grace.

An emcee tapped on a microphone. "Can the people in the back rows hear me?" The reading was beginning. I tried to fake what I've seen people do when they are affectionate with a child. I ran my fingernails along Shushu's legs and arms. I stroked her hair. I hugged her close. I whispered in her ear that she was the prettiest little girl in the whole wide world. I never stopped. Normally fidgety Shushu collapsed, limp, silent, heavy, against my chest, as if she were some addict receiving the drug she's been craving.

I picked the wrong poets this time. They were boring and pompous white boys, the kind who give poetry a bad name. Shushu slid off my lap and wandered around, asking women for goodies from their purses, lifting up her shirt and displaying her naked chest to men. Dexter darted through the audience, chasing the one other boy his age there, whom he had managed to find and with whom he had managed to cook up some mini boy war: intricate enough to compel, limited enough to truce with one correctly pitched shout from a mom. Shushu kicked one of the poets. I summoned her back; she nestled into my lap; a festival photographer snapped our photo.

We smiled and said thanks and went to look for Martha.

"Well, it was just as I expected. They threw me out!"

"What?"

"Yeah. I was sitting there with Sparky, and he was quiet as a mouse. Then some honcho with a clipboard and nametag told me I had to leave, simply because I was in possession of a child. That ruined the whole day for me. The only way I could get through was to go buy some chocolate in the food booth, sit on the hill, and eat it. Let's get out of here."

As the car was pulling out of the parking lot, I began to panic. I had wanted to take it with me, but I didn't even know yet what it had been.

"Martha."

"Yeah? What?" she said, turning to me sharply.

"Shushu. It really bugs her when you lock her in her room."

"I know. That's why I do it. It wouldn't be punishment otherwise."

I stared at the cows and silos and rolling fields of Sussex County. Thought about how teams from Sussex always whipped the pants off of us in high school football. "Farm boys," we called them.

Those people on the platform just talked. They were talking entirely too quickly to be editing in advance of what they were saying, to be making sure it was okay.

"You know what's the first thing I noticed when I got back from Peace Corps? I mean, I didn't even have to be on an American street to notice it? I noticed it as soon as I was in the airport and I saw Americans?"

"Size. Americans are bigger," Martha guessed. "Or maybe teeth. It always seems to me that when I meet someone with a foreign accent, their teeth are different. Sometimes better, sometimes worse. But not the same, not like ours. Well? Am I right? Is that it?"

I spoke. "The hostility Americans show their kids. The disrespect. The lack of tenderness. That it's public. I mean, it's as stunning, as take your breath away, as much of an affront, as if you walked into a room and saw a bunch of people naked. And I'm not just talking about the obvious slaps. I'm talking about sharp, rude comments, questions honed to trip a kid up, or humiliate him. But then there are the slaps, too. It's a different world."

"Take the wheel," she ordered. I did. She reached into her tight jeans pocket and pulled out a cigarette and lighter. "These kids act up, Miroswava. They're not like they are with you. Dexter's already following in his father's footsteps –"

"Oh, no."

"Oh, yes, thank you very much. Dexter has tortured his first chipmunk."

I turned around to the back seat. Dexter was humming and looking out the window.

"So," said Martha, after retaking the wheel. "What do these people over there do when kids act out?"

"They just . . . love them more. Mothers or uncles or grandmothers or whoever is around pulls them in and cuddles them. Murmurs to them – they have a special set of words that you use only with kids. So they murmur those words. They stroke the kids. Comfort them. Hold on to them. In general, just love them more.

"See – and I'm not saying that this is everybody and I'm not saying that this is all the time. But I saw it often enough that I noticed. And I got the idea, that is I concluded, that adults acted this way, that their philosophy was, that kids don't act out out of malice. And that it wasn't some malice that needed to be punished. I got the idea that their philosophy was that kids don't act out out of some flaw, some perversion, that needed to be hidden or corrected or amputated. And maybe they do. For all I know maybe kids do act out out of malice. Maybe it is a flaw or a perversion. But, see, I noticed this different way. The idea, the philosophy, behind loving them more, seemed to be that – that kids are newcomers. That they don't get all the protocols, just yet. And that they were screwing up more out of ignorance than anything, and that it probably bugged them as much as it bugged anyone else. So, they loved them more."

Martha looked down at Shushu, now asleep in my lap and drooling on my blouse. "I just couldn't bring myself to do that."

"Oh?" I asked, so eager not to let go of that energy, no matter how far away we drove from the poetry festival, no matter how close we got to home. "Why's that?"

"Because, Miroswava," she said, peering out her window as she negotiated Dead Man's Turn from two-lane country road onto interstate 23, "I hate my kids, and I hate my life."

It's ten o'clock now. It's been seven hours. It's because of you, Diary. "Oh, I hate my kids; I hate my life:" Martha's normal greeting. It's so perfectly in tune with this Irony Age that I never felt the words I was hearing. But I'm keeping these appointments with you, Diary. So that I will have something to offer you I inspect my day, reflect upon it. I report these gleanings to the ears of an other who may hear things to which I know enough to remain deaf. The ears of an other who may ask, "*What* did you just say? Explain, please." And so I try.

"I can understand your mom, maybe," Martha said on the drive home. "You know nobody wanted me, or the one who wanted me died. I was so empty, so lonely as a kid. I used to dream of this. 'Someday I'm going to have babies and they'll love me and not leave me and we'll all be a family and support each other and it will all be wonderful.' Well, now I have them and I can't stand them. It's not at all what I thought it would be at all."

When we were bedding the kids down, Martha forced a "dear" to Shushu, the "dear" of a substitute teacher or ax murderer. Then, when Shushu was safely behind another wall, in her bed, Martha turned to me and made a face and said, "I try." I recognized that face. I knew the taste of the "love" Martha offers Shushu.

From image management staged to look like love, or maybe duty, like Martha's forced good night kiss with Shushu, I wove this myth: "I am really loved. The love I receive is shallow and forced; it lacks enthusiasm and warmth. I receive it only when I can work up the energy and stomach to imitate the girl I am supposed to be. The love I receive makes no reference to the parts of me that get me most excited, to what I read, the movies I watch, or what I imagine when I'm wandering in the woods. Therefore, these parts of me that get me most excited have no value. I must punish my moments of joy, stray stirrings of power, and jettison them." This is how "if-only-you-were" love trained me in squandering my best time and energy frantically auditioning to play handmaid to those who despise me.

D EAR DIARY, IT'S four a.m. Friday. When I had that nightmare about the monster I thought, okay, good, I've got the whole week. After writing it out, I worked not to think about it. It's four a.m. now, and it's Friday. In five hours I'll be a giver, a teacher, a representative of the state.

I'm writing today's entry with taped hands, like a boxer. The eczema has split open my fingertips. They're swollen and covered with loose, numb scales. These look like lizard scales, or the bark of a tree. The only sensation my fingertips register is pain, from when skin as parchment, skin somehow mummified horrifically quickly without ever maturing, tears away. Red flesh is exposed, too raw to function as skin. Sometimes I'll be grabbing something – a sheaf of paper, say – and look down and see blood all over it. I don't know how to explain this to people.

I can't locate my keys in my bag when standing at the door of my apartment building at night. I can't make change, or even separate bills, while standing in line in a supermarket. Everyone stares; says things like, "Well, I'm glad *you* have all day." I can't hold a pencil because my fingerprints, and any moisture from oil or sweat, are gone. The blood all over the typewriter keyboard makes it slick; my fingers slip and slide. Grooming, makeup, have become their own little obstacle course. I can't touch myself. The mandate that I must not feel has zeroed in on these ten tiny portions of my body. I don't have a hint of eczema anyplace else. Frying these ten islands of sensation, I've replaced overeating, my other obedient regime for not feeling.

DEAR DIARY, I heard footsteps behind quick and shallow as panted breaths. Finally Munal was at my elbow.

"Ms. Hu – I mean, Mira."

"Good morning, Munal. Aren't you grateful for mornings like this? It's almost cool, and there's no humidity."

"I'm sorry. I don't know that word."

"Munal, you don't have to apologize for not knowing a word. 'Humidity.' It means the amount of moisture in the air. Palestine has low humidity. New Jersey, especially in summer, usually has high humidity, but not this morning. If you don't find a way to work 'humidity' into your next essay, I'll be crushed. What's up?"

He fumbled in his bag. "I brought my camera."

"Wonderful. You want me to take your picture?"

"*My* picture? *No!*" he exclaimed so forcefully I turned and stared at him. Then, flustered, he said, "It's not a very good camera."

"Oh?" I said.

"Yes, I could afford to buy only this cheap kind. It's not a top notch camera like you probably have."

I laughed.

"You are laughing at me."

"Yeah, but not because of the kind of camera you have. So, so far I know you have a cheap camera and you don't want any photos of yourself. Anything else?"

"You are always picking on me," he protested, hanging his head. I put my arm around his shoulder, reached up and tousled his Brillo hair. He jerked away. "So," he pleaded, "Is it all right with you?"

I looked at him, eyebrows high. I spread my arms wide and shrugged.

"Oh," he said. "Can I take photos of us? Of our group? Of our SSNoS class?"

Whenever I want to reach out and hug one of them I glance downward and speak formally. I did so, and even began walking at a quicker pace. "Munal, I think your taking some photos of our group is a most excellent idea. In fact, you can be the official class photographer. How does that sound?"

"No! I can't be the official photographer. What are you thinking? This is not a good camera. This is not a proper camera where you can adjust the focus. It doesn't flash. And I hardly know how to work it. I took some snaps at my cousin's wedding and everyone in the family was angry with me. And not just in this country. People in Gaza, people I've never met, cursed my name. My poor mother was so ashamed. I cut off my uncle's head. I will screw it up. If I have to be the official photographer, I'd better not do anything."

"Munal, in some cultures it's considered proper to cut a respected uncle's head off in a photograph."

"You are always laughing at me."

"Take the photos, Munal. If you don't I'll have to give you extra homework."

"Oh! That is not fair!"

"Anything to keep the customer satisfied." I saw maybe my best chance up ahead of us. "Munal," I said. "Excuse me," and I began to run, to catch up.

I recognized him from behind by his long, thick, shiny black hair. Damn if that hair doesn't smack of East Asia. "Lee," I said, only when I was right next to him. I was afraid that if I had called to him he would have run away. Attendance regulations guarantee that he come to class, but not that he talk to any of us outside of class. He's refused to remain in the room even long enough to be served a summons to one of my student-teacher conferences. Lee swiveled his head, like a mantis, toward me, focused briefly, and just kept walking.

I hadn't any idea of what style would work on him – drill sergeant, good buddy, goddess? So I was reportorial. "Lee, you tell everyone your name is Lee and you are Chinese. Sometimes. Sometimes you are Japanese, or Korean, but always a martial arts expert. But I've discovered in the Office of the Registrar, after being alerted by some of your fellow classmates from Newark, that in fact your name is Alejandro Sepulveda and you are Puerto Rican. I've been told that you have no martial arts training. I'm curious about this. I'm available to discuss and help in a situation that might result in invalid transcripts for you, among other problems. For example, recently some boys challenged you to demonstrate your martial arts skills and you were injured in the ensuing encounter . . . "

Lee continued looking dead ahead, but he reached into his bag and pulled out a spiral bound notebook. He put the notebook between his face and my face, and kept walking. I stood still.

Munal caught up. "Are you sure?"

"Munal, I'd be heartbroken if you didn't. Let's get to class."

Lee was there. He's always there, usually early, in the seat nearest the door. He always hands in his work, always on time. I suspect much of what he writes is copied from the side of a cereal box and made to conform to the assigned topic through quick workings of the word game, "Mad-Libs." His language mechanics are acceptable. He's passing. I want to fail him. I want to fail him and Troy. I want a column in my grade book to record evaluations in something other than use of the past perfect. Troy will be failed for the error of not wanting anything. I can't believe that Lee's never speaking to his fellow students, that his peers' treating him as if he were a universal allergen, isn't something it behooves his teachers to notice. But then, I've not been asked.

Instead I'm under implicit orders to keep going through the motions, acting like this emergency is less urgent than the others that immediately stop the gears of the machine. Troy threatens violence; we call in the palace guard. Lee comes, day after day, chronically weird, and we continue to minister to him as if his greatest need were infusions of the most up-to-date literary theory.

Maybe it will never be a newspaper headline. Maybe, years from now, I won't be sitting in front of a TV and my regularly scheduled programming won't be interrupted by a handcuffed Lee being lead out of his basement bunker by men in navy windbreakers with the letters "FBI" stenciled on the back. But someday, years from now, I have to believe, this karma catches up.

I was walking to the blackboard. Etta threw one of her textbooks on the floor. It struck with a heavy thud. This was Etta's most dynamic academic gesture to date. No way I would not pounce upon this opportunity.

"Yeah?" I asked, after spinning round.

"I don't wanna talk about this."

"Right. Etta, class hasn't started yet. We weren't talking about anything."

"Whatever it is. Even if it ain't started yet. I don't wanna talk about it."

"Okay." I walked from the blackboard and took a seat in the circle. The door swung open; Suarez, coming in, late. A rush of relief; thank you God, he'll still go to college, I have not lost him, in spite of the past couple days of such unreadiness I have to convince myself that I don't hear it when I hear him call my name. I stared ahead. He sat down next to me. Damn.

"Damn." Why "damn"? I don't know why "damn." Okay, fear. Of? I don't know. That's why I'm writing. To find out.

He sat down next to me.

But I say this: I'm gonna go to the fancy "can I help you ma'am" boutiques in the mall. I'm gonna purchase Gray Flannel, the expensive men's cologne. I'm gonna present it to Suarez. If he's gonna come to *my* class, if he's gonna sit next to *me*, it may as well be a smell I've selected.

Don't get me wrong. Suarez's bodega cologne doesn't arouse me. That's not what I'm saying. And he's hardly the only one. Anwar's another one. None of these guys' colognes turn me on. It's that even as I look away from Suarez, as I should, I am arrested in a halo of invisible contact.

I stiffen in my seat, slide, imperceptibly away, with no creak of nut, bolt, or wood, and, I escape nothing. Just as when a bug or leaf skims my arm I can't help but conjure what touches me. He's in the shower. It's hard for him to lay claim to the one bathroom. I know it's only the one bathroom. I know it malfunctions. I know pop is cranky and erratic about fixing it, and I know pop uses fixing the bathroom as currency in family politics. So how hard was it for Suarez to lay claim to the one bathroom this school morning? Is that why he's late? How quickly he must undress, the fumbling over buttons.

"You're not the only one who has school today, Gabriel!" Or what is her nickname for him? Or does she speak her protest and her love in Spanglish, a dash of Spanish, and some English? Secret words they've pieced together. This scold is the only ardent speech life will spare her for him today; he never punches and plays with her like the old days. It's this bathroom's fault. It's clear to her that she began to lose her brother around the time he began spending so long in the bathroom, and coming out smelling like a girl. What could anyone think up to do in a bathroom for so long? At first she thought he might be sick; she worried and wanted to get help. But now he's in there all the time, when he's home, and he's hardly ever home anymore.

He is applying so very much cologne, as he tries to ignore his sister just outside the door. Was it the name that called out to him from the dusty bodega windowsill, from the seven layer lucky candles, Santa Barbara statuettes, colored lights and bruised plantains? What do they name bodega colognes, anyway? "Chango's Bongos"? "White Businessman's Love Call"? What's going through his mind as moistened fingers meet his neck, his cheek? That this will mask him, or announce him? That this will excuse him, or allow him? His body glistens. Yeah, he's already toweled off, but the shower steam surrounds him, condenses on him, clings to him, mingles with a fresh layer of sweat. This building dates from before they installed fans, and the small window won't open. The shirt slides on over delicate beads of moisture.

"You smell like a girl!" She swings away from a devastatingly aimed towel as she finally claims the bathroom. She sees a side of him no one else sees, any more. Certainly not the police, nor his teacher. In the back of his mind, he accepts that she loves him in a way that no one else in the world ever will, again. This makes her very precious, thus he struts like a matador before her, silent, never glancing down, but sparing an unspoken thought for how naïve that girl is. There's one last reconnaissance in the hall mirror. He kisses his mother – he's no Boy Scout – he just comes from the kind of people for whom it takes more thought not to kiss your mother than to kiss her – and he opens the door, and he becomes very hard, except for this ridiculous but undeniably sumptuous scent, which is so damn distracting. So, "Damn."

And "damn" because he was sitting right next to me.

There was quiet for a few moments in the classroom. Finally Troy demanded, "Wha?" I said nothing, not even a hand gesture. In fact, I was trying to imitate Lee's classroom presence, to see what that felt like. Sometimes relinquishing absolute power, if it's Friday and you've had a long week, can feel just right.

"Etta, it is you. You must teach us now," announced Abdullah, looking up from the dog he was modeling out of a folded bit of notebook paper. God, I love him. Our kaffiyeh-draped Hephaestus. Munal pulled his camera out of his bag, shot me a pleading look. I winked and nodded. Munal got up and began to pace the perimeter of the room. His body took on new movements. He could have made a convincing photojournalist.

Abdullah had his back to the light; good, that would work, with him. He's one of those people who carry in themselves the gravity of winter. He looked as dark as a vulture's wing, as a slice of chocolate cake, as Hephaestus in bellow smoke, fashioning a dog hip, or a human's, for their mysterious ends. Munal snapped that.

• Reminder: be sure to get a copy of that shot of Abdullah.

"You so sure, Ms. Hudak, that this stuff mean something," Etta was in touch with her inner geyser. "You tell us, Ms. Hudak, that this stuff we're reading is supposed ta mean something in real life. 'Apply it to real life problems, like a Band-Aid.' You said that. Nothin we talk about mean shit to me. You talk about stuff mean somethin to Abdullah and Gabriel your little pet, but mean nothin to me. How about we talk about me for a change? I'm in this class, too. I pay money, too. I got real life problems, too. And I need a Band-Aid."

Abdullah nodded. "Tell us the who, what, when, where, why, and how. Show us the details that will make us able to see what you see. What is the back story?" I had to struggle not to beam at him. How does Lee do it?

"I'm sick of my niece father," Etta announced. "Sick of him. Just sick, well and truly tired, fed up. He is such a sorry ass loser."

Sharifa shook her head. "Telling, not showing," she said. "You tellin us what you feel. You gotta tell us the facts, and we decide for ourself."

Etta jutted out her little chin at Sharifa. "I got an eight year old kid," she reported, defiantly.

"No way!" Dave shouted.

"Actually, she my sister's baby. I raise her since my sister's dead."

"Oh, no. How did she die?" Sharifa asked.

"Her man kill her," Etta said.

"*Que triste,*" said Carolina, the look of a medieval Madonna on her face; Munal caught it. Unless he chopped her head off.

"And that's the problem. My sister's old man keeps coming around. The baby's father. And he –"

"He not in jail?" Victor asked.

"No, silly," said Etta, mightily put out. "You don't understand. He's not the one who killed my sister. This is her husband. That was her boyfriend. Anyway, he comes around and he aks like I'm his maid. He put his feet up on the furniture. He just walk in the kitchen; he don't aks. He grab the chips and the salsa and he put the TV on. He gots his own home. He gots his own woman. Why do I gotta be his maid? And you know what else? Whenever he feel ready, he go into my bathroom, and he use *my* toothbrush! I know cause I go in there after he been in there, and it's wet."

"Etta, did you hear what you just said?" I couldn't keep silent any longer.

"Wha?"

"'He gots.' It's 'He's got,'" corrected Suarez, somehow spitefully.

I ignored him. "'He's got his own woman. Why do I have to be his maid?' It sounds like you're making the two terms equivalent. Is a woman just a maid to you?" I shot a glance at Suarez. He raised his eyebrows, cocked his head. A concession.

"Not just," she said. "Just mostly."

"Oh my God." I stood up.

"There she goes," sang Dave. "You got her started."

"Oh, man!" whined Etta. "This ain't gonna be *class*, is it?"

"Etta," I sat back down again. "Etta," I thrust my arms out, palms up. "What's class? It's a place to learn. You're hurting, somehow. You have a lack. You want something you don't have. Class is the place where you heal the hurt, fill the lack, get that something you don't have."

"In your dreams, Ms. Hudak. Not your class."

"Well, then, make it that way!" I shouted, letting the anger show. "Lessons are all around you, Etta, just plug into them. The class you go to should be the class that's teaching you what you want to know. Like how to lay down the law when it comes to assholes" – general gasp – "using your toothbrush! And you get those answers here, if only you'd attend to them. Think about all those women that Dr. Rothenberg has you guys reading about. Shirley Chisholm, a *black woman* presidential candidate. Barbara Jordan, another black woman, a highly respected political leader. Were they maids?"

"When they man come home, then they maids, yes."

"Not Barbara Jordan, Etta," I said, growing spiteful myself. "She was a lesbian."

"I don't wanna hear about no more faggots!" Troy.

"Nigger, nigger, nigger, nigger," Sharifa, under her breath.

They've both grown old, along with this routine. It died down of its own.

Etta, "A woman can be as phat as she wants, she can be all that, and when her man come home, she a maid, or she in bed."

"Phat?" I asked. "You mean that with a 'p' 'h,' right? What does 'phat' mean, exactly?"

"Physically attractive," purred Carolina. "Physically, you know, 'p' 'h.' Attractive, 'a' 't.'" And then, just by sitting there, she demonstrated.

"I don't think so," said Etta, pulling herself up to all her four feet, ten inches. "It mean 'pussy, hips, and tits.'"

"That's disgusting!" Anwar unrolled the words over the curled lips of a displeased sultan. Munal caught it. Fabulous! "You should not be speaking like this. Ms. Hudak, you must stop her. She is a woman; you must stop her from saying such things."

But I was worried about Supreme, the Puritanical Black Muslim.

What if he heard Etta talking like this? I looked for him; absent, as he had been all too often, lately.

"Etta," I said, "I admire your very precise and attention-getting use of language. Now if only I could get you to *write* this way, eh?"

Puffing out her little chest, Etta insisted, "Tstrue!" to Anwar, who was apparently more compelling than I, and Munal caught that.

Anwar regained his composure, reclined against his chairs. "It's not a good thing for you to say, and, anyway, it's not true. Only a woman's mind make her beautiful."

Etta defied him. "No. It's clothes. It's make up. You know it!"

"Students! Exactly what we've been discussing here, exactly what everyone's talking about with such wonderful energy and interest, exactly that topic is one of the hottest topics in academia today . . . " I related Etta's outrage to current scholarly debates on gender. The women nodded. They adduced their own life stories and the stories of their mothers, sisters, and friends. They were with me; they were getting that they are part of it: the campus with its chimes, the vast green lawns, the books, and the power.

But would academics ever admit them? Martha had lent me a pile of scholarly articles she'd photocopied for her A+ term paper on postmodernism. In one of them some so-called literary critic made a faux daring reference to beating his wife. Why is his sorry personal life apt fodder for the academic mill, while the first-person storytelling of the world's Ettas is proof of marginality and intellectual retardation? I was trying to solve that puzzle. It wasn't even occurring to me that we were telling story after story in which all the evil characters were male, all the victims female, all the problems involved men, and none of the solutions did. And then I was slammed into a tiny, familiar hole, my legs scrunched against my chest, so I would not offend, not earn another beating.

"Men are animals! That's what you think, right? Say it. Say it right now. Say: 'Men are animals.'"

I jerked towards Suarez, my mouth open. "*What?*" I had just brought up one of Dr. Rothenberg's assignments, *The Color Purple.* It's a book, a book. You don't talk about books that way. You don't interrupt discussions of books to scream, "Men are animals," in a voice that won't quit till it sees fear. You talk about Walker's use of metaphor. Why couldn't he have stayed in that chair he'd dragged out of the circle on the first day? Tough. Self contained. Now so close, he'll see that I'm not what he needs. I wrenched my hands back and hid them in my lap. I looked away from him, trying to be invisible. I looked back at him, to check. Suarez still saw me. Munal shot that.

"I'm not gonna say that," I said, hating the little girl in my voice, hiding under the kitchen table, begging permission.

"No. You just gonna think it. Right? Say it. You get us in here, you act nice to us, and you want us to act polite and write nice but you think we really animals. Right? No matter what we do. Right? Say it. Say it. Say, 'Men are animals.'"

I swear to God that I am not this person. No one before has ever made me feel like this person. But the words pooled and eddied around my tongue: "Men are animals." I kept swallowing the words, disciplining my tongue. The words burned in my gut, my gut became transparent, and he read there.

I tried to buy time. I knew that the other students didn't care what I said one way or the other. I thought of that day that I had said something funny and only he and I laughed. "That's not been the thrust of this discussion at all," I said. "The position you've taken fails to give the discussion credit for the complexity of what's been discussed."

"I ask you a yes no question," he said. "Yes, no."

"No. That's ridiculous. You are precious. Never forget it. And stop trying to scare me!" I couldn't say that either but it flickered in my heart and he read there.

"Lay off her," screeched Etta.

"I ain't *on* her, Etta," Suarez snapped. Etta recoiled and looked scared. Suarez can be scary. Suarez was scary. I began to rise to protect her. But he said: "I ask her a question. Yes, no." He turned back to me.

The key to my survival in Their world where nothing is real is the amputation of my passion and the camouflage of how much I care. If I open my mouth and talk now it will be passionate enough to get me fired.

Etta got her wind back. "Yo –"

But Suarez spoke again. He spoke in the soft voice that sounds very gentle, with the rising inflection at the ends even of declarative sentences.

"Don't you check out on me, now. I say something important to you and you check out on me."

"It's time," I announced. "Class is over. You can ask on Monday. Ask Dr. Rothenberg. I won't be the teacher Monday."

"Oh yeah? I'm gonna get you outside and then you gonna be the teacher," he said, soft enough now that only I could hear it over the students rising and gathering their things and leaving. I watched Suarez leave, too, watched his broad, male shoulders in their black shirt, and I exhaled. That's all he did; he just got up and quietly left. I envied that.

I wanted the poetry festival to be the hinge. Its beauty. Serenity. Its feeling of rightness. The scary things and the scary people would be slow to find me there. It didn't ruin the good feeling to know that the scary things and the scary people still exist, that I hadn't conquered them, and that they would eventually get around to the poetry festival in Sussex County. And that, when they did, I would be led off without public protest. But there I was blessed by geographic indulgence, provisional safety, enough anonymity to forestall immediate eviction. It was like what I used to feel around Miles. Today with Suarez was its exact opposite.

That day when it was raining, and he came to see me. I have never been more determined to protect, to nurture, anything, even myself: someone who was honest; someone who was trying. Protecting him, nurturing him, was the ultimate act of resistance against the scary things and the scary people, the ultimate self-assertion, and victory. But today a dybbuk hijacked my desire. This demon feeds on one thing only: the pain of a heart I could love, no other heart. This pure hunger demanded that I say, "Yes. You are animals." That I say it to him, no other person, in this perfect little sadist voice, that I twist the words till I see his face crumple, and that I relish that disintegration.

I pull myself back. As I do the dishes. As I sweep the floor. As I stare out the window at the sumac. "Men are animals! Say it right now. Say: 'Men are animals.'" I pause. I can do this. I know I can. Just give me a minute. I weigh potential replies as if they were gold dust and I were operating in a big wind. But though I've been pulling off this juggling act all my life, suddenly the answer that is both safe and true, and will satisfy the audience, does not immediately come to me. I move on to the next thing, fixing dinner, sponging out the fridge. "Men are animals! Say it right now. Say: 'Men are animals.'" I pause.

Apparently, the places where I'm paralyzed, are exactly where I have to grow. Where I am blind, where I can't even feel, I have to do my most vital work. I am immobile as a target, but everything around me races on its own elemental trajectory.

Oh, get over it. He's a teenager. A teenage Puerto Rican male. He's at some club tonight. La Piñata on Market Street or that awful Tropicana Palace and Go Go Bar on River Street. He's with that tramp, his Lolicita. He's thinking with his cock. I don't have to come up with the answer; the boy who asked has already forgotten the question.

I just rested my arms on the typewriter platen and gazed out at the sumac, my face a ghostly reflection in the window. Right now I want to sprawl out on my tummy on the parlor rug in front of the TV. Raw-boned Kai is right behind me, wearing a hollow in the couch where he lies watching Star Trek, his favorite, with the only quiet concentration I've ever seen him display. It's that episode where the starship's magical molecular transporter goes on the fritz. Heroic Captain James T. Kirk is split. There are now two Kirks, the one kind but ineffectual, the other ruthless, but a great kisser.

Kai, at moments like this, and they are rare – I feel you soak the room. It's not the return of a word, or of an action, but, rather, of feeling. When I was at the sink doing dishes and you were behind me eating spaghetti. That felt different than doing dishes in an empty kitchen, or with Daddy or Evie or anyone else there. It's that feeling that I feel now. I feel it so very strongly my only question is not, Kai, are you here, but, rather, why? What have you come to say to me? And that's why, Kai – I know you were a guy, and everything – but I wish that when you were still alive that you had talked to me once in a while. Then, when I get these feelings, as if you were here, there could be dialogue between us, not just the plots of old TV shows you watched while I sprawled out on the floor, practicing mute, unilateral adoration.

DEAR DIARY, TOPH had asked what time he might try calling Saturday morning. I'm just realizing in typing this that he didn't ask whether or not to call Saturday morning, just what time. I said, "Nine fifteen." He called at nine fifteen. Martha bitched me out. "What does it take to satisfy you? A nice guy calls when he says he's gonna call. Women record events like this in their diaries, Miroswava. They report them to CNN." That's my problem, then. I'm a woman and what's supposed to satisfy women doesn't satisfy me. His reason for calling remained a mystery; without an agenda, I just talked about what interests me. Our conversation became an interactional eczema. The energy grew old and died too quick; raw, unready energy was exposed, only for it to fail; everything itched.

"Toph, didja ever wanna trade with the students? Like, they be the teacher and you sit back? Ever wanna submit? I did it Friday. Let Etta take over class. What is it with Etta, anyway? You know, she's in love with one of the other students, Supreme, the Black Muslim? The one with all the ridiculous bow ties? But he won't date her cause she's white. But she's blacker than he is. She speaks Black English; he speaks scrupulous Standard." I wasn't hearing any "Uh, huh,"s nor "Mmm"s. Okay; change topics. "Have you ever called a student at home? Like, what if a student asked you a question, a really hard question, and it took you a while to figure out the answer? Would you call him at home?"

"That's dangerous," Toph finally begrudging me two words.

"Oh. Sorry," I said.

"Role reversal. You know 'Oedipus.'"

"Heard of it," I said.

"The Greek king who kills his father and marries his mother. Freud did lots of work on that. It's the great tragedy – role reversal."

"Yeah, yeah, yeah," I said, suddenly excited to experience some tension and contact in the conversational tennis ball. "Like why kids of alcoholics go crazy. They had to parent their parents. Never got to be kids."

"Could be," he said, abruptly spitefully lax again.

I ignored his distance from a phone call he had initiated, and continued, red and raw. "But how do you know, really, what is your role? What's the real tragedy? Reversing the role assigned to you or reversing the real role? And how can you find out except by challenging it? Stepping outside the lines? Have you ever wanted to do that, Toph?"

"Hmm? What." he asked, absent, a passenger gracelessly invited into an alien conversation during a long plane ride.

"Have you ever learned anything from a student?"

"Sounds like a recipe for disaster."

"Well, you know more about this than I do. I haven't even read Oedipus. I'd better cut it out."

"Cut what out?" he asked.

I couldn't respond. I was still reeling from what I just heard myself say. I could take it back; Toph wouldn't even know what I was taking back.

"I can see the raccoon now," I ventured, shaky.

"I'm beginning to worry about you," Toph said. "Is everything okay with the students? You do have that certifiable juvenile delinquent in your class –"

"He's not so bad. Not like you'd think –"

"Still defending them. I think we should just send losers like Troy directly into the military."

"Oh, Troy. Right. He's running up and down along the bank, now. I wonder if there are crawdads in water that polluted?"

"Naw. Paterson raccoons are strict Dumpster divers. This one's probably just jogging."

I laughed, and thought, okay, what do I do next time? Tell Toph I'm moving out of state, quit the job, wear a wig till he forgets me, and walk only in alleys? Explode, "Shut up! Cosseted simps like you should have to pass comprehensive exams before receiving licenses to speak!" That wouldn't be okay to say. Meanwhile, I couldn't stop gasped, forced laughs at his bogus witticisms. Couldn't stop telling him how smart he was. Couldn't stop enduring his paternal arm around my shoulder. He finally hung up; his hanging up was as lacking in plot development, climax, denouement, as everything that had gone before. Another step closer to our having sex.

DEAR DIARY, I wondered what anonymous incest survivors would look like. Only three ladies showed for the seven thirty meeting. They all clutched frosty, hospital-vending-machine-fresh cans of Diet Coke in their fists. These women were as round as basketballs. I have never been as fat as these women. I sat up straighter, smiled and greeted each graciously. I was glad I had worn my teacher clothes. These women were obviously needy.

In order to set a good example, I spoke first. "Hi, my name's Miroswava. You can call me Mira; that's easier for most people. Oh, and, I am a survivor," I said, mindful of Twelve Step protocol. "A couple of recent events have inspired me to come to my first ISA meeting tonight, even though I had to borrow my friend Martha's car to get here." I chuckled, made eye contact all around. They smiled. "Well, first, I've been having – mmm – dreams. Nightmares, really. But they're not like regular nightmares." I looked up. Would they get it? I suspected that they were getting it all too well. But it was too late to come up with a new story. I fumbled on. "And, there's a kid at school – but that's . . . . And this guy at work is flirting with me. He called this morning and I was really annoyed, but I – what? I couldn't. What? What am I trying to say here? I couldn't – See, when men flirt with me, I assume I have to – I assume – I just give them everything they want . . . "

Saliva pooled under my soft palate, as if to prepare for vomiting. Pinpricks of hard, chilled flesh pushed my hairs up away from my arms. I covered my belly with crossed arms. The women tilted their heads, smiled, murmured. Their facial expressions convinced me that these women were hearing each word for what it really means. I was sharing vocabulary, not translating a foreign tongue as I went along, withholding or distributing meaning according to what suited me. I began to sob.

I have never been as fat as those women. I have never cried like that in front of strangers. I have never cried like that in front of myself. And I've always had sex with anyone I could.

We'd been in Nepal a little less than a month. Yes, I am still telling this story; I hope thus to come to its end, someday. It had been a little less than a month when I saw it on Miles' face for the first time. Or when I imagined that I saw it. The best I can do here is tell the story in the first person singular. Well, shit, this whole diary is in the first person singular. Why add *caveat lector* here? Because my recovery depends on reporting the truth. I report elsewhere things people have done and said that could be testified to by witnesses. But the point of this story is my interpretation of the look on a man's face, and I am the only one who still interprets it that way.

At the time, Emmie indicated that she saw it, too, but men are forever dismissing women's stories in which the whole point is the look on a man's face, as told by women. In *Sharia*, the Muslim legal code, women can't even testify in court, except in special circumstances, and even then it takes two women's testimony to equal that of one man. Women were the first to witness Christ's resurrection; male apostles pooh-poohed their testimony as nonsense.

I'm no Mary Magdalene and this is not the Good News. I'm just a woman telling a story about a man, as best I can. And so, I report, caveat lector; I can remember, understand and tell this story only in the first person singular.

We'd been in Nepal a little less than a month. There had been a sing announced at the training house but I'm not really into that sort of thing – guitars and bongos, Grateful Dead songs, herd instinct – so I was halfhearted about going. Well after it had begun, for reasons I don't remember, I showed up. Everyone was lounging round in a rough circle on the floor. Miles was against the far wall, playing guitar. I stepped out of the night, into the open doorway, he looked up at me, and I received it as a telegram. The news was rushing from his face like light spilling from sun-struck gold. A rich gold that rendered the white light from the pressure lantern a flat aluminum glare. And surely every watch there registered the rent in time. I slid down; he continued playing. There was no thought to resist, any more than you consider reverse when flying down a slide. He was playing "Uncle John's Band," not a song in my repertoire, a song I felt no need to know. But I knew I would come to learn it, by heart, without trying. I snuggled into Emmie, our exuberant Berkeley flapper, to whisper the breaking news to her; she preempted me. "It's so obvious," she giggled. Entangled in each other as kittens in yarn, she and I collapsed against the whitewashed wall behind us.

When the sing wound down, I rose to go. Miles dropped what he was doing – picking up after the sing – and followed me out into the night. I was bunking just across the street; he wasn't losing me; I was going as far as a weak man can throw a stone. Miles said one of those one-last-things you say to an evening guest before she departs. I promised to do my homework or nodded or produced a one-liner. I don't remember what I said but I know they were words honed to meet his and please him, and then I turned to go. And then I heard my teacher say another one-last-thing to me, and I stopped still in the dirt yard. I responded, again, pleasing and in kind, confused, but paralyzed by the habit of obedience. Trainees filed past; Miles released them with a one- or two- word goodnight; they kept moving, and soon, I was the last trainee still there. Even cook was snoring and the houseboy had long since bedded down; the pressure lantern died; the stars were my only remaining witnesses. Starlight was the only light by which to capture this image: my teacher saying more and more one-last-things, aural filaments binding me within his web of vision, of earshot, of impress.

As Miles spoke, he stood at the edge of the cement apron surrounding the training house. He was not above me, not Juliet on a balcony, not separated from me by any physical barrier, no immigrant on ship deck. Yet I sensed so strongly then, and do now in remembering this, him as if above, us as if separated by perilous sea, by foreign element, him leaning forward, yet never touching.

On that night I was not so reverent of such details; they were all part of the passing sensory confetti of my days, over which I felt no control. I never invested in the final resolution of their pattern when the confetti ultimately dropped. All I remember thinking is, "Okay, okay, we love each other. Okay. But I gotta get some shuteye!" Hovering in the background of this memory, though, is a feeling waiting to be inhabited and given voice. Silenced and shadowed then, like a dissident, this exiled anxiety vectored forbidden ideas: "My superior is not flawless; I have some value." I inhabit this anxiety now. I give it voice: "You are my teacher and you are a married man. I am young and defenselessly in love. What you are doing now is poisoning me." The anxiety has eyes as well and draws to my attention this detail: Miles never letting me go, Miles never touching me. Apparently the point of this story is not the look on a man's face, after all. So often I have to tell the story to arrive at its point.

But I've never thought of myself as that kind of a woman. I've always had sex with anyone I could. Yes, yes I have. But when it comes to the man I loved, as far as I know, Miles' groin could be as smooth as a Ken doll's.

I think of the circle and cross dream, the one that I had when all this began. I don't want to be in this circle point, circled round in this womb, anymore. I want this to be a hot stove that ricochets me into action. I'm sorry that right now I feel it as movement *away*. I hope some day it becomes movement *toward*. I'm ready to be the line bursting from the point, the turning crankshaft, the racing sail at right angle to wind. If this is what it takes to get over this, to get to the end of the story, I'm gonna do it. I'm gonna have sex with Toph.

D EAR DIARY, I swung back doors I have passed every day but whose thresholds I have apparently been declining to so much as place foot upon heretofore. It's only now that I have crossed these boutique doorways that I see my consistent refusals as methodical behavior. Airs redolent of patchouli, rose, musk, or frankincense marked each territory. Yes, frankincense, apparently dressing a female body is ritual akin to midnight mass. Notes of harps and chimes meandered out of fern-hidden stereos. Time was studied calm; there were no clocks. Cloister quiet was a universally chosen discipline. I slithered through curtains of roped beads and walked beside an undulating wall of silk scarves. I had not moved in such a harem tent since I was six years old, no one was home, and hope chest and jewelry box lay unprotected. Beautiful clerks attended to me with deference. No wonder women so adore shopping.

But I'm not a woman, not really, not yet, because I was enjoying this as an anthropologist jotting in her journal. Because some of the fat is gone but the plow-horse bones remain. Because the things I truly loved with the ardor infant Bambi felt for his mother – a taupe suede jumper, a scarf made of, colored by, the water that bathes coral reefs and their over-floating sky – these things I loved were priced strictly for the pocketbooks of Cinderella's wicked step-sisters. To torture myself, or, what? I don't know. I tried on the taupe suede jumper before suicide-inducing three way mirrors under "confess now" lighting. I saw a thinner woman in exquisite dress I could not ransom and age. I am older. I am not the girlish dreamer I promised this to. What did I do with all those years? I spent them crouching on a closet floor, holding my breath until the sounds of the scary people had died away, until I was ready, until I was safe. What toll free number do I dial to correct this mistaken deposit, to redeem years wrongly banked?

The only thing erect in my body or my spirit a white flag of surrender, I turned to go – but first witnessed Venus rising from the sea. A white gown, some scattered roses, blowzy, blush-red, clung with the insistence of skin. Warm architecture flaunted tensile blooms touch might dimple but not compress. My eyes could not avoid these very large, perfectly globular breasts. Their recipient was young; these may have happened yesterday, these may still be, to her, nothing more than impediments to softball, sleep, and free passage down high school halls. A bit of a tummy, which would concern her, "Do I look fat?" She couldn't know how that mound practically pulled fingers to trace creamy peak to its promise down. This architecture also advertised a fragility that a caress could buckle; there were pinched waist and ankles and knees. Her wrists were behind her head; hair flowed over them, folded forward over muscular, ivory, shoulders – a glossy aureole. Her eyes implored. Her look was hinging. She was deferential, but certain: of all the m/patrons in this shop, she had singled me out. I could prop her up; I could let her topple.

"Well?" she asked. "What do you think?"

"What do I think. Well. I think you are one of the most beautiful earthly creations I have ever seen. I think, if I had what you have now, and with my current attitude, I'd take it to the big city, and name my fortune. I think the correct reaction to you is to kneel, begin at your toes, and lick up till Eden is retaken." Stating these basic truths would do neither of us any good at all.

Instead, I nodded a connoisseur's nod – she had requested expert reassurance – and I coolly pronounced, "The dress is good. The best you'll get in that price range. You in the dress? Spectacular. Never doubt it for one heartbeat."

"Thanks," she said, with a sweet gratitude I am not used to receiving from kids. Does this go on in clothing stores everyday, I wondered. "I needed another pair of eyes."

"My pleasure," I said, and, before I made any one of several of the available options of fool of myself, I moved on.

Back home, I raced up to the loft and began strip-mining my clothes closet with the kind of hysterical determination to find appropriate disguise that I usually feel when receiving a last minute invitation on Halloween. I turned up two things I'd never worn: a midriff baring black blouse and a wrap-around cotton skirt. The skirt was from a Rajasthan bazaar. You have to buy one if you go; you become a patron of the arts, of an art form that's been around since the Rajput courts. These skirts are printed with hand-carved wooden blocks; the dye is turmeric; it's fixed with mordants of mango bark and myrtle flowers. Buying one is not frivolous or vain; it's no less a cultural mission than visiting a museum! And the black blouse I had bought in an underground boutique in Warsaw, under Communism when beauty was still subversive. I had marched; I had chanted "Soviets go home!" I had purchased cool clothing in dissident boutiques.

I focused on my lashes as I slathered on mascara. I focused on my legs as I shaved and slipped on pantyhose and dropped the skirt over them. I focused on my midriff, as I, for the first time, wriggled into that belly-skimming black shirt. Eyes scrunched shut tight, as if before a firing squad, I positioned myself before the new full-length mirror and, ready, aim, fire, opened wide. It wasn't me, of course, standing before me, but the sorceress inhabiting that mirror.

Those mirrors in the shops had been all wrong. With this light, with these shapes and colors – is it all light? The right light? The right pair of eyes? *I* wanted to have sex with me. To do every dance club in the city, flooring helpless males across Manhattan with my totally unfair cornucopia of beauty and smoldering sexiness that just might combust the very air. I wanted to sit on the floor and cry for years dedicated to despising my own flesh, slinking past mirrors, not getting dressed up, not dancing, not fingering silk colored by sky.

After a full night of club hopping, Toph drove me home. I didn't get out; but just sat still in his car. It's been my experience that if a woman is immobile long enough around a man, eventually he will jump her.

"Are you thinking hard about something big?" he asked.

"If I'm lucky," the obvious answer, I didn't dare say. "No," I lied, never having seen thought in a woman act as an aphrodisiac on a man.

"Well, why aren't you talking?"

"You talk," I said. They like that.

"I've been trying to talk to you for five minutes, and all I get are monosyllabic replies."

"Sorry."

He sighed. I waited. Stretched a bit; in stretching I exposed my neck, throat, breasts, my white and naked belly – just generally splayed myself out like a deer ready for gutting.

"What was this all about, my being a boy?"

"*What?*" I blurted, blindsided.

Toph smirked in quiet triumph. "Martha said you and she were deciding who the men were and who the boys were. She says her plumber is a man; you're undecided. Said you'd have to see how he acted in a fire or other calamity. Be merciful, Mira; give the man a flood."

"Since when do you talk to Martha?"

"Since you won first prize," he replied coolly, enjoying himself. "She's now one of the people one must talk to."

"God, what else has she said to you?"

"Nothing. Not any of the stuff I'd really like to know. Just that you're both decided that I'm a boy."

"I'm sorry," I said. "I take it back."

"You can't take it back," petulant; flirtatiously so.

Yeah, yeah, yeah, who cares; I thought. What is the shortest possible route between my fingernails and his chest hairs? I was seeing him the way a heat-seeking camera sees. Lost trappers in the far north slit open their mush huskies and stuck their hands inside to stay alive for another moment. I wanted that. "Okay," I stretched again and swiveled my entire body toward him. I wriggled forward. "So, I can't take it back." I closed my eyes and dropped my chin. I swept my hair up over my head; it cascaded down from my brow. "The back of my neck is soo stiff," I whimpered.

"Oh, really?" he sang, not fooled at all. His arm reached around my shoulder. He tugged me into the hollow of his side and rubbed his stubble into the back of my neck. That felt remarkably good. I liked that. Can't say anyone's done that to me before. I'll ask for it again, as if for the first time, and when I get it, I'll raise a silent toast to Toph.

But I pulled away. This was still doing it wrong. Somehow wanting and touching were not enough. I was missing something. So I pulled away, and he didn't resist. I looked out the window of my side of the car. Stop it, Miroswava. I wasn't at all aware of what it was, but I knew I had to stop it.

"Is it time to go upstairs?" Toph asked.

Shocking even myself, I jerked toward him, angrily.

I got out of the car. When I realized I had reached the front door of the building without Toph, I turned around. "Well?" He was still in the car, looking as if he had run out of usable expressions. Finally he parked the car in the lot across the street and followed me up.

As soon as I got my apartment door locked behind us I moved into him and stuck my tongue in his mouth.

"Whoa," he said.

"Whoa?"

"Let's talk."

"Okay." I took his hand and lead him to the couch; didn't put on the light. He got up and switched on the overhead. I got up and turned that off and turned on the lamp on this desk.

He actually sat on the floor. "Miroswava Hudak," he began, as if this were a practiced speech, "where have you been all my life? I've never met anyone like you. I'll never forget you."

I guess I smiled. I figured this is how he revved up and it wouldn't last long. I wanted to get the show on the road.

He gazed at me, encouraged me to produce anecdotes of the fascinating places I've been, things I've done. No, I didn't eat the termites in Africa, yes, I did tour Burma on the profit from smuggling Johnnie Walker and Marlboros. I talked; I charmed. It was just like hitchhiking. You owe them for the ride and you want to keep them distracted from the crowbar under their seat. My mind raced: the second he leaves I'm going to the night market, the one near the projects with the drive-by shootings. I'm going to buy: butter, brown sugar, walnuts, coconut. I'm going to mix them up. I'm going to eat them. Nut bulges nudge, sugar melts, on my tongue. I swallow. Their texture salutes my throat. I receive them with familiar joy. They surrender their sweetness and warmth to my flesh, transubstantiate into me. Ninety per cent of my creativity and libido is a mile and a half from here in a sticky-floored night market, and he's sated on the ten per cent of me he can imagine. Damn you. Do something to compel me into this moment. Isn't that the least we humans owe each other? To tug each other into the moments we live?

At three a.m. the phone rang, piercing the air with a somehow more unnaturally jangling alarm than it uses in the daytime. I suppressed a little jump. I dreaded hearing Mommy's cries, the graphic, hospital-fresh particulars of slow, horrible death by cancer of a beloved Babushka, (whom I hadn't visited lately), after her thankless lifetime of hardship, never redeeming that nauseating, cramped, trip across the Atlantic in steerage. "Excuse me," I said to Toph. He nodded as if he understood.

"Hello?"

"Ms. Hudak." Funny, I guess that was a question, but I noted that the inflection did not rise, not like when he uses the gentle voice, the one with the rising inflection at the ends even of declarative sentences.

Diary, I don't know if I can share, even with you, what it did, to my whole body, to hear Gabriel Suarez's voice on the other end of my phone at three a.m. But you're gonna have to forgive me for recording – I mean I started you to talk about my addiction to food, after all – that the obsessive thoughts, the craving for comfort or a summons to this moment of my life, evaporated, that quick.

"It's three o'clock in the morning!"

"I know. But I know you wake."

"How?"

"Your light's on."

I sighed. "Give me the number," I wrote it down. "I'm calling you back."

"You don't gotta."

"Right. Good-bye for now; you'll get a call within the hour." I hung up.

Toph didn't say anything. "Toph," I began.

"That's okay. I heard. Family emergency?"

I nodded. I escorted him to the door. He kissed me, open mouth. I didn't get the point of that. I had thought he was trying to communicate a desire for a Platonic relationship. Sonnet readings, savoring the moment, that sort of thing.

"See you tomorrow?" he asked.

"Sure," I ad-libbed. I had half the clothes off and on the floor before the door was nested in the jamb. I gathered them up and grabbed some paper toweling from the kitchen and a glop of Crisco and began rubbing all that crap off my face as I walked to the bathroom. I stood in the shower for a long time. Toweled off. Rubbed hard. Turned off all the lights. Grabbed the phone. Plugged it in upstairs. Got into bed. Wondered what mamacita would make of this. But – this wasn't his home number. I knew because I'd been toying with the idea of calling him myself. And if he were in Newark, he wouldn't have known that my lights were on. Dialed. Bet, though, that wherever he was, he'd pick it up before the first ring was finished. Bet right.

"Gabriel Suarez, if I teach you nothing else, let me teach you this: most people would consider it pretty socially inappropriate for a student to call his teacher at three a.m. in the morning."

"Oh, yeah? You just call me and is now three thirty."

"No extra points for cuteness. Did someone shoot you? Is it drugs? Are you in trouble with the cops? Give it to me straight, and quick."

"Nah. Thas na me."

"Suarez, if you are going to call me at three o'clock in the morning, you are going to pronounce every goddamn final consonant."

"That's not me."

"Thank you. How do you know I have my lights on?"

"Had," he said, with a quick certainty.

"Ooo kaay," I said slowly. "How do you know I *had* my lights on and have since turned them off?"

"My friend she live across the lot from you. The big vacant lot – you can see her building out the window."

"How do you know which apartment is mine?"

"You don't got no curtains. And beside, everybody, we all know."

"Double negative. Double subject."

"Yeah, right."

"So what's up?" I asked. "You know it's weird to call people at this time, no? So why did you call?"

"I keep thinking about Friday, what I said."

I watched my hand reach out from under the blanket, reach out into the darkness, and make as if to touch. "Yeah, me too," I confessed.

Long silence. I still had no answer. This silence accused me, weighed on me, revealed me as a failure to him and to my vocation. I struggled to fill the black stage of silence with my significant answer; mute paralysis accused me further. Only my hand kept dancing against the darkness, feeling it, its edges and its soft places alike.

He finally spoke. "I'm sorry."

I assumed he meant for calling so early.

But he continued, "I could see that I upset you. I scared Etta. When I was talking to you, I felt the way I used to feel in jubie – Juvenile Detention. I felt –" long inhale, "like I could hurt somebody. Like I would like to hurt somebody. Like I would enjoy hurting somebody."

"Yes, yes, yes," I said, very quickly. "It's immediate. It's too fast for anyone to lie. People lie, people are phony, all the time, even when they're being nice to you, even while making love. And the thing is, Suarez, one is so rarely lying or faking it when one is – beating the living shit out of another human being. The trick is to tell the truth, to be real, when things slow down, and get – you know – softer."

"You got it," he said. "So now I bet everybody scared of me. I feel like I ruin the whole class."

I grabbed the darkness hard. "Gabriel."

"Yeah."

"I forgive you. And I bet Etta will forgive you, too, after you apologize to her, and I hope you do, because – you guys are just a great group, and . . ." another long silence.

He said, "Yeah . . ." and then another. But there was no awkwardness now, but faith enough to be generous with time, to listen to the other breathe.

When I was ready, I said, "Gabriel?"

"Yeah."

"I am sorry. I apologize to you."

"What for? You gonna hang up on me?"

"Yes, I am. I am going to hang up on you. But first – I apologize for failing as your teacher. For not having the answer to your very good question. For blowing you off."

"You tryin be nice."

"Auxiliaries, Suarez. Auxiliaries. 'You *are* trying to be nice.' And, no, I am not. Good-bye. And, unless you have just been shot or are in some other dire distress, don't ever call a teacher at this hour again."

"Okay, chief," he said. I think I was hearing a smile, the kind of audible smile that you recognize through sound, even if you see the man, right in front of you. Suarez may be too unutterably cool for visible smiles right now.

There was another long, patient silence during which neither hung up.

"Your girlfriend's – I assume it's your girlfriend – she's gonna worry about this," I said.

"Nah. She sleep," he said.

I suddenly confronted a sinkhole in me that I hadn't even suspected when he didn't rush in to explain, "She's not my girlfriend," or, even, "She is." Something. Some gift to meet my needy invasion. No matter what; I would have felt even.

"*'She – '*" I began

"*' – is asleep.*' I know," again, the audible smile.

Silence. Now definitely the silence of neither hanging up. Suddenly I realized how wrong that was, and, so, giddy, I wanted to do it more and more and more and more. To say things, one-last-things, that sounded safe, but as you thought about them, for days, would come to be taken in all the wrong ways.

"Good-bye, Gabriel," I whispered; though I had no intention of whispering. I hung up the phone. After a few seconds, I rose up on my elbow, and my hand reached out from under the blanket, reached out into the darkness, and unplugged the phone, as well.

D EAR DIARY, HOW do I make amends to a diary? How do I reassure you and convince myself that those trashy dramas that suck time owed you really mean nothing to me? Do I proffer candy and flowers? No. It is only my own gratuitous self-flagellation that drives us apart, stiffens muscles, shoves away appointed hours that become days, makes you hard for me. Just in wetting you now with ink, I sense your jubilation. I open you. I touch you. I put you to your proper use. You are satisfied. I am convinced. I really want to be here, with you. You are uniquely wise to treat my inexhaustible ignorance as a natural resource. You invite one blind report after another, and never interrupt. Ignorance accumulates until I understand what it is I'm trying to say.

A lot has happened since last I wrote. Where to begin.

When I commission myself to write justice for the weight of events, to honor every nuance, I can't write at all. Moments saturated with feeling demand a counterintuitive tactic: I must become like a robot. My only ability and duty is to focus on the next binomial choice, the next yes or no, and thus to accumulate isolated facts until they bend me double as gray birch under heavy snow.

Okay. Small facts first. Toph and I are having sex. Not every day, or anything, nor even every time we see each other. I don't think it means much and it will end, eventually, without any drama, I'm sure.

Next. Gabriel Suarez . . .

Just report the facts, Miroswava. Play over facts as a percussionist plays over her instrument. To linger is to cheat the next beat of its chance. Obey the dictate of William Carlos Williams, Paterson's biographer: "No poetry but in things." Facts move in machines called plot: and then, and then, and then . . . Facts are only clung to as long as they are novel and as long as they advance the machine. Then facts are dropped as cleanly as the woman a player has finally nailed down. Facts don't outstay their welcome. Feelings do, like an equatorial doldrum that has captured some mythic, cursed galleon. That doldrum never lets her go, never lets her move on.

When I file stories by feeling my right brain leads me down the primrose path. I filed that training-house sing story under my intuitive feeling: "Miles' revealing love for me for the first time." I should have focused on facts. I should have focused on Miles never letting me go, and never touching me. It's facts, not feelings, that make the world go round.

But it's hard for a woman like me to report just the facts. I unplug telephones. I preemptively strike facts down. I allow no facts.

No, Miroswava. Stop getting lost in feelings. Focus on facts. If you don't, you'll give up. You'll abandon your diary and never try to write this story again, because, whereas you've already survived all the facts, recording the feelings is just too hard.

But can facts ever honor the sum? Will you bend, diary, after I record my paltry facts? An old man spinning yarns of World War Two; a student and a teacher seeing each other?

There goes my right brain again. Jumping ahead, not being linear. Being spontaneous, being intuitive – all those qualities that have gotten me into trouble. Not organized and detail-oriented, like the left brain – all the qualities I need. Mira, just record the facts. In some kind of order.

Okay. I began with something small, manageable; I'll move on to something a little bigger, a little tougher. I'll end with the fucking impossible.

A fact: I'm such a stickler about correct pronunciation of foreign names, when I say his, "Gabriel Suarez," I almost sound like one of them. "Gaa brree ail:" I sound to myself like a red-lipsticked, purple-miniskirted Chiquita in a TV PR soap opera. "Suarez:" I sound to myself like the hacienda-hothouse, yearning virgin in one of those fat, magical realism novels that are so trendy nowadays. It's scary. That's okay; as long as I don't start *acting* like one of them.

What else? Nothing, really. My paltry facts: he comes to class; he is the student; I am the teacher. Sometimes he is unavoidable; other days, I have to ask myself, "Is he here?" and I scan the room, and spot him. Sometimes we make eye contact; sometimes we do not. I prefer the latter. Then I get to watch him work, study the top of his head as he bends over his paper, take in his phenomenally black hair.

But I feel something – hardly objective data – emphasis "I" emphasis "feel" emphasis amorphous "something." The first time he and I make eye contact that day, I feel something. The first look is a microcosm; it's too unexpected to domesticate. When I first see Mommy my eyes are cast down, always; hers penetrate the far distance. We do all the juggling we need to maintain blind position. Gabriel's first glimpse of me is unexpectedly intent in a boy so young, searching as if he had an inkling of places he's never been, and smarter than I'd ever given credit for. Mine of him is joyful and helpless. When I find this hard to survive, I tell myself most people aren't me, and they ignore the first look. So I smile and say something about school.

Okay. Now. I've come to the impossible. The thing that's kept me from writing all this while. If I reduce it to isolated, sequential facts, not conceive of it as a feeling I must inhabit, allow to waylay me, maybe I can write it all down. And then drop it, cleanly, and sail on, in my own little self-sufficient plot.

I borrowed Martha's car to attend the Incest Survivor's Anonymous meeting in Montclair. The car got a flat. I knew enough to root around Martha's trunk. When, amidst the animal crackers, greasy rags, three ring binders, Styrofoam picnic hamper, and a fourteen-year-old copy of the *Suburban Trends*, I found a spare and a jack, I knew enough to conclude that I had what I needed. But of course no one's ever taught me how to change a tire.

I was halfway to the phone booth in the weeds beside the interstate when I remembered that Martha and the kids were down the shore. I called Mel at the shelter where she volunteers. Damn I'm lucky, I thought; it was close to her time to get off. She could easily drive by on her way home and tell me what to do.

"Good evening, Safety House." Mel's voice was as slow and rich as the butter in a Tibetan Buddhist lamp. If I were on the lam from a loved one, that crooning singsong is exactly what I'd want to hear.

"Mel, it's Miroswava. Listen, I borrowed Martha's car and it's got a flat, and, uh – Could you possibly swing by here on your way home?"

Mel's voice immediately switchbacked into lets-get-this-over-with-as-quick-as-ever-we-can American jive. "Hi. Sorry; can't. Chris and I are having Owen over. He just won the Herman Hewitt Peale. You know, the humanitarian award? For his book about women's cooperatives in Bangladesh. Listen, if you do get that tire fixed, come on over later. They'll be plenty of free wine and cheese."

"Okay, bye." Dialed the next number. "Toph, it's me. Listen, I hate to bother you, but I borrowed Martha's car and it's got a flat. I'm not far from your place, actually."

"Well, isn't *this* interesting," he spoke in the voice of a connoisseur indulging a rare pleasure. "Synchronicity."

"I'm not following you?"

"Oh, come on," he said. "Sure you are. Remember what I was telling you the other night? Remember? I kept telling you what a powerful, creative, woman you are, Mira. And you kept telling me that I didn't know what I was talking about. Remember that? Now you've created this opportunity. And you can use that same energy to create a solution. Yeah, sure, I could show up; I could change the tire. But if I did that, I'd cheat you of the chance to learn this valuable lesson. About what a powerful, creative woman you are."

I think I said something like, "Mm hm," before hanging up, but all I was thinking was: that's twenty-five cents I'll never see again. Without thinking very hard, I dialed the next obvious number, a number that I know as well as I know my own name. I know I know it as well as my own name, because the one time I had surgery I came out of the anesthesia repeating this number. I move so often I'd need a phone book to call myself. They've had this number for fifty years. Daddy just asked where I was and hung up.

At Wanda's wedding, Jennifer, the stranger who married into the Hudak clan, adjured me to "Just look at your father. Do you people appreciate how good looking he is for a man his age? I don't think you do. You're used to him, so you don't notice him. How many men his age have all their hair, like he does? And it's not gray. Look at that. He still has black hair."

Not all, not now. As he walked toward me on the highway I noticed the silver threading through.

Jennifer gushed on about Daddy's sharp, symmetrical features, his fit physique. "That's what you get when your father is a working man. You can tell that just by looking at him – he's no desk jockey. You can see all those years of work in his body."

Yes, I could. And it's not just years; it's generations. It's that whole damn country. Daddy's a short little Polak, I was noticing, yet again – it's always surprising how short – but his broad shoulders are wider than his trim hips; his legs assert definition under baggy, old-man pants. His arms are muscled and rangy. Everything that's there is there to be used. And it's more than the material, I could see, as he was walking toward me, rolling a tire beside him, a jack tucked under his arm. "Hand-to-plow:" the language his body was speaking. As Daddy moved, the language traveled with him. In the book of Luke, Jesus advises one who would be excellent to emulate the plowman: work; keep straight as a furrow; look neither to left nor to the right; and never look back. Jesus could have found all the illustrative models he needed in Poland, whose name means, "dwellers in the field." "Hand-to-plow:" a language with very few jokes, or maybe an abundance; I guess they just don't translate. No symphonies; hand-to-plow demands unbroken focus on dirt and the rear end of an ungulate, after all. Yes, there are lots of dirges, but at moments like this, one is glad to be the intimate of a speaker.

"Hi, Dad. Sorry to bother you like this."

"You went out without a jack? Or even a spare?" He dropped.

I didn't try to explain. "It's not mine," I said, hovering over him, hurting for his seventy-something-year-old body, suddenly tiny and defenseless on this chaotic, speedy stage: the hollow glare of oncoming headlights, the cacophony of horns and yells, big, fast, expensive cars. "It's my friend Martha's."

"No excuse. You check before you drive." He was working away, apparently oblivious to the traffic. "You got your mother very worried."

"I'm sorry."

"You can tell her that when you get home."

"Actually . . . I was gonna go back to Paterson."

"*Paterson*? Why *Paterson*? What are you gonna do in *Paterson*? Oh. Wait. That's right, you live there now. So, how are you? How is everything? Your old man worries about you."

"Fine."

"Roll the spare over here, would ya?" he asked. "Or are you gonna get your nice clothes dirty? No, wait. Stand aside. I got it. You look nice. What are you so dressed up for? You're lucky your mother let me come out here."

"Why?"

"She don't wanna let me drive half the time any more. I don't know what it is."

I had heard Mommy and Evie using the word "senile." Well, they've used even worse about me. I couldn't imagine Daddy not driving everywhere and anywhere – to cousin's weddings and magical caverns, stalactites, stalagmites that glow in the dark, Bear Mountain, Chinatown. He's an explorer. Just hand him a map. He'd know how to fold it, too.

"She wouldn't even let me go to my reunion. What do you think of that?"

"What reunion, Dad?" A question asked not out of interest, but quelled terror. This is how I learned what I'd been doing that night with Toph. You owe them; you want their mind off their crowbar.

"Of my men! My men. They wanted me there. Last time, I wanted to go, but we couldn't afford it then. It was around the time of your brother Kaiyetan's funeral, and there wasn't enough money to go around. So they passed the hat, took up a collection, got me a ticket, so I could go. But this time, your mother wouldn't let me go. 'No way,' she said. No way. So I couldn't go. But they called, they called the house. Those men, when they first met me, all they could do was make fun of me, I tell you."

Cars whizzed past, honked, lit us up like lightening, left us in urban, no-man's-land, carbon-blue electric night. "That's right. They made fun of me, cause I talked funny. Couldn't pronounce tee haitch. I was the Polak. You used to make fun of me for that, too. But I tell you, they were all on the phone, last week, Jimmy, we used to call him Jimmy, his name was Gimigliano, private first class. Red-haired Ira Feinberg, quartermaster, Monty – what was his last name? Or maybe that was his last name. No, it was Montgomery. All of them. The ones that are still alive. They apologized. 'Sarge, we gave you a tough time at first, but, God damn it,' that's what they'd say, you know, 'God damn it,' that's what they'd say to me; that's how soldiers talk. 'God damn it, Hudak, You were the best – I don't like to hog the phone . . . I don't like to say stuff like that in front of ladies, but you were the best God damn first sergeant in the Pacific theater . . . ' Now, you gonna make it home on this tire? You want me to follow you to make sure you make it all the way back to Lenappi? It should hold, but I can follow you."

"Thanks, Dad," I said.

"What. Don't be ridiculous. I'm your father," he said.

I drove the car to Martha's, rather than to Paterson. Martha's is just up the county road from Lackawanna Avenue. I couldn't abandon him to the night and the highways, Diary. Daddy followed me all the way up there. He got out as I was parking. "What's going on? What are we doing up here? We're practically to the reservoir."

"Dad, this is the house of the lady the car belongs to. My friend Martha. Like I said."

"You mean this isn't your car?"

"No, Dad, it's not my car. Look, it's okay. It's my friend Martha's car."
I walked over to his car and got in, driver's side.

"What are you doing?" he asked.

"Give me the keys," I said.

He laughed a dry little laugh. "You're getting to be like your mother,"
he said.

"Give me the keys," I said. He did. He got in. I drove us home to
Lackawanna Avenue.

Mommy was standing in the kitchen in her housecoat. "You got your
father out of bed! He's not sharp enough to do stuff like this! Aren't you
eating? You look too skinny. There's ham in the refrigerator. You'd better
not let this happen again!" Then, even louder, sharper. "Mee!" as if
she'd found me out in a crime. I turned. She was staring at my hands.
"It's back!" The eczema. She exhaled a cloud of cigarette smoke, shook
her head. "You'd better get rid of that!" She returned to bed. I squatted
down and stroked Benjie. He merely rolled over a bit, granting me better
access to his belly. "You're getting old, Benj."

I walked into the parlor and began sifting through the straw basketful
of the mail I still get at the Lenappi address. Daddy, as he always does
when I'm doing my mail, hovered, stood in front of me when I tried to
move, fretted about certain pieces. "Better open that one. Looks
important." Even mail intimidates Daddy. Did I learn this, or did I inherit
it? Each white, business-sized envelope might contain the command we
cannot fulfill in spite of hand-to-plow. Then, of course, the sender of
white, business-sized envelopes, the quick and clever, native-born suit-
wearer, equipped with a head capable of three hundred sixty degree
swivels, will eviscerate us. This is what I feel when I go through my mail;
this is what Daddy feels. One reason why I sometimes still call this house
"home" and why men like Toph and I can have sex and never touch.

I tuned Daddy out. It's my best trick. I've practiced it for years. It's
how I learned to live oblivious to facts. If he spoke, I barely responded
with "Uh huh." I dropped my eyes when he stood in front of me and
waited stoically for him to move. I was no longer a needy female on the
highway. I no longer had to feign interest. So, safe, I suddenly confronted
this fact – had it been outlawed? Or had it been just too cognitively
dissonant to entertain?

Ah, now, I cry. Am I breaking the rules? Because I am crying now, am I wallowing in feeling, and again, like a coward, a woman, avoiding, rather than reporting, fact? No. Even feeling has its plot. This feeling's plot transpired in three seconds. Me looking through my mail. Daddy hovering beside me, as he always does. My suddenly realizing that he shadows me, that, on the highway, he rushed into that story about his men, because he is lonely. Contact with me is the only contact he's had with another human being all day, maybe for many days, save Mommy, who works her tongue on him as a hagfish eroding its host. Rasping with insult and bile, she never lets the wound of his disappointing her close. My suddenly realizing that Daddy wants to hear, "Well done, Hudak," before whatever it is that's taking his mind takes his life. That he wants to hear it from me. Me, who has, through the years, perfected ignoring him into extinction when he stands only inches away. Me, who erases every fact of his unique humanity, his height, his handsomeness, his inability to pronounce "tee haitch." Smug, cunning, righteous, I perform this microcosmic genocide. And why not? After all, I am the powerless oppressed; he, the omnipotent oppressor. It's by me he's begging to be seen, pleading to be heard. Me, who when miles away, surrenders to tremors at the mere, inescapable thought.

I lurched into the kitchen, ready to open the refrigerator and pull out as much food as it would take. I had my hand on the door handle. I looked up; Daddy was looking at me.

"Getting a midnight snack?" he asked.

"No," I said, more adamantly than I had planned.

"Don't let me get in your way. Have what you want. It's your house," he said.

"Dad," I said.

"Yeah? What."

"Are you doing anything tomorrow?"

"No. Why? You got something you want me to do?"

"Yeah," I said. "It'll take a couple of hours, and we'll start around nine, okay?"

"What are you gonna do?" he asked, with a little laugh, a little nervous, but game.

"You'll find out. I'm going to bed." I grabbed Benjie and climbed the stairs.

I placed Benjie on the foot of the bed, knowing this was futile. No matter how carefully or insistently I positioned him there, before the night was through, he'd be grafted to my soft, warm butt. I crouched down and burrowed into the crawlspace under the eaves. Tunneled past winter coats in plastic bags and my old Barbie dolls and a full folk costume from Czechoslovakia. Flush in back, there it was, like Tutankhamun's sarcophagus: Kai's old reel to reel. I don't think I'd seen that thing since I was six years old.

I pulled it out, blew off dust, unwound swaddling plastic. Put the plug to the outlet – hesitated – maybe I shouldn't do this. Maybe something has changed with electricity in the past couple decades, and the house will explode. Mentally flogged myself for being such a lame spaz when it comes to anything technical. Plugged it in; grabbed the microphone, switched on "Record." Smiled when I saw the tape go round. "Testing one, two, three, four." Switched it off. Hit rewind. Watched the eager tape spin drunkenly backwards. Hit "play." "Testing one, two, three, four." Felt set. Felt excited. Felt I had done something with the energy that would make it possible for me to sleep.

DEAR DIARY, OKAY, first. The way I transcribe his words. Listening to this tape was fabulous. I would have bought a ticket. I'd had no idea. I'd set out into the backyard with a beach bucket. My toy shovel turned up rubies, unearthed diamonds and emeralds. I wouldn't risk nicking one facet. I would be sure to copy it all down, and to copy it down exact.

My pen hit the page. The reel to reel began announcing its own version of history. I couldn't bring myself to write the things that I was hearing. Daddy talks wrong, Diary. I had never noted this speech that had been surrounding me all my life. Then the tape machine reported it, and I focused on recording it, accurately. My father sounds like a gangster from a Warner Brothers' flick, black and white, grim, about the Depression and immigrants.

My father grew up in the Depression. My father is an immigrant. And I'm trying to understand him in terms of Hollywood films.

I'm doing the best I can! This is all so foreign, so new; I'm so unpracticed. Daddy pronounces "t," "h" as "d." He says "dem" instead of "them." And he uses "them" as an adjective. "I saw dem boys," instead of "I saw those boys." He doesn't pronounce "i," "n," "g." He says, "talkin," "runnin," instead of "talking," "running." He uses present and participle forms instead of the simple past: "I come yesterday." "I seen dis kid."

Daddy kept referring to Uncle Rocky, who's alive now, as Uncle Vwadyswaf, but Uncle Lad – that was his American name – he's not alive anymore. He died during the war. Place names were lost; they became "here" or "there." Nouns were "things" – "tings." "We were advancing on the Philippines, and I had to make sure that my, my," snap, snap, snap; he clicks his fingers, "darn it, the word was on the tip of my tongue. I had to make sure that my thing –"

"Your rifle? Your bayonet? Your helmet?" a woman's voice urges him on.

He claps, percussive, on the tape. "Helmet! That's it. Now, what was I saying? Refresh my memory."

He looks like me, you know. A man, and older, but like me. And he's my father. In charge of the world. To witness his struggle for *words* . . . I watched him, all my life, struggle for work, struggle for money. I watched him struggle for dignity. Words should be the one thing we can have for free. If I transcribed accurately, Daddy's speech would look like a parody. I will not write my father's speech as a parody.

The Miroswava conducting this interview surprises me no less. When Daddy's answers don't satisfy, she presses, polite but determined. She isn't playing the hitchhiker game. She isn't being generous and she isn't afraid. She wants this story, in its every exotic detail.

I decided not to be his victim while conducting this interview. I decided not to look at or question my perpetrator. I decided to surrender the self-serving delusion that I know anything about this man. The primary quality of every human being is that he or she has a story; that story is vast, and we don't know it. The best thing that can happen between two human beings is that they share some of the story. I would give no one detail more or less attention because it had more or less to do with my pain. I wouldn't ask, listen, work this puzzle, because I already knew and

I was gathering justification for my judgment. I wouldn't ask, listen, record, in order that evidence for people to pity, admire, or excuse me would accrue to me. I would ask, listen, care, because I knew nothing, and I was willing to know. I would tease out his story so thoroughly that I could discover its bone structure, the underlying mathematical equation, its own unique beauty, symmetry, and inescapable demands. To do this, I could not look at him with in-spite-of eyes, hear him with if-only-he-were ears.

"Miroswava, I have had a wonderful life. Skunk Hollow was a wonderful place for a kid to grow up. The people there were beautiful, just beautiful. The only thing I wish was different, is . . . It's a shame that your brother Kaiyetan went the way he did. That's the only thing."

The woman on the tape wouldn't have Kaiyetan. She would prod her interviewee to provide facts, not feelings, and in proper order. "Let's start at the beginning. Why did you call it 'Skunk Hollow?' The real name is Carbonburgh."

"Well, the name of the town is Carbonburgh, like you say. The reason it got a Skunk Hollow tag on it was, you understand, the sewer drain emptied out there. Right near your grandmother's house. You remember your grandmother's house? The little thing. You said you couldn't hardly stand up straight. First you had the slag heap, and then the Lithuanian cemetery, and then there was Skunk Hollow. Right there, from the, from the thing. They pumped the water out, and it became a black stream. From the colliery. Then the city put sewers in for the affluent people. For the English, Irish, Scotch, and Welsh. They got the improvements. They made it so that their sewerage come out right by the Lithuanian cemetery, where the Polaks and the Slovaks, the Hungarians and the Lithuanians lived. You see, it was all sections. There was the Brown Road section, cause the roads was made of clay. There was Pig Alley, where an Irishman kept a hundred pigs. There was Smokey Town, with the slag heap, that was always fuming. And because of the rich people's sewerage, there was Skunk Hollow."

She craves antecedents more romantic than this. Fancy people doing fancy things. Perhaps one of her ancestors was a knight, an ulan, or an insurrectionist. "Do you remember anything about life in Poland? Did your parents ever talk to you about what life in Poland was like before you left?"

"Miroswava, you understand, there was nothing. That was why we left! So yous kids could have it better. In Poland, all it was, was grubbing. Grub, grub. There was no really – nothing. And it was getting worse. We were slaves, you know? Slave. Slav. Same word. You could look it up! Where's that dictionary?"

"Dad, please come back here. The tape's running! We can look it up later."

Sheepish, obedient to this interviewer and her recording machine: "All right," he says.

"So? Life in Poland?" prods single-minded Brenda Starr.

"Life? There was no life! That's why we came to America! Slaves for the Russians. Slaves for the Germans. And neither one of them ever went to one day of school."

"Grandma and Grandpa, you mean? They didn't go to school? Hmm. So how did they learn to read and write?"

He laughs. He laughs so hard. "What, are you kidding me? They never learned to read or write, Miroswava. Neither your grandmother nor your grandfather could ever read or write one line."

"No way!"

He laughs.

"How did you travel?"

"On the sneak! And with help. From town to town, by horse and wagon. They'd put like a mattress on there and they'd have the farm goods, cabbage, potatoes, some of that stuff, on top. We didn't have to do that all the way, just enough to get away from the Russians. It's not even in Poland anymore, our village. It's in Russia now."

"Wow."

"Hey! I'm telling you."

"So, you're in this wagon, and you're traveling . . . "

" . . . from town to town. The people would take us in. Enough to get away. We didn't have no papers, so, when we got here, we had to hide sometimes, too. But your grandparents knew how to hide. They learned that in Poland. They learned that from the Russians. Even without school!" and he laughs.

"Dad – are you telling me – wait. Are you telling me you were *wetbacks?*"

"It depends on what you want to call it. 'Wetback' is just a word, right? Hey! Let me tell you. Them people had to be fast; they had to be smart. You had the federal agent coming in the front door, they had to fly out the back window. They did it, and then later, after we were settled in, we had boarders who did it, too. I'm telling you. The English, Irish, Scotch, and Welsh. They wanted us Hunkies to mine the coal, but every now and then, to make themselves happy, they'd round us up. Your grandmother was very good at this. All of them were. They had to be. She could hide twenty men in plain sight. I tell you."

"So, who was this who wanted – what did you call them? Hunkies?"

"The coal companies! They wanted the donkeys. That's what they called us. 'Strong backs.' The men would go down to the town square, and the company man would show up, and he would say, 'Get me a Hunky; I need a donkey.' And so, he – your grandfather – would have work for that day, and we could eat."

"Who were these men? The ones who called you donkeys?"

"Americans! The English, Irish, Scotch, and Welsh. They controlled the town. But we didn't just work the mines. Nobody could survive on what they got from that. We was also moonshiners. If I don't tell you that, I'm not telling you the truth."

"Grandpa? Made *moonshine?*"

"Not your grandfather. Your grand *mother.* Your grandfather would work one or two days, and before you knew it, he was fired. He was always getting into trouble, beating everybody up, drinking. He was not what you would call an obedient man. And he hated the mines. And the mines weren't steady work in them days. We had, what they call, 'over-production.' The men could only find work a couple days a week, if they were lucky. So my *matka chrzestna* – what's that in English?"

"I have no idea."

"What, are you kidding me?"

"Dad, I don't speak Polish!"

"What do you mean?"

Crescendos of defensiveness unreel from the audiotape: his for not teaching her his language, hers, for not speaking it. Finally, to cut this Gordian knot, she takes a wild guess: "Godmother?"

"Yeah, that's it. See? I knew you knew. Finally, my *matka chrzestna*, like you say, my godmother, she figured it out. She got my mother the corn and the sugar, which was illegal, she got her the mash, like oats, you know, and rye . . . and a big kettle. It worked pretty well for a while there, but when the raids – oh, that was terrible. We were the laughingstock, because when the police came, everybody, you know – they let the word out first. They let the word out they're going to go down there and raid the Hunky moonshiners in Skunk Hollow and we were the laughingstock. There must have been like one hundred people out there watching them, the English, Irish, Scotch, and Welsh, how they dumped out our barrels of mash, and axed our stills . . . "

"What was it like in the mines?"

"Nobody in the world should work in a coal mine. There should be no such of a thing as a coal mine."

"What was it like?"

"In them days, it wasn't like it is today. We didn't even have respirators, I tell you that right now."

"What was it like?"

"It's cold. You sweat and the sweat freezes right on you. You go down and down and down. You might as well be going to hell. You're black. You're black like them shoes. You blow your nose and it's black like them shoes. If you're lucky, if you got a friend, you get high coal. Kids like me, we get four foot coal, then three foot coal, then a shaft eighteen inches high, wet all the time. Dripping wet. But that's exactly why they want you, you know? That's exactly why the foreman fingered you that morning, instead of some grown man he sent home. You're a kid, scrawny, and small. You fit in there where a grown man don't.

"You're crawling, on your belly, and it's in that position, you dig. Four foot wasn't bad. You kneel down and can really throw it far. But that makes it tough because now all that weight is hanging on your waist, and you're twisting around, back and forth. And sometimes, the company don't even pay you! They say, 'Wait a minute, we give you twenty ten cars – ' or, they say, 'You didn't clean out the rock.' Or you work with some Irishman, three-handed coal, and he speaks English and you don't. So you don't get paid. What are you gonna do? You start a fight, that's it for you, mister. No work for you next time. They remember, believe me. And there ain't no unemployment. Ain't no disability. No nothing. God never should have made the coal mines.

"That's why, when my father – you know what I'm talking about; when my father – when he died, it wasn't so bad for me. Nobody my age had a father. Some men, Hamrik's dad, they died stealing the coal. They weren't really stealing it; that was just an expression. 'Stealing the coal' means, you work without pillars. There should have been pillars, to hold up the – the thing. But, no pillars, or the pillars were old, and already rotted. They had a big order, they wanted us to work fast. Next thing you know, the thing, you know, you know, the roof, the ceiling, it collapses. Or, with the bootleg mines, the whole thing caves in on the men. A whole crew lost their dads that way. It was awful, digging them men out. Some men, Koormass's father, he fell into a fan. They had these big fans, half as big as our house here, with no screens, nothing between you and the – the blades. The man took one false step, fsht. That was it. His whole body goes in a thousand different directions. Some men, Bolek's father, he died breathing gas. Other men got burned from gas. They died slow, their skin all bubbly, screaming, oh, it was awful. There was the black lung. Emphysema. You see a thirty-year-old man can't get up enough air to make it across the street. Explosions. So loud, those explosions. The whole earth shakes. The windows in the sills. You think they're gonna . . . shatter. Everything. Nobody past that age had a father at home. So, it wasn't so bad for me."

"You said Grandpa was always beating people up."
"Always."
"What was that about?"
"He was a little guy, your grandfather. So Pan Spyt, that louse, the man who bailed us out at Ellis Island; he was the one who paid the bribes. He got us out of there."
"Pan Spyt brought you to Skunk Hollow?"

"That's right. He's the one who brought us to Skunk Hollow. Showed us where the work was, for the Hunkies, like us."

"Okay. Dad, you were about to tell me about Pan Spyt and Grandpa's fighting."

"Oh, that's right. I'm sorry. Anyway, it was him, that guy, Pan Spyt, that louse, who got your grandfather to fight. And your grandfather was a very small man, Miroswava, even smaller than I am, if you can imagine that. But he would not quit until he won, and he always won. So Pan Spyt, that louse, the guy who picked us up at Ellis Island, he spoke English. He would walk up to Johnny Bull and say, he would say, 'See that little Polak over there? He can whip your ass and your friends' asses, too.' And they'd put the money down. And my father would fight. A little guy, smaller than I am here, but he wouldn't – your grandfather would not quit until he won, Miroswava. And he always won. And then Pan Spyt would collect the money, all the money that the men had laid down. I tell you, Miroswava, no matter how big they were, nobody ever came back to fight your grandfather twice."

"Did you say that Grandpa didn't get any of this money?"

"Miroswava, you understand, your grandfather never learned to speak English. And Pan Spyt, that louse, he took us on when we didn't have any papers. So your grandfather owed him. It's too bad he ended up paying with his life."

I'm not ready to transcribe that part.

"Do you want to know about Saint Michael the Protector?" he asks. This business of being interviewed is fun; he's beginning to enjoy it, and to volunteer stories.

"What's that?" she asks.

"When I was in jail. That what's Mrs. Rinsler called it, jail, cause she swore she'd send me to jail. But it was really just reform school."

"You were in reform school?" she's shocked, but a bit titillated.

"Should we not put that in there?" he asks, amused, but polite, eager to abide by the rules.

"What do you think, Dad? It's up to you."

"You know what I think," he says. "What I always told you. Tell the truth. That's what the Bible says, and that's how I always told you. If you don't have that stuff in there, about the still, about how your grandpa died, about your old man's time in jail, you don't have the truth."

"Okay," she says, "Go for it."

"Lad got into some kind of trouble, and this lady – she worked for the county, you know, with delinquents and everything else. Mrs. Rinsler – that was her name – she came to the house to get Lad, but I didn't want her to take him. He was older than me, but he was a scrawny kid; he had – whaddya call it –" the sound of fingers snapping frantically – "consumption."

"Do you mean tuberculosis?"

"That's it. Right."

"But that's a serious disease!"

"Yeah, I know, Miroswava. It's a serious disease."

"Didn't you guys – something –"

"We did what we could."

I think I sat there blinking for a long time. Finally, "Tell me the story of Saint Michael the Protector."

"Mrs. Rinsler came to get your uncle Lad. So I says to her, I says, 'You goddamned bum, you get out of here. You're not touching my brother. Who the hell do you think you are?' My mother and father didn't know what I was saying cause they didn't know anything in English. So, I told her, 'You just try taking him out of here, you just try. I'll bust your head!' So ever since that day, she had it in for me.

"Everybody had fireworks. I asked, 'Where the hell did you get them?' I went and I broke in, me and another guy. I got out. I seen where the police was. I crawled up high where they couldn't see me, but the other guy, he got caught. He turned me in. They took me away. I served a year's time."

"What was it like?"

"It was beautiful. It was a wonderful place for a kid to grow up. The sisters were beautiful. That's the nicest place I ever been. The sisters took care of us," he laughs. "And did they ever! I'll tell you, we used to get what they called 'bendovers.' Bend down, touch your toes, fwt!" The sound of hand striking flesh. "A stick about that thickness."

She gasps.

"Hey! I'm telling you! What Sister Della Reese did I would never wanna see it done again. She dunked a guy's head in! When his nose was bleeding that bad. The guy's name was Sheldon and he was a big guy! Right in a bucket of water! We thought he was gonna drown! She couldn't have been more than four foot eight. We called her 'The Devil.' His nose was bleeding that bad and she dunked his head in there again and again – maybe it was a dozen times she did it. If you ask me, and this may be wrong for me to say, but I think she was just jealous.

"But I'm glad I was there. They treated me like they did in the army. None a this, 'Yeah.' You answered with, 'Yes, sir!' and 'No, ma'am!' You didn't dare smile or blink your eyelashes. Man, you froze. When that nun blew that whistle you better not be the last one there. Sister Cecilia, we called her 'Cowboy,' cause she was bowlegged. She punched me in the nose, got me all bloody. I didn't move. I stood still, arms at my sides, just like this. 'Master Hudak, don't you think it's time you did something with that nose?' 'No, Sister.' 'And why not?' 'Because, Sister, if I do, you'll just punch it in again.' I'm glad that happened to me."

"Glad? It sounds –" She couldn't say "Dickensian;" they had to keep speaking the same language. She couldn't say "like Hell;" she would never swear in front of her father. "It sounds very hard."

"It was beautiful."

"What!"

"Miroswava, c'mon. All of our meals was furnished. And didn't you hear me tell you that they had a *swimming pool?* Can you imagine that? Your old man, from Skunk Hollow, getting a chance to – Hey! Did I tell you that this guy Sheldon made it to *college?* That's right. The sisters sent him to college."

"They sent him to college?" she repeats, astounded. "Why?" Thinking: why him, Dad? Why not you?

"Sheldon was very passive. He would never get in an argument with anybody. If they had dunked me in like that, I woulda fought 'em. And now that I remember, either he did, sexually, but I'm damn sure he didn't start it. She must have started it with him."

"One of the nuns?" she exclaims.

"Hey! I'm tellin ya!" he vows. "Here we were, eight, nine, ten year old boys in St. Michael's, and here was Sheldon, nineteen years old. What do you think was going on?"

"So that sent Sheldon to college. Full scholarship too, I'll bet?"

"Yup. It was a Catholic college, too," he says, meaning: it was the very best.

"Well, I'll be," she responds, laughing. "How about you, Dad? Did you go to regular school at all?"

"Very little."

"Why?"

"I just didn't like it. And, until I had Mrs. Legemza, I never had one of us for a teacher. It was always the English, Irish, Scotch, and Welsh. So, I hookied school."

"Did they give you a hard time?"

"What, are you kidding? They hated us Hunkies. When one of them came drinking to some of our stills in Skunk Hollow – and they did come, even though they wouldn't want you to know it – they're so stuck up! It's ridiculous. The English, Irish, Scotch, and Welsh – they got the stuffings kicked out of them. They knew the English language and they would get away with things with the police. So, we showed them. We kicked the stuffings out of them.

"One day, they were making me diagram sentences. And I said, 'Who are you kidding? You're putting them lines every which way. That's no learning.' If my folks would have had money for college, I would have buckled down. But what was school to me? So they wanted to send me upstairs to Mr. Malcolm. But I says, 'No. I'm not going up there. I know he can't take me, so he'll get his helpers to hold me down while he beats me.' Cause that's how he beat up the Hunky kids, you know? He couldn't take us, otherwise. I was small, but I says to Mr. Malcolm, I says, 'You're tough in here, but you're going to have to go outside, sometime, and then I'll be the toughie. We're Hunkies, and we're small, but we got quick hands. I pick a lot of berries, I pick a lot of coal, I pickax the coal out of the stripping, I pick mushrooms up in the mountains miles and miles from here, and I carry it all home. I can take you. I could kill you, but I won't, but I will take you.'"

"How old were you, Dad?"

"Fifth grade. So Mr. Malcolm says, 'Wha wha wha –' and I says, 'You're the one who brought this up, sir.' And he says, 'This boy is a hellion. Send for his father.' So they brought your grandfather in. So your grandfather comes, he says, 'My son he tell you what I say.' Mr. Malcolm says, 'Why can't you just talk to me yourself? Do you have some kind of a problem? Can't you talk right?' 'No! My son he tell you what I say.'"

Daddy, then, begins to speak as his father speaking in Polish. Daddy didn't speak Polish to me, but translated into English what Grandpa said. Daddy did this in precisely pronounced Standard English. I had to rewind the tape three times to make sure I wasn't hallucinating. And then I realized – he's quoting Grandpa speaking in Polish. So, since Grandpa spoke fluent Polish, Daddy speaks fluent English here. Every "t" "h" sound is enunciated flawlessly.

"'I have worked in your coal mines for many years now. I have beaten up a lot of you son-of-a-bitch, Johnny-Bull bastards. I don't do this because I want to. I do this because I have to. Just to get to work, I have to walk through the English side of town. My boy is not a hellion. My boy is good. If you touch him, and he kills you, it will be your fault. And if he doesn't kill you, I'll come up here and throw you right out of that goddamned window of yours.' So I told Mr. Malcolm that that's what your grandfather had to say."

"So you're telling me that Grandpa beat Grandma?"

"Yeah. And I would have to come between them. I'd break it up, give him a hard talking to. And then, when he was sick, she beat him. So then I'd break it up, give her a hard talking to."

"Oh my God."

"They made up real quick, though. Miroswava, understand, they made up real quick."

"It wasn't any better in America."

"Don't ever say that. It couldn't have been any worse than it was in Poland."

"Everybody was constantly beating everybody else up!"

"Yeah, but, you understand, once I got old enough, and big enough, nobody could take me."

"Oh my God."

"I had to, Miroswava. Your grandparents, they made it clear to me, 'Don't you dare come home crying unless you got the other boy going home crying.' And after the third time that I got a lacing with that barber strap you better believe I sent the other boy home crying. It was a way of life! When the men come over here, they had the same situation. If them English, Irish, Scotch or Welsh saw one of our men alone, they'd attack. So, you had to. You had to teach them a lesson. 'Don't mess with that crazy Polak!'"

"Like I said," says the woman on the tape, "mindless violence. And you lived in a crappy little place called Skunk Hollow!"

"Don't ever say that, Miroswava. You'd be surprised how many people want to go back to Skunk Hollow. Everybody knew everybody else. Everybody helped everybody else. There was no welfare in them days. There didn't have to be. There was a guy, used to steal the apples off of your grandmother's trees. I said, 'Mamma, why don't you stop him?' And she said, 'I see him all the time. He looks so funny to me. It's fun to watch him.' That was the kind of person your grandmother was. She didn't want to make no trouble for nobody. If somebody was so hungry he had to steal her apples, and she was lucky enough to have apples, that was okay.

"We always found a way to work things out. Like, one time, with Mr. Malcolm, I used to deliver papers in them days, too. And fat old Mr. O'Hara, he was over all the teachers, he was one of my customers. So I went to him and I says, 'Mr. O'Hara, I'm sorry. I guess I can't keep bringing you the mushrooms and the berries and the free coal like you like so much, because then Mr. Malcolm will feel that I bribed you.' And fat old Mr. O'Hara, he says, 'Wha, wha, wha?' So I relayed everything. And fat old Mr. O'Hara says, 'Don't you worry, Master Hudak. I'll handle this. I'm sure Mr. Malcolm and I can come to a happy understanding.' Mr. Malcolm never hit another Hunky kid the rest of his life."

"Tell me about your time in the army."

I was anticipating juicy yarns. Squirting blood, exploding guts, hairbreadth escapes, Pacific Islanders ululating in gratitude. Daddy joined the army when he was only sixteen. He used Lad's papers. It was the Depression; Grandpa was dead; somebody had to support the family.

Lad was too feeble, so Daddy went. He had to get used to being called by another man's name.

I wanted the stories behind the luscious black and white snapshots in our family albums. The man in these photos is stunning; he could be a movie star. Time is a nation, too, with borders, capitals, and its representative types; Daddy is one of that era. He's posed under a fedora; he's ridden the rails; he's dancing to "In the Mood;" he's commanding a mongrel squad of Italians, Bohunks and Jews. He looks like a cross between Errol Flynn and Clark Gable, only real. His eyes crease as he squints into the sun; his belly is flat; his abdominal muscles rise clear. He stands, smiling, triumphant, under palms with wide-smiling, bare-breasted natives, next to dead Japanese soldiers, next to pyramids of helmets and bayonets rammed in sand. In one snapshot he rides the same jeep with that General who smoked a corncob pipe – Mac Arthur? The one who would return.

"Dad, tell me about your time in the war."

"I'd rather not go into that."

"Oh, come on."

"That's a long time ago."

"Dad! You guys saved the world –"

"Miroswava, you know how bad it was in the coal mines? War was that bad, and then it was worse. Nobody should have to go to war. There never should have been a war. If you ask me, God should never have invented war."

Close to the end, the woman inquires, "What about Polish culture, anyway? Why didn't you pass it on to us?"

"What, are you kiddin?" he protests, bombastic.

"No, I'm serious," she replies, daintily insistent.

"Miroswava, there's no such of a thing as Polish culture."

"Don't tell me that –" she rises, ready to duel.

"How can you beat American culture?" he asks. "We really had no culture. The Polaks, the Slovaks, the Hungarians, the Lithuanians. All the schools, you understand, was based around the English, Irish, Scotch, and Welsh."

"It's not just school!" she shouts. "You're wrong," she says. "Look, Dad, culture is not just fancy people doing fancy things," she corrects and instructs the misguided old man. "Why haven't you told us any of these stories before? Why didn't you ever speak Polish to us? Teach us Polish? I don't know how to find these mushrooms you find –"

"But I did. Don't you remember?"

"You never did."

"Think about it," he urges.

"Believe me, I have," she insists. I gasp at her audacity and ponder his forbearance. This is the kind of comment that would normally earn her a slap.

"You don't remember, Miroswava. Don't you remember? I used to say to you, '*Chodz tu, Mirechka moja.*'"

"What? What did you just call me?"

"Sure. And you used to call me '*Tatoosh.*'"

"I never called you '*Tatoosh.*' Did you really call me 'Mirechka'?"

"But your mother told me to knock it off."

Her mind is racing. "It's – it's not that," she blurts out. "It's just that she wanted what's best for us. For us to be American."

"Of course," he pronounces. "That's what I was saying. Your mother wanted the best for yous. For yous to be American. So – no more 'Mirechka.' No more '*Tatoosh.*'"

About a year ago, Mr. Wrobel was getting tired of being a drunk. He taped up the doorway in his kitchen. He turned on the gas and stuck his head in the oven.

Daddy hardly ever talks to anyone any more. He mostly just vegetates in that recliner, watching sports on TV, reading his paper, and going for long, solitary walks. But Daddy got a feeling. He crossed the street to the Wrobel house. In Lenappi no one locks his door, even while taping it up for a suicide try. Daddy walked in right before it was all over. That night, his shirt wet with another man's tears, Daddy had Mr. Wrobel in an AA meeting. No one ever mentions it; no one ever has. But you can tell by how she acts around him that Daddy is Mrs. Wrobel's personal Nobel Peace Prize laureate.

Growing up, we tried to make sense of the Daddy who saved derelicts' lives by shoveling them into AA, the Daddy who drove us around to see Christmas lights with such patience, eagerness and joy, the Daddy we were pee-in-our-pants terrified of.

In Evie's analysis it was primarily a problem of fashion. The very day that white lipstick came in, it was on Evie's lips. It didn't survive there a nanosecond longer than it did on the covers of the elite, trend-setting magazines. Mommy bought her a Singer and Evie clocked sweatshop hours sewing with a hand-to-plow determination. Everything on her back was one step ahead of the catwalk models. Anyone in Lenappi will tell you so.

For Kaitek, our problem was that we had been snookered by papism. If Mommy and Daddy had just not been raised Catholic; if they had only not sent us to Catholic school . . . "Our natural development was severely warped!" Kai urgently confided to me one night while we chauffeured home a pizza. Wool uniforms, starched white shirts, punished movement. "And worship of the Blessed Virgin Mary! Get real. Any anthropologist will tell you what's going on there. That's a female deity! That's what that is." Kai had just completed his first semester of college. "Female! A female God! Think about it. Do you realize, in that fat little head of yours, that that's the kind of perversity they're ramming down your throat? I mean – what is that supposed to do to the libido, to the ego, of a growing boy? Look. I've worked out a scheme that's gonna get me out of here. Don't tell Mommy this, or Daddy, either, but I have figured out a way out. I don't know, Mee, if you're ever gonna see me again, so I want you to listen up now. You still seem brain dead, but someday, you'll remember. So I'm telling you."

For me? Food. Fat. Better nutrition. One year I got Daddy a canister of brewers' yeast for Christmas. Alternately, the solution was to be found in self-help manuals. One year I got Mommy a copy of *I'm Okay; You're Okay.* She returned it to me, at high velocity.

Both Evie and Kai used to work summers at the Club. They saw how the rich men whose bags Daddy carried treated him, and how Daddy took it. They'd come home emotionally all bruised up; Evie cried one night. She was never the same to Daddy after that. It was as if Daddy were something unclean and she were wearing all white. And it was, of course, his freshman year of high school, his first summer of work at the Club, that Kai broke into that house. Kai didn't steal a single thing; he just tore the place up, pissed on it. Neither the cops nor the *Suburban Trends* had any explanation for that. Kai had been in there for an entire afternoon; he was landing himself in jail, anyway. Why not pocket some of the abundant crystal or gold surrounding him, and then slip away, anonymously, rather than grinding things into the carpeting, flinging things off of the dock, making great, big splashes and then deep sucking sounds? My response to Kai's and Evie's almost pre-verbal agony was simply to vow never to work at the Club. And, for a while there, setting some small, discrete fires. The way that the rich men treated Daddy, and how Daddy took it, was never factored in to any of our analyses. It festered in our guts, without being worked out in our brains.

I have a college degree. I've spent thousands of hours watching PBS and listening to NPR. I was in grade school during the sixties. We read books about oppressed minorities in inner cities. I was trained by the Peace Corps. I know how to sell Green Revolution rice strains to maharajas. Nothing, nobody, has ever suggested to me that I might want to examine my assumption that my grandparents were literate suburbanites who could stroll hometown America without fear of molestation at the hands of their fellow citizens. After all, Daddy is a straight, white male, and political correctness insists that straight, white males are the omnipotent, universal oppressors. This is not my country, and it won't be, until it tells my story.

I'm pausing again. I'm writing around it. I'm trying to convey feeling without the essential and unspeakable facts.

Diary, I can't tell you the story of how Grandpa died. And how Daddy saw all of it. And that he was just a little boy. And that, with his little body, he tried to stop it. And that he failed. That's part of why I went so long without writing.

Am I discovering a new level of anomie in myself? I think my diary is American in a way that I am not, and that I must thus hide from my diary facts it could never feel as I feel them. I must explain these facts to you, without letting you know what they are. I must spell it out to you, while hiding the letters. Because, with the facts, you'd never understand.

"Insane," "crazy," "mad," "deranged," "lunatic," "berserk," "amok," "hysteric," "nuts:" all these words, rooted in a variety of tongues, have the same etymology: "This life expresses a truth I refuse to confront."

Daddy is not an American. Had he been, his story would have changed. At some point, in Saint Michael's, in the Army, in AA, eventually, someone would have said, "You have value. It is wrong that every time you have turned around, someone has beaten you or someone you love. It's got to stop before you pass it on." There would have been a Declaration of Independence, an Emancipation Proclamation, a nineteenth amendment, a stick in the spokes of the wheel. Daddy would not be nuts; he would fit into the master fiction that is America. He would not have spent his life acting out on me and on himself truths neither I nor anyone I know has ever wanted to confront.

As I was getting out of the car, after Daddy drove me to Paterson – so that I could transport the reel to reel comfortably – he said, "Come by more often. I may not be *edge jay kay ted* but I miss my children."

My heart cracked. I could feel the cool trickle of my heart's fluids spill out into my central body cavity, washing over vital organs, which had no use for these chilling liquids, and no method for mopping them up.

Quickly, so quickly it was almost after I opened the Mill Street door, almost after I ran up the stairs to my apartment, I leaned over in the front seat and kissed Daddy good-bye.

I did do what I could do, Diary. I did do what I could.

"You should talk to someone about this," prescribes the woman on the tape, in the voice of a case study's heroic, compassionate psychiatrist.

"About what?" asks the man. He genuinely doesn't know.

"About all of it. Everything. About Grandpa. Don't tell me that that doesn't hurt you. It does. Find somebody. Talk about it." Aha. It is more than academic to her. She has let the pain invade. Her voice is urgent.

"Why?" he asks, open, but still unclear on the concept.

"To relieve your heart," says the woman on the tape, with a simplicity that takes my breath away. She has something of those festival poets on their stage. That sentence had never occurred to her before; it was not vetted or pruned before it was spoken. She says it with no speed, but pronounces it with all the full weight of its conviction.

"Miroswava, the hurt is gone, but, you understand – what – what I – the wish is still there. The hurt is – Oh, let's see. It was after, I guess, it was after I joined the Army in Lad's name when I was sixteen and I had a different – I had grown up. It was in the Army, you know, you gotta grow up. Or else. And I grew up and I thank God for that because it helped me during war time."

Okay. He has at least mentioned his hurt, even if he can't build a noun-verb-noun sentence with it. He fails to mention his offspring's inescapable inheritance, his rage. "Dad, they hurt you. You were always getting attacked, physically attacked. The nuns at St. Michael the Protector –"

"Miroswava, no" this is the voice that closes doors, that ends things, that frightens. She resolves not to challenge him again. "You understand, they taught me my place. It's a very important thing, knowing your place in this world. That's why I taught you. Didn't I always teach yous kids that? How to say 'Yes, sir' and 'No, ma'am.' I taught yous that, didn't I? That's right. I took the time to teach yous that. I remember we usta practice, around the kitchen table at night. I figured if I didn't have the – the time, to teach yous kids anything else, I was gonna teach yous that. 'Yes, sir.' 'No, ma'am.' Cause if I hadn't learned my place, Miroswava, I wouldda ended up just like your grandfather, and you wouldn't even be here."

She has no argument. Perhaps there is none. "Well, I gave you some good advice. If you don't wanna take it, it's not my fault," she says, after consulting her inner lawyer.

"Well, what do you want me to do, Miroswava?" it's the pleading in his voice that gets me.

And the certainty in mine: "Find someone. Find some wise, compassionate person that you can relieve your heart to, so you don't have to carry it around."

"Hey. I told *you*," he says.

"Yeah, but I'm your *child*," I insist.

"Miroswava, if I have to go out of my house, to get any satisfaction, I don't wanna tell anybody. It's a family matter." There is a long, mumbled pause on the tape. And then the man speaks again: "Huh? You don't think so? You mean you would tell just *anybody*?" he voices the gentle disbelief of a little boy encountering something forbidden, the inconceivable, mentioned as if possible, as if everyday.

"Wait a minute. I don't want to record this," I say. The next sound is the abrupt *clack* of "record" pressed off.

D EAR DIARY, YEAH, I know, I been a b a a a a a d girl and I haven't written in a l o o o o o ong time, but . . .

I can run one mile.

I ran one mile yesterday.

I ran one mile the day before yesterday.

I ran one mile the day before the day before yesterday.

I will run one mile today.

It's baby talk, okay. I'm a baby handling wonder: I ran one mile!

I – I – I – I – I went to the track. I – I didn't think about it. I just told myself, "I'll run a couple of yards, and then I'll stop. I'll do that a few times, and then I'll quit." But I didn't stop. I didn't quit. I didn't quit! I didn't have to!!! No hurt, no side stitch, no panting pulled me down to ground. *I* ran *one mile*!

No words. Just dawn, crisp air, atomized light exactly as I'd always imagined it. Just me. Just my legs. I just start. And then, I just keep doing it. A little part of me waits to drop. When I don't drop, amazement floods me. I run one mile. My God! I experience runner's high! I don't want to stop! I don't stop! I run one mile and a quarter! I can't believe I've been living my life without this! I want to do it again, and then I want to do it again, and then I want to do it again.

I ventured into the women's locker room. A jock smiled at me. I was thinking too hard to reciprocate. "Is she a lesbian? Will I be sending the wrong message if I smile back?" The ones who have smiled at me seem really nice. They haven't quizzed me about sports stars to authenticate me as a member of their tribe, and not some enemy plant among them on an espionage mission.

Now I don't even think about it. I strip. Naked, I stand and move publicly. Rather than feeling clothing insulate my body, I feel the room itself sheath me. The locker room encases me more distantly than clothing does; it is metallic, the rows of lockers; and cool, the tile floor; and Spartan, the wooden benches. I take a public shower. I do this in a facility lacking shower curtains. In four years of high school gym class, I never took a public shower. I weigh less now than I did in ninth grade. I take public showers, long, leisurely, servicing all the right spots.

I can't wait to run. I leapfrog over activities scheduled before it. Thoughts of the pleasures those activities promise, the needs they fill, evaporate when I anticipate hitting the track. When I'm doing chores I should, and they get to boring me, during moments I used to think, "Let's bag this and eat," I now think, "Let's bag this and run."

As I circle the track and encounter my shadow in its own orbit: to my right, long before me, to my left, gone, as if I were a gnomon and the track a sundial, I know. I know that this is it. This is the very substance I sacrificed when I banished food. I know I have it now and I feel full and fearless.

As I shed clothing in the locker room, I tear off others' condemnation of my body. I inhabit that body, like meek Clark Kent changing into his power-bestowing Superman cape. As heel strikes dirt track, I escape Their shackling underestimations. I focus on my body and my untrammeled enjoyment of it. "**Trammel** n. 1. A shackle used to teach a horse to amble." I cast that shackle off, I escape class, I am nobody's horse, I do not amble, but I run, and it feels so untrammeled good. It's hypnotic; dreams are released.

DEAR DIARY, I'VE been touching myself. People who catch me at it must think I have some kind of perversion. I'm too focused to apologize, explain, or even to stop. I find my fingertips stroking each rib and the spaces between, as if combing. I seize my thighs, try to grip to bone. I slide my hand along my jaw and tilt my palm back and forth to test the angles and the planes. I, while climbing hills, massage my gluteus maximus, the alternation of bundled explosion and taut, stretched reach that propels me up. I wake in the night and find my hands inspecting an intruder's ass, hard, smooth, and start – just who exactly are *you* entangled in my sheets? Only when I'm fully awake do I realize – it's *me*. Like some savage mother getting acquainted with her own offspring – she sniffs, she licks, she nudges to settle possession – I, clumsily, establish some relationship and history of us together.

DEAR DIARY, REBEKAH called. "We've been worrying about you. We haven't seen you in a while."

"No," I replied. "I guess you haven't."

"Just wanted to check in . . . make sure everything is okay . . . " Rebekah said, open-ended.

I didn't want to be recruited into providing her end for her. "I can understand that," I said.

"Sometimes the first meetings are really hard on a gal. You meet women who really understand what you're talking about. It's like going through the early experiences all over again."

"Yeah, it is," I agreed.

"So, what's up with you?" she finally demanded.

"I really liked the incest survivors' meetings I made it to," I said. "And I liked you all. I really did. You especially. But you know, you are in Montclair, and I don't have a car."

"I'm worried that you might be in denial," said Rebekah. "You can always take a bus."

How do people come up with these fantasies? "No, I *can't* always take a bus, Rebekah. There is no bus between here and that meeting. The suburbs don't want to make it easy for us Patersonistas to infiltrate."

"One of us could drive you," she suggested.

"Maybe," I said. "But that sounds like more of a hassle than it's worth. You have to go begging, and people never show up."

"These issues are very important," she insisted.

"I don't doubt it, Rebekah," I agreed, "and I really appreciate your concern. I do. If the meetings were here in Paterson, maybe I'd still be going, or maybe not. I don't know."

"How are you with the incest now?" she prodded.

"Whatever it was, it's in the past," I replied.

"Well, of course," Rebekah said, at the end of her patience. "Of course it's in the past. But that doesn't make it any less real, or any less vital that you –"

"I know, I know," I agreed. "Rebekah, listen. My parents have a story, too. Quite a story. They were on the frontlines in three of the big traumas of this century: immigration, the Depression, World War Two –"

"That doesn't give them the right –"

"I wasn't saying that. In fact, I never said that. But Rebekah, there's a position between excusing people and condemning them, and that is knowing their story. Right now, at this minute, and this feeling changes, I am very not interested in judging my parents. I'm not interested in blaming them. I'm not interested in punishing them, or even in thinking about them. What they did to me is in the past. What they did to me is *their* karma. It's not my karma, and I can't do anything about it. It's *my reaction* that's mine, and that's happening now, and that I *can* do something about. So, if you want to know what I'm doing, that's what I'm doing, Rebekah. I'm consciously dealing with my reaction. And, for this moment, consciously dealing with my reaction doesn't include schlepping to Montclair to whine about what happened to me in the past and how sad I am about it all."

DEAR DIARY, LAST week, without instructing myself to do so, I began calculating how much change the supermarket checkout clerk owes me. Then I started counting my change. Calculating change I am owed, feeling that I am owed change, were, in the old dispensation, impossibly arrogant and taboo. The checkout clerk was one of the Gods of money. Revealing that I could add, and, what's more, subtract, invited superior powers to smite me. But I *can* add. I *can* subtract. I can demand what's coming to me. I can feel that something *is* coming to me. And money doesn't belong only to Them.

Calculating change, the first time I did it, felt good. It felt like riding a stallion naked through a pink and blue sunset.

I guess. I can't say for sure. I've never ridden a stallion even with clothes on. Me or the stallion.

DEAR DIARY, SOMETIMES, now, I pause and envision the grain I'm about to internalize sun-saturated, gilding a distant Dakota; squinting farmers fold it under and in with combines and skill. In my mind's eye I accompany blind carrots tunneling into dark loam; peaches dangle, ripe and heavy, the wind slightly slowed by their clinging fuzz. I'm saluting the food, thanking it for coming, meditating on its incorporation it into my physical rivers and plains and factories.

D EAR DIARY, A fat woman entered the Writing Center. Fat women are often difficult. Fat women are often not that way with each other. There's the unspoken camaraderie: "It's okay; you're one of us. We're in this together." That's understood. But the fat woman who came into the Center today didn't react that way to me.

She stormed in, lips pursed, fists cresting hips, vinegar-voiced. It was clear that she was invading enemy territory with every step and that I was to deny her every request. She bristled like a one-woman phalanx, ready to fight and win every last shred of righteously wrenched tribute she had coming to her.

I merely stood up from my chair. I didn't do or say anything else. I just waited for her to see, to realize: "Comrade! *Tovarich*! *Compañera*!" It never happened. She just kept treating me like one of Them.

Later on Monique was in. She demanded all the statistics. "Well, I have been noticing all this while of course, but, you never brought it up, so I didn't either. Now, and especially in that cinch skirt, it really flatters your waist. Where did you find it? Exactly how many pounds is it now? What plan are you following? Could it be the pineapple diet?"

"I have a tapeworm," I was ready to blurt. Then I bit my tongue. This is the kind of person I was doing this to impress. "Oh, I just haven't had time to eat, lately . . . " I mumbled.

Monique earnestly whispered to me the details of her anorexia. Before she left, she invited me to a social evening with herself and her banker boyfriend. Well that cinches it better, even, than my skirt. I don't have to bond with fat brunettes like Rebekah about the misery and torment of being an incest survivor. I can bond with bug-thin Monique about the misery and torment of maintaining a socially acceptable feminine figure.

As Monique was confiding in me, Martha was staring from a distant table. I went over to her after Monique left. "What's up with you, Martha?"

"Do you know how long I've been working the SSNoS programs?" Martha hissed. "Do you know that that curriculum packet you guys use, *I* put together? They never so much as put my name on it."

"Okay. You were just staring while Monique was talking to me –"

"Why you? Why is she so friendly to you? I've been here way longer than you. She treats me like a peon."

"I thought that you had said that –"

Martha got up and left, then.

But I do not desire Monique's confidences. Her thinness and blond hair are not valuable to me. I can't imagine loving a woman who wears silk all day and never gets a sweat stain. What I want from Monique is I want to know: "What goes on in your armpits, honey?" She could be a circus geek. What I want from Monique is I want to know: "Isn't it kinda weird, that the only way a woman can get to the top of the food chain, is by refusing to eat?"

I want to call that fat woman back.

DEAR DIARY, I don't know. I don't know. I don't know. Everything is new. "What time is it?" "Are you hungry?" "Do you want something to eat?" "Have you ever been in love?" "Have you ever been loved?" "Do you want to get married?" "Do you feel okay?" "Is anything wrong?" "Are you happy?" "Are you working?" "Have you ever had serious disease?" "What do you do?" "What are your plans?" "Do you want children?" "What makes you sad?" I pause, as if to consider the biographical data of a research subject. In this pause I hearken to the sudden, new answers that surprise and challenge me no less than they startle my questioner.

I flush with a warm gratitude for the familiar. I look up to the center, top, back of the classroom, and spy the industrial clock fixed into the cinder block wall, and pray, "Thank you for being there, as you have been in almost every American classroom in which I've taught or learned." Van Ness, the farm-stand across from Martha's house on the county road; they got their first red peppers in yesterday, same time as last year, and the year before. "WE BUY RAW FUR." That hand-lettered sign still swings from its rusted iron bar in the dirt lot. It's been there at least since Kai stretched gutted muskrat, squirrel and deer in our Lenappi cellar, and made music money selling skins to the Van Ness clan. Yesterday the temperature dropped to fifty, and I encountered only one mosquito in four hours of hiking. That night was the first night the heat kicked on, the first time I've worn pajamas in months. Thank you, Earth, for not accelerating or reversing our course. Benjie still paws out the steps of the primal doggie dance when he hears the word, "walk." Kids still watch Saturday morning cartoons. My eyes are still blue. Thank you, thank you, thank you. Constants I fix on as the rest spins.

I couldn't ride a bike. It was concluded that I was a natural spastic dry of the inner ear fluid that suspends hominids perpendicular to earth. But I kept trying. Every time I straddled one of my siblings' bicycles counsel pelted me. Daddy: "Keep your eye on one fixed point dead ahead of you!" Kai: "Stop being so afraid of falling!" Evie: "Be sure to push hard the minute you're on, and, after that, don't think!" Mommy: "You'll never do it! You're a schlump like me! We didn't have wheels in the Old Country. You don't need them here!"

I failed. I failed at all of these tasks. I just couldn't do it. I couldn't ride a bike. I steered the bike toward the jumble of words and tumbled, over and over. I resigned myself to being much less, more random, than others. I could feel urges and hints of what I was supposed to be, targeted, mobile, I could feel my body as shreds of actions it was expected to perform. These teasing sensations were brutally futile. I was a puzzle that would never come together.

And then one day Evie released her grip on the seat. The winds of the earth or fate were right. I pushed off down Lackawanna Avenue, and, oh, the magnificence of this! I was progressing like an arrow in flight on two hard, black narrow wheels and my own sudden, dominant, balance. "Ah. So, *this*. So different from what I'd thought." I realized that I was being ravished by, participating in, action. My action, nobody else's. New action, true because now. Action, not words. Action clean of inherited instruction. I struggled to summon the lessons, frantically tried to bandage my action with scripture. This would insure that I was keeping my eyes on a fixed point in front of me here, stopping being afraid of falling now, pushing hard, not thinking ever. This phylactery would comfort, would insure that this action done so effortlessly and joyfully was indeed what many had banged their jaws together about, and that I was doing it right. But no matter how I tried as I pedaled, I could not coordinate movements with words. It was happening. That was all. I let go. And the talking and the doing separated as permanently as the body and the soul at death.

When did it happen? What did I do? Was it the healthy breakfasts that made interviewing Daddy possible? Was it taking vitamins that enabled running one mile? I didn't have either on my agenda. Did I do it or did it do itself? What, if I stopped doing it, would change things back to how they were before? What happened to my old self? Is she out there shucked off in the Pine Barrens somewhere, like that snakeskin Sparky found? How should I feel about it? Is ritual called for? And, if it should come up, how does one appease this dead?

DEAR DIARY, I was walking through Paterson. I was approaching the crew stationed on stoops, milk cartons, and overturned garbage cans. I pass them, in front of the same burned-out building, every morning, and, again, every evening. What these men do is, they converse. They converse constantly, warmly, rhythmically. It's as if they're reciting a very long poem. They break off as my retreating ankle is pulling out of their circle of sidewalk turf, to say, low, mellow, "Hey, lady, good mornin'. What pretty legs you got." Or "skin" or "barrette" or whatever. Suddenly, today, just today, it occurred to me: these men are derelicts. The broken glass on these sidewalks they place here, after downing bottle after bottle of fortified wine.

Now, before today, all I'd ever thought about when confronted with the sight of them up ahead was their maleness and my fatness and my femaleness. Would I be able to carry myself in such a way that they wouldn't know that I was born to be hurt, and hurt me? When I was able to, day after day, pass these men without acquiring visible bruises, I breathed a sigh of relief: I've fooled the ones in power once again. It never occurred to me that I have any right on the sidewalk, or that these men are bums whom most women would simply dismiss. Or would most women? When walking past any group of men, do all women in some way acknowledge we're tiptoeing on a trap door before implacable judges demanding deference?

This felt like some kind of final Promethean awareness that transubstantiates all. It always does. When I saw myself counting money, I thought, "Okay, that's it, I've got it, I've got fire." And also with running and then with entering the locker room. But on all those days I was still cowering like a refugee in front of sidewalk drunks. What am I doing, right now, brave, new, proud me who runs, publicly bathes, counts supermarket change and doesn't cower before sidewalk drunks, that, when the next awareness hits, will shame me into an eagerness to disown some past morsel of self?

D EAR DIARY, I want. I do. I want.
What do I want?

I discover a shadow up ahead, a suggestion, a line drawing. She's doing things I want to do. She's being someone I want to be. She's not Nancy Drew or Evie or Mel or Konrad's wife or anyone else I feel obligated to try to be but would hate being. She's not anyone who could never be me. Forced to affix a nametag to this phantom, I blurt out, "She's me, but a future me, after I lose weight. After I stop doing everything wrong and learn to do everything right. After I'm finally ready." But that knee-jerk blurtation knocks my internal plumb line dizzy. Only the gravity of truth tautens that jigging string: this future me is all of me, but – *and* – loved.

This phantom I imagine as inhabiting my future is performing acts so taboo not only can I not name them, I can't even focus on them. But, apparently, I want them. Dumb, eyes averted, sneaking the occasional glimpse, I inch forward. Movement forward is an act of faith. This faith has been heated and cooled so many times it has been purified. Alloys like reasonable hope, training, encouragement, or allies, have been driven off. Thus this faith is tempered to defiance. Perhaps if I finger through enough rubble I will eventually lay hand on the brush that can flesh out, with color and dimension, the alluring silhouette up ahead of me. Perhaps if I hang out with those who seem to know I will be instructed in the route to and animation of her poses. Perhaps if I keep opening my mouth I will eventually voice the aria or screed or choral text that can grant aural substance and definition to that siren's echo. Or perhaps I will end like one of those babies developmental psychologists study – the babies who crawl off tables because they don't yet get the concept of "edge."

Another discovery: right now, in this very journey toward my future self, I do have something of a companion. I do have something of a guide to consult. She's like poet Donne's fixed compass foot. After I stray too far, she leans and hearkens and draws me home. Yes, in this she is a stereotypical female: she is the homebody. She does keep those home fires burning, burning so bright that home is a lighthouse. But I must say, how she defines "stray" and how she defines "home" turn me inside out. I want to remain safe and silent and she commands, "Stop straying. Speak up. Home, for you, is reporting, out loud and in public, what you see." I want to quit and she urges, "Stop straying. Keep trying. Home for you is further than this soft couch and more exotic than this TV show; your home deserves more mindful work than easy answers." My companion, my guide, my fixed foot whose firmness renders my running compass' circle just, is the little girl.

Like all oracles, though, her pronouncements can be as Delphic as any newspaper horoscope. I puzzle over their proper application. Is my sudden swerve toward the pink, fluffy, and floral, an itch I scratch at risk to my true self? Previously I had anything good to say only about Shaker design. Severe, ladder-backed wooden chairs evidenced that the craftsman's hand never wavered into frivolity and waste. Within the past week I've veered from hankering to live in a barn to lusting to dance at Versailles. I am a pair of laughing eyes behind a flirting fan. I daydream my new body decked out in raiment so rich with embroidery and lace its stitching would blind three needleworkers. While touring the Versailles palace years ago, in Vibram rubber lug boots, I strode rapidly through the Hall of Mirrors and made faces at the guards. I refused to enjoy any of it in memoriam of all the peoples whose oppression made such decadence possible.

What do I want?

This much is clear: I want to yell when I dance. I want little morning-after bruises scattered up and down my wrist. I woke up very hoarse after dancing with Toph. I couldn't figure out why. I mentioned this to him – maybe it was a cold coming on? "You give off these – I'm not sure what to call it. Loud cries? – when you dance, Mira," he said, assuming his Dr. Freudian air. He pulled my hand by its fingertips toward his chest and pointed out the little bruises that had so mystified me. "Those bracelets you were wearing." Aha. The brass and ivory bracelets I had bought in Ladakh so long ago and have not worn till now. So. I want to do that some more – to rattle bracelets with enthusiasm, to yell and to dance.

I want *The Sunday New York Times* and another paper that has the decency and the common sense to print comic strips.

Long exhale. How to enumerate this next want? I went to a garden store, for the first time in my life. I bought some dirt. I really never thought I'd ever be able to bring myself to pay good money for dirt. I bought a packet of seeds. I really never thought I'd ever be so corny as to buy a packet of seeds. Today Martha gave me a plastic greenhouse she found in her cellar. Full of dirt and seeds, the greenhouse now rests in my windowsill.

I want to do seasons. I want to pull them off, like very complex and demanding, foreign-language verb forms. I want to penetrate them. Ever since this experiment began I've been religious about not missing foods at their peaks. In summer I pounced on the cherries, then, the peaches. Now I'm eating red peppers, and eggplant. I want to curl up in the short round curve of the year, like a conch in her shell. I want to stretch out like a cheetah, fully extended, in long days, letting heat shoot through my open spaces.

I want a dog. Dogs, really. There's the hardy one, a Rhodesian ridgeback, say, for woods hikes, his sleek pelt and high step immune to hooked chestnut, sticky tick trefoils, and that vicious vine well dubbed "doghobble," "devil's shoestrings," or "trip-toe." And then there's one for cuddling, a demanding imperious lapdog, maybe a peekapoo like Benjie, or a Lhasa apso.

"I want a dog" is the four-syllable version of a confession much more complex, as is "I want seasons." Both are admissions of my eagerness to retire my identity as a traveler, and to go home; and to retire my identity as an addict, and to enter time. Dogs need home. Seasons need time. These are related. The substance of the seasons is time's action on home. Time is created when change is noted from home. Time, change, and home are impossible to the addict and to the traveler. The addict's brick wall of terror forfends, absolutely, the unexpected. To the addict, change is impossible. To the homeless traveler, change is understood as the product of a choice to board a vehicle and travel from winter to summer, from night to day, from this century to a medieval village high in the Himalaya. To the traveler, change is an infinitely modular block on an itinerary.

When change is understood as the product of time, not a traveler's choices, when change is treated as blessed, not as the addict sees it, as catastrophic, narrative can result. Both the traveler and the addict lack narrative. Neither yesterday nor tomorrow would fit in the traveler's backpack. She is bereft of time. The traveler passes children and the old, the successful and the victim, and all these phenomena appear as static tableaux, or revolving dioramas. The traveler does not witness the rise of the successful man. She cannot follow the tragic decline of the cancer victim from vigorous youth to bedridden shell. The tableaux merely shuffle, because the bus has moved from site to site to site. The addict also lacks narrative. Change is terrifying and is not allowed. The only movement possible is that from fix to fix to fix. For both the addict and the traveler, for example, no one ever has children, children just are, and they stay children, in the same way that blue remains blue. Narrative cannot happen.

Travel's packaging of flow into static tableaux explains why, though I like travelogues well enough, they don't compel me as novels do. A novel unreels an integral strand of narrative that I must follow to its inevitable climax, to the end of its time. Travelogues are episodic, choppy; I can close a travelogue and put it down at any point without being deviled by that spur to take it up again. Addiction is similar. I can visit an AA meeting and hear the same addiction plot hitting its same brick wall of insistence on the impossibility of change. Unlike a flowing narrative, addiction reduces life to static and predictable ritual, infinitely repeated.

Just as the traveler sees no change, she is similarly inert to everyone she meets. Each witness to the traveler, each set of eyes who glimpse her, is seeing her for the first and the last time. She is always a snapshot on holiday. If the traveler is laughing, she has never been sad. If she is old, she was never young. She never had a special brother who died. She has no narrative. She is a face behind a bus window, shielded by her transit from the investment that narrative demands. Locals overcharge; morality invented for stationary neighbors doesn't apply to moving targets. As if she were an episode in a travelogue, men bed her, women love her, but feel no compulsion to take her up again after putting her down at any random point.

This casual exploitation of the homeless traveler by locals more rooted demonstrates one powerful misunderstanding of the word "transit." Transit is misunderstood as complete freedom of movement. In fact transit is a drastically reduced realm of movement. Like a line, transit has "one degree of freedom;" that is, like a line, transit occupies one dimension only, from A to B, the Main Drag in and out of town. The addict is similarly misunderstood. Her abandon is read as completely free indulgence of will. In fact, though, her freedom is limited to traversing a tether to and from her drug of choice. I've seized and exercised the freedom of the traveler, the abandon of addiction. I want to test the freedom of home, and from that point to demand commitment.

I crave, with all the fervor of a bodice-ripper heroine craving man enough, a location that compels me to naming it "home." I hunger to be met, engaged, accepted and pinned by position. I yearn for a stance from which sunsets and sunrises, moonsets and moonrises are calibrated against notched hill or neighbor's roof, against dolmen, menhir, or power line. I long for a situation that demands the kind of rooted alertness that gave us the potential for astronomy, forgiveness, memory, healing, narrative, all these gifts and substance of time. "Give me where to stand, and I will move the world," said Archimedes, one who understood that change requires home and time, that to move, one must stand still – in the right posture. I fantasize a spot with a name, that one can give one's name to, and, just, practice the verb, "to season," the discipline, "to stay," the changes possible as one times.

Mommy was born in a country whose national anthem was titled "Where Is My Home?" That country no longer exists. Daddy's national anthem, in a non-existent country, was, "Poland Is Not Yet Lost." But Poland is lost to my father's village, which was cast outside the borders of its long-imagined home, into geopolitical no man's land. My parents were migrants who, according to two folk songs they knew by heart, went *"za vodo," "za chlebem,"* across the water for bread. I think these homeless people imagined home as retreat, as protection. I am a traveler, and, when it comes to home, perforce, I take others' word. But I know that there is no environment more protective of retreat into internal turmoil than a bus depot, or an airport, or a pier, or a highway, or exile. Exactly because home nurtures it challenges. Or so I would imagine.

I want. I want to have a job where I am allowed to do what I can do. I want people who can, and who do. I don't want: "I can't do this; I've never heard of it;" "I can't do this; I don't understand;" "I can't do this; I have a meeting on how to save the world in half an hour;" "I can't do this; I don't deserve it;" "I can't do this; my people have never done it;" "I can't do this; others will laugh," "I can't do this; it's *their* responsibility." I don't want any of those people. "I can do this. Let's *go*." I want these.

It's a bleak, scary moment when "Barbie doll" seems an apt metaphor for "human." You throw Barbie into a new situation: job search, leaving home, death, and you pull the string in her neck that makes the words come out, and all she can say is, "Will we ever have enough clothes?" and "Let's plan our dream wedding!" It is so scary when you've known someone for a while and you realize you could reduce his every reaction to everything from global warming to orgasm to a stock repertoire of twenty rotating phrases.

I remember once I was bored at a party. The conversation of regurgitated words and ideas was like salad in one of those restaurants where they make them out of scavenged, wilted greens previous diners have left on their plates. I was offended. And then, suddenly, a man used the word "stilts." Not just for the heck of it; he was really talking about walking on stilts. I was so grateful to him. I thanked him for it when we ran into each other weeks afterward. It was the first time a person had spoken the word "stilts" within my earshot.

I try to do that here, with you, Diary. I reach to use the word I haven't used before, and not just for the heck of it, but because I have encountered the thing I haven't encountered before. I do go to the dictionary, and to people who know things I don't. If I find an arrowhead made of what looks like rock to me, I am willing to be told that it is "fossiliferous chert." I will use those words, though they are new and hard to spell and, since I've never used them before, I must be a child when I speak them. I do this because I want to be able to give that arrowhead to you as precise and substantial as the frost-heaved earth gave it to me, and for that I need to use the new word. I do this because I don't want to insult the world by reducing it to my stock repertoire of responses. Seeking pronunciation of the new word in others, demanding it of myself: I want that.

I want my finger right *there* where the globe of baby head bursts from stretching branches of mother limb. I want to feel the gnaw, the grind, the snarl of generation vibrating just under the surface I touch. I want to work on the bridge that people take between what they are as circumstance decrees, and what they are willing to be.

I was homeless when I was doing my undergrad student teaching. After a beating, I had fled the house with nothing. I was sleeping here and there. Student teaching was a blur; most of my life is a blur, with brief and unexpected moments of clarity. I was presenting one of those lesson plans I threw together in an all-night bar posing for its Edward Hopper portrait. It was a seventh grade class in Schuyler Colfax junior high. The boy was in the row near the chalkboard, in the middle of that row. He had brown hair and clear skin. I don't remember his name. I don't remember what I was teaching; if somebody had asked me at the time, I might not have been able to reply. But I can see his face. The look on his face kidnapped me into that moment and made it unransomable for me – that moment will forever belong to my memory of this: the boy got it. Suddenly, because of what I saying, he had gotten it. He crossed that bridge. That's what I want.

I thank God I have you Diary; I confess to you what I wouldn't even imply to others. I want a child.

I don't feel regret when I look in the mirror and see wrinkles, suddenly sharp now that the fat isn't there. Wrinkles connect me to everything because everything is captive to time. As such these wrinkles are as beautiful as the frost just now dusting the pumpkins suddenly exposed by the wasting and the withering of the garden corn. That corn was so flush just a month ago. In the midst of it, when you cut through to get to Martha's quicker, it was as overwhelming as an ocean. Now it's as if the earth is inhaling the energy it once pumped through those bright green shoots. My wrinkles are a holiday whose arrival has rounded to me for the first time. I don't know yet what myth they will recount to me, what tune they will play for me to dance. But I do know that their truth will resonate in the marrow of my bones. I do know that things I'd heard before, sterile of comprehension, will return to me, and I will suddenly understand them and feel them, too. This is what happens when one is introduced to all exotic and true feasts and their lore for the first time.

But I am a pragmatist, a working class Polak. I look at these wrinkles and think, how do I make soup out of these? Dare I say this? They store wisdom. I have stories. I suddenly find that I have patience. How is it that when one is older one is more generous of the less time that one has? Patience manifests as smooth as a polished doorknob; it feels as familiar as a memorized recipe. Wherefrom that polish on surface I don't think I've ever touched? The comfortable confidence in the recipe I'm sure I've never tried? Just recently I was complaining that I have no patience.

But there it is – as fresh as the bite of the first apple just off the tree. Every year, that first apple startles. That new taste disappears in a few weeks, and is forgotten. It's stored somewhere? And every year it returns to the trees, to my mouth, to my wonder. The question is, how can something so old taste so new?

When I do, now, things I've learned to do with competence – shop for groceries, separate my laundry, put socks and underwear in their proper drawers – there is someone with me, the one I want to show. When a story comes to me, a good story, about the family, who lived in a world that has been erased, that world of ox carts and kitchen violins, there is someone with me – the one I want to tell. Ideals – for them, if for nothing else: self-sacrifice, honesty, kindness, seeking, hand-to-plow, "*Jeszcze Polska.*" Surely, someone wants to learn these lyrics. The Doppler Effect – essential physics for any hitchhiker. It took me so long to get the Doppler Effect down, but now I've got it: the retreating car, the one that has already rejected you, always sounds fresher, most inviting, just as it is about to sink below the horizon. Cocks. Way easier than the Doppler Effect, but they took so much longer to figure out – no doubt because of the public relations juggernaut they've got working for them. I didn't penetrate the mystery of cocks until Danny Baca, from across the street, told me this story. I had been bragging to Danny about how hard I had gotten an especially unattainable boy. "Aw, that's nothin," Danny insisted. "Once, I put a quarter into a gumball machine. I was supposed to get one gumball back. I got two. And, I got a hard-on." Cocks, the Doppler Effect, laundry: am I deluding myself to think that I can pass these life lessons on, to a child, to my child? Or is it too late?

I cried at Martha's. A brief, "Who turned on the lawn sprinkler by mistake?" almost horizontal spit of tears. I saw Sparky and Shushu in their fall jackets for the first time. Cotton-candy Shushu's was hooded, quilted, lavender. Sparky, ruddy, green-eyed, his hair a blond cock's comb, wore a quilted russet vest. Both garments were vintage, sprinkled with white lint balls, trailing strings. The kids looked so ready for fall. Not mine, but their fall, a caramel-apple fall I had had once but haven't even thought about in years. Powers greater than they would abruptly cut off their summer by decree. Heat and afternoons of chlorine-filled noses at Fountain Springs swimming pool would be usurped by the smell of sharpened pencils, strict bedtimes and scratchy plaid wool. Bells would ring recess. Child herds explode into an empty field. Without ever stopping their feet from running as fast as they can they reach out their hands and fill them with other tiny hands and form a human chain and snap it around on itself and break and spill like loosed beads and roll and tumble and get bumps for Martha to "tsk" over. Mitten-shaped sassafras leaves, internally aflame with infinite, unnamed, heat-giving shades, would be carefully selected from bushes that burn, but are not consumed. Under the tutelage of sweet-smelling teachers the season's best leaves would be pressed between sheaves of wax paper. As the days get shorter the craving for Reese's peanut butter cups will grow stronger and finally climax with pillowcase-sized gluttony on Halloween night. "Winter's over, Miroswava. It's spring." And now it is almost fall. And I am still with them, my friends.

One of the reasons I traveled so much was I didn't want to let Them cheat me. The last line of Kai's obituary read, "The man lived in the area all his life."

This Fourth of July, Sparky sat on my lap as we watched fireworks. I stared at each explosion, willing myself to be awed, thrilled, and satisfied. After the first five, I noted Sparky's breath on my cheek as he "Oooooed," and "Aaaaaaed." Slowly, careful to keep the corner of my eye on the sky so I wouldn't miss anything, I lowered my head to look at him.

His pale, downy face, open-mouthed, blank of any precomposed reaction, was bathed in light that rapidly faded to blue dusk to gray night again, then, with the next explosion, his skin ignited with the pale green sheen of lightening. Miniature twin explosions shimmered into thousands of scattering embers in his eyes. I sacrificed witnessing the rest of the show first-eye, and watched it all reflected in Sparky's face.

D EAR DIARY, SSNoS is over.
The lunkheads in charge got the bright idea of a final field trip. When every remaining, budgeted moment was precious. When, soon, we'd be letting them loose, and everything we could teach them would no longer be an an I-can't-sleep-till-I-get-this-worked-out inspiration, but just another yesterday, eternal, a perennial spring of quiet, measured, rejoicing, or a pitiless thorn of regret.

So some pee haitch dee lunkhead in the bleachers decides we need to devote a whole class day to a field trip. Great! Give us the field trip! But let the kids decide! They'd pick something fun like Chinatown or Great Adventure. But, no. Some well-meaning social engineer who's never been so much as sneezed on by a student goes and buys a couple hundred tickets for the highly symbolic, very deep Broadway play, "The Piano Lesson."

Whoever made this decision has never asked Anwar, "What's up this morning?" and heard him confidently reply, "Quarter to nine." Has never entertained Etta when she's in the mood to test the aeronautic properties of textbooks. Has never clocked Dave's knee bouncing up and down under his desk at a hundred bounces per minute when he has to listen to more than ten sentences together of someone else's speech.

I know why Dr. Hemings, or Dr. Rothenberg, or whoever it was, thought this was a good idea: the guy who wrote the play is black. Anything he writes, then, will automatically osmose into SSNoS students like some hereditary disease. Oh, please. This is a work of art, not sickle cell anemia.

I'm so weary of living by the decisions of lunkheads. I am so sick and I am so tired of witnessing my students fallow or fester under the decisions of lunkheads. What is it? Is it the magical properties of the three letters: pee haitch dee? If they follow your name, are you empowered to live out bizarre fantasies? Or does the job description go on to stipulate: "Must have a pee haitch dee, and, and this cannot be overstressed, must also be a lunkhead"?

Anyway, it was magic seeing the kids all dressed up. Okay, I'll admit it, I teared up. How could I help it? They were gorgeous. The SSNoS kids are pristine, always; the best-dressed kids on campus. But that day, that big fat tour bus released a flock of peacocks in midtown, a generation of princesses.

"Man, oh, man, Etta." A silky, jade-green blouse perfectly accented her red hair and freckles; an elastic white skirt so small and tight I could have used it as a headband all but snapped over her derrière.

"Wha."

"Have you ever considered modeling?"

"Oh, you wack!" she blared, pushing me. I almost fell over; damn it, that girl is small, but strong.

I went back for more. "Has Supreme noticed?"

And, that quick, Etta's feisty dynamism crumpled into an atypical expression of defeat. "No," she pouted.

"He's right over there." I winked. "You've got it, girl. Why not work it some?"

More in testimony to her vitality than my wisdom, that was all her balloon needed. Pumped, she rose up, and wafted off, in the general direction of Supreme.

The sophistication of Sharifa's Marlene Dietrich style cross-dresser ensemble astounded me. The artful juxtaposition of culturally loaded signs that compels and changes a reader that Sharifa has not, just yet, achieved with words, she effortlessly achieved with clothing, her face and body. Carolina, throughout the day, hovered over Sharifa's face like a hummingbird over a flower, touching up, or just admiring the few spare hints of makeup that transformed Sharifa from vague girl to woman sharply defined. I couldn't address Sharifa as I usually do. I found myself deferring.

Lee's hair, glossy, smooth as still water, almost waist length, was gathered in a low, black ribbon. Anwar, I noted, wore gray silk, which, alas, did not increase his visibility to Carolina. I had half a mind to swipe some mascara on his lashes and assigning Carolina to doctoring it.

I rushed to the front of our group and grabbed Munal. He was striding at such a spry clip he might have been our tour guide. "Lend me your camera," I said. He immediately handed it over.

"Is it really true," he demanded, "that there is a room in this city where a whale hangs from the ceiling?"

"Yup, Munal, it's true," I said. "I've seen it. But it's way uptown. We wouldn't be able to get up there today."

"I don't believe this," he protested. "How do they keep it? Doesn't it go bad and smell?"

I sighed. "Well, ya know, I've never asked myself that. Maybe we can take a trip in someday and check it out, okay?"

"Is it really true," he said, "that we traveled through a tunnel to get here? A tunnel under a river? Isn't that dangerous?"

"The thought of it always gives me the heebie-jeebies. Now, Munal, you've gotta excuse me for a minute. I gotta discuss something with Dr.

Rothenberg, okay?" I lied. I settled down to the back of the crowd, along with Lee and Troy and the rest of the sediment.

Munal's rough features worked with the fine clothes he was wearing: nubbly earth-toned slacks with a sharp crease and deep cuffs, and a classically tailored man's shirt. Set in such richness, his large nose and pock marks took on a new authority; they were simply doing it right. I got in a few snapshots. Munal buying a hot dog from a street vendor. Munal talking with some cute little girl from another SSNoS class as they passed under a peep show's giant neon eyeball. My last shot: Munal with Abdullah, who, gesticulating, speaking Arabic, looks to be explaining the moving headline sign in Times Square.

At the theater door, "Thanks," I said.

"What did you take pictures of?" he asked.

"My friends and Manhattan's landmarks," I said. "Can I get copies?"

"Of course," he said, putting the camera back in his bag.

The matinee began at one. The kids were in the first row of the first balcony. At one, everyone was erect, eyes front, hands in lap. Everyone, that is, except Lee, our gymnast of catatonia, who, tucked into his Walkman, was proving that one can be supine in a cheap theater seat. Some students were even nodding knowingly at scattered lines of dialogue.

The play was great. I mean, "The Piano Lesson" is a truly great play. I have no doubt that it deserved its Pulitzer Prize. A brother and sister fight over an inherited piano. The piano is a great big symbol for history, identity, destiny, all that stuff. Very profound. If only it had been a rap song, or an episode of the Ricky Lake Show, devoted to the same themes.

Etta was the first to break ranks, of course. As she passed me Etta rolled her eyes so exaggeratedly toward the ceiling I thought she might lose them up there, and she made a pumping motion with her tubed hand, which, I think, mimes masturbation and, metaphorically, anything uncool. I didn't see her again until the bus ride home. There were whispers that she'd been making out with one of the ushers; I don't know. Carolina, at one twenty, gazed up at me, one of her patented "*que triste*," looks. I resisted producing any meaningful body language, thinking: "Carolina, this is the real world, not class. You cannot mitigate the tragedy of your walking out on this great play by acquiring a hall pass before you leave." By one thirty all the girls were MIA. Some of the boys snored and drooled; others began those hierarchy-building contests that juvenile male primates spontaneously generate, even silently, in any environment, even a Broadway theater showing a Pulitzer-Prize-winning play. Based on my field observations, I concluded that winning involved placing the winner's fist on top of the loser's fist fastest and hardest. No sudden upsets here: it looked like Abdullah was winning. Toph, though, appeared to be making a good showing, to the others' general surprise and admiration.

I guess – I guess I haven't wanted to record that he has a cleft chin. I don't worry about where I'd come to a halt when I start talking about Anwar in silk or the diagnostic personal excellence demonstrated in any tale starring Abdullah. I can notice and report that Etta does red and green as glorious justice as a Christmas card. But what, Diary, what if I were to record here that one Gabriel Suarez's chin has a lovely deep cleft? Which it has. What if I record a further truth: that that cleft chin, and his remarkably large, dark, richly brown eyes, and, let's not forget these, his celebrated nostrils, are the features that the viewer is noticing when the viewer is deciding that Gabriel Suarez is handsome?

Not, not, stop-you-in-the-street, dead-in-your-tracks handsome, not that at all. Not the kind of handsome that would be cited first in any effort to identify, as it is with Anwar: "You know, the handsome one. The Arab, who's drop dead gorgeous. Pity about his missing teeth." In any case, immediate visual thrill so often frustrates lasting satisfaction, as do visually stunning diner desserts, the kind you see in glass display cases as soon as you walk in the door, before you've even been able to give the lentil soup a fighting chance. When men graced with that rank of meringue so much as twitch, they risk decomposing the portrait. The flummoxed viewer, suspecting a cheat, rejects any change as a withholding of promised perfection. Immediate beauty must be imprisoned, fossilized. "Be as delicious as you were before, in my imagination, when you were still, and unattainable."

On the other hand, when the viewer starts noticing, if the viewer were to start noticing, something like, oh, Suarez's cleft chin, say; when the viewer starts questioning exactly what element in features as common as brown eyes creates that haunting complexity, a different beauty is taking place. Some beauty waits its turn; some beauty bides its time. Some beauty allows its impact, like snowflakes, by silent accumulation. The viewer's job: to show up, punch the clock, invest time. Some beauty is camouflaged in life, as a young deer is unobtrusively folded into a thicket of sun-shot saplings. Even nowadays with deer so common you practically run into them on commuter trains, you still have to spend a lot of time in the woods for a good look at a fawn. It's another hike. You're absent-mindedly staring, staring, staring, resentfully, at the same old temperate forest: oaks and maples, maples and oaks. Why are there so few *orchids* in New Jersey? Why no birds of paradise? Without notification the vision steps out of its surround, coalesces; light is newly defined; beauty drops its last veil.

So I don't tell you, Diary, what Suarez was wearing that day. But you can imagine it, can't you? You know of his coloring. I've already reported to you how he smells. You are using your empty pages now to imagine him, at the play, in the theater, the attention someone like him would pay to apparel for such an outing. The accoutrements, like cufflinks, like an immaculate pocket-handkerchief, that a more easily born boy would never consider indulging in, that this boy would attend to with the deliberation of a museum curator. Converts *are* the most zealous. Diary, you are using your empty pages now to run swatches over surfaces, to test color and complement, creases and folds. You are, aren't you? Never mind. I'm not telling you. Okay, one small hint. Think, suspenders. Fresh hair cut. All right now, stop.

But I have to tell you this – Teaching means offering another the chance to be born again. It may mean other things, too, but if it doesn't mean this, it means nothing. Forgive me for saying what is so obvious – giving birth is a terribly intimate thing. But it's all about feeling, more exquisitely than you'll ever feel again, the presence of another, and using that realization, that sensation, to thoroughly let go.

He sat five rows in front of me. He betrayed no awareness of the other guys and their games, of the girls in their finery. I wondered if he was aware of the space his absorption in the play created around him, the cushion of things unshared between himself and his peers. He perched on the edge of his seat, nearly falling out of it. Every time something made him laugh, or outraged him, he turned around and looked up and shared his smile with me, or his outrage. I know that he did that, because I automatically looked down at him at the same moments. I am mindful, as I write this, of the dark all around us, the surrounding wood and velvet and hush. I am mindful of how excited I was by this play's use of language and props and ghosts to talk about heritage and destiny, excitement that felt like a live coal. I am mindful of how bright his face was when he turned to me, in the darkness, mindful of how I registered his face as if it were a source of light.

I guess it had been the day before, after everyone had left. I was in the Writing Center. I was alone. As the last student's laughter died down outside, and the light in the room diminished and became concentrated in a few remaining golden flecks of dust, the teacher shred and fell to the floor. Without a shower, a stretch, or even a quick trip to the ladies' room, I sat down at one of the computers to do some writing in solitude, and I became myself. I shattered like a brass band struck by a hand grenade when Gabriel Suarez's fingers contacted my shoulder.

He lurched backward. "Sorry," he said, looking confused, surely having no idea what he was apologizing for.

Grab for a towel to conceal wet nudity, jettison shoplifted earrings from pockets, spring off lover's body, out of the flashlight beam: these tactics for getting ready were not adequate. I was fully clothed, doing nothing evidently wrong, as I slowly came to realize. But I still wasn't anywhere near ready, and I wasn't anywhere close to figuring out the tactic to getting ready for this. "Gabriel," I said, and my own voice shook me.

He stepped back further. "This is a bad time?"

"For what?"

He smiled. It was a charmer's smile, cooked in advance and being, right now microwaved, a smile I had not yet seen on him. The kind of smile that's accompanied by a wink. The kind of smile I have come to expect from Dave. I felt it beneath Suarez.

He looked toward the door. He looked scared. I waited. "Ms. Hudak, do you think, uh, you could take a look at somethin I wrote?"

"One of the reliable pleasures I have in my life right now is reading your writing, Suarez," I said.

"Yeah, uh, just one thing. I don't want you to tell me it's no good. I don't wanna hear that I fuck – that I, that I screw up."

He looked worried. It wasn't the rational, controlled worry of a good pool player estimating the available shots. It was the impotent worry of someone who's been cheated for no good reason before and safely assumes he'll be cheated for no good reason again.

"You're the best writer in the class," I asserted. "Now let me see this, whatever it is."

"Naaa. I screw up."

The part of me that wants to be Mary Tyler Moore wanted to comfort him in advance, as he seemed to be begging me to do. But I said, "Make up your mind; if you don't want to show me, I've got some writing to do."

I don't know how to speak straightforward truths except to sound castrating. I don't even know if there is a way, given what women are expected to be, given how straightforward truths are treated when they come from women's mouths. I shut up. I folded my hands in my lap. The setting sun's gold was endangered. It would soon become extinct. One of us could have risen and put on the electric light. Fearful of breaking something, neither of us did. He sat down, and pulled the writing out of his bag, and handed it to me.

I looked it over. His name didn't appear on the page. At some point in SSNoS he stopped signing his name. I pointed this out to him and asked him to please do so. "Yeah. I don know what's goin on. I always sign my name ta papers." I adjusted; when I got a paper with no name on it, I assumed it was Gabriel's. And I noted his handwriting, too. Then that began its own shift. His writing goes from script to print, from right slant to left, all on one sheet.

I tilted the paper toward the remaining flecks of gold. I began to read. What I read made me flush and shiver as if the seasons had miraculously and permanently changed.

Our first confrontation behind Pitcher Hall had been dead easy for me. This Suarez is so hard. Why couldn't he give me something easier to correct? A redundant subject, a dropped final consonant, identity as a teenage Puerto Rican male?

I have struggled so hard to make this language his. But I've failed. It's not his, it's not his at all. Today I am his only audience. I read: "I don't know if I have what it takes . . . I have been told that I am no good . . . I want to give somebody else the love and courage I never received . . . To do that I must sacrifice, and I must work and, I will . . . I have a dream." I know who is speaking these words. I know where he was before he could write them. I read these words over and over and every time I read them I feel the same pity and thrill and pride. But my job is not to be his only audience. My job is to prepare him for other audiences.

How do I tell him that I fear how his most likely reader, an academic, will react to this, Suarez's new writing? I fear the other audience who will read these earnest, stripped down, technically flawless sentences and say, "'I want to give love.' Yeah, yeah, yeah. This needs some irony. Where's the *hook*?"

Week after week I have processed his language with the relentlessness of a louse comb eliminating nits. I have refused him the heat, the immediacy, of Spanish. I have refused him the music, the fluidity, of native accent. Gone is the signature, the idiosyncrasy, of backyard terms for foods, objects, locations; talismans infused with his own soul and the souls of those he loves. I have crippled any spontaneous urge to speak and saddled it with second, third, fourth thoughts.

I urged his surrender with the promise that he would receive something greater – access to wider communication. Instead I have left him only the base vocabulary a traveler can carry in a deracinated, cobbled-up lingua franca understood in any bazaar up or down the route of trade. Like all lingua francas, it is a language tailored to serve strangers in buying or selling goods. Like all lingua francas, it cannot speak poetry. While traders share the same idea of "horse," "gold," or "microchip," they have no common memory, and thus no common understanding, of "love," or "sacrifice." What professor on this campus would understand the word "courage," as applied to attending a college class, as Suarez understands it?

The call and response common to cultures where even a declarative sentence ends with a rising inflection, I have refused him. The chorus's shared history would add the power of resonance and response to even the stripped-bare sincerity which I have left him. That chorus has been silenced. Silence after calls like: "I have a dream," "I am a survivor," "You would tell just anybody."

"What is this exactly?" I asked.

"Professor Hemings, she got this scholarship, at a place called 'Princeton' –"

"*Princeton?*"

"Yeah," he said, his body steady but his brow furrowing at my strong reaction.

"That's an Ivy League school," I said.

"Yeah?" he said.

"I mean, it's a good school, an excellent, an ex – excellent . . . are you thinking of going there?"

"I don't know. There's this scholarship, Prof. Hemings say I might get it."

"And this is your application?"

"Part of it. They wanted me to write something." He paused. "I sent it in already," he said. "But I wanted to know what you think of it." He paused again. "Why are you cryin? Why do you always cry?"

"I am *not* crying," I snapped, wiping my face. "And I do not always cry." I got up and walked to the window. "You'll get your BA at Princeton, then? Not here at Tillman?" I asked.

"Yeah. I guess. If I get this scholarship."

"Princeton is so far away. Inaccessible, in fact," I whispered.

"You kep givin my papers to Dr. Hemings. Telling her I was . . . good. A good student. She told me that."

"Yes," I said, turning around. "She told us to do that." I looked up at the clock.

"You in a hurry for somethin?" he asked.

"No," I said. I was just trying to ascertain how late is too late.

During most of that staff meeting I had been wondering what was happening to Esther Hemings' body underneath her dress. Below her hem stretch the attenuated calves of a Somali famine poster child or a high-fashion goddess. But then, somewhere under her dress, her body balloons and twists into arthritic fat. Her hair is all white. Her face is as pocked and irregularly puffed as a moldy loaf of bread. She's got twice my energy and is one of the most powerful women in Wayne. Color, age, fat, ugliness, no matter. I was trying to understand how she was doing it, so I could apply her system.

Esther Hemings was exhorting the troops. Tillman State Teacher's College had done its job by the old immigrants like the Irish and the Jews, she told us. Those had passed through its doors and had now fully realized the American dream. Now it was Tillman's job to work similar magic on those the American Dream had passed by: our SSNoS students, she told us.

We were, though, to remember that Tillman State was unable to meet the needs of certain students. She was referring, delicately, to Tillman's reputation as an undistinguished school. Rutgers kids mock Tillman as "the best high school in the state." Everybody knows it's where poor and therefore unpromising students get degrees that mean not much more than what a high school diploma used to. Dr. Hemings – she will not allow anyone to address her as anything else, not even "professor" – told us to be on the lookout for the especially gifted, and to send them to her. I immediately thought of Gabriel. And, I thought of something else.

After the meeting I followed Dr. Hemings to her car. She did not slow her pace to accommodate me.

"Dr. Hemings, if you don't mind, I'd like to ask you something."

"Why, certainly, darlin."

"I'm Miroswava Hudak."

"Well, of course I know who you are, darlin. I never forget lovely, colorful, ethnic names like yours. I've heard all about you, and the very fine work you are doing for us here in the SSNoS program." She opened her car door. "It's a shame that innovative techniques like yours don't transfer. But it's been my experience that unusual techniques work best with unusual, charismatic individuals like yourself. So, for the time being, we will continue with Martha Streichart's curriculum packet."

Dr. Hemings entered her car and sat down behind the wheel. She reached for her briefcase; I handed it to her.

"That's fine," I said, "I'm not part of the movement to get my methods enshrined in the curriculum packet. That wasn't even my idea; it was Monique's. I wanted to – I want – I was thinking of something else –"

She put the key in the ignition. I hate it when people talk "down home" to me and then behave like this – rush-hour pressure. "Do you remember me?" I finally demanded.

"Darlin, like I said, you are Miroswava Hudak. One of our best tutors. At the end of the semester, you can count on a fine letter –"

"Dr. Hemings, you were my teacher. Here. At Tillman. Years ago. I had you for Freshman Comp."

Her face registered no memory. She was looking at me with unchanging down-home noblesse oblige and revving BMW impatience.

"Dr. Hemings," I stumbled on, "for our first assignment, I wrote a story about *wigilia*. About – about Christmas Eve in Polish households. You seemed to like it. You gave it back to me and you told me to stop attending class. You told me that you couldn't teach me anything. You told me that you would just give me an 'A.' And I was a kid, I was happy, you know? That many fewer classes I had to attend, that many fewer papers I had to write, more time to play, an easy A. But my mother – she got really mad. She said, 'You're paying to be taught. She's letting you down. If she has nothing to offer you, she needs to find someone who does.' And the thing is, back then, in *those* days, well heck, *today*, the thing is, Dr. Hemings, I – I – I really needed a teacher. I just wonder, now, why you didn't attend to me the way you were telling us to attend to our SSNoS students?"

"Is that it?" she challenged, removing the key from the ignition. Apparently she was no longer in such a hurry. "You all through? You followed me all the way out here for that. You another one of these white folks who have a hard time seeing us get ahead? Well, I tell you something, young lady. I have worked too hard, I have labored too long, to endure this kind of – . You need to read some of my books, young lady, books written before you were even born. We have not carried the cross this far to be held back by the ideas of – pfft. The ideas of people the likes of *you* about what we can achieve!"

I walked back to my swivel chair, across from Suarez. I sat with the back of the chair against my chest. "Two things, Suarez," I began. "You say, 'I have a dream.' Readers will assume that's an allusion –"

"Wait," Suarez stopped me, and I smiled. "What's a lewzhun?" he asked.

"An *allusion.* An allusion is a reference to another work. Martin Luther King gave a very famous speech in which he said, 'I have a dream.' It's as if the words stop being words and become a brand name, like 'Ford' or 'Sprite,' or 'Seven-up.' The words belong to King, now, and since you're not actually making an allusion here, you'd be best not to use them."

"Okay," he nodded, and crossed the words out.

I tilted my head and I beamed.

He caught me. "What?"

"Nothing," I said, trying to hide my delight.

"You said there was two things wrong with it," he said.

"No," I corrected him. "I said 'two things.' I didn't say 'wrong.' Okay. Well, you report that you doubt that you have what it takes. Now you listen to me. You have what it takes, Suarez. You are what it takes. Don't ever forget that."

He pressed his lips together and stared at the floor. "Oh, yeah?" he said.

"Yeah," I said. "My best teacher taught me that. 'The kingdom of God is within you.'"

"You got that from the Bible," he said, relieved.

"See?" I said. "You got my allusion." The gold had decayed to lead. It would have been so easy not to get up. I stood and walked toward the door. He followed. "Be careful at Princeton, if you go," I said. "They've got alotta lewzhuns there."

He punched my arm. "You bustin me," he said. "Don't you bust me."

"I ain't bustin you. Word." I assured him, in the voice I've been struggling all this while to find with him. I turned left, for the walk home to Paterson. He accompanied me. Our walking together felt easy and good, an event that had been waiting for us to move into it. We walked through the shadows and sun of quiet campus buildings and the grassy patches between. There was no appointment, no plan. None was necessary.

We would keep walking till we got to the edge of the campus, the little hem of cafes and bookstores. He would ask me if I wanted a calzone, or a glass of tea. I would say yes. He'd select the café, after consulting me. He'd pay. We'd sit and laugh and be polite. An old, old motif, a chestnut, but all but paralyzing to those living through it: we'd discover that underneath our gruff exteriors we'd both been hiding the tenderness and decorum of convent novices. We'd have to split the calzone. No one can eat a whole one of those things.

He'd reveal his nervousness about the scholarship. Oh, but they'd accept him. Yes, Princeton would be difficult at first; it's unlike anything he's ever experienced. But he would be identified as an "Hispanic," or maybe they use the word "Latino." His maladaptations, throwing his chair against the wall, expressing himself simply and earnestly, would be understood, not as malice, flaw, or perversion, but, rather, as indications that he was a newcomer. He would be assigned a mentor invested in his success. Our little Gabriel Suarez would become another great Hispanic American, like Richard Rodriguez, or Geraldo Rivera or George Chakiris – well, you know what I mean. He'd resist at first, but eventually he would become a Princeton man. Lolicita would soon be history. A more appropriate mate would appear, someone like him, with glossy black hair, similarly gifted, and chosen.

We'd exchange addresses, write polite post cards and updates. And as he progressed, I'd appear to be standing still. He'd report newer and better jobs, the arrival of children. I'd be in the same questionable neighborhood, just getting by. And the Princeton man would come to ask why a woman "with so much potential" spent all her time writing in her diary, something for which she isn't paid; no man falls in love with her for it. And she's still talking about trying to lose some weight. And one day he'd figure out who this was who had seen him, whom it was he had impressed, to whom it was he was writing.

"*Mira*," he said, suddenly, "*no sé –*"

"*What?*" I exclaimed.

"What," he said.

"What did you just call me?" I demanded.

"What? I don't know. Oh, that. It just Spanish. Kinda weird, huh? I usually only do that, start speaking Spanish like that, with, uh, people that I know. So, look," he said, quickly, "Look. I don't know. What it is that I do that gets you going so strong. I gotta tell you, nobody's ever – before you, Ms. Hudak – this is all so – will people there – or is it – is it just *you?*"

I stopped walking. I stood still. "Listen to me, Gabriel Suarez." I said.

"This has nothing to do with me. Nothing. It has nothing to do with Dr. Hemings. Listen to me," I said. "This is you. You are so damn smart it's scary. You wanna hear something really weird? Really, almost . . . Sometimes . . . All the time, I photocopy your assignments before I give them back to you. Okay, it's true. You, Gabriel, you. Not the other students. You. I do that – I do that so I can keep them. It is – thrilling – to me to watch how the way you use language gets better with each and every paper. I lay the pages side to side. There are things you do now that I taught you that you couldn't do when you first got here. You do them now as if you'd been born doing them. But the real excitement comes from the things I didn't teach you, that nobody could possibly have taught you. Martha – your math tutor – Ms. Streichart – she's saying the same sorts of things about your performance in math class. The simple fact is that Princeton will be lucky to get you.

"But, like I said, it's not about me, or Martha, or Esther Hemings, or Princeton. Suarez, somewhere inside of you I know you know what you have. The proof of that, strange enough, is that you keep asking me. If you didn't sense it inside, you'd just write me off as a kook, or it just wouldn't matter to you at all. The next step, the step you have to take, is to stop asking me, to stop looking for it from the outside, and to invest in that tug, that pull, that wrenching something that you feel inside."

He was looking at me. His facial muscles had gone limp. His mouth was slightly open.

"Now you'll have to excuse me," I said, briskly. "I just remembered that I have some writing I have to do. See you –" I was about to say, "next class." Suddenly realizing, I just said, "See you." I spun around and began stepping, with an exclusive rapidity and direction, back to the Writing Center.

D EAR DIARY, I haven't written in a while but I gotta get this off my chest.

I had gotten a call and was asked to come in. Now remember, I'm not on their payroll. I did apply for the fall positions; no go; *fine.* I have only a BA. I was good enough to teach all those classes that the PhD couldn't show up for; by the end Dr. Rothenberg was out more days than she was in. But I'm not good enough for fall. Fine. But she asked me to come in, so, I went in.

"Oh, you're here. You have some problems," she said in lieu of "hello." My final evaluations were splayed out over her desk. "Mira, were you aware that these would go into each student's permanent record?" Dr. Rothenberg looked at me as if she were waiting for my permission to slap. "I'm sorry to have to say this," she finally said. "But we've caught up with whatever was going on." She paused. "You know, Mira, I know. I know all about it. And on top of everything else, you don't have an advanced degree. But I wanted to give you a chance, you know? But just look what you've done with the chance that I gave you. Just look."

I peeked at my coworkers' evaluations. Monique's were as arid as her armpits. A series of small, shut boxes crammed with the codes we had been invited to reduce our students to. "A" didn't brand an "adulterer," but, rather, someone with an "Unacceptable number of absences." "R" was a student destined for, "Remedial classes," and so on. Monique had penned one or two sentences next to a minority of student names. "Lee attends math class regularly," she risked recording in a typical insight.

"Yes, Monique," Dr. Rothenberg cooed. "She's quite something, isn't she?"

My evaluations did, indeed, present a very different picture than Monique's. Over my blow by blow accounts of Troy's threats, Dr. Hemings had scrawled, "What I want to know is, is he passive enough to sit through fifteen credits in the fall?" A full page chronicled Sharifa's ongoing efforts to master the Standard English simple present tense "s." Quotes from her papers demonstrated her progress so far and the work she still needed to do. I had closed with full citations of scholarly and newspaper articles on the ongoing controversy around Black English. Dr. Rothenberg said, "Your assignment, Mira, as far as Sharifa goes, is, did she attend the mandated number of hours, or didn't she? Mira, look at this. You used up all the form space and you couldn't even tell us that?"

"I am so sorry. I am such a scatterbrain . . . Thank God we have clever heroes like you to clean up messes made by schlumps like me . . . It was so generous of you to hire such a silly fool . . . I hope you don't withhold my last paycheck. I needs it so bad, Ma'am." With the implacable fury of soldiers besieging an enemy, these sentences formed and reformed, stormed my organs of speech. I bit my tongue.

I did not pronounce them. I hadn't the agility or goods to compose any other statements.

Urges to clown wormed through my muscles. I'd mess up her desk; I'd slump. My cloddishness would provide her face-saving absolution. She could, then, release the room's tension, rescue me, and conclude with a happy ending: "See? I have to crack the whip over these people."

"Mira, you should have kept a minute-by-minute log of students' comings and goings, rather than this . . . whatever it is that you've turned in here. Why didn't the stu – You should have had them interrupt. You should have had them make sure you recorded exactly when they arrived and left."

I demanded erect posture of my spine. I expanded my lungs, took in air, exhaled. "Again, now. Do it again," I instructed, "and keep doing it." To my muscles: "Assume the elegant calm of Baryshnikov lounging between acts." To my tongue: "Maintain radio silence until any word or gesture of self-abnegation is incinerated."

Then I began to puzzle out the problem: Why had I done these perverse things? Why had I inconvenienced this well-dressed, super-confident, nice lady? What *had* I been thinking? Something like this: "I had thought it – I had given it priority – I gave priority to teaching and to learning. Those were my priorities." I struggled to pronounce these words in a clear, steady voice, not to whisper them, not to whine them. Yes, yes, that is right. That was it. I didn't do this because I'm a spiteful clown on a vendetta against this poor, blameless, nice lady. I didn't do it to give her extra work and headaches. I didn't do it because I have it in for the students. That's not it at all. Discovering more, I added, "I didn't want to communicate that my focus was on minutes and seconds. I wanted them to – I wanted them to get that this, that teaching and learning, that they're as vital, that they are *life*. I wanted them to, to do their whole persons and their progress as persons. That's why I wrote those long pages. That's why I added all those details. And for whomever is teaching them next. So they'll know where these kids have been, and where to begin."

Dr. Rothenberg noted that I was not saving her face. I was increasing the tension in the room, rather than sacrificing myself to its release. She spoke. "We – Dr. Hemings and I, the facilitators-in-chief of the SSNoS program – we didn't distribute these timesheets as some sort of a joke, Mira. Minutes and seconds are the building blocks of learning, Mira." She stopped. And began again, "I'm really sorry," she said. "I am *really sorry* that this has to go into the students' permanent records." She nodded. "*And* into yours."

I scurried into the apartment, sure passersby knew. Shivers pelted down my spine as I undressed; I hunched as if observed. I didn't take out the garbage. I wrapped myself in a blanket and camped in front of the TV.

A fool! That's what I've been. I had been moving and acting in the world as if I were okay, as if I were ready, as if I knew about knives and forks, where they were, how to use them. I had been so wrong. Apparently, all this time, I've been making scabrous, evil, lunatic errors. I've shamed myself. I've disgraced my family. Everyone has seen. Everyone has known. They've been totting up my vulnerabilities in Their little black books. They've been tittering behind my back. They've been accumulating ammunition to bring me down when I am least ready. And I haven't known, haven't had any idea. I've just been cruising along, hanging out or working hard, thinking I was knowing the warmth and safety of acceptance into community. I have been so naïve. I've just been exposing myself to Them.

I unplugged the phone, curled up, held my breath.

DEAR DIARY, I received a summons. Staff who had worked the SSNoS program this past summer would trade ideas on updating the curriculum packet. I was in the Writing Center's vestibule, shaking cold rain off my coat. I could hear Martha. She was saying something about abuse and addiction and what did you expect from these kinds of people who come to this country with no idea of what it is to be civilized? I thought, wow, that's harsh, even for Martha, and how will it go over with Dr. Rothenberg, who, I knew, was there. I had passed her very memorable auto in the parking lot. It was under a lamp, next to the security telephone. Would she let even her pet talk about SSNoS students in such a politically incorrect way? But something slowed me down and heated me up, bid me listen unseen.

I heard a sisterly "Mm hmm," from Monique.

I heard, "Now, you see? That just proves what I've been saying all along," from Dr. Rothenberg.

Then Martha said, "And you would not believe how her grandfather died."

I walked into the room. Martha's mouth hung wide agape. Dr. Rothenberg and Monique rearranged their derrieres in their scoop-seat plastic chairs, and shuffled the forms in front of them with an admirable sense of purpose. I sat down. There was a long silence. No one looked at anyone else. "Are we waiting for Toph?" I asked.

"He can't make it," Dr. Rothenberg announced.

There was another long silence. Monique put her papers down and sipped her coffee, which she takes black, with saccharine.

Finally, Dr. Rothenberg said, "I think we should talk about what just happened."

"I don't," I said.

"I'm sorry, dear," Dr. Rothenberg said. "But you're just proving my point."

I looked at her.

"A program like SSNoS relies on teamwork," she said. "And, dear, a team is only as strong as its weakest link. You know, Mira, Dr. Hemings told me to watch out for you. I asked her why, and all she would say is, 'Watch out.' You shut out Monique's overtures of friendship. And you've just been rude, here, to Martha, who has been a very good friend to you. Now, I think all of us can agree that 'diversity' is a key concept in SSNoS. And the wondrous beauty in diversity comes from the all the fabrics in the weaving. That's why we wanted *you* on our team, Mira. Just like a mosaic." Monique nodded in agreement.

Dr. Rothenberg went on, "Mira, there's something I think you should know. You've brought a lot of energy into the SSNoS program. There's been a lot of talk about that and there's no denying it. Now we're here for you, dear. It was poignant, really it was, your admiration of Monique's final evaluations. We can help you with that. We can help you hone whatever gifts you may have.

"But you've been a very difficult team member, Mira. We're making decisions about who we'll invite for next summer's program. We'll be needing team players who can play their part in the weave. We'd like to help you."

I looked at Martha. "911" was written all over her face.

"Dr. Rothenberg," I said, "I'd be happy to contribute to any enhancement of the curriculum packet. I might as well let you know now, though, that I won't be doing SSNoS next year. I'm going to be . . . someplace else."

"I'd advise you to wait till you cool down before you burn your bridges up," Dr. Rothenberg said. "Don't shut us out, Mira," she said. "We care about you. And we can see the calls for help you've been sending out." She glanced at the eczema on my hands. "We're in this together, Mira. We're all victims, dear. There's so much in common between you and I. It's just that I'm a little bit further down the road than you, that's all, so I can be a help to you, like a guide.

"This is the year that I'm finally admitting that I was horribly abused by my parents. I was always pushed to be the princess. Do you know what that did to me? The ballet lessons, the special enrichment classes. My mother would never let me leave the house unless I was picture-perfect. If I came home with an 'A' it was, okay, you can have the ice cream sundae, but no whipped cream, because it wasn't an 'A' plus. It was so humiliating. I had to be the star who proved that the whole family was perfect. It's only cognitive therapy that's made it possible for me to go on. We create our own realities, Mira, we really do. Feelings aren't facts. You've got these tapes in your head."

I rose. I said, "G'night, ladies," and I left.

DEAR DIARY, I'M sorry. I can't make it more flowery or complex or worthy. In the following entry, I'm going to reveal something that I haven't told you. I haven't known how. You and I share the deepest language I know. I don't yet know what the essence of this is. Please believe me when I say that I wish I knew how to talk with you about it.

There is language to talk about this on forms, in telephone interviews and statements of purpose. It's a nauseating, insipid language I have only, heretofore, ever heard, ever mocked, never spoken. I've heard it used to cheat and humiliate people like me.

When I speak it it's just like a puppet show. I get stage fright; I buck myself up. I crouch under the stage, homemade from a cardboard refrigerator box. I slide the puppet over my hand. I muffle giggles, tears, and contemptuous snorts. I'm thinking: I'll allow my mouth to form these sound not to communicate, not even to be present, rather, merely as means to an end. I want to be the one who decides what field trip Etta Yearwood gets at the end of summer school. If this little puppet is what it takes, so be it. The button-eyed sock speaks and is greeted with a warmth and respect I've never known.

I've been thinking, I'll finish this up, and then I'll go back to being me. But that's not how it works. Allowing the puppet to receive applause has altered some delicate setting in me. Since I've abandoned, however briefly, my native tongue, and surrendered my mouth to alien sounds and the world they create and demand, my fluency has eroded. I try to talk to you. Guttural syllables result. I destroy the page.

I was watching a PBS special about the solar system when I heard the knock. I looked through the peephole and couldn't see her for the "Harvest Colors" bouquet. I opened the door.

"Hi, Martha," I said.

She goose-stepped into the room. She unloaded the flowers, the fruit basket, and large, matte school portraits of Shushu, Sparky, and Dexter. Then she turned and stared at me.

"You're going to have to excuse me," I said. "I was just about to learn why Copernicus is up for consideration as making the single greatest scientific contribution of the millennium." I went back into the living room and lay back down on the couch.

"I told you!" Martha said. Fists punctuated stiff arms at her sides. "I told you this would happen! I can't believe I did this, to a person as good as you. I told you you're too good for me. This is how I am. I'm not gonna change."

I nodded. "Did you know that Copernicus was a Polak?"

"This isn't gonna work," she said, stomping around the kitchen. "This isn't going to work, Miroswava! Listen! I've been a good friend to you! I gave you my house key. It's too long, man. You never called. You knew what kind of hell I was going through." She raised up the kids' portraits, waved them around. "And you know what this is doing to them. It's not their fault. Think about it. Things had better go back to the way they were before. Tell me what it's going to take."

I reached up and put my hands behind my head. "You know, Martha, you pressed really hard to read that transcript. My interview with my father, I mean."

She leaned on the counter, glared at me. "Where is this going?"

"I think something about myself that isn't true," I said. "I think of myself as being worthless. I think I have nothing of value. But I've been thinking about how eager people are to hear each other's stories, how we fight a tug of war to get at each other's story first.

"It's not true that I have nothing. I have my story. Stories are commodities. Even if we don't want a person in our lives, we certainly want her story. We all let everyone know as soon as we can that we know that Monique is anorexic. Oh, yeah, and we know that her man is a cross dresser, too, giggle, giggle, giggle, pious show of phony concern. We all have to let everyone else know that we know that for all her talk of what a bodhisattva she is, Rothenberg still takes her bastard ex's booty calls.

"I come from people who don't tell their story publicly. Or maybe don't tell their story at all. I don't have to tell you that. You know that. And we think that keeps us safe and invisible. We'll hide out until we're ready. But we got that wrong. Cause when you don't tell your story, other people do, and they tell it totally wrong."

"You know how crappy they treat me!" Martha said. "And you know damn well that it's you I love."

"Please," I said. I turned my attention to the TV. She'd leave eventually.

And then she said, "Snow orgasms."

I looked at the floor.

"The trip to the Pineys," she said. "Our first trip. We found that spot of unmelted snow under a grove of pines. We were slipping and sliding. We really had to struggle to not fall down. You asked me, 'Martha, do you ever get snow orgasms?' And I thought, okay, this woman's nuts. But you told me that if you're hiking in snow and ice, after a mile or so the scissor action in your inner thigh muscles – you're trying hard to keep from falling – that that gave you snow orgasms. And, once, when you were slipping and sliding to St. Francis School, you had to cut a quick snow angel on Lackawanna Avenue to make it stop."

"I can't believe that you remember that," I said.

"I remember everything you say, Miroswava," she said. "Sometimes I write more in my diary about you than about myself."

My eyes grew wide and I shook my head. I looked down at the floor again. "Did it work, Martha?" I asked. "Are you now *in*? Did Dr. Rothenberg finally put your name on the curriculum packet? Has Monique invited you over to her place for dinner? What do anorexics serve, anyway, Perrier and ipecac?"

Martha laughed, weakly. I laughed, weakly, too.

"See?" she insisted. "We're friends."

I got up off the couch. Apparently I was destined never to learn why a fellow Polak was up for mind of the millennium. I embraced Martha. She squirmed, awkwardly. I let go.

"I'll make some tea," I said. "I'm having peppermint. You? How about some peppermint tea? It's very good for the tummy."

"You know I have a steel gut," she said.

"Some Rust-oleum, then?"

She smiled. I put the water on. "I might still have some Earl Grey in here somewhere," I said, reaching up on my tiptoes to search the cabinets over the sink.

"You've got to understand," she said. Brace yourself, Diary, this is it. "You've got to understand," she said, "how it hit me, to hear that you're leaving us for Berkeley."

That's it, Diary. And even now, now that you know the fact, I still don't know how to talk about it with you. To continue:

I spun around. *"What?"*

It was the first time I've ever seen Martha look scared. Everything fell; nothing of consequence was left in her face. "Wait," she said. "Wait. Are you getting mad again? We already made up. You can't get mad for the same thing twice. That's double jeopardy."

"You're telli – this is about Berkeley?"

"How did you expect me to react?" her face was again formidable in its anger. "You're going to graduate school. To a fancy graduate school. Berkeley. You're going to get a PhD from the University of California at Berkeley." She sang all this as if it were the lyrics to a country song about a new form of love betrayal.

"You fucking bitch. Get out of my house. Never come back." I wanted, very badly, I could taste it, to hit her. Instead I handed her the photos of the kids. I turned off the gas jet under the teapot and emptied steaming water into the sink. I walked into the living room. I turned around. She was staring at me, drained again. I felt contempt. She couldn't even hold on to her own anger, and that was, so evidently, all that she had. I *would* hit her after all.

"You . . . loser. You *are* a loser! You know that? You call yourself my friend. You give me the key to your house. And I sit with you in the welfare office and I hold your hand through every monthly crisis.

"I called you. I tried to talk about it. How all my life, I'm dyslexic and everything else, I just always assumed that I am a little bit retarded. I haven't known what else to call it. I see a big, red barn and somebody says to me, 'That's not a big red barn. That's a small blue frog,' I am so ashamed. I think, Christ, when will I ever get it right? Cause I am always so wrong.

"Martha, you haven't got any idea, thank you very much. I shit my pants bussing to the test. I had to clean up in a gas station bathroom. I had to sit in a room full of kids young enough to be my kids, if I'd ever had kids. They didn't look scared. They looked like inflated balloons. I went to your house first thing. You blew me off. You changed the subject. So much for giving me your fucking key.

"Sixteen years of my life I spent in classrooms afraid to open my mouth cause I was so goddamned stupid. And everybody let me know, too. Then this test puts me in with the top two per cent of students who took it. I squandered my life trying to see small, blue frogs in big, red barns. Talk to me about regret, Martha. Talk to me about rage. You have no idea. You shut me up.

"You focus on the one thing, the one thing that you think I have that you think you don't have. You ignore the everything that you have that I've never had, probably will never have. Shushu is worth a million acceptances to graduate school.

"I'm so lucky? Tell me where the money is supposed to come from. I've already got a bill, for more than I've ever earned in a year . . . " I guess it was around this time that I realized I was talking to myself. Martha wasn't so much listening as, just, waiting.

"Miroswava, I'm sorry," Martha rushed out the words. "I couldn't stand the thought of losing you," she said. "You and me . . . you are the first . . . this is the first 'I and thou' relationship I've ever had." And she sounded human, and as if she had some real compassion, real feeling. And that was just too bad, because there really is such a thing as too late.

"Get out," I said, lying back down on the couch in front of the TV.

I was feeling as if she had already left when she said the strangest thing.

"You know, Miroswava, you were right about Maurice Sendak," said this woman, still in my apartment. To me she was no more alive than a toenail I had cut off and failed to get down the drain. "I'm not surprised; I mean, you're right about so many things. Remember? When I was looking for a book that I could read to all of them at once? Dexter, who's already in *Playboy* stage, and Shushu, who's, well, Shushu – so you told me about Maurice Sendak. You said he was a favorite of yours. So that's how I'm going to do it."

When she said, "do it," the woman became animate again, and I reentered time. I sat up a little straighter and listened. I would listen for details and know best how to stop her.

"They all like *Where the Wild Things Are,*" she said. "Just like you said. They are so entertained by it, every time I read it. I haven't been reading it to them as much, lately, because I wanted to store its impact on them.

"So, yeah," she went on. "I've got the hose from the vacuum in the trunk of the car. It just reaches, between the exhaust pipe and the back window. You've got to secure it with duct tape. *Where the Wild Things Are* is in the glove compartment. I know the spot down the back woods. We'll all be sitting up front, reading from the book, and we'll all, just, fall asleep."

"Martha," I heard the voice that interviewed Daddy, "I'm going to call the mobile psych unit at St. Joe's. I'm going to call the cops, too."

"Yeah?" she said. "How amusing. You think that anything official is going to change anything in the lives of people like us."

"Martha," I said. "This isn't your only choice. You're so smart, Martha. That's what you were born for. You would make a great professor –"

She sauntered into the living room, sat in my one comfy chair. "'You are so smart,'" she repeated. "Let me get this straight, Miroswava. You mean, that I'm smart, and that there's all kinds of goodies out there for smart people, and if I just raise my hand and identify myself, they'll let me in on it. And everything will be all right. Is that what you're saying? Oh, fuck you and fuck your incredible phony arrogance, too." She sounded very tired, but, now, in control.

"You whine to me about thinking you are retarded. Poor little Miroswava. 'We shall overcome.' At least you had some defined thing you could focus on and blame and overcome.

"'You are so smart, Martha.' And you're just figuring that out now, Miroswava? How observant. And you want some kind of gratitude for telling me this? Dear, when I was in grade school, the teachers didn't know what to do with me, so they put me to work tutoring high school football stars. When I was in third grade I was doing my father's taxes. I taught myself to play the flute by listening to records. Then they found out who stole the flute from the band room and that was the end of that.

"Idiots are in charge, Miroswava. Scum get the big piece of the pie. It's in the Bible. Those that have a lot will be given even more by God. Those that are just scraping by; God is sure to take what little that they have, and leave them with nothing. That's not just the lyrics of a rock and roll song. That's Biblical. That's God's law. That's the way it is.

"And I'm charm-impaired. You know that. If I were somebody, they'd be talking about how 'feisty' and 'energetic' and 'strictly business' I am. But I'm nobody, so I'm a 'hyper bitch,' I'm a 'social cripple.' So, please, just, just don't tell me how smart I am as if it's some solution I've been too lazy to consider, some justice I have so far refused."

"I love you," I said. Perhaps that wasn't the moment to speak that truth. Because I couldn't give her anything that she wanted. "And I'm going to call St. Joe's and the cops."

"Miroswava," she said, quietly, looking at me, squinting, "you will never see my children again. And I know how important they've become to you." She looked sad.

"You're not gonna kill those kids –"

"Maybe not," she shrugged. "It was just an idea. I've got others, too. Do you know what happens if you combine bleach and ammonia? This is really interesting, because they're both around the house all the time, right? So this is what happens. Actually, it can occur in three levels. First you get mono, then you get di, and then you get trichloroamines. You inhale it, and it's just like mustard gas – the stuff that was banned after World War I. Say good-bye to the mucosa of the lungs. Just with household chemicals! That is, it kills you. But, like I was saying, it's just a plan. But whether or not I do it, you will never see my children again, Miroswava. I'm gonna make sure that they know how you abandoned us, and turned on us, and betrayed us."

"Martha, you're not thinking straight. Listen to me. St. Joe's can help you –"

"Why don't you just shut up?" she said, still no more energy in her voice, but authority. "What do you know? These are *my* kids. You never had kids –"

"That's not the point! The focus isn't always on you. The focus isn't always on the mother. The focus is on the kids. And when you ask that question, the right question, yeah, yeah, yeah, I have been a kid. And I have had a mother. So I know! Martha, why, why, why don't you use what you have? I mean I honest to God don't get it! Why not be what you could be? You are so much smarter than Rothenberg. You could –"

"No!" she sat up, animate with a red anger. "Don't you dare start on her. She's different than us."

"You hate the way she treats you –"

Martha was shaking her head violently. "You wish. She is different than us. She's got, she's got – something we don't have. Don't even think about it. We're lucky just to work for someone like that."

"I cannot believe this bullshit you are feeding yourself."

"Is it bullshit? Look at us, Miroswava. Then look at her."

"That poisonous cow? She uses words like 'wondrous.' How can you possibly respect her?"

"Don't you dare start on her."

"What is this shit, 'don't you dare start on her'? I've already finished with her."

"As if you knew," Martha shot back. "You are so goddamned smart, Miroswava. You have an answer for everything, don't you? You have no idea! Miroswava, you never put up with a drunken husband who'd as soon beat the crap out of you as fuck you. You've never gotten up at three a.m. to change a diaper full of slimy green shit. You've got all the time you want to read your books and go walking in the woods and traveling around the world. You never had to sit still and fume while some asshole in a suit calls you and every other woman an airhead when you're running a whole house and everything and you've got the weight of the world on your shoulders – you ever do any of that, Miroswava? No. You have no idea what it means to be a woman."

"Gloves off? Is that you want? With *me*? Or are you just trying to get me to say something as vicious as you just said to me so you don't have to blame yourself later? Okay, Martha. You're my friend. I'll do it for you. What does it mean to be a woman? It means," I said, "speaking up when some asshole calls women 'airheads.' It means that if you marry someone you don't love just so you can get social approval or money you don't go around whining about it and blaming everybody else. It means –"

"Why do you do this, Miroswava? Why do you have to do this? Why do you have to be so complicated? Do you think it makes you more interesting? You think I don't know where you're from? Why do you always have to be different? You bring it on yourself. Look at yourself. You're so high and mighty. Forget it. You'll never get a reference letter from Rothenberg or from Hemings, either, and I tried to help you, there. What did you do with Hemings, anyway? She's one of the nicest people in Wayne. You can't get a letter from your last job, either, unless you go back and let that guy Jim feel you up. You probably brought all that on yourself, too.

"Your mother and I were talking about this last night," Martha said, and the thing that amazes me is that when she said this, she used the same voice, the voice I had come to associate with my friend. She didn't switch languages or anything. "I've been going by there a lot, lately. She's really good with the kids. She loves you a lot. I don't know why you torment her. You know she's not well. She's probably not going to live much longer. She misses you so much and you never come by and visit her, or anything. Lenappi too good for you?"

I got up and got the phone book and the phone and I called. "Hi," I said. "I'd like to report a plan for a murder-suicide. It's a woman and her kids. I'm gonna give you her name and address and phone number and I want you to get somebody out there tonight, okay?" I heard the door open and then slam shut and I heard myself alone in the otherwise empty apartment.

D EAR DIARY, I remember the plummet's speed. My body was suddenly, uncharacteristically, fast, its direction arrow-clean. My medium was no stray dirt path or road or school hall crowded with competing dense bodies demanding my compromise to their trajectories. As a bird's is, my medium was air. I remember my body in reverse. Head due south, as sure as a fishing line's sinker; feet were flopping fecklessly up above. I think I remember this part, but it could be a later insertion: the sudden thud of the flattening top of my scalp and skull against unyielding earth.

I can gather that Kai carried my limp body into the house and lay me out on the couch. I can gather that they thought I was dead. I regained consciousness to piercing screams. "Oh God! Don't let her die! Please God! Please God! I love her!" Mommy was kneeling beside me, wringing her hands, swaying.

I remember concluding it best to reverse the journey from black obliteration into busy light. I frantically struggled to arrest the mechanics rapidly knitting me back together, to scramble the neurons falling under conscious command, to slacken the elastic reflex into life. I yearned to just lay there, limp, helpless, blind, finally knowing what it is to be loved.

I contemplate the roster of those I've loved and lost. The first name on the list is mine. Miles would love me if only I were Buddhist enough, or was it WASP enough? I was never really sure. Men would love me if I could be small enough. Mommy and Daddy would be redeemed if I would fail enough. Dr. Rothenberg would look good if I apologized enough. Martha would sisterly bond with me if only I got knocked up and let my cheatin-hearted lover-man treat me achey, breaky mean. If only I could just agree that all those big red barns are small blue frogs.

No. I have been thoroughly dead and it has earned me no love at all.

D EAR DIARY, I told Chris and Mel about Berkeley. We'd received an unseasonably warm weekend forecast. They invited me to one of their Indian summer barbecues. Owen would be there, and other academic colleagues. It could be my debut.

The weather was sublime, the sky clear blue. As I trudged in the sun along the shoulder from the bus through four-foot, bee-bothered boneset and sneezeweed I was tricked into high summer. While reclining in the shade of the apple tree I broke out my sweater. This tree is meant to be a soothsayer, to plunk fruit according to karmic design. Dick, who, Mel insists, has a persecution complex, sustained yet another direct hit in the tree's venerable history of precision bombing. Owen never came close to being hit, although they say if he sat under it with his mouth open the choicest fruit would find its way to his tongue. When I was still living with Chris and Mel, I had overheard their gossip of, but never witnessed, this tree's William Tell aim. Now I was being woven into its legend. Apparently during the barbecue I was nearly struck several times. Blithely unaware, I always escaped unscathed at the last second. Mel clapped and laughed and adduced, "See? See? That's cause she's always living on the edge."

Owen deigned me his warm and crinkly grin. After he dies, I swear, that grin is going to the Smithsonian. "She's a scapegrace, all right," Owen chuckled. I excused myself in order to scribble "scapegrace" into my pocket notebook. I would be sure to bring that word to you exact.

When I returned to the table Chris asserted with a woozy, beer-lubricated vehemence, "You guys have it all wrong. She's a *free spirit.*"

Well, I thought, okay, but "scapegrace" and "free spirit" didn't seem rigidly exclusive. And then I noted that a placidly self-satisfied Owen and Mel were on one side of the table, a combative Chris, the other. Heavens, no. Mel trading Chris's bed for Owen's? But Chris continued, "She's doing it right, Mel, not like we did. She was young, traveled the world, had her adventures, and now that she's seasoned, she's getting the degree. What did we do with our youth?"

Chris' redaction of my biography distracted me from ruminations about the recipient of Mel's favors. I remembered Chris's response to living with me, a roommate in constant posttraumatic stress. How much it put him out when I requested he not stomp on the stairs. Now my slouching toward a Ph.D. had to be reduced to the strategic maneuver of a wisdom he had lacked, rather than seen for what it really was: agonized, desperate and slightly screwy. My imagined wise planning was a tool to help him feel bad about himself, as had been my chronic nervous breakdown. I thought of a subtitle for Chris', the would be liberator of the peoples, projected magnum opus: *The History of the World and How It Inconvenienced Me.*

However I was being imagined, this imagined me was now accepted in a whole new way. It was as if our moments of awkward tension had just never happened. I had to wonder if the acceptance to Berkeley had anything to do with it. I had to wonder if I was imagining it all. But which half of our history was I imaging? In a way I was disappointed. I had been prepared to put more work into acceptance.

I sat back and waited. The social circle and the apple tree, the trombone and the oboe, were playing their parts to perfection. Nothing, just nothing at all, was wrong. Nothing ugly was happening. I wasn't in a DMV line. I was waiting to feel . . . happy. Dare I use that word? Too big? Okay. How about . . . content. Comfortable, at the very least.

I went down the list. I couldn't find even comfortable. My torso was tight as if gripping, as if I were reverting to some former evolutionary stage during which my species had prehensile shoulders. I was perching on the edge of the picnic table's bench. I noticed that I was holding my breath. I forced myself to exhale. That sounded as if I were an Omaha beach veteran visiting Normandy's graves for the first time. Everyone stared at me as if to say, "*Yes?*"

"Bless me father, for I have sinned. Time is a duty, not license. With a bit more sufferance, the clock goes faster. Away? To? I don't know, but thank you, God; this minute passed; with a few mores' passing this day will end. I will have survived the goodness of it all, the clement weather, the pleasant guests. I can escape, alone, to my reward of bed. Let me chew some gum, play some Scrabble, sip my diet drink, to pass these trying seconds quick. Oh, if only I had food to make them go quickest of all."

When I got home, I found that I had locked myself out of the apartment. The super had to let me in.

When I castigate myself for doing something wrong, the eczema begins to itch and exude pus. The itching becomes more and more intense. I simply can't resist scratching. Scratching unties all the knots in my body. The pleasure is close to orgasm. I scratch so furiously I open skin. I force it to bleed, to bleed out the pain, the disease, the past, me.

DEAR DIARY, THE contact points of my body – joint-crowded socket, skin-smothered muscle, hair-jammed follicles – are very sore. It's a gritty sore as though they've been abrading each other, methodically, like lapidary files, insistently, like glacier over rock.

I'm safe alone at home in my own little apartment, my own *big* apartment, no one is hurting me, no one is even touching me. I am years away from Miles, Mommy, Daddy or the English, Irish, Scotch and Welsh. I can earn enough money to live. I am well-fed and clean. Rain does not come in.

There are people in this world who have a right to suffering! There are starving people now. There are homeless people now. Girls actively raped right now, children actively beaten right now; I'm not even legitimately crazy.

DEAR DIARY, AS soon as I finish typing this sentence, that's when. It'll be the all night market: meager pickings, ex-con clerks and a greasy floor. All's it takes is a little imagination, a little gumption, a little can-do attitude, that's all. No, they don't have premium or fresh; they do have butter, brown sugar, even vanilla. Potato chips and chocolate-covered peanuts. These won't find bits of me like lint that I must pick off before I can be loved. I'll exhale. I'll come down off my tippy-toes. Sure, the act earns me brief spells of acceptance, one day with Martha, one with Mel. These are not enough. These are as conditional as coins thrown on a sidewalk bought with a street performance. I want pleasure in which I can drown.

I'm not writing anything that makes any sense. Why don't I just get up right now? Why not? Why not end these obsessive thoughts the only way I know how, and free my mind for other things? Why not? Why not? Why not? Why not?

I will. I will. I will. Just watch me. My poor, sweet, innocent self. I'm here to put a stop to this. This punishment. I will overturn this coffin lid pinning me to a terminally humiliating identity.

Real things are happening to real people. Real women have real children. Real woman have real jobs. Real women have real relationships. My relationships are saltines. One tap and they crumble.

I don't have to wait. Fuck typing the end of this sentence. I have peanut butter. I have flour. I have honey and milk and oil and spices.

All's it takes is a little imagination, a little gumption, a little can-do attitude, that's all. I could make a passable cookie dough from these.

Would anyone with any dignity be thinking like this? The world is going to end soon. Atomic war, chemical weapons, global warming, Y2K. Compared to that, a few pounds of fat? Nothing. This is my last chance. For sweet, at peace. It's too late for all that other stuff.

DEAR DIARY, I'M in bed now. I can't even read.
I ask, "What's going on?" I find nothing particular. In fact, I find no feelings at all. I know the pressure a dam feels on its broad flank.

I overwhelm Them who never see my vulnerabilities. I am too "difficult." "You drive everyone away." They threaten me: I'll end alone. But I am not alone, not at all. Hurt knows, intimately. Hurt sees what human beings choose blindness to. Hurt is certain: "Here, exactly you are soft." Hurt drives there to nest and feed. Hurt never abandons me.

I'm not doing it now. I don't have a good reason not to. I want, just once in my life, to feel this all the way to its end. I don't know what its end might be. Right now it feels like punishment for being alive. Every smile, every time I skipped as a little girl, the shine in my hair, any good I thought I'd do, melts into bleak mess of monster identity. The only sense I can make of this is elaborate curse. The only God I can imagine, who is by definition creator and audience, is a sadist.

I am clean as a cleaned blade. No one would share this with me. No one would so much as cross a room to understand.

DEAR DIARY, TODAY same. All same. All give up. The mind rock. No move. No think. Every word pronounced to another, every touch dropped on another, a lie. This soft, pink flesh, how it doesn't begin to convey rock troll, boggles the mind. Others contact only mask. Me, just: eat.

It is bad when life is a noun, again. When you can't the verb.

Why not a more active suicide?

DEAR DIARY, YOU'RE in a hospital waiting room. Your loved one lies inside. Doctors, orderlies, nurses, hurly-burly, whiz past, fetch shiny equipments, shout theories and commands in precious vocabulary, encrypted so as to be incomprehensible to you.

You sit. You wait. That's all you're allowed to do.

Was it in grade school? Kindergarten? Or before? What was the one wrong move, maybe a smart-ass trick, never meaning any harm, or maybe there was some malevolence in that fateful word or action – should you feel guilty? Do penance, request absolution? Or used? And get angry, and protest, "For Christ's fucking *sake!*" Wasn't it just yesterday, or was it the day before, that the loved one was okay? Then, suddenly the wrong move was made, whatever it was, and real life stopped. Pinpoint your last normal moment before nightmare.

People outside the window are laughing, smiling; there are kids playing and beautiful women. You marvel at their feats, the range of movement and expression. Bodies so like yours, so like your loved one's. But, wait. Those abilities are not so alien. The loved one used to be able to do that. The loved one used to do it regularly. And you. You used to be one of those laughing people, going about your day, never imaging how badly a human body can break. Now no matter how calm you appear as you flip through your fresh copy of *People* magazine, even if you nod off to sleep sitting up in your steel and leather waiting room chair, you never stop: "Is this divine retribution? Is it stupid chance? Is it ever going to end?"

The beast laughs. "I have forever. You have just one day at a time."

D EAR DIARY, I don't feel like a warrior. I feel like a battlefield.

D EAR DIARY, IT'S over.
As it happens, it wasn't cookie dough, as I'd always assumed it would be. It was peanut butter. One night I was doing stretches on the floor. I heard myself say, "I can't take this anymore." I have no idea what "this" was. I can say that it wasn't physical hunger or the exercise's exertion. I rose and walked into the kitchen and pulled a jar of peanut butter down from the cabinet.

To report that I spooned the peanut butter straight from the jar into my mouth would communicate nothing to you. Listen: I talked to that peanut butter. I poured my heart out. An avalanche of words. I may have even cried. The peanut butter didn't interrupt each point in precious debate that proved how smart it was, and how wrong I was. It didn't swing the subject round to its own woes. The peanut butter, thoroughly present – I mean, what could be more present, more substantial and absolutely *there* than peanut butter on the roof of your mouth? Thoroughly present, the peanut butter listened to me. The peanut butter permitted me, lubricated my rocky desert. Yes, I had battled long, against mighty foes. But the peanut butter was there, supportive, patient, and sweet.

I know what you're thinking, Diary. "But I do that. I hear you. That's what I do." Yes, I know that you do that, Diary, and I'm grateful, but, you see, I wanted so badly to be touched. "Want," "need," "crave" don't begin to tell you. My entire body was yearning upward; "hungry," "thirsty," "itch" – they don't begin to convey. "Demand," "command," communicate nothing. I needed the physical, against me, solid, rooted, implacably obedient to the laws of matter. Something that would alter me, rechannel fluids, rumple planes, physically register my being to refute thorough erasure. I had to have something that would do back to me, wrench me, bend me around it, and right then. Right, then, real, hard, but, yet, at the same time, soft and sweet and all-enveloping.

Peripheral reality disappeared. The four walls of my apartment could have melted into Fiji, waves and palms; I wouldn't know. There was no world of winners and losers in which I was designated loser, nothing outside of my mouth and my need and my immediate gratification.

For a long while since I haven't been able to bring myself to write in you, Diary. Ashamed and afraid to go home, I've been cheating on you. I've been scribbling around.

• On a paper plate:

What did I lose? I'm nothing, anyway. That's why so many people I can't forget find it dead easy to walk away from me. I don't care I don't care I don't care I don't care I don't care I don't care I don't care. I'm nothing so I have nothing to lose.

Anyway, it's too late. The sun set, the workers laid off for the day, the race run, the horse stolen. I didn't learn how to be human fast enough. No matter how hard we try, we'll never make it. There's too much catch-up. While I'm applying bandages, those trained to be aggressive are out making the kill.

This is it, then. The yes/no decision I've put off all my life, I've made today, and invested in it. I'm gonna get that job at K-Mart that pays just enough to maintain one human life and spend every dime on food and sandbag my door and eat and watch TV. I could live off the video of that "Dr. Joel-rescues-Maggie-when-she's-sick-in-the-wilderness" episode of *Northern Exposure* alone for one whole week.

- On a few schedules grabbed while riding the 86 bus to the Wayne supermarket (the bus driver gave me a dirty look for grabbing so many):

I need to pee or shit all the time. Every piece of me hurts. Not just my stomach but also my arms and legs feel stuffed with food. It's hot and tight, just like how I used to feel during Mommy's enemas. Even imagining other actions – jogging, reading, going to movies – is impossible. I drop my eyes in front of mirrors. I squirm when grooming or hygiene demands I touch myself. I flinch away from others' fingers and eyes. I will not confront my reflection in others' eyes; I avoid the awareness triggered by touch. I'm driving myself further away from whom I want to be. I am going deaf to music I'd learned to hear.

The tension of abstinence is nothing compared to that of using. I need to be near food in time and space. I'm on the leash. My entire being is a tensiometer. All senses are marshaled to measure tension until it reaches critical mass, justifying the next hit.

Even the pain has its use. Food grounds elusive, airborne phantoms in a knot I can knead under my fingers. Even if I can't address loneliness or bad dreams, I can rub a sore tummy. Food transforms taboo pain into social grace. If I dare break a date because of one of those nightmares about stuff that may or may not have happened ages ago, I get so beat up for it: "Move on!" "You probably imagined it!" "Don't talk about such depressing things!" A chorus line of stomach problems star in their own TV drug commercials. If I claim one of those as reason for canceling a date, I am okay, I am doing it right. I receive tenderness: "Take care of yourself tonight. I know what torture gastric reflux can be. We'll see you next time." If there were anything else, I wouldn't do food.

- On the back of junk mail:

[I apparently established an identity by calling all those *Sierra* magazine eight hundred numbers. I still get junk mail from those companies and others like them that they passed my name along to. This identity is between twenty-five and forty, a homeowner, with a wood burning stove. She is Politically Correct and religiously New Age. She drives a sport utility vehicle to a ski chalet at Tahoe. It's all so poignant. I feel like calling the companies and saying, "Guess again." But I don't. I like getting glossy, slick mail addressed to me.]

"If your eye troubleth you, cast it out." Very clean. Oh, but Jesus, think of all I do with that eye. I don't just sin. I see sky, its blue that can never be replaced. There are lots of shades: cerulean, midnight, sapphire, but no synonym replaces "blue." No activity synonyms sight. I see not just what hurts, but what feeds, what vivifies, what loves me and what I love. How dead do I have to be before I can be okay? How self-blinded?

Seeing is essential. It touches all I do and know and am. As I cast out my eye, I kill me. I mute myself of "See for yourself," "Seeing is believing," "Out of sight out of mind," a whole lexicon, a whole culture. I become a new thing, one that doesn't see. How can I know if I will love that, will want to be that? Who will teach me?

- On some relatively blank spaces in several consecutive picture ads in the yellow pages, bleeding into a few sheets of paper toweling:

Assiduously honed awareness of past and present has adulterated the essential fuel called faith. I have no joy for new enterprise. I have pained regret over apparently infinite past wrong. I am exquisitely sensitive to how badly things can go. I quiver, suspended, a mass of jellied wounds confronting hot stoves, grit, lye, and sharp sticks. When I was using, I wasn't crippled like this; I could accomplish anything, with the right food at my side.

- On a note magneted to the refrigerator:

What are you feeling? What do you lack? What is your statement? Talk to me in words I understand. Here's a whole page of theme paper. Fill it up! But in a shared tongue. I'm so weary of orders encoded in muscle and desire that I must obey on pain of death. And you; don't you tire, ever, of unilateral command?

- In black ballpoint ink, on a crumpled scrap filched from the recycling bin. The print gets tinier as the frayed edge nears, as if this were written in some prison camp where paper is gold:

Everyone saw. Not one person did a goddamned thing. How can I suddenly join? I loathe the tent of those who sacrifice little girls.

My skin weeps. My right hand is frozen into a claw; it is lobster red, and covered with death yellow scales. The scales fall off at all the wrong moments. Although I guess there really isn't a right moment for scales to shower from one's hand. My latest hygiene imperative: disposing of bits of myself. The swelling prevents even a tiny finger flex. Just to scribble this out I had to soak my hand in brine and bandage it with cortisone. All those science teachers were not kidding when they insisted that humanity evolved to the top of the heap thanks to the thumb's ability to bend in opposition to the other fingers. Write one of those long papers Mel says you have to write in grad school? Ha. I can't even brush my teeth.

But I am beginning to wonder if going this alone is impossible, sort of like deciding that I don't need air. Sure, I can be tough and stop breathing, but I'd also stop living. I'm beginning to question if, to recover, I need to look at the face of someone who is feeling for me sorrow; I need to be held by this person. Maybe I don't want this, maybe I need it, I need it precisely, as someone with scurvy needs vitamin C. I have never wanted to choreograph this. I have wanted this to come spontaneously. I didn't arrange the pain. It came spontaneously. I want to believe that the world that can so methodically and accurately cripple and wound can also touch in a sweet, a good, a healing way.

I've long wanted a teacher. Not another Miles but what I wished Miles to be, a teacher. I've wanted to hear: "Your qualities which, if there were a fire in your soul, you would bundle under your arm and save first, these are witnessed by me, and they delight." I don't know if I've wanted, lately, anyone to come between me and my despair. When you know you're going to live someplace for a long time, you decorate. And so I abide in a lived-in luxury, a familiar resort. I once did crave and shout in my prayers for someone to come between me and my despair, that is between me and my addiction. Was that a long time ago? After long times like that, you scar.

- On the inside of a kandy-korn carton grabbed from the Dumpster:

Kept waiting for it to taste good, for me to get my hit. It didn't happen. I trashed it outside. Went back inside. Was inside for maybe two minutes.

Went back out to the Dumpster again to dig it out. It still didn't satisfy. I didn't say, "Aha, I'm seeking satisfaction in the wrong place;" I said, "Aha, this is proof that I need more food." Now that addiction has me, it never has to deliver again.

I know that if I stopped eating I'd be overwhelmed by regret and shame and I'll need to eat again to survive the regret and shame. Addiction is an internal guillotine that chops off sane me.

- I began to apostrophe the food, the way I do you, Diary. I wrote this in pencil on the kitchen countertop:

Even Sparky, Shushu, or Dexter, wouldn't be enough. They should be the real thing, but, for whatever chemical or psychosocial reason, they *aren't.* You are. When they touch me, I rejoice. I'm a leper who planned to never receive any touch so fine. Translucent fingers, animate and real, are allowed to spatter my skin. I am silently grateful. And I know. Their touch doesn't go deep. There is some barrier. I hit the barrier before I perceive the person beyond. Perhaps the deepest part of me was never ploughed by humanity. I am intimate with the deepest part of me. You plumb it, effortlessly. You mean more to me than the dearest person has ever meant.

Except, maybe, Kai, or maybe not. But, certainly, Miles . . .

Miles – oh, blow me, fool.

No, I'm not copying that from the countertop. I'm just saying, fool, blow me.

DEAR DIARY, TOPH came by. He communicated that I had been out of circulation for some time and that that meant that he hadn't been getting any and that I owed him. I trooped up to the loft and took off my clothes and lay down for a while while he relieved himself inside of my body. Later we went to a café in Montclair and he talked about some writing he's been doing and how many miles he can run without stopping. Last Sunday he did ten miles, in spite of the rain and his being out late the night before with some of his high school buddies who have chosen different life paths than he and who make more money, but who seem tragically limited and pussy-whipped by their harpy spouses who have sure lost *their* looks since twelfth grade, *I tell you.*

I said, "This is great. I hope you *do* try to get it published. It reads like Hemingway, without the overweening macho. I especially like how you use the word 'carbine.' I've never used the word 'carbine' and, boy, have I wanted to." And I said, "Wow. I'm so impressed. And in the rain! What dedication. But do be sure to drink some Echinacea tea just in case you were exposed to something. Remind me when we get back to Paterson. I've got teabags in the apartment." And I said, "Well, everybody makes the choices that's right for him. You did what's right for you. In the long run, you'll be happier."

I'm not writing the standard version today, but I know how. I would write about the certain tousle of his blond hair; the wheaten cowlick that springs vigorously from his Apollonian brow no matter how brusquely he swats it down. I would focus on that with a Vermeer-like exclusion, elevating standard-issue to the sunset glow in a gentrified neighborhood. I would describe how sturdy and thick his wrist looked against my doorknob, and how I noticed how differently put together men and women are as he shouldered his pack in a brief *contrapposto*. I would spit on my palms and take on that challenge writers always do, the challenge that always defeats them. I would struggle to materialize the evanescent in this ink, to capture the intractably wild on this paper. I would attempt to bring his smell to this page. It's acrid, like the tannin in crackled oak leaves that work up into your nostrils while you're hiking a sun-dried ridge. But don't get me wrong – it's more ochre than mahogany. There are slim-hipped sweats and Nike running shoes warmed to body temperature. There is some core that has nothing to do with soap, his comfortable class, or civility. I would attempt some cute macho anthropomorphism about his scent's conquest of my apartment which had been, for so many days, exclusively feminine. I would mention that when I rubbed my face after this evening's exceptionally vigorous shower a passing sense of defeat shuddered through me: "I'll never escape." I didn't realize till just now that that was because I was smelling him on my towel, still. Excuse me while I start some laundry.

I would report live about the satisfaction of, at long last, being the object of a man's adoration. Believe me. This is how women tell and live the standard version. I've stayed up late with enough other girls. I've watched enough TV and movies. I did it myself, with Miles. If I would only perfect it, I would finally summit my peak experience.

This storytelling technique demands ferocious single-mindedness. Its practitioners must betray language. We must torture words. I'd have to swindle my Diary. I'd demolish my hard-won bonds with the best friends I've ever had: language, words, you, Diary, to tell this story in a way that made it one variation on the sanctified myth. I'd store up all the rage those lies would engender and vent it in on women lower caste, more honest, fatter, than myself. But Toph would come out smelling like a rose. He would be made up entirely of fetchingly tousled hair and manly wrists, pungent odors and masculine powers that satisfy me by erasing me, masculine needs that drive him to his knees begging for friction in my feminine folds. He'd be the masculine attention that finally fulfilled. I'd know what love is available for women from men, this seal of approval: "You've been looking so beautiful, lately. I can't keep my hands off of you. The line of your neck, the sound of your voice, the colloidal jiggle produced in your mammaries when they are jostled; the tickle these give me render you worthy. You have achieved the pinnacle of your identity: you are a pretty enough thing to make a cock go hard and get soft again." I wouldn't write him asking for a cunt in pedestrian monosyllables that, with a few substitutions, could be used to demand a TV's remote control.

I was doing this experiment to be wanted, to be loved. I was at least wanted; at least I turned a man on, finally. But when it struck it wasn't the hankered-after fulfillment. It wasn't even new. I suddenly recognized that I've lived every second of my life quelling the reverberating terror of knowing that there are people who get their greatest pleasure and release from intense contact with my flesh. I thought of Mommy's and Daddy's hands on me. I thought of the hands of that bozo in Texas. He had pulled off the highway, into the woods. He said: "You fucking bitch; you goddamned whore; you are so goddamned fat and ugly; I've got a gun." Even as it was happening, the irony struck: he's telling me how ugly I am, and he's perpetrating a felony in order to have me.

Oh, give me a break; that is not what I'm saying at all. I am not saying that a man's self-centered demand makes him a bad guy and a woman's passive acquiescence makes her virtuous. If I had found bad guys or good guys in any of this I wouldn't be writing in you, Diary. I'd be running down the street naked shouting "Eureka!" I'm just reporting that it's not the peak experience. I'll tell you what a peak experience is: wrestling a revolver from some rat turd who's trying to rape you and turning it on him and hearing *him* beg. That's real womanly fulfillment. What do I feel about what I did with Toph? I felt like what I felt with Mommy when she came after me. I was as remote in insulation as an ice fisherman. I can't even speak about them in the first person.

They're like a couple arguing publicly. I admire neither, but I *do* watch. Why? They frighten but fascinate me. I can't look away. Is this ugliness a distorted reflection of anything in me? Are they a crystal ball telling my past, or my destiny? I keep score on each one's errors that perpetuate the agony. I'm trying to find someone to blame. I'm trying to finger the solution. It's not just him. Why does she put up with it? Why doesn't she tell him what's going on? Why doesn't she ask for what she needs? Why does she have to be so difficult?

"You seem distracted," he says. "What's up?"

"Oh, nothing," she says. See? See what I mean? She's just being difficult.

"You want another Diet Coke?" he asks.

"No, that's fine," she says.

"C'mon, let me buy you one. You never let me buy you anything."

She is confused. She had been unaware that there was an ongoing, concerted effort to buy her beverages, an effort she had been resisting. Had she really ever turned down a free beverage? But the subject is changing already:

"Yeah, so Bryce is pulling down six figures. Hard to believe that a chronic nose-picker could do that before thirty. Do you believe this economy?"

"I guess I am distracted," she mumbles.

The man closes his newspaper. "How about a movie? That Danish film I've been waiting for is in town. It'll never survive out here in the suburbs for more than a week. It's that new Danish avant-garde I've told you about – remember, I told you? That I'd seen the other one already? These guys are pushing the envelope. They're talking about things that have just been absolutely – that nobody treats cinematically. The risks –"

"It's – my cousin," she blurts. "I'm worried about her."

The man slaps his folded paper onto the wire lattice tabletop and drills his fists into widely spread thighs. "Your cousin. Okay. Which cousin is this? You have so many. Is this the one whose wedding you were at?"

"No. Another one. You don't know her. I haven't talked about her. I'm worried about her."

"Oh, yeah?" he asks.

Mentally, frantically, she fingers through her bilingual dictionary. What do They call it out here anyway?

"She's – an addict. She's uh – I guess what They might call – an incest survivor. She's going through a bad time right now. From what I understand she's not leaving the house. She's just holed up in there, using her drug of choice, all the time. Bad dreams, bad TV, crying spells, no hope: that sort of thing."

His face is kicking in. He is engaged. Is this working? Is it this easy? If so, why the hell has she waited this long?

"Well, let's go," says the man, fingering his car keys. "Let's go right now. I can catch the movie another time. I can catch it in the city. It'll play longer there. You probably didn't want to see it anyway. It's not your thing. Not like – who's that old guy? Frank Capra?" Has he just snorted? "So let's go. We do an intervention."

"What?"

"We intervene. It's a technical term. In layman's language it means we – snap her out of it."

"Toph! . . . That's – you're being great, really, you are," she pats his arm. He doesn't like it; the arm is withdrawn from the table. The keys jingle at the end of the arm. She struggles to continue, though she has just been told to shut up. "It's – it's – it's just that I don't know if – I'm not sure that –"

"Look, Mira, I know it's confusing. I can see by how you talk about this that it's probably all new to you, probably hard to – to assimilate. But I've read a lot about this. Do you know Gary Null? Tony Robbins? Look. What it comes down to is this. We all create our own reality. All of us. We're doing it all the time. Depression is just another – it's just another head trip. It's just another illusion. It's something we create, when we wrap anger around fear –"

"*What?*"

"Look. We'll talk about it in the car on the way over. And we can stop and get some wheat grass."

"Wheat grass?"

"Yes, wheat grass. It cleanses the second chakra. Where the wounded inner child lives."

"Toph!"

"Yeah?"

"Could you please come back here for a minute?"

"What? For what? Are we gonna fix this, or aren't we? C'mon, Mira. Time's a wastin'. She's your cousin. You owe it to her."

"Toph, please come back."

Ah, there she goes again. The woman has made him angry. Now why did she have to go and do that? Here he was, ready to give and she has thrown a monkey wrench into his best intentions all over again.

She is talking very quickly. Maybe if she talks quick enough, she can travel back in time to before she made him angry. "Toph, maybe, uh, before we drive over there, um, maybe we could, uh, maybe we could talk about this? Like, listen, we could . . . practice? Maybe? Like, like, uh, what if it were I. I'll role-play. I'll be her. Okay? And you say the stuff that you would say."

"Mira." Mira, period. It's a whole sentence, noun, verb, and noun. That's how long they have been together: long enough that he can say it all with just her first name, and then period. But he continues: "Why are you being ridiculous? You said she's an addict. Tell me. Do you know anything about addiction? You haven't even heard of Gary Null *or* Tony Robbins. Have you ever seen an addict when they get like this? Do you have any idea how dangerous this is? Mira, look. I took an abnormal psych class, and I'm telling you, we could be dealing with life or death here." He sits down again. He looks a bit beat, but he is smoldering. He will be proven right.

"Toph –" she pleads, in as feminine a voice as found on any porn video.

"Look," he says. "Forget this role-play idea. It wouldn't work with you, Mira. You've got to understand that this is a whole, it's a whole different thing. Not everyone was raised like we were. These women – you're too strong. You could never know – even if you tried to imagine."

She shows, finally, assertion. It's the assertion of someone who has given up. "Okay," she says. "We've just arrived at the house. My cousin's on the couch, in her pajamas. She's sloppy. She's – angry. She's gross. She's not anyone you'd want to get next to. You walk up to her. What do you say to her, Toph?"

"You're so good at this, Mira. Why don't you start?" he replies.

She pauses, for a long time. In that pause there is nothing. No look, no sound. A director once gave a peculiar, memorable direction to film idol Greta Garbo. The character she was playing had lost everything. This was to be Garbo's final close-up, the last scene in the movie. Garbo had to communicate all that loss, that near death, and whatever the future might promise – from suicide to renaissance. "In this close-up," the director instructed, "what I want you to do is look straight ahead, and, mentally, count to ten." This woman's face is blank enough that perhaps, mentally, she is counting to ten. Finally, she speaks.

"Okay, Toph, I'll go first." The woman reaches across the table. Perhaps because of her quiet assertion, the man does not flinch. She places her hands over his face. "Toph, tell me. What color are my eyes?"

"This is ridiculous," he pronounces, into her palms.

She drops her hands. "Ain't it, though," she agrees. "Oh, by the way, blue. Always been. Toph, what's my confirmation name? Oh, wait a second. You're not Catholic. One of the biggest days of my life, but you don't even know what the word means. What's my middle name, Toph? Who's my patron saint?"

He is giving her a look seen in nature only on the faces of either lovers tightly sandwiched between urgent sex and ugly good-byes, or professional assassins.

She continues placidly, or, simply counting, two, three, four: "Therese. After the Little Flower. I'm Miroswava Therese Hudak. What languages did my grandmother speak? What did my grandfather, both my grandfathers, do for work once they got to this country? How many brothers and sisters do I have? What are their names? When I was eight years old, what did I want to do when I grew up? Did the Salvation Army Santa ever visit my house? Did he ever get me alone and reach up my dress? Are any of my uncles wanted by the FBI? What's my favorite ice cream flavor? I'll give you a hint. Chocolate chip mint." Eight, nine, ten.

"You're starting to imagine things, Mira," he says, gathering up his newspaper, and, not quite standing, just rising like the mercury in a thermometer. "That's the problem with women like you. Okay, I'll admit it. I am impressed by your intellect. I have to admit that's why I've stuck it out with you all this while. But from now on, I'm not making any more excuses."

She looks at him; she looks to be counting from ten to one. After a long while she observes, "You are so American."

He fully collapses into the wire chair. What the hell is she talking about? What's the fun of the joust when your opponent goes and makes incomprehensible non sequiturs like that? Ah, wait; she's continuing.

"Someone else is in pain. You're not. That makes you the elite. That means you have the answer. But that's not what it means, Toph. Toph, didn't – don't you even think about this? It's all been given to you, Toph. You're ready to go rescue someone you never even met, with some dubious scheme. Cause you've got this one qualification: you have had a lucky life. You are so American."

"As I was saying," he says, "I'm not making any more excuses for you, Mira. Paula was right."

She bursts: "*Paula?*"

"Paula. She's a woman, Mira. You wouldn't know what that is, so I haven't told you about her. But she's been right about you, all along. I kept insisting, 'No, no, Paula, you don't understand. Mira's really gifted. It's worth it.' But you know what? It's not worth it any more. If I want insights, I can get a subscription to *The New York Times*. I don't have to swallow your incessant abuse."

"*Paula!*" she is laughing, hitting the table laughing. "That's so great, Toph. I mean, it is just so great."

His body had been verging upward; curious, eager to not capitulate to what he understands as nothing but an upped ante, he surrenders to gravity and the wire café chair.

"I mean," the woman continues, *Paula*. She's got a name! So often they're so and so's . . . whatever. *Konrad's* wife. *Miles's* wife. But this one has a name. A real, live name. I guess that's a sign of progress. I guess that's a sign of the emancipation of the feminine race. Whaddya think? Oh, thanks, Toph. I mean, really. Thanks for absolving me of regret."

"I am not going to miss any of this," he says.

"Miss *what?* Wait a second, okay?" she says. "'Incessant abuse.' Is that what you mean? What you're not going to miss? What is that? Are you being serious, or are you being mean? What incessant abuse? Are you saying that I abused you incessantly? If I was abusing you, why didn't you tell me so I could make amends and stop? And how did I abuse you, anyway?"

"I thought that if I gave you your head," he says, nodding, gravely, relieved that this truth would finally have its hearing. "I thought that if I demonstrated to you how patient and loving a man can be, that eventually you'd feel secure enough to tire of your little dominatrix game."

"'Gave me my head.' Toph, do you have to do that to language at moments like this? Okay, so the whole time we've known each other, you've been feeling dominated, and not doing anything about it. So let me get this straight. You felt that if you were completely artificial with me that that was the only way we could have a genuine relationship. And what's all this about a subscription to the *New York Times?* I am a woman. I am not a library card. Were you really unclear about the difference between the two? Okay, I'll confess. I have no idea what you're talking about. 'Dominatrix game?' Toph, I'm scared to death of my own shadow –"

"It's too late for that, Mira. It's too late to manipulate me with your feminine wiles."

"*What?* Feminine wiles? You think by drawing to your attention the fact that I'm terrified of you, of me, of life, that I constantly feel like I'm – I'm confessing my faults here, not trying to seduce – Oh my God. That's disgusting. That you interpret my exposing my weakness as an attempt to – And to think, you came this close to convincing me that I was the crazy one." Exhausted, she rests her head in her hands. When she's ready, she asks, "So, who's Paula? You spend all your free time playing with yourself on the computer; how does a man like that meet a woman? You can't have met her at work . . . Oh my God. Toph, say it isn't so. You're not fucking one of the students, are you? Toph, no. Oh, no, Toph, no."

"The program's over, Mira. She's not a student anymore."

"Which one?"

"I've mentioned her to you."

"But you only ever talked about – no. Oh my God, no." She wishes she could be taking an exceptionally vigorous shower, right at that minute. "Prema. The one you told me about. She wanted an American name. She asked you to help – 'Paula'? You named her after Paul McCartney? No, wait. You named her after Paul de Man. The Nazi!"

"He was a brilliant literary critic!"

"Did you get to feel like Adam? Naming all God's little creatures? But wasn't Prema always whining to you about – about her fiancé! The one engaged to the guy she was always whining to you about. She's a teenager! You said she was using you. You said that she was using him – that she was gonna marry him just to get a green card. You said that it was a drag to be around her because she never got any of your references, that it was such a relief to talk to me after . . . You said, I remember this, you said, 'Every idea in her head, I put there.' Toph?"

But the man is not defending himself. He doesn't see anything to defend himself against. Nodding again, he says, "I know what you think of her. What your feminism makes you think of her. Strange, isn't it, how feminists are so vicious to other women –"

"What I *think* of her? I can't think *anything* of her. I've never even met her. All I know of her is what you've told me. And based on that I don't so much think of her as smell her. From what you told me I just envisioned this pair of spread legs and men shoving in cash and valuable prizes like green cards. When you first started tutoring her, I remember, you said, 'Some women, as wives, are a man's better half. She'd be a man's lower half.' . . . It was such a good line I memorized it . . . " The woman is practically in tears. "It's like *Invasion of the Body Snatchers*. Exactly that. You meet a man, he seems cool, not the love of your life, and you're not the love of his life, either, but you could be fuck buddies, it could be pleasant and uncomplicated, and then you find out that the pods got him, too."

His face has settled into an undisguised, pugnacious scowl. "It just cranks you so hard, doesn't it, Mira? Some people are simply able to love, commit, and throw themselves into a relationship. But it really bugs the shit out of you. You're an intellectual and your life, your whole worldview, are founded on logic. Our life is founded on passion. We're passionate people, something you don't know anything about."

"You know," she pronounces, through fist at her chin, just barely supporting her head, "even you don't believe this crap you're spewing."

Disappointed that his profound theory didn't deck her, he fills time till the next dig comes to him. "Sarcasm," he diagnoses. "We've talked about it. I hope it works for you, Mira. I hope it gets you past the pain, at least today. I know you won't have anyone to call." The next dig has come to him. "I know you can't call Martha anymore." And another. "We've talked about it. '*Perversity.* 'That's what Paula calls it. Your perversity. We don't understand why you choose to be so hard. Women like you always end up alone. That's what Paula said. She has a simpler way of understanding these things, of getting to the essential truth. We understand –"

"Look, Toph, this is Mira you're talking to. Remember me? The woman who found the error in the first sentence of your celebrated Hughes paper? I have heard, noted, and been appropriately stung by your devastating use of the royal 'we.' You blunt its impact by belaboring it. Oh, God. I can't believe I'm taking my red pen to your pathetic efforts to wound me with your happiness."

The man silently rises and walks away. The woman's head is down. Suddenly, she senses something, and looks up. The man is back. He is at her elbow.

"You showed such contempt for me," the man has apparently returned to say.

She says nothing.

"Such hatred," he says.

She sighs. She knows that this annoying person, too, will pass. She figures she'll just keep sighing till he does.

"You fight like a tigress," he says.

She turns her head sharply away from him.

"Let's fuck again," he suggests.

She jerks her head up toward him. "*Ty kurwi waselina,*" she spits out, without hesitation.

He walks away. He's understood the general rejection, though he's unaware that he's just been called a "whore's Vaseline."

DEAR DIARY, WHEN I heard the doorbell, I expected Martha. I wondered what had taken her so long. But through the peephole I saw Rebekah, the round, fat woman from the Incest Survivors' Anonymous meeting, the one with the Diet Coke. As opposed to Betty, the round, fat woman with the Diet Coke, and Willow, the round, fat woman with the Diet Coke, at the Incest Survivors' Anonymous meeting in Montclair.

I opened the door. "Hi?" I ventured.

Rebekah didn't waste any time. She is, I suspect, a woman who knows about wasted time, and is its enemy. She reported that she'd been having feelings. She'd be driving to work and flash on an image of me falling through space, and so she came by.

I ushered her in. I proffered the open jar of peanut butter, a fork projecting out its top. She declined. Standing next to it, her hand on the off button, she suggested "we" turn off the TV. I lay back down on the couch. "Oooo kay." I smirked. "You're wearing a poncho, Rebekah. I haven't seen one of those since the sixties."

"It keeps me warm," Rebekah said.

"So would a coat," I said.

She didn't bite.

"Have a seat," I said. She released her great bulk noisily into my one comfy chair. I was relieved when it accommodated her.

She asked, "Do you want to talk about it?"

"It's just pretty much what you said," I replied. "There's a lot of falling through space that's been going on in this apartment the last little while."

She nodded. Her car keys were still in her hand. "I can drive you to the mental health unit –"

"Oh my fucking God," I said.

She just looked at me.

"Look, Rebekah, I don't mean to be unkind, but I just don't feel like wasting my time and energy. I know it's what I'm supposed to do, but I can't enable you. I can't donate myself as the raw material to make someone who isn't risking any spontaneity or compassion look heroic."

"Oh." She sucked in. The additional weight of inhaled air seemed to knock her head further back on her neck. Then, "I'm not here to be a hero," she said, softly. "I'm here because it was uncomfortable for me to have those feelings. And it would be comfortable for me if I could do something to help. I want to do the right thing."

"Of course you do," I said.

"You're humoring me," she guessed.

"I was raised not to be rude to guests," I explained.

"I didn't come here because I needed some peanut butter," she said. She slipped her car keys into her woven straw bag's wide floppy mouth. "Look, Mmm – tell me your name again."

I kind of laughed. "Miroswava."

"You'll have to write it down," she instructed. "I learn things visually." I got up, reached into this desk, wrote my name down on a sheet of paper, handed it to her. Rebekah muttered over the paper a couple of times, as if conjuring an incantation. I suddenly felt anxious for having been so hard on her. "Thanks," she said. "Miroswava – I'm saying it right now, right? Miroswava. I don't think I'm better than you, if that's what you're thinking. I look upon us as a kind of a sisterhood. I lost two years of my life to incest. My adult life, I mean. I'm not even counting what happened when I was a kid. I couldn't leave the house. I was a basket case. All right. You laughed. I didn't remember your name. But I know things about you that people who know your name don't."

"Maybe. And Maybe I'm better than you," I said. "I can leave the house. I just don't feel like it right now. And the psych ward? I mean, you see that I'm feeling lousy and you think the solution is to dress me in a flimsy rag that exposes my ass to strangers and put me under fluorescent lights and have other strangers stick me full of needles and drugs."

She sighed, angrily. "No, I don't think that that's the solution."

"Well?" I looked at her. "What have you got that's better than peanut butter and TV? I'm listening."

"What do you want?" she asked.

"That's a good start," I conceded.

"Maybe we can go to a café?" she suggested.

"Yeah, I know a nice one in Montclair. Come to think of it, no, thanks," I said.

"I just thought it would be good – if you've been in here a while, away from people –"

"That's the idea," I said.

"You want to be alone?" she asked.

"No! I hate being alone," I confessed. "I just don't want to be around people."

Rebekah's expression was one big question.

"Humanity is a cult that won't let me join," I said.

"That sounds pretty grim," she said.

"It has its pluses and minuses," I replied. "I mean, who wants to sink so low as to join a cult?"

"It sounds like you've been hurt," she said. "I know what that's like. You get hurt and you hole up and you isolate. But eventually –"

"You know what they say in program?" I interrupted her. I was referring to Twelve Step Anonymous groups, like Incest Survivors. I could speak her lingo; I know all their scripture by heart. "They say, 'doing the same thing over and over and expecting different results is the definition of insanity.' I keep trying to do humanity, and I keep failing. I have no friends, Rebekah. Not a single one. That's pretty exceptional. Even Hitler had a girlfriend. People meet me, they love me to death, they hang on my every word, and then, kaboom, they are permanently gone. I'm forbidden so much as to refer to them. My great fantasy is to walk into Miles Aldrich's – this guy I used to know – Miles Aldrich. I wanna walk into his office and announce the unspeakable to his colleagues: 'You know what? I know that guy. He bared his soul to me.' But I can't do that. I'm his Admirable Crichton." Rebekah was giving me a blank look. "Doesn't anyone read any more?" I asked, rhetorically. "But that's not my point. My point is that my whole life is forbidden territory. I can't take it any more. I'm tired of living through one Holocaust after another. And you know what? I have no idea why it happens. The sudden love. The inevitable, and permanent, hate. And since I don't know why it happens, if I walk out that door, there's nothing I can do to prevent its happening all over again." I looked at her. I was hoping she would look as confused as I was feeling, but, alas, she did not. She knew. She knew why everyone had to hate me. It was that obvious.

"Spill it," I ordered.

"I don't have the answer," she said.

"Like hell," I said.

"It's just that . . . "

"C'mon, c'mon, c'mon," I urged.

"It's just that . . . well, we talked about this at the meeting."

"You g*ossiped* about me? That's completely against Twelve Step rules!"

"People are only human," she shrugged.

"Oh, my God. Just tell me," I said, screwing up my lips.

"Miroswava, you're an intimidating woman," she said.

"What the hell is that supposed to mean?"

"Just what I said. You're intimidating. You intimidate people."

"No way! 'Timid' is my middle name! I live my life in permanent adrenaline overdose. Every time I pull back a shower curtain I brace for Norman Bates. And *you're* intimidated by *me*? *I'm* intimidated by *air*."

"I don't know what to say," Rebekah said. "You don't seem that way," she said. "We all talked about it. We all felt it. I mean, women come and go from those meetings all the time, but you – you struck us. So maybe this Miles person – that was his name, right? Maybe he was intimidated."

"Yeah, right," I snorted. "I am not intimidating, Rebekah. I am sitting here on this couch. I am hiding out. I am shaking. I am not intimidating." I worked the scalloped hem of my crusty afghan through my fingers, and then I spoke again. "You know the difference between us? Polaks and Jews?" I asked.

Rebekah's chin jerked down, and to the side. "I don't remember mentioning to you that I'm a Jew," she said. "And I don't see what's that got to do with anything."

Already she was ten exit ramps beyond what I had been talking about. I could have said, "Don't be ridiculous. You can't hide it. I can always tell where somebody's grandparents came from. And it has everything to do with everything." But that would have gotten us twenty exit ramps beyond what I was talking about.

"Rebekah, my father said to me, 'You would tell a stranger.' And that's what we envy about you. You talk to anyone. About anything. I don't mean you, personally. I mean the culture."

She wasn't getting it. I kept trying. "People see me when I'm writing in my diary. Like, when I take it to a café and write. Or, they'll hear me typing in the Writing Center. Strangers. They stare at my hands. They say, 'God, you type fast. Are you a secretary?' Or in a café, 'You write so furiously. Do you publish?' But, Rebekah, the stuff I type so fast, the stuff I write so furiously, it would be death for anyone to see that."

"And that's because you're Polish?"

"Do you know who we can talk to?" I asked. "We can talk to someone we're related to. Blood relation. That's it. That's why I can tell my diary all these things. If I didn't have my diary, I wouldn't be able to talk at all. Do you know where we can talk? We can talk in a home. Not a house; a home. Do you know what we can talk about? Wait, wait, wait. This is it. *Her!*" I tossed a magazine at Rebekah. "Do you see that? Do you see who's on the cover of that magazine? Of course you don't."

"It's Martha Stewart," Rebekah informed me, quietly, slowly, perhaps testing her impression that I was fully over the edge.

"That's what you see, Rebekah," I said. "To you she's Martha Stewart of Westport, Connecticut. To me she's Martha Kostyra of Nutley, New Jersey. Jersey. Polak. Working class. Woman, for Christ's sake. Do I need to add that all up for you? The disdain, the jokes."

Rebekah placed the magazine gently on the floor. "Miroswava, I'm not one to read a lot of news magazines, to tell you the truth. And, I'm not really into ethnic heritage. We even get a Christmas tree, so the kids won't feel left out. I'm sure this is all very interesting to you. But – we're here to talk about incest. I don't want to co you in denial. According to program –"

"Look, Rebekah, I think it's best if you just go," I said.

"Tell me what I'm doing wrong," she said. "Do you need to talk about . . . Martha Stewart?"

"I need to talk about Martha Stewart. I need to talk about a lot of things, Rebekah. And I'm just really tired of enabling people who try to channel me into psych wards and graphic discussions of incest and recipes for closure and changing my name to Mary Huxtable and all the other square holes round pegs get shoved into so that someone else can look heroic, can look like they have the answer. Thank God nature is amoral. Thank God only humans try to act the savior. Can you imagine what a monkey wrench social engineering would have thrown into the march of evolution?"

Rebekah's eyes raked my face. I would guess that she felt herself to be taking a great risk by considering following my lead. "What purpose will it serve?" she asked.

"I have no idea," I said.

She paused. She looked at her watch; her brow was furrowed. Finally, "Talk," Rebekah said, suddenly, sharply, amazing me. I immediately wondered what had transpired in the very brief moments I had spent with this woman to inspire her investment.

"Okay," I said. "Martha Stewart. She's Polish. She's Jersey. But she can talk. She can be on the cover of *Newsweek*. And I ask myself, how the hell does she do it? How did she translate herself? Rebekah, everything she says is Polish Gospel, Polish *woman's* gospel, no less. The kind of stuff I always assume I have to keep hidden, or change, or forget, if I want to get anywhere in this country. 'Keep your household clean. Keep your stock and people fed. It is a shame unto you to buy readymade at the store; the decent woman makes it at home, by hand. Do it all hand-to-plow. No bellyaching.'"

Rebekah's face wore the folds and focus of someone fully engaged. "So are you saying that you don't want to talk? We don't have to –"

"Christ, have you heard anything I said?" I shouted.

"What?" Rebekah asked. I would have taken a bullet for her right then.

"Thank you," I said. "Rebekah, I don't think I said anything about *not wanting* to talk."

"All right. I don't know if this will help," Rebekah began, "but we do have an anonymous program. Nothing that you say will leave the walls of this room."

"But that's just *it*, Rebekah," I said, hitting the couch hard. "Of *course* I want to talk. Of course I want to leave the walls of this room. I want to be like Martha Stewart. I want to access what is essential in me, what is rooted in me, and translate it in such a way that the world embraces it and is fed by it. And I never want to be like Martha Stewart. I never want to pass.

"And I will never forget what my father asked me. I interviewed him, and he said to me, in total disbelief, he said, 'You would tell just anyone?' He wouldn't. That was honor for him. And I respect that, Rebekah. I do. I love him for it. I do. Can you understand that? Do you believe that what I'm saying is real?"

She nodded.

"I just wouldn't want you to interpret anything I do as meaning I don't love my father. That I don't do what they did doesn't mean I don't love them. That I do what they forbid, what is the worst thing in the world to them . . .

"The way you tell your story, your audience's response, can make you sick. Can bind you as if you were in jail. Can kill you. The way you tell your story, your audience's response, can heal you. Can free you to move. Can resurrect you.

"Whoever you are, whatever your story is. 'In the past, you did the best you could. Now, you have the strength you need. In the future, you can fly.' Why do we begrudge each other these words?

"And it's more than that, Rebekah. The story that your community tells you can sicken you, imprison you, kill you. Whether you love someone or not and whether you are willing to entertain their story are two different questions."

"How do you tell your story," she glanced again at the sheet of paper, "Miroswava? Who's your audience?" Rebekah was leaning forward, her arms thrusting out of her poncho. I was ashamed.

"I'm a terrible hostess. Let me take your coat," I said.

"In a minute," she said, firmly. "Now tell me. How do you tell your story? Who is your audience?"

I shook my head violently. "That's just it. I don't know, Rebekah. And so if I do what my dad said, not tell the story to anyone, I'm stuck. I have to tell the story to someone who can hear it and say, 'There. There you have it. Evidence you can fly.' But I have no idea who that audience is, so I keep trying, random, taking on the terrible risk of serial storytelling . . . I told Miles, in sign language, anyway. I told Martha, that is, I connected the dots that she already had. It didn't work out. Those people took their existence and their memory away from me. I can't tell you how great is the risk of this work."

Rebekah sat back in her chair. "I guess it's my turn," she said. "Tell me. I want to hear your story."

"Okay," I said. "First let me take your coat, and get you some tea."

Then, Diary, I told her. Fact by fact, and then, and then, and then.

I wasn't conscious then, I'm not conscious now, of any drama or pathos or even interest in other life forms in anything I said. But when I focused on her face after I was done, I could see that she was crying.

"What's going on?" I asked.

And the weirdest thing – she just repeated everything back to me. I watched her face. I think I will remember this moment forever. Orange and green, blue, yellow, red, emerged from black, white, and gray. Everything began to move. Life was a verb, again, life; even stones were verbs. I knew the hinges hidden in rock.

D EAR DIARY, I am in a room. There are four blank walls. There is a blank ceiling and a blank floor. There is no door. There is no window. I don't want to be here. I want to be anywhere else. I ask, "How do I get out of this room?"

False friends, false teachers, say, "Leave."

"But you don't understand," I say. "There are no doors. There are no windows."

"Then die a little, and you won't notice so much. And do us a favor; shut up about it."

True friends, true teachers say, "Be there."

"But you don't understand," I say. "There are no doors. There are no windows."

"We didn't suggest escape. We said, 'Be there.'"

I hate being here. I refuse.

One day my resistance is low. I have no choice but to be in the room. I am terrified. I know being in the room will destroy me. Then, when I still exist, I dance the dance the room allows. I write its poetry. I tell it to all of my friends, and my friends are the people who stay and hear.

Suddenly, I am in a new room. The former is only a memory.

D EAR DIARY, I tried to get Rebekah to stay. She said she had to get home, though, to get the kids dinner; her husband was working late. How strange; angels have rugrats whom they must feed. She made me promise her one thing. You impressed her, Diary. She made me promise to dig out your ancestors, dig out the old diaries again, and old photos of myself. She deputized them as my guides and companions until the next ISA meeting. (She'll be coming by to pick me up.)

"I have faith in you, Mirechka," she said. I taught her that, "Mirechka." But she did ask – "Does anyone ever call you anything besides the whole four syllables?" She was delighted to learn it. Her people were from Vilno, she says. I lent her one of my Roman Vishniac books. "I have faith in you," she said. "You won't do anything to hurt that child. You won't allow anyone else to hurt her."

I smiled and nodded but I was lying. Rebekah was innocent; she was wrong. When Rebekah dimpled and sparkled at me when speaking of the child I once was, she was imagining a normal girl, I'm sure. Rebekah could never have known. I didn't correct her. Rebekah wanted to feel secure, before she could leave, that I would see something lovable in these photos, and safekeep it, till I could be in her healing presence once again. I would give her that, in spite of knowing otherwise.

But I did know, Diary. I knew what discipline it would require to disinter photos of myself and view them. I would confront the lizard scales, the mucus-smeared flesh, the gooey stigmata, whatever it is I never confront, because I never look at photos of myself.

But my predictions proved wrong, Diary. Once I pulled down the cardboard box I found that the discipline required was so very different. I didn't have to steel myself against photographic documentation of an error worthy of hate. It's simple, really; I saw a pretty girl. I saw shining hair, sparkly eyes, deep dimples. I saw more than that. I saw the girl's humor, decency, and adventure, as she haunts the threshold of life. I saw what Evie used to call my strawberries-and-cream complexion. I thought she was implying that I had strawberry-shaped blotches and an excess of fatty pallor. The nicest thing my big sister ever said to me, and I couldn't hear it. I see that skin now because I don't have it any more. I was encased, once, in what I now so envy: the skin of a pretty girl. I never experienced this, my own flesh; I never exercised its gifts.

The discipline required to view these photos is very different than I had thought. I wonder, do we refuse to love abused children because we cannot stomach the injustice we must swallow with the love?

I similarly steeled myself to confront the absurd creature I knew inhabited the old diary pages. I had always promised myself; "Someday I'll get out, and I'll make up for all of this." As if to provide maps and documentation for that someday, I was a compulsive observer and recorder. The facts are all there, minus the understanding that feeling provides. Selective numbness was my part of the bargain. It kept me physically alive and true to those I loved. Like the transcripts of the trial of Joan of Arc, these diaries waited for a time when someone had enough courage to feel the facts.

The oldest entries are the freshest and most nervy; later entries have evolved a clever but stale style, like the articles in *Seventeen* magazine. Since I could make no sense of it and no one else was interested, the detail-by-detail transcription of Joan's trial abruptly ceased. My diary, the potential reflection, school, and proving ground of my soul, had been successfully pasteurized and homogenized. On paper, I was Mary Tyler Moore.

When I write "Mary Tyler Moore," I'm not writing about the real human being, an actress I respect. From what I know of her, I'm sure I would like her and I would never slam her. When I write "Mary Tyler Moore," I'm referring to an archetype in my own, personal mythology. This archetype was created out of others' uses of Mary Tyler Moore and the characters that she played on two hugely popular television series when I was growing up. In the media and in the public mind, the woman and the characters blurred into one powerful persona. I experienced that persona as the embodiment of the admonition: "If-only-you-were like her, we could love you. You are not like her, and so you cannot be loved."

I was a young girl. It was the nineteen-seventies. I was desperate to know whom I could be. I was seeking a channel for the pounding energy that made me jump out of bed at three in the morning to clean house – to clean house because there was nothing else I was allowed to do with that energy.

A professor in college noted my enthusiasm for art and literature classes. He warned me, "When a woman of your ilk develops a taste for refined things, it often ends in suicide. You'll have to guard against that." He saw no channel for my energies. He couldn't even *name* my energies. One couldn't be "intelligence." That quality was found in people with ancestry very different from mine. That quality was found in the handsome youth who reminded the professor of himself when he was a lad. No, I was just "stubborn, like a lot of you Polish people. Your people have problems with authority," said another professor, after I questioned something he had said. He said this in front of other students, at two o'clock in the afternoon, in late October, on a clear day. I turned red and shut up for the rest of the semester.

My own people were no refuge or encouragement. I remember this from our trip to Slovakia. We were strolling through sun down a dirt and dung road. This was Mommy's home village. The village was tiny and an hour's travel from movie theaters or indoor toilets, but smack in the palm of history. Foreign letters, Russian, fluttered over the road. Mommy told me that these banners had been hung all over the country in the wake of 1968's invading tanks. I asked her to translate the banners for me. Mommy, with a defiant contempt, said that each banner conveyed the same message: "Don't try anything stupid. Big Brother is watching."

We turned a corner. Three limber, leggy boys in caps, white shirts, suspenders, clambered up above us, high in a roadside row of cherry. The acrobatic cherry-pickers hailed Aunt Tetka as we strolled beneath them. A boy's upside down head swung to greet us. Suspended from a branch by his knees, the boy handed us a sack, and then, to my open-mouthed amazement and sudden, bursting love, he pulled himself back up, free-handed, into the tree again.

This was the first fruit we'd seen during our trip to Slovakia. We'd been surviving, as the locals did, off of doughs – breads and dumplings – and grease in various forms. Uncle Steven kept us updated on how many days he'd go without a bowel movement. We plunged our hands into the sack and began gobbling cherries. After splitting a cherry open with my front teeth and pointing out the wriggling white worm working its way through wound-like cherry flesh, I swallowed it all down. Sweet juice radiated into the road dust in my throat. I was a child, and used to eating wild fruit in Lenappi; I didn't much care about worms.

Later that same day, we were pushing our way through fields of standing grain. This was always hypnotic, so like walking through the ocean. You could almost feel oceanic pressure batter your thighs, the suction of swirling tide and sand on your ankles as you moved forward. An iridescent scarab beetle the size of my thumbnail landed in Aunt Tetka's Christmas-angel white hair. I stopped her, bent her down, and picked the beetle out. Tetka straightened. She fixed me with a stern stare. She turned to Mommy. "Your daughter saw the worms in the cherries. Now your daughter has found a bug in my hair. She notices things, and then tells people about them. This quality will not do her any good."

Stay with me, Diary. Don't you leave me now. You heard me say how desperately I need you to be my audience in order that I may heal. I know, I know. The audience wants an action hero. You don't want an inventory of resentments seethed in self-pity. But that's not what I'm serving you.

Look, Diary – I've climbed to eighteen thousand feet. I've lanced my own animal bites in tropical jungle. I hitched coast to coast. I based my action-hero checklist on National Geographic expeditions, Jack Kerouac novels, and listening to Kai dream aloud. I did it all alone, shouldering my own pack, with a compass I never learned to use, a snakebite kit I never needed, and an overworked Swiss Army knife. I *have* been there. I *have* done that.

And you know what? Action hero is the safest role I've ever played. Tarzan action disguised the passivity of my brain, and the inertia of my spirit. Action excused my tunnel vision as war excuses censorship of the press. Heroic action protected me from confronting my scariest enemies. My scariest enemies were not the black mambas nor the green mambas I ducked in Africa. They were not malaria or those motorcycle soldiers who tried to kidnap me when Bangui was falling and I left the safe house, alone and on foot, because I'd never seen a state of siege before and I wanted to check one out. I was never less afraid than when dispatching those African soldiers with the street moves I had picked up in Lenappi rumbles under Kai's tutelage.

Punching and running, I was paralyzed. Going and doing, I was frozen, rigid, day after day in the same position. If I stop and think, I may begin to move. Nothing in my life has required more courage than granting myself permission to see and record. I have never needed to be fleeter of foot than in evading tar pits of blame and regret, the snapping jaws of rage.

But I may lose you now, Diary. I cling to you with one hand while typing with the other. Go ahead, Diary. Say it: "You're a hostage taker, not a storyteller!" Yeah, well, tell me the difference. You want suspense, a love story, someone to hiss. But there is suspense. It is the suspense of life or death. This is about love. Will you receive my rush of moist and panted words, or will you turn away? Diary, I confess I've finally come to realize that all the men who have drunk my bodily fluids eventually abandoned me not because I am fat, but because they refused to hear my story.

"It's not that we hate women," society assured me. "If only all women were like Mary Tyler Moore, we would love them." In Mary, I didn't see an accessible role model. I saw a woman who was thinner than any natural born woman I had ever known. There *was* a fat woman on the show, Rhoda. But Rhoda was not as good as Mary. There was a fat man, too: Lou Grant. He was also old, bald, alcoholic, and rude. He was also powerful, sexy, and wise. Oh, and he was a man.

Mary's pedigree could pass any Third Reich test. There *was* an ethnic woman on the show, who had a messy, passionate family: Rhoda. But Rhoda was not as good as Mary.

We were told that Mary was a model of the liberated woman. Mary addressed her boss as "Mr. Grant," while his male underlings called him by his first name. When Mary had to talk about anything serious with Mr. Grant she smiled and stammered and waved her arms and made self-deprecating comments and often ended up shooting herself in the foot. There *was* a direct, articulate woman on the show. She called Mr. Grant "Lou" and never stammered: Rhoda. But Rhoda was not as good as Mary.

Mary was white collar and richer than I could imagine being. I remember awe at the wide swath of clean, white space she had all to herself in her studio apartment. If anyone in a Hudak household had staked claim to so much lebensraum they would be greeted by hoots of cruel laughter. Then an elderly relative would be put up in all that territory; winter clothing would be stored in it; perhaps some bacon or other parts of a dead pig would be hung from its ceiling. And the vast expanse of Mary's windowed doors! I could hear my mother: "What are you trying to do? Heat the whole city?" Chinking would be shoved into those windows for insulation; furniture would be braced against the doors. There *was* a woman on the show who worked with her hands and who lived in a cluttered, dark, tiny apartment: Rhoda. But everyone, even Rhoda, acknowledged that Rhoda was not as good as Mary.

I watched every episode of "The Mary Tyler Moore Show," but I didn't watch the "charming," "innovative," "liberating" show beloved by its fans. I watched with the same despair felt while reading Kafka. I watched, and I understood: "These are the parameters. This is what a woman can be. She can be skinny. She can be ethnically correct. She can be rich. She can defer to men. There is no promise of life or community, dignity or significant work outside of these parameters. If-Only-You-Were-She, you could be loved."

"If Only You Were She:" The If Girl. The If Girl is the designated survivor. During the Holocaust a handful of Jews who could pass, Jews blonde and blue-eyed, were designated by their communities to survive, so that they could someday tell the story. The If Girl can pass, so she's allowed to survive, only, here's the difference: she is forbidden from ever telling the story.

The If Girl goes along. The If Girl gets along. She's one of the guys. She carries her own portable glass ceiling. She calibrates, with mathematical precision, where to station it above herself. She then poses under it so that she can never threaten the alpha male on the premises. Her much admired vision and integrity stop short at the barbed wire keeping her sisters in. She says things like, "I don't like shrill feminists," "My best friends are men," "Women bring these things on themselves. I'm nobody's victim. If he mistreats me, I walk out that door."

I internalized The If Girl. My internalized If Girl decided that the abuse I received was all my fault. The If Girl couldn't believe that others were irrational and cruel. She couldn't believe this because They had power, and I did not. The If Girl always knows which side bread is buttered on. So, to avoid offending the powerful, she had to scapegoat some aspect of me to justify the hatred and abuse They subjected me to.

She didn't have to look far. The If Girl zeroed in on the most transgressive body, the body most deserving of punishment. This was a no-brainer. Everyone knows that the fat female body is the bad body. I was fat. If only I would change. If only I would obey. If only I would lose weight.

My internalized If Girl concluded that this fat, monstrous Jabba the Hut was the pariah that kept me bad, hurting, and alone. Jabba wasn't me, my internal If Girl decided. Jabba wasn't anything important. Jabba was only some expendable growth, some parasite, or cancer. Jabba was a grotesque deviant who shoved food into her face. Jabba didn't work hard at maintaining good public relations. Jabba didn't do any of the nice things that girls must do to calm misogyny's itchy trigger finger. Jabba didn't stammer. She didn't wait for permission. Jabba declared, "I want it NOW." And one of the things Jabba wanted was love. But without love, she refused to charm or seduce anyone. Jabba did not surrender the requisite deferential feminine smile; instead, Jabba's flat eyes interrogated, "What have you done for me lately?" Such a monster deserved punishment. If only I could eliminate Jabba, I would finally be doing it right. I would, finally, know love. I would finally receive identity, the only worthy identity a woman can have: The If Girl.

Until the If Girl was able to demolish Jabba, she hid Jabba. While Jabba was hidden deep down inside, The If Girl operated in the Real World. The If Girl did a woman's work: she smiled and charmed, though receiving no love in return. The If Girl enjoyed some provisional successes. But her successes never had the feel of depth or permanence about them. The If Girl blamed Jabba for these imperfections. And yet Jabba has always touched me, fed me and compelled me in ways that The If Girl never has. How to account for this? I *can't* account for it if I continue to talk about Jabba through the language of The If Girl.

I must see Jabba as she sees herself. I must allow Jabba to have words, in her own language. I must allow her to speak these words, fluently. An actress once told me, "I don't perform villains as objects of the audience's hate. I perform them from the inside. I perform them in terms of what they love." Jabba, what do you love? Speak up, Jabba; speak up. I surrender the keyboard to you.

"I am your protection. I protect the Little Match Girl. The Little Match Girl is a starveling. The Little Match Girl is on the outside while They feast within. I break Their rules. Breaking Their rules is no crime or sin. The Little Match Girl will never be rewarded for keeping Their rules, unless she kills herself, as Marilyn did. Their rules exist only to cheat her. I grab. I feed. I do it all to keep that needy starveling. My devotion to her is animal, my protection fierce. I'll never let anyone get close enough to bruise her again, not even you."

Jabba opens her voluminous robes and spreads them wide. They arch around her like a bat's wings. Crouching there inside is The Little Match Girl. The Little Match Girl is very young, stick-thin, charred black, blue-veined, pink- and tender-hearted. Deep, deep inside, she has a red, molten core of anger.

The If Girl was partly right, after all. Jabba, it turns out, was the source of everything in me that would get me beat, hated, burned at the stake. Jabba's goads were the deprivation, pain and fear The If Girl refused to register. While The If Girl was shaking pompoms and chanting cheers for the enemy team, Jabba was under the bleachers, picking through dirt to find fallen candy and crumbs for dinner. Their blind and empty smiles could never feed Jabba.

Since The If Girl condemned Jabba as damaged, bad, and best hidden, to have intimacy with myself I had to contact something damaged and bad. That desire to contact something damaged and bad built up huge amounts of shame. To overcome that shame required huge amounts of energy. Jabba couldn't just say, "Excuse me. I need to go to the bathroom . . . That man is standing on my foot . . . I need to plan the rest of my life in a way in which I can use my intelligence." The If Girl would simply swallow back down any of Jabba's words. So, to get any attention, Jabba had to shout, "Give me food now or I will not allow you your next breath."

The If Girl loves the world and wants me to enjoy it, even if I have to kill myself to do so. Jabba doesn't hate me; that's not why she buries me in chocolate and peanut butter. Jabba hates the world. I don't want to spend the rest of my life seesawing between The If Girl and Jabba. I don't want to spend the rest of my life hibernating in this apartment and eating all day. I don't want to abandon myself in order to achieve success in The Real World. Somehow I have to make peace between Jabba and The If Girl. I have to interdigitate them in one person.

Excuse me for a moment.

I just pounded the shit out of my pink and sky blue Salvation Army couch, pounding into its motif of flowers and ribbons and shouting, "I will kill Them, kill Them, kill Them if They ever come near that Little Match Girl again!"

Then I put on lots of cheap perfume, which I think Jabba likes, and heavy make-up. Then I kissed myself in the mirror and said, "Jabba, I think I like you."

My God, I looked beautiful! That's the face. It's the face I've been waiting for.

I want to role-play Jabba for a whole day. She'll wear red. She'll push people who get in her way. She'll yell across rooms. She'll be great with kids. She'll get into fistfights. She'll sleep deep, and snore.

Jabba still doesn't like sobriety, but I think I can get her to like exercise. You want nice strong legs to kick people with, don't you, Jabba? There, girl. There, now.

For so long I've been asking myself two questions: "Other people can protect themselves; why can't I?" and, "I have so much anger inside; what would I do with it if I let it out?" Sobriety doesn't mean, as I thought it would, a new or different me. It just means that all the me's move. It's as if every car in a vast parking lot were changing position.

D EAR DIARY, THERE are clumps of orange in the hills now, like the clots of interrupted color on a leopard's back. The reservoir is low; its breakwater brim of uneven boulders lies exposed. Far out, too far to identify, a cormorant – or maybe a grebe? – bobbed in tweed waves scalloped with lacey foam. He stretched. My fingers kneaded each other lightly as they nestled, folded, in my lap. They wanted to work this bird's portrait, to stitch his dragon neck and slender, fish-hooking beak into a big, woolen sky.

• Reminder: buy some embroidery floss.

My ride dropped me one mile south of Ringwood Manor. I thanked Phil – that was his name, and we knew some of the same folks – and then I walked the rest of the way along the estate's long, stone, tumble-down wall. The pond was to my left; the mansion rode the crest before me. My muscles surrendered their kinks; I drowned in the natural beauty.

How much of this vista did Peter Hasenclever see in 1764, when he and other speculators, like filings to a magnet, were drawn here by Ringwood's ore? The German-born Hasenclever, an ironworker since age fourteen, had convinced rich Londoners to give him tens of thousands of pounds to produce pig iron, hemp, pot and pearl ash in North America. Hasenclever's plan was to recreate a medieval European manor on these new American grounds, which he set about taming with bridges, roads, and dams. He was to be the lord in his mansion on the rise; peasants and workers in forges and furnaces would labor below. The rented forest would shelter professional woodsmen.

Well, "The best laid schemes," as the poet said. Hasenclever was history by 1767; he returned to London bankrupt, charging his partners had conspired against him. Some of his American mines would last for a hundred years, but Minnesotan iron began edging out Jersey's in the 1880's.

Eventually Ringwood Manor was ceded to the state. The manor's contemporary habitués are more likely to picnic and snowboard than sweat in forges and tug their forelocks before their lord to the manor born. The green uniformed park service employee in the tollbooth let me in for free. They charge admission only for cars, not for sneakers, and, a hitchhiker, I had shucked my temporary wheels a mile back.

The sugar maple in the parking lot lived up to expectations, created in previous autumns, for flaunting the most flame-like of all foliage on the property. I swear it doesn't stop at flickering through embers' every shade. I swear if you watch it long enough you'll glimpse lavender and ultraviolet. We are neither so powerful nor so rich; nothing manmade captures the ore in a strangled leaf's colors and makes it portable, or durable, makes it something you can have if you stay in city doors these few crisp nights and clear days.

I strolled the path past the plaster copies of ancient Greek statuary to the hill overlooking the pond. My hands behind my head, I lay back and I watched. Scoops of heavenly vanilla clogged the sky. Heavy-bottomed, caramel-topped dollops gridlocked. When enough of them came together for some momentum the jam broke; clouds flooded away in a rush, leaving clear but melancholy sky, and room for more jumbo clouds to meander in and jam and return the light to pearled, the air to cool again.

The black walnut hard by the pond was stark naked. Walnuts lose their twigs in late summer, as well as their leaves, and must grow new sets every spring. I marveled at how tall this scion had grown. I remembered finding its towering parent splintered and flat after Hurricane Belle. I had cried. Evie and I used to dye our hands olive and madden ourselves twisting its kernels out of labyrinthine shells. Black walnut husks contain a dye, and also a pungent poison that kills bedbugs, tomato plants, and apple trees. If all a squirrel does is crack those rock-hard shells, and torture out nutmeat packed as tight as screws in wood, he's a better man than I am, as far as that goes. Evie and I grew lazy and decadent; we abandoned the old tree, and store-bought our walnuts. When the old tree crashed a couple of summers later, I took it personally, and cried. But that was years ago, and now a shoot from that titan's roots had grown up into this new nut-bearer challenging me now.

The maples, birches and ashes smoldered, but were not consumed. Crows dipped with the symmetry of notes delineating a fugue while flying two together across the water. Goose feathers stretched over plump goose breasts. The geese were busy and brown, honking as if in vast migration when waddling from one side of the pond to the other, their path a counterpoint to the going of the crows.

Everything glowed, with a reserved ferocity. Everything sang, but one of Bach's Passions. The stripped black walnut, the crisp filigree of Queen Anne's skeletons, the wrought iron gate in the eighteenth century graveyard: every item on beauty's invoice pronounced its name with a visual precision that drew a lubricating blur of tears from my eyes.

The light and feel was of Colonial days, when life was forbearance in candlelight, and reflections of dutiful actions swam in burnished ebony. I can only imagine that high polish in quality ware rendered the dutiful inescapably sensuous, as in that old John Singleton Copley portrait of a pensive Paul Revere palming a pewter vessel.

I lay on the smooth round hill. I didn't bolt up the straight, steep mountain to be athletic. I didn't study the cameos in the pond to seek interesting out-of-state migrant birds for my life list. I tested myself: "Hey, wanna chew some gum?" I'd tempt my mouth with gum; my mouth spat the gum back out again. Putting something into my mouth seemed irrelevant. I kept offering myself cinema, plays in New York, even an opera ticket. I suddenly realized I hadn't eaten all day. I didn't offer myself food. I didn't want any.

But I felt like I was doing something. That something felt like important work. Something was sinking into me, and I was allowing it. Maybe it was a seed sinking into the level of earth that must accept it before it can germinate. Maybe I was sinking into truth. Maybe I was just sinking into time passing felt as time is felt as it passes to insanity or death.

I wasn't afraid of this because it was real. I don't know what that means. I knew I would just have to live the sadness' duration, the way one lives out a cold. I knew that sense that lovers have: this one other is everything and anything else is extraneous; everything I require and have searched for is contact with this one other. I would encode the wisdom of this sadness from the split ends of each hair to the ticklish cells lining the soles of my feet. I didn't want to have to discover some foolish, inexperienced part of me years from now and explain this sadness to it. I didn't want to ever again make the kind of mistake that not knowing this sadness made me make over and over and over.

I didn't feel like an addict. Food and fat were immaterial. Another deity replaced them. The stimulus hitting me with the force of a storm of the century became *me*. I know what you're thinking, Diary: "But you always write about yourself." Not so. No matter what else I've written, every one of my entries can be reduced to: "Today I ate," or, "Today I didn't eat." Examples of their codes: "Today I seduced Konrad," or, "Today I exercised for one hour," respectively. On that hill I had a moment, and I don't know if it will ever return, when there was a Miroswava Hudak without reference to: "Today I ate," or "Today I didn't eat."

I wasn't born an addict. Addict isn't essential me. I was fashioned into an addict to accommodate others' fears and failures. Fat me isn't wrong me, unlovable me, me who needs to change. Fat me is perfectly okay. I haven't been eating all these years because of the inherent allure of eating. I've been self-medicating. Life hurts me and I don't know how to do it, because I don't recognize, value or exercise my own strengths, and I see everyone else as omnipotent. All these years I thought the key was a "no." "No, Miroswava. Don't eat! And everything else will fall into place." It never occurred to me that the key was a "Yes, Miroswava." All those months and months I'd been entrenched at home, stubbornly not eating, mind boggled that the magic didn't happen. I kept waiting and waiting and thought that I must be a very bad girl. I used to think that our bodies are limited and define us; that our minds are plastic, and can go any way we choose. My body changed. Something in my mind remained rigid.

I selected the lumber for the stage. I drew up the blueprints and I hammered the nails. I supervised costume design. I typed the script. I certainly starred, though I scouted out and directed my supporting cast. I exercised all those powers. The one power I never exercised was the one power that could have saved me: the power of being awake.

But, the diaries. Some understudy waited offstage. Some spirit mother stored my most precious possessions in a hope chest, ready for her daughter's exile's end when she could return home to claim her own.

I rose up on the hill and walked, slowly. I pondered what this new discipline might entail. What would be the hours on this, my new job? When would I finally get a vacation? Workers do think that, even on the first day. When could I retire? What would my salary be? What respect, what punishment, would being this sad person earn me? I was ready to accept and incorporate the answers to all of these questions.

DEAR DIARY, TODAY was one of those crazy change-of-season days when the wind blows the clouds or even just a mess of leaves over the sun and you're wondering why your warmest sweater is still in mothballs, why you were fatuous enough to wear shirtsleeves. You curse yourself for being too much the grasshopper and never enough the ant. The shortsighted, childlike way you've been throwing your whole life away receives a District Attorney grilling. Your parents were right; you should think more about the serious things. And then, the wind shifts. It blows from Jamaica, or someplace generous of its breath and south. You melt into the postcard and murmur, "Why, I'm turning into a grinch. To think I almost wore a sweater on a chrome yellow beach day like today." But night always falls; and night dictates season. Do you have enough faith in your testimonial of thermal abundance to dive naked under just a top sheet for the next eight hours of vulnerable unconsciousness? Or will you molder into a hoary fiscal conservative and invest in the wooly blanket?

DEAR DIARY, I want to tell you something. I'll inform you now that I will speak with both pride and pleading, in case you miss your cue to coo, "Oh, good girl, Mirechka; I am so impressed." In all this recent *Sturm und Drang,* I have not missed one of my scheduled sessions with Etta. And in typing that I suddenly realize that I haven't yet told you about sessions with Etta. Okay. So let me tell.

It's always a surprise, for a teacher, after the semester is through, to see which ones return, and what it's like when they do.

Dr. Rothenberg had granted me the task of informing the kids who wouldn't be allowed to register in fall. Etta was one of our failures. She cried. "I so stupit!"

Grasping for any truth in what I was about to pronounce in faith, "That's not true, Etta," I protested, quickly.

"Oh, yeah?" she challenged. "Then how come I couldn't pass this bogus program that's cake even for wacks like Lee?"

I was grateful she asked me an easy question. "Maybe Lee can't be honest, or real, which you are without even trying. It's not what they've got that you don't, Etta; it's just how they're using it. Look. I kept inviting you to come for a one-on-one, and you kept declining –"

"I figured you was just gonna tell me I stupit. Right?" she demanded.

And I was ready to say, "Right." I bit my tongue, of course. But time had come to interrogate that. I *did* dismiss Etta as stupid. And she did have me pegged; that *was* what I was going to say, in a dressed-up sort of way. Once again, Etta clued me in to her smarts and my phony piety. I scrambled for encouraging words. "C'mon. You know you can try SSNoS again next summer."

"I be just as stupit next summa."

"Look, Etta" I said. "I'm always using the computers in the Writing Center. If you want, you can come by, and we can review some skills. You can learn all about Old Ironsides, America's most beloved frigate . . . "

Before I could do anything to fend it off, Etta's ribbon-thin arms circled my neck, her red curls tickled my nose and her lips left a kiss mark of what looked like Maybelline "Sunlit Bronze" on my cheek.

Etta comes clean. She comes on time, her writing utensils in a plastic "Little Mermaid" pencil case. It's a challenge to get her to focus on the work at hand. She's Evangelical, and proselytizes me. "What's more important? This dumb rule or your immortal soul?" She wants me to confess Christ, get married, or at least have some kids. Her obstinate faith in life's warmest and fuzziest promises frees me to fantasize. Sheltered in the walled city of her belief I find myself exposing dreams I might not confess to a more sophisticated person. "Oh, sure, I've thought about it, Etta. What would he be like? Well, first, of course, he'd have to make me laugh. And be compassionate. Not just the easy compassion of politically correct words but a committed kind, the kind that takes in homeless kids and works in a soup kitchen after hours. But not a wimp, you know? No. Strong. A man. I need a man who is at least as much of a man as I –" I cut myself off, and glanced at her.

Etta's expression was eternal, female, and kind. "You'll see. You'll find him," she patted my hand.

I was sitting next to her as she did a computerized, multiple choice, fill-in-the-blank exercise. She had to choose between, for example, "I might have gone," and "I might of gone." I had purposely made this too easy, a review of material we'd covered, and she'd mastered, last summer. I just wanted to get us both used to working at the computer together.

I studied Etta's fingers. They'd hover over the correct choices. "A, " for "I might have gone." "C," for "He goes," not, "He go." "A" again, for "It worked well," not, "It worked good." Over and over, after hovering, they'd suddenly dart to select the wrong answer. My jaw dropped. I sat and watched her for twenty minutes. I wasn't imagining it.

"You see, Ms. Hudak," she said, throwing up her hands. "I not so smart."

I stared at her. I considered our opponent: the Byzantine back-room deals Etta's brain pulls off with every act of intellectual self-sabotage. I have no idea how we're going to bring that energy around to our side.

But we must. Etta is a genius. Her genius allures and humiliates me. She survives. She's a beautiful, ninety-pound girl-woman in a city that generates arson and gunfire like orchards generate apples. She inhabits her skin with a wriggly exuberance, as if it were a favorite nightgown and she were always a six-year-old just slipped into it after her weekly Saturday night bath. She snaps her fingers and trumpets "Screw him!" in thorough dismissal of the incestuous father she escaped years ago.

We shared a bus home once. Etta brought her son up on her lap and coddled him and talked to him about his day as if nothing else where going on in the world. As if we weren't bussing through menace and ugliness testifying loudly that she was one of those Patersonistas it's okay for society to abandon. Nothing in any gesture, except maybe for her occasional mooning over Supreme, says, "I am alone. I have no future. Pity me."

Her genius humiliates me. Since I can't diagnose or locate it, I can't teach it. I try to figure out a way to bridge the silence between her verve and fearlessness and survival and books about verve and fearlessness and survival. Because of my own lack and its lack, Tillman College and I had to identify Etta as a failure, rather than ourselves.

I told her one day that I had run into Supreme in downtown Paterson. He was selling the Nation of Islam's *Final Call* newspapers and vegetarian snacks. He and I chatted about his plans. He had passed on college for this semester, but told me he would consider going next fall. I believed him. He seems to enjoy wearing a suit too much not to get a college degree. I told Etta that before I moved on, under the guise of being the village gossip, I had "let slip" to Supreme that Etta is really black.

"You shittin me!" Etta protested. I wasn't sure if this would enrage her, and she'd knife me, or if she'd see the window of opportunity I was trying to open.

"Well, why not?" I argued, quickly. "I made a lot of noise about errant plantation owners and a darker brother you have in Paterson and the tragedy of families torn asunder along the color line. You know he's a socially conscious kind of guy. I thought he'd go for it."

Etta punched me so hard my arm is now black and blue. But then she started laughing, and then she hugged me. And then I realized that that was what I had been working for all along.

Let's see; who else. Right. Lee turned up. I was in the cafeteria and there he was, a slender, t-shirted desperado of geekdom. "You wanted to talk to me."

"Yes, I did, Lee, during the summer when you were in the SSNoS program and I was your teacher. You blew me off."

"We'll talk now," he said.

"Fine. Great. Sit down," I said.

"No. We gotta meet in a class, like with the other students. At an appointed time."

I didn't try to hide how bored I was with his addiction to drama. But I was curious. "The man wants an appointed time; the man gets an appointed time." I reached into my backpack, and pulled out my Mary Engelbreit date book. "Next Friday. Six p.m. The Writing Center." Wanted to add, "Dueling pistols or sabers?" Decided not to.

He nodded, silently, and walked away. If he didn't show up, it would be no skin off of my nose; I'd have the Center to myself at that time and day, and could use the computers to write.

He did show, exactly on time. He walked up to me, and handed me a beat-up paperback: *Zen Flesh, Zen Bones.*

I took it. I smiled. "Wow. Gosh. Thank you so much," I looked up at him. "I love this book, Lee. Is this copy for me to keep? Thank you. I've always wanted my own copy. I've only ever just borrowed it –"

He practically spat. "You ain't never seen that book."

"That's not true, Lee!" I said. "I love this book! It's one of my favorites! I read it practically cover to cover one afternoon on the bank of a river in . . . in Asia. While . . . the book's owner washed out his shorts . . . "

"Bogus," Lee pronounced, and he turned and was walking out the door, when I said,

"*Pendejo.*"

You bet he turned around.

"Oh," I said. "You understood. So, *Lee,* is '*pendejo*' a word in Burmese or Thai or whatever it is you're claiming to be this week?"

"I understand some Spanish. You Polish, but you know that word."

I didn't want to waste time. "A monk asked Tozan." Reciting resonantly, I surprised myself. *Merde,* would I blow this? Did I even remember how these tales went? I pictured Miles milking river water from his sock. I heard the nasal, slow-motion explosion of lowing water buffalo. I felt ineffable sweetness . . . "I remember. I remember! Okay, it's like this. Okay. A monk asked Tozan how to cope with hot and cold. Tozan said, 'Go to the place where there is no hot and no cold.' The monk said there is no such place. Tozan said, 'When you are hot be hot; when you are cold, be thoroughly cold.' Okay. Another one. A monk was polishing a little bit of potsherd. Another monk said, 'Why are you doing that?' And the first monk said, 'I'm going to make this so shiny that I can see my face reflected in it.' And the other monk said, 'That'll never work! It's just clay!' And the first monk said, 'Well, you're doing the same thing. You meditate and meditate, but you'll never attain the flawless perfection you desire.' I've got more; you wanna hear 'em, Lee?"

And then Lee smiled. A real, honest to God, human being smile. And then he left. We'll always have that smile.

Troy and I ran into each other – literally – on a campus sidewalk. Among faceless, rushing strangers, rather than in our familiar classroom, Troy was bereft of an audience for whom to act out a tense, adversarial relationship. In fact, as he hooked onto my face out of the crowd, slowed, focused, placing me, he didn't look tense or adversarial at all, just like one human being recognizing another. He rushed to cover his Biblical nakedness. "Oh, tsyou, you sorry-ass, so-called teacher."

"Hi, Troy," I said, stopping.

"You know what? I'm gonna tell you sommun," Troy began bouncing back and forth on the balls of his feet, like a gangsta rapper, like Jimmy Cagney playing George M. Cohan, for that matter.

"Glad to hear it," I said.

"You are the worst teacher I ever had. You know it? Lousy. Embarrassing lousy. And you know what else? Everybody say so. Oh, not your so-called pets."

"Thank you for sharing that, Troy," I said.

"Dr. Rothenberg? She cool. You? You suck."

"I'm glad you had the experience you wanted with Dr. Rothenberg," I said.

"Yeah. You suck," Troy reaffirmed, as he bounced off.

Well, it's just perfect that Troy liked Dr. Rothenberg. Dr. Rothenberg will never disappoint anyone's expectations of a Politically Correct, Buddhist, Jewish, divorcée professor. Troy is everybody's idea of a scary, urban, black boy. What systems they'll function in are built around accommodating the clichés they both present. Neither Troy nor Dr. Rothenberg will ever confuse his or her audience, which will always know when to gasp, weep, or rise in a standing ovation. Neither will ever confront the audience with its own ignorance, or remind it that virtue can prove itself only when it is taken by surprise. Neither will ever suggest that the painstakingly hammered-out script, describing how past atrocities should have been avoided, is superseded by each moment's hungry or lonely or merely annoying human. Neither will ever demand that virtue be proven through risk as a verb, not pinned to the chest as a rank-bestowing noun. And then, of course, I wondered if I were just telling myself this to comfort myself because a former student just told me that I suck.

Nah.

I was sitting in an empty classroom one day waiting for the Writing Center to empty out, rereading my very own copy of *Zen Flesh, Zen Bones.* Sharifa came in. "Hi, Sharifa!" I said.

"Hi," she said. "Dr. Hudak."

"I'm afraid I'm still just Ms. Hudak," I corrected her.

"Yeah, right," she said. She tried again. "Ms. Hudak, I just wanted to let you know how much I liked our class this summer. It was the first time I got to talk about some important things, things that are important to me."

"That's great," I said. I patted myself on the back for how I had handled Sharifa's use of Black English, never questioning but that that was her "important thing." We chatted some more. She confessed to being in love. I said how happy I was; how she ought to bring the young man around, so I could meet him. She went out into the hall and came back in with Carolina. I said something like how nice it was to see what good friends they had become.

Sharifa is a workmanlike scholar who compensated with diligence for what she lacked in spark. Her obsession with hypodermics and glucose levels may serve her well; she wants to become a nurse. I have no doubt that she'll stick it out and earn her BS at Tillman. Carolina, on the other hand, had failed. She and I had talked for an hour, during which she refused to believe that nothing, not even her brother-in-law's bribing me, would change her grade. Afterward Carolina, projecting a pitiful pathos while demonstrating the frightening determination of a stalker, tailed me all over campus, raccoon-eyed from running mascara. Anwar followed, demanding, unsuccessfully, that I "act like a woman" and "show some compassion" and pass Carolina. I was glad to see that Carolina had survived that trauma, and wasn't so put off that she couldn't hang out with her SSNoS buddies on Tillman's campus.

Sharifa gave me a curious look. I just kept looking up at both of them and smiling. And then Sharifa turned to Carolina and turned her open mouth on Carolina's open mouth; they kissed. And I thought, my, what an unusual thing for Sharifa and Carolina to be doing.

It was well into the kiss before the word popped into my head: *Lesbians!* These girls are lesbians! What Troy insisted on referring to as "faggots."

I guess I was wearing my ignorance on my face. "Is this horrible for you?" Sharifa asked when the kiss finally broke.

"No! I just think it's so wonderful that you two found each other," I lied. Lying not because there's anything wrong with being gay. There isn't. Lying because I was too rattled to experience anything as wonderful.

Sharifa and Carolina were wearing their own shock on their faces. I didn't understand their shock any more than they understood mine. Finally, Sharifa spoke. "We thought you was one of us," she said.

"*Sí*," Carolina agreed.

"You always be talking about Willa Cather," Sharifa went on. "You old. You not married."

"Well, I like *that*," I said, not disguising how affronted I was at that last bit. Sharifa and Carolina registered my affront not at all. My only hope now is that I run into them again so that we can create a new memory, one in which I display my newly practiced suavity when confronted with Lesbians.

The whole thing still bothers me.

It doesn't bother me that I never addressed the lesbian Sharifa, though I talked to Sharifa every day, that I never wrote about the lesbian Sharifa in my diary or in my grade book, that I never taught the lesbian Sharifa. It bothers me that I never addressed the Sharifa who *could have been* a lesbian. It's as if my mind had room for only one identity for each student. Sharifa was "the-inappropriate-use-of-Black-English-on-an-academic-paper-black-girl." Carolina was "tragic-airhead-beauty-desired-by-Anwar-and-from-a-war-torn-Central-American-nation." Those are the identities I said "Hi" to. Those are the identities I taught. Those weren't the identities most prized by Sharifa or Carolina, at all. Since I allowed them only the identities I concocted for them, I didn't see the evidence in front of my own eyes: Sharifa's courageous resistance to Troy's homophobia, Carolina's hovering over Sharifa at the play. Her Marlene Dietrich ensemble, for big blue heaven's sake!

- Reminder: Don't do this again! See. At least, try to see. Or, at least, be aware that you aren't seeing everything.

Munal has seen the whale, and not just that; also pterodactyls and a Peruvian pre-Columbian stone calendar. He called. God bless him. I love it that he dialed the information operator and got my number and called. He apologized twenty times for calling. That's okay. Desperation can give courage that confidence would never supply.

Toward the end of the conversation, when it seemed clear that it wouldn't come up unless I brought it up, I said, "So, how did the pictures turn out?"

"Oh, ho, ho. *Those* pictures," he said.

"Yeah, *those*," I said. "Remember, you promised me copies."

There was a long pause. I formulated his outraged protests in my imagination. There was even more of a pause. Finally, "Yes, I will bring them to you," he said. I smiled.

It was a cold and blustery night when I ran into Abdullah. I was at the Cedars of Lebanon deli, buying my weekly fix of baba ghanoush. Abdullah ordered a coffee, small and dark, like himself. He got a peppermint tea for me . . . I've got no ready metaphors for that order. I don't know if I'm seen as weedy or unsweetened. He pulled out my chair. We sat at one of the little metal tables.

In the brief wait, before our orders arrived, before, relieved of anticipated interruption, we launched our conversation, our eyes did not rake across the shelves of merchandise or focus on the paper carnations in a vase at the table's center. Our eyes met, and lingered warmly. Our waiter, really the deli owner's son, arrived with our drinks. Abdullah thanked the boy in Arabic – I know that much Arabic, now. As the boy stepped away Abdullah turned his gaze back to me. He pronounced, "You're the best." I blushed and looked down, but not so rapidly that I couldn't enjoy him tilting his head, and smiling at me as if I were a newborn, or a puppy.

We smiled exclusive smiles. We said things like, "Your papers were a delight to read;" "Your assignments were the most inspiring I have ever had, either here or in Palestine," under the watchful eyes of invisible women shrouded in black who wafted in to the deli with each chilling gust of night wind.

I waited. I was waiting for a moment of uncomfortable but titillating tension born of teacher-student affection and born, too, of his across-the-water wife. But neither titillation nor tension ever arose. I've been wondering why. Is it because Abdullah comes from a culture where love is okay? That he feels no need to engineer strong emotion, no need to make it more cerebral by making it more complicated or forbidden? I remember seeing him and Anwar holding hands as they walked. I remember the quiet testimony in Abdullah's papers of his mother's, aunts', grandmothers' and sisters' love for him. What was remarkable was that this love never starred in Abdullah's compositions; he never trained a spotlight on it; it was just always in the background, reliable, the assumed four walls and furniture of his life.

I don't know. I do know that his eyelids didn't tic or cheek muscles jump. He didn't tell me that I was probably a codependent who ought to seek counseling, because I was obviously just too emotional and he just wasn't ready for a relationship and he had commitment issues and abandonment issues and the last girl he'd been with was just like his mother and they were still trying to work things out . . . He didn't proffer any of the disclaimers I've heard from men for whom I've shown even feigned, merely pro forma appreciation. Rather, Abdullah wore my open enthusiasm for him as graciously as silk. I exhaled; I expanded. I felt no need to mime the emotional inertia I do when I am trying to pass as an American.

Abdullah updated me on Anwar. "He selling candy now. His uncle's shop. I show it you; you can visit him there. He will be happy to see you."

I nodded, and tried to imprison my pique behind pursed lips. Anwar's academic evaporation irked me. By the skin of his remaining teeth, Anwar had passed SSNoS. He registered for fall classes, and then he just disappeared. A catatonic can get ahead on a college campus, if he plays his cards right. One cannot jerk around the bureaucratic dragons in the cavern of the registrar and hang on to any chance of earning a baccalaureate. Anwar, by registering, disappearing, and not officially withdrawing, had royally sabotaged himself.

"Do you ever hear news of Suarez?" I asked, and immediately

regretted that impetuous and self-exposing question. There was no reason for Abdullah to know of Suarez. To my mind, there were in the same Linnaean category: "students on whom I've had an inappropriate crush;" they were not in comparable categories in Abdullah's system.

Abdullah said, "No. He's from Newark."

"Of course," I said.

But a need had been expressed, a desire. Abdullah would not allow himself to fail me. "I hear he going to a school in South Jersey. Maybe down the shore. Maybe Monmouth Community College? I gotta cousin going there. If you ask Dr. Rothenberg, she know the name for sure."

"Thank you. I'll check that out." I smiled at him. He settled back, relieved. "You worked really hard, Abdullah. I can't tell you how much I admire that."

"Yeah," he said. He glowered into his coffee. "I want to tell you something."

Okay, I thought, here it comes! He'd finally confess the reason his Brontë-hero face looked so stormy and inconsolable some days. Just, please, Allah, let it not be that he has to kill his wife.

"I had some trouble last summer. So I wasn't always my best on Fridays, your days. I regret that. My father, how to explain you, back home, he needed eighteen thousand dollars. I had to work extra to send it to him. What are ya gonna do? It's family. Ya gotta take care of family. So I sent it. But it was a hard semester for me."

"You blow me away, Abdullah," I breathed.

One of the shoppers, a slender but fit looking young man, broke free from the crowd and approached our table. He bowed to me and said something to Abdullah in Arabic. Abdullah replied, and then turned to me. "I gotta go," he said.

Suddenly I realized that this man and Abdullah had arrived together, that this man had been killing time patiently that Abdullah might provide his teacher with a proper greeting. Of course. They never do anything alone, these people; they never do anything without sentiment, without ceremony. They? SSNoS students, Arabs, Patersonistas, the gang back in Skunk Hollow, those doing it wrong? Those for whom everything matters, for whom everything is real? I don't know. But they never do anything alone.

I nodded to Abdullah and his friend. Abdullah muttered something plaintive to the man, and the man went back to perusing shelves of macaroni with Arabic script on the boxes. Abdullah studied the dregs of his coffee. The air grew thick. We had both told each other how wonderful we were; what else was there to say? Abdullah can suck up a room's energy like a cyclone by hitting his book with the flat of his hand, and staring at it, uncompromising, when he so chooses. I was impressed that both of us let these seconds pass in long, unedited silence. I was ready to say, "Yes."

"Yes, you guys should have a state. Why not plant your flag on Main Street and Railroad Avenue from here to the Garden State Parkway? You're entrenched here already with your halal butchers, jute sacks spilling pistachios, and that sinuous music that blares from open doorways. Women singers belt out sounds that require no translation, defy and subvert any notion of the veil.

"Yes, I will edit all your papers for you from now till you graduate.

"Yes, a woman, she crazy, she not human, if she not want any man, and you already have one wife. I'll be wife number two."

"Will you be my teacher again, ever? At Tillman?" Abdullah finally asked, his face grave as if so very much depended on the reply.

"No," I said. I couldn't begin to explain why.

He looked very dark. I felt almost afraid. I felt almost that he would slam his open hand into the metal table between us, and with that gesture set right my life of chaos, and render it into a gleaming model of rational architecture, as cleanly functional as any artificial hip, dog or human.

He sighed. "I gotta go," he said.

I sighed, too. "Good night, Abdullah," I said, offering him my hand.

He surprised me by helping me up. "C'mon. We give you ride home."

"Abdullah, you don't have a car."

"Tsno problem. We take you by taxi."

"But I'm really close –" his look shut me up.

"*Habibi*!" he called to his companion, and we were off for the block and a half taxi ride back to this apartment.

DEAR DIARY, I was rummaging around in this desk drawer for my staple gun. Was overturning spools of adhesive tape, pricked by loose pins, toppling dominoes of flashcards in Polish, Spanish, and Arabic. I set to flight one homesteading spider. Stumbled, if fingers can stumble, upon a little paper flag. It was unmistakable. The red flag of the Kingdom of Nepal is unique: two triangular pendants, rather than one rectangular one. I hurriedly buried the flag under some envelopes. I continued rummaging while, now, carefully ignoring a slow, well-worn, panic.

And then, I just stopped. I stopped and I asked, "What is going on?"

"Access to your memory denied. You loved something you're not entitled to. Because you didn't deserve it, you lost it so thoroughly you're not allowed even to remember it."

"Oh. I see. Thank you for the explanation of how that works."

I took the photos out again. I summoned The Countess. I commissioned her to help Most Fragile remember, to honor her own narrative, to lay claim to her own memories. I re-inhabited these photos, or, perhaps, I inhabited them for the first time. I took them, square frame by square frame, as if they were enemy-occupied territory. A radical irredentist, my battle cry was whatever the girl or woman in the photos was thinking and feeling. I spoke her words aloud.

"These nights are hot. It's hard to sleep. It's fun when Miles teases me right before I fall . . . Miles, why let everything go so far? You get the teacher's salary. Why not do the teacher's job?"

The Countess and I moved on. "I'm proud of how pretty I look in Konrad's t-shirt. I'm leaning against his charisma, so solid it supports me. Konrad, you tell yourself you've succeeded because you have an indoor toilet, and none of your betters now knows you've ever gone without one. But you aren't the success you could be, not quite yet. You can't bring yourself to respect what you love."

And we moved far back in time. "Gosh, this is a neato afternoon! Oh, yeah, we're poor but, we have the greatest times no matter what! Kai is the coolest dude in the universe! Evie is the toughest girl!"

I'm not in the last photo; it's one I took. "She glares at me, predatory. Open your eyes, Mommy. I'm not any of those Americans who hurt you. I'm your daughter. I love you. But I can't let you tear me any more."

Suddenly I am young, very; sensations flood my cell; pen and paper float, shoes; my hair swells with the wave it wraps. This is air, how it feels; I remember! This is Saturday night in my home state – the crickets, crack of ball on bat, sizzle of hot dog on backyard grill, the lawn mower dying down, this is how it sounds. This is tile. A tile floor. A speckled pattern. Black on white, next to it, white on black. I've seen this before, square and regular. I remember. This is glass. Glass does just this to light; nothing else does just this. Glass. Light. Glass. Light folded in glass. Shadow captured in light. The light is clear and white. Black shadows delineate. The architecture, the flavor, of light in glass on a kitchen countertop. This is me. This is how I smell. This is how I taste. This is my circumference. I am here. I was young when I last knew this. Then something happened. Something knocked me out. I've been out for a long time, practicing to be alive. Now, in this moment, I am alive. It is okay.

I remember. What a lovely thing: I remember.

I want to rescue everything. Sunset strolls through jumbled temples and fruit pyramids in Kathmandu, my mesh market bag suspended from fingertips like an oriole's nest. Greeting Rajasthani studs who perch fold-legged in box stalls, wrapping necklaces round their fists: the bead market. Tapping, white magnesium flame: the tin market. The folk lyrics of the work song Aunt Bora sang as she harvested rye. Riding a motorized bicycle through an African country at war. Stopping and kicking down its stand and staring slack-jawed at a dark green rain forest tree. Puffs of sky blue rose and fell with the buoyant ease of hot air balloons. These were blue plantain eaters, rain forest birds. I could tell you how beautiful they were, but you could not believe me. I could not believe myself. That's why, though gunfire was constant and I was alone and equatorial night was pacing and near and Sudanese smugglers ran onions and women up and down that road I stood still, long and longer, staring. I would wring those moments of the belief they allowed that anything could be that beautiful. An afternoon when Chris, sitting at the kitchen table, suggested that I don't talk to him enough. The glow-in-the-dark planets Kai stuck to our bedroom ceiling. Kai's entire life, or what of it overlapped mine. An Argentinean, whose name I never got, picking me up and twirling me round till my hair described a fluid circle. "Jose! Juan! Esteban! That was fun!"

No, it's not just men. I'm finding I've got two lists:

List # 1.) I'm sorry, but you're a garden-variety jerk. I put up with you, I acted impressed by you, I was deferential to you, solely due to decades of bad training. And I've got to inform you now, even if only in this diary, how pompous, and boring, and ridiculous you are.

List # 2.) I'm sorry. What I did to you was despicable. I cringe. I'm offering right now to make amends, but, I don't know where you are. I tried looking you up, no luck. I don't blame you. I'd lie low, too, if someone ever did to me what I once did to you. Please know that it wasn't about you or hate or destiny; it was about physics. I was ricochet. I suspect you've gone on with your life and you may not even remember what I did, although I can never let myself forget it. Even so, it is my hope, that somehow, even though you've never heard this apology, that somehow you've found a way to forgive.

D EAR DIARY, OVER and over, I return, over and over, through effort. At best it is bushwhack, at worst, forced march. Over and over I return to the center and I ask there, "What do you call this? What is it to you? Is what I've put down true? Or am I just confessing dogma, and do you burrow into a more numb hibernation? Are you waiting for the next catastrophe to hurt you alive or knock you dead forever? Don't do that. Respond to me. Teach me to spell."

Tonight, instead of using Tillman's computer, a typewriter, or even a ball pen, I print these words across this page, not write but print them, in pencil, which I periodically pause to sharpen. I value and use, often, the eraser at the end of the pencil. I examine each word as it falls. If that drops my plumb line center, the word stays. A jigging string? I feel my hand rub against the word and consider the why of writing it and what reducing it to elongated pink crumbs implies as I rub it out.

When I began, I wanted the big thing. If the proverbial blind "can't see the forest for the trees," I didn't want any trees, no bark, nematode, morel, nor deer scat. I wanted forest. I wanted the sum of forest from Maine to Alaska. I wanted command of forest essence. I didn't want to be slowed down by trees.

Approaching you, Diary, tonight, I am grateful to God that my language is divided into letters. With my sharpened pencil I slice even these into smaller elements. I will equip my consciousness with a revolving door; it will welcome one guest at a time, but no packed crowds. If the bits I record threaten to coagulate into a theme, I may be forced to adopt a postmodern, confetti, cut-and-paste diary style. One letter at a time. That's all I can deal with tonight.

I went north before dawn. Hiked the Norvin Green State. Deer sprung clear of brush, its tangled thorns, as winged things. A merganser dove into water, pumping up popping bubbles. (So is that what I saw? This merganser? And neither a grebe nor a cormorant?) The progressing sun hammered the back of my head. I bulleted up the blue-dot trail. The strategic targeting of boot, the push of ball, toe, calf, against rock, soil and moss, nothing, nobody holding me down: I wanted to live forever. I felt I could.

I perched on the rock bald. The watershed below auditioned for a New England calendar. Nappy red and orange ridges sliced across red and orange ridges. Off and down to my right silver breathed: tufts of wispy mist hovered over the smooth plate of reservoir. Farthest east something like Oz rose just high enough to scratch the dome of a snow globe: the skyline of Manhattan.

I descended like the resigned sigh escaping from my lungs and caught a bus going south. Walking down Lackawanna Avenue, I passed the Baca's. They were all out on the stoop; I couldn't resist the gravitational embrace of their silent, inevitable invitation.

Nina had been gazing out the screen door when she caught sight of me. She exploded from it, setting its flimsy weight awobble on rust-throat hinge. Then she suddenly stopped dead in the yard.

I smiled, shook my head. Will that girl ever grow up? I hope not. That was exactly how she used to bound out of the house to greet me, fast-forward energy, and the sudden snapping back, when I was half my age and planning what are now my reminiscences, and she was ten. I remember her feverish dreams from those days, and nights, as well. All the spectacular feats she might accomplish someday, and in what sequined bustiers. I had trembled with terror for that little girl. And asked her, "So, Nina, when do you get started?" And she had replied, "Don't be weird. Girls from Lenappi never do stuff like that!" And I had breathed a sigh of deep relief.

Mr. Nina was out on the stoop, too. I forget his name and appearance between encounters. All I remember is that he's not good enough for Nina. Now widowed Arnulfo dandled Nina's toddler on his knee. And Danny was there. Danny's a man now, a Lenappi man, and so what we once were to each other has hit its dead end. I looked at him and smiled; he mumbled and looked away. As is right. And I knew that as soon as I turned my gaze from Danny he'd begin catching glimpses of me out of the corner of his eyes, or gaping outright, up and down. Those are the rules.

The men were lounging on the stoop in hammock position as if the hard cement could swing, showing off their various paunches, rolls, and spare tires. A flattened pizza box rested before them. Pollen-gold peanut M&M bags littered the stoop. There was a two-liter plastic bottle of bargain-brand cola.

My arrival was easy, though I haven't been here in years; though, for reasons it would take at least a paragraph of hemming and hawing to work up to, I've been avoiding them. I've been avoiding them the way the Frank family avoided the Gestapo. I go around the block the long way to evade detection. I wear dark glasses. I concoct alibis. It's all the worse given how grateful I am. Arnulfo never asked any questions. He loved my mother; they went to the same church. But he knew and he took me in. No matter. Their greeting was warm, as unseasonably so as the day itself. My arrival slid right in there, disturbing not the trajectory of one descending leaf.

Nina's in the factory now, one Mommy worked in, and Kai, one I always assumed I'd work in, but somehow never did. She and Mr. Nina are renting an apartment above a store on Ringwood Avenue. Arnulfo got Danny a good job with the town. He'd be able to move out soon, buy his own house. I glanced up at Danny by way of congratulation, but, really, to check up on him. My eyes intercepted his perusal of me and he looked down at his cigarette ashes and I gave up too and turned away.

"So, Mira. You gonna tell us why you living in Paterson? I couldda gotten you a job right here in town," Arnulfo reminded me.

"But I can't type," I informed him, for the thousandth time. "Not professionally."

"I don understand. A smart girl like you."

"It's the dyslexia —"

"Pfft." Arnulfo studied the sky, not out of any interest in meteorology.

I shut up. He continued. "You are not safe in Paterson. Don ever think you are safe there because you are not. And you know why, don you?"

I shrugged and waved my arms and smiled insipidly. I knew what was coming. I braced myself. I would pull the covers over my head till he was done.

"You got a gun?"

"No!" I sounded so little girl.

"You buy a gun, Mira. You like a daughter to me. You buy a gun. Don kid yourself. These goddamned Espics from Puerto Rico – no one has more respe for a woman honor than the Espanish man, from España, you hear me?"

"Yes, sir."

"But these Espics. Don even think about it. You buy a gun. You listen to your Tio Arnulfo."

I smiled, big and broad. Because he let me know that he was still my Tio Arnulfo.

There were the usual fart jokes and gossip, baby brags and come-around-soons. I gave my Paterson address and it was immediately decided that I live closest to Uncle Fernando, though Uncle Chick would do in a pinch. "You have trouble, you go to them." As an excuse I said I needed to catch Mommy. I slipped away.

I felt the hole in myself the shape and density of a stoop holding up three generations and an empty pizza box. Why couldn't I be like them? My own people? Why did I have to be different? If I were like them, I could eat pizza now, and peanut M&M's. And I'd be in the factory, all right, but I'd know where I belong.

I walked in the always-open back door. She was in the garden. My heart beat fast. This was it. I finally deserved what I've been waiting for, for so long.

I called out the kitchen window, "Hi, Ma."

As if I had just critiqued, "You should have picked those in August!" She asserted, loud, edgy, "These aren't any good until after the first frost."

"I know," I agreed. "You've told me that a million times."

She wasn't looking at the window, but at the persimmons in the tree and on the ground. "All right. Now what did you do to that Martha

Streichert girl? She's a good girl. She's been good to you. We're not the kind of people who forget things like that. You remember that, Mee."

"Mee" sounded very hard. I sort of gasped. Had I been hearing that all my life? How had I survived it?

"Did you hear me?"

"Yes," I whispered.

"What? I'm coming in there." And suddenly I realized that that was a threat.

She slammed her rear into the door and flung it open; her hands were busy holding up the corners of her apron. She pivoted round and caught sight of me. Her face went gray. She stumbled back three paces, right into the door.

"Hi, Mom." I smiled. I realize now that smiling is not the natural response to someone going gray and stumbling back three paces at the sight of me. I respect, again, the work of telling the truth. My mother was staring at me as if I were the avenging dead. Several seconds went by. I walked up to her, and for the first time in years, kissed her cheek.

She rolled an apron-full of persimmons onto the table, selected a small, sharp knife from its wooden block, and sat down. She took a drag on her cigarette, then glared at me, while never missing a twist of her knife in the fruit's errant flesh.

I waited. Would she hit me for attempting to usurp Evie's status? Was that it?

Finally, she snapped, "All I want you to do is give it to me straight. Have you got T. B.? Or this new AIDS thing? I'll make an appointment with Doctor Patel."

"No! I've just been really busy, lately," I lied. "Too busy to remember to eat."

"Don't be ridiculous. There's ham in the refrigerator."

"Well, there's a news flash," I said. "But, really, I'm not hungry."

"He's a good doctor."

"Of course!"

"You just don't want to go to him because he's an immigrant."

"*What?*"

"I know. I know. You said you don't like Dr. Patel because he's an immigrant –"

"I never said any such thing!"

"Yes you did. I remember. Years ago, when he first came to Lenappi. You saw him at the A&P and you said, 'That guy's from India.'"

That was all I'd said, though. I never said: "That guy's from India so I don't like him." I could have "corrected" Mommy, but I didn't. She can be so insistent. But you believe me, don't you, Diary?

She just kept staring at me. I've never seen her stare at me that way – as if I were a complete outsider. One of those strangers out there she knows she can't control. And, thus, immaterial. Have I always been immaterial to her? Perhaps. But she has never been immaterial to me.

After I'd removed the crowns and rot from half of the persimmons I asked, "Can I borrow your car tomorrow? I've got Kai's old reel to reel in Paterson and I want to get it back to the house."

"Just don't go hot-rodding around," she warned.

"And then, later, will you have any free time tomorrow afternoon? After mass? Maybe a few hours?" I asked.

"For what?" she barked.

"You'll find out."

Before heading back here for the night, I stopped at Tillman to get some writing done at their computers. While drying my hands in the ladies' room I noticed myself in the mirror. I was wearing baggy cut-offs, an oversize denim shirt, and a cotton sun hat. If I stood under the light just right, I looked better than I did in my twenties. Not younger, but better. "Ready."

Maybe if I hiked a lot once I got to Berkeley. Maybe if I made sure to stand under the right lights. Then, maybe, I would at least not look so weird. Though, of course, I would still be so weird, weird, old, working class, my fellow students young enough to be my kids, rich enough to be my boss.

I have these worries. But when I've just come from hiking, they do not show. The air shows, my love shows, and my willingness. That was what I saw in the mirror, and it looked sweet to me.

I had a question for the lady in the mirror, a question that's been on my mind. "You vowed to go home, and stay there. Now here you are, once again, giving your possessions away, packing till your backpack is full to bursting, asking too much of its zippers and compression straps; asking your landlord back for the deposit, bidding farewell to the woods you adore –"

"I know."

"Well? Are you, again, a traveler? Sacrificing home, the white picket fence of your dreams, Archimedes' fixed point of perfect power?"

"To tell you the truth, I don't know. But, maybe, going to graduate school at Berkeley is the least traveler act I've ever performed. Maybe I've always been home but I just have to inhabit it."

Another human female entered the ladies' room. She paused and gazed in the mirror, also. I could not escape to my comforting musings. The two of us were shackled, captive, within the bounds of the mirror. I confronted in that flat square what I've seen a million times and am powerless to change. I do not look like Them. It's not so much about fat, now. I can't put my finger on what it is. Any support my positive interpretation of my reflection offered shattered. I crashed back down to earth. I rose, dusted myself off, shouldered a familiar but no less heavy resignation, and left.

The Writing Center was stifling, pungent and chaotic with humanity. I aimed my energy, an arrow, directly at the machine. I tuned out extraneous noise. I thought I heard something like my name, but I reminded myself that I no longer belonged here. I was a woman with no name, between identities, and pirating the computer. I did not turn from the machine. But then I closed my eyes to stretch, to take a deep breath, and then I smiled. That ridiculous, but undeniably sumptuous, scent.

I turned around and beamed an ecstatic, Lenappi-hiking-girl smile.

"You look very happy," he observed.

"It's good to see you! I think . . . why are you here? Princeton?"

"Had to come back. My sister, she sick."

"Oh, no! What happened?"

"She got the appendix."

"Say it right or don't talk to me."

"My sister had appendicitis."

"She did that just to get you back, I'll bet. I bet she misses you a lot."

"Yeah," he said. "But . . . I never told you about my sister . . . did I?"

Not knowing how to answer, I just smiled. "You look so good, Suarez,"

I said. "Princeton is good to you." I felt some relief. When he left here he was still dressing for 1963 – the leather jacket, the pointy boots. But he had learned at Princeton. He was wearing good quality, clean jeans, broken-in running shoes, and a white shirt, open at the collar. Everything was glow-in-the-dark immaculate, but, eventually, I hoped, he'd relax and get over that last shibboleth.

"Why you always here?" he asked. "You don't work here no more, but I figure I find you here."

I smiled again. "You'll make a good cop someday."

He didn't like that but he let me get away with it. There were other things on his mind. "I was thinking, wondering," he said. "The night of the party. There was a goodbye party, you know? For all of us. And I got an award at that party. You weren't there. I was wondering if you was in here that night."

"Um, no," I said, quick. "I was not feeling good that night. I called Dr. Rothenberg – I was hoping she'd tell you guys . . . But, your sister. She's okay?"

His was still searching my face. But he answered my question. "Oh, yeah. She just a baby. Way younger than me, and she not used to being by herself, not used to me being away. It's new for her." The searchlight switched back on. "I go back tomorrow."

"Oh!" I said.

"You disappointed?" he asked.

"No, it's just – it's nice to see you."

"Oh, yeah?" he asked.

"Yeah."

I hadn't realized how valuable it was, or how lost, till I failed to find it. Oh, these lines, angles and planes announced "Gabriel Mateo Suarez" unmistakably, the short, close hair, the cleft chin, even those expressive nostrils. But that face of summer had apparently also been a unit of time, time now passed. However I might interpret how I had used it, that opportunity was now irrevocable. That face had been my daily life, every weekday, five hours a day – profligate enough of a presence that familiarity eclipsed the temporal nature of my privilege and power.

I used to be the one petitioned for advice and permission. I used to be the confessional. This face recorded my redundancy in those positions. Since I last saw him, events had transpired in his life. These events had been significant enough to leave tracings on his face, as the thread of a melt-gorged river inscribes its delicate bed of sand. "Events:" I use this neutral, blind word because of the nature of this river, I knew nothing . . . And suddenly I realized that we were dangerously close to doing that thing where you just gaze at each other and smile.

I sat up straight in my chair. "Auxiliaries! You owe me auxiliaries, Suarez! It's not 'She just a baby.' It's 'She's just a baby.' Okay, look. We're gonna practice. You and me. Right now. You have time? Good. Let's go. I'll ask a question; you answer it. Then you'll ask me. Ready? Good. First question. Do you live in Princeton?" I asked.

"Yes, I live in Princeton," he said.

"Are you staying in Princeton now?" I asked.

"No, I am not staying in Princeton now," he said.

"God, listen to those final consonants. Gorgeous. You been going to an elocution teacher? Or you practicing to be one? I'd hire you. Okay, your turn. Ask me."

"Do you live in Paterson?" Gabriel Suarez asked me.

"Yes, I live in Paterson," I replied.

"Are you in Paterson now?" he asked.

"No, I am not in Paterson now," I replied.

"Do you like me?"

"Thatsapersonalquestion.Imateacher.Ilikeallmystudents."

"Das good," he said, and he rose and walked out of the room.

I'm writing "good," but he didn't actually say "good." He said, "guh-" with a glottal stop at the end, a pronunciation typical of Black English. And I thought, what's going on down there at Princeton? He didn't do glottal stops before he left. Anyway, realizing there was nothing more for me to do in the Writing Center, I, too got up and began my walk to Paterson.

Threads of plastic and metal scratch and pit my soft white thighs. Black and gray, colors of the dirt in an ashtray: the upholstery in the backseat of Mrs. Horthy's boxy, white Ford Falcon. The windows are rolled up. There is air outside. If we open the windows, air is liable to enter. Air's foreign, willful stunts with temperature and humidity, could, like a Gypsy, rob us, with one tap, of any equilibrium we've managed to stockpile. Mommy is smoking. Mrs. Horthy is smoking. I am holding my breath. Mrs. Horthy is driving. Any blood remaining in her body has wormed deep within. Mrs. Horthy's scuffed facial skin is as thick and distant from fecundity as the sole of a sneaker from the rubber trees of Malaya. Mrs. Horthy occasionally mutters oddly juxtaposed words, her own tabloid headlines: "U.F.O.'s Land in Lenappi Reservoir;" "Local Girl Sees Blessed Virgin Mary in Knee Scab after Fall at Saint Francis Playground;" "Too Frequent Abortions Cause Case of Nymphomania." Mommy says, about Mrs. Horthy, "Good friend," "Good Catholic," "You can rely on her," but, also, "Thorazine," "Greystone Institution," "Electroshock Therapy."

Mrs. Horthy drives. Her body is squeezed dry by a quiet, white, poverty of such puniness and limitation that her skin-vested grandmama back in sheep-bitten Szabolcs-Szatmar couldn't have imagined it and an invisible husband whose only palpable contributions are visible welts on Mrs. Horthy's face, neck, and forearms. Whatever is left in her ignites when Mrs. Horthy grips a steering wheel. Her pedal to the metal, we have hit three church rummage sales so far today.

The boxy, white Falcon mounts a gentle, grassy slope; the emergency brake grinds into service. I whine and puke and am no fun, so they leave me. Oh, poop! I crack open the heavy door, and escape to the migratory bazaar come to rest in the church parking lot.

I snake through flanks of heavy coats hanging from rows of metal rods. They sway like slow, dark, rancid water. Their stench sways, too; it stalks me, the odor of the hundreds of smelly rich people who once owned these coats. When garments become saturated with stink, the rich pass them down to this migratory bazaar and its transient shoppers in a ritual called "charity." I struggle to evade the odor, to move up, out, into clean, cool air. I weave my head and shoulders, sniffing, testing. I bump into a shopper. She stares. There is something wrong with this woman. There is something wrong with a lot of these people. Mommy would have them laughing and human in a second. They'd relax and confide the stories of their latest surgery and she'd be feeding them. I am too afraid and move on in search of someplace far enough away that I can access clean, cool air, but not so far that Mommy and Mrs. Horthy can maroon me.

There is a long, low table, above it, cool air. I stand here for a long time, and encounter, amidst the broken strings of beads, solid evidence that the world I live in is real.

Two little wooden birds. The heads are smooth spheres, the bodies, smooth ovals. Real feathers, real, emerge from the wood on the head and tail. The feathers are bright pink, purple, vivid green, yellow, and fluffy. So fluffy. Automatically, I test the fluff against my cheek; my eczema-numbed fingers are not even tried. "How did you get here? You are the first ones from the magical world that have made it here. How long will you stay?"

"You can't play with them unless you buy them," croaks the woman behind the table.

I cleave to them, say nothing. She doesn't understand that these birds are mine, and I am theirs.

Mommy, who is always there, without being summoned, and always knows, without being told, gives the woman the appropriate sum and I am free to do what I will with these birds. I wander back to the Falcon. I pull, pull, yank, and finally the stiff, heavy door yowls open. I climb in, and kneel on the scratchy upholstery, my tummy against the back. I blow on the feathers. They billow like no other substance I've ever seen. Their colors alone are proof. These birds are my first true companions.

I jerk the feathers out of the first bird. For a substance very special, it is comically easy to break. I turn on the other bird. I pull, hard. The feathers come out. I grind them against the rough upholstery, like spice on a mortar. I knock the wooden birds together. This is not enough.

I climb outside and find a rock. I pound and I pound. Still not enough. Though mangled, the feathers don't stop being feathers; they still have that identifying magical substance. Though crippled, the birds don't betray their original design. A weird man is staring. I swallow my tears and pants. I position my body to block his view. I dig a hole with my hands, and bury the birds.

"Gabriel!"

The other kids at the bus stop stared, but stupidly and slowly. I was a mess, sweaty, hair all over. I tried to comb it back with my fingertips.

He didn't move. He looked at me as if down, though I'm almost as tall as he, as if over a barrier. "My bus," he said.

"Too bad," I said. "Get the next one."

His face exposed no affection, no respect, no connection. He could have almost convinced me that we'd never met. The kids mounted the bus. He stayed. We were alone. I grabbed his arm.

"I have to tell you something," I said.

"Oh yeah? What?"

I took a deep breath. I turned inward, seeking the courage and fluency I imagine I demonstrate when I am writing in you, Diary. Instead I confronted the hard marble of paralysis, the tightfisted miser of fear. I would not give him anything.

He had less time than I. He jerked free of my hand. He walked away.

Well, that's ridiculous, I thought. This is his bus stop. He can't walk away. He can't walk the twenty miles back to Newark. But there he is. He's walking away.

I chased after him and grabbed him. Shame burned my cheeks. I was sure I was way out of bounds, whatever the bounds were; I was sure he'd tell me so, and, what's more, file a report with my superiors. But he turned and looked at me as if this were all expected, as if he were just waiting for me to return the ball in some game. What the heck was going on? *Why does everybody get issued a rulebook except me?* I dare not move or speak. I would just get it all wrong all over again. No. Say it. Just – "Thank you."

He was silent. He looked away. After the appropriate number of seconds, "Bogus," he said.

I spun him around. "It's not like that."

"Do you thank all your students?" he asked.

"You know it's different with you."

"How?" the reptile demanded. "You tell me how it is different with me. Tell me."

"You changed me," I said.

He turned away again. I knew it was time to let go of his arm. Lots of cars passed. We stood in the broken macadam, him looking away from me, both of us watching cars, occasionally swinging our arms, or staring at the dirt, and kicking it. That was the most important thing; it was our task for that moment.

Gabriel looked back, not the reptile. I wanted to bring all of anything I've learned here to that moment. Wondered how to do that. Realized that just as I surprise my audience, life would go on surprising me, superceding my painstakingly hammered-out script with each new moment's animate human. Realized that so I am offered the chance to prove any virtue to which I aspire, or at least to practice humility. Noted what the horizontal shafts of setting sun were doing to his coal black hair. I wished I could . . .

Yes, yes, I'm fully aware that "could" is a modal auxiliary, inadequate to the task of completing that sentence. All I can offer is a punctuation I despise. The ellipsis: "the omission of a word or words necessary for the complete syntactical construction of a sentence; a mark (. . .) used to indicate such omission." The definition is dry. The etymology says more: "Greek, *elleipsis*, a falling short, defect, from *elleipein*, to leave behind." I hate it when women use ellipsis. It's always women – the same kind that dot their i's with circles. It's such a fem punctuation. I demand, "Don't insult language by implying that words are not up to the task! *Just spit it out!*" But I can't complete that sentence, Diary. I lack the verb of predication. I must expose my defect, and leave it, eternally unfixed, behind. And, so, "I wished I could . . . "

When Gabriel's eyes met mine, they looked sad and scared. I think I knew what he was thinking: "What have I done since the last time I saw you to fall short of your best hopes for me?" He targets with a fighter pilot's precision my pathetic little performances. But the pressing conviction of his own inadequacy saps his focus. I guessed this because I have been the one who has needed to change to deserve the love of the apparently superior teacher, and that is how that goes. I wasn't going to burden him, not right then, with a full invoice of my failings.

"Talk about Princeton." I suggested.

He actually nodded. "I don't know," he said. There was a long pause. "You know, my father, he work on the line. He so tired some time. And here I sit on my ass ten hours a day –"

I nodded feverishly.

"None of us ever do anything like this before," he said.

I nodded. Rubbed his back a little, dropped my hand, looked at the dirt, kicked it.

"How do I know –"

"How do you?" I drilled him. "Because you do. You do, or else it wouldn't torment you."

He looked at me. "I worry about time," he said. "This semester, it didn't work out so good. It took so long to feel like I'm settled there. Then I gotta come up here. How'm I gonna catch up?"

A bus was coming. It would be his. Neither of us would allow him to miss it. We hugged good-bye. My cheek swiped, lingering, against his in the hopes of collecting a memento of scent. I was frantic for something worthy to say. I said, instead, something I've been puzzling over ever since. Was it good enough? Did it sound like a cliché? But it wasn't a cliché, not for me. Had our form of communication been a letter, instead of conversation, it would have been one that sits on the desk forever, a letter that is never sent. Not because the correspondent hasn't enough to say, or doesn't care, but for the opposite reasons. I have revised these words over and over in my memory and I am never delivered of their superior. When I am, you know that I will tell you, Diary. Although, I wish I could tell *him*. Anyway, these words were very real for me at that moment, and that's part of why I've been thinking about them ever since, to taste again their certainty: "That's okay, Gabriel. It'll be there when you're ready. School never ends."

Printed in the United States
1393100001B/255

9 781401 092429